LYNNE PEMBERTON

Platinum Coast

Grafton

An Imprint of HarperCollins*Publishers*

Grafton
An Imprint of HarperCollins*Publishers*
77–85 Fulham Palace Road,
Hammersmith, London W6 8JB

Published by Grafton 1993

1 3 5 7 9 8 6 4 2

Published simultaneously in hardback by
HarperCollins*Publishers*

The Author asserts the moral right to be
identified as the author of this work

ISBN 0 586 21859 9

Set in Times

Printed in England by Clays Ltd, St Ives plc

To my father.
The past is past,
lost forever,
only the memories survive.
I miss you.

Prologue

It was dark when the small fishing boat slipped unnoticed out of the shallow-draught harbour. There was a strong sea breeze and spray flayed the skin of Christina's cheeks. She turned her face away from the wind and caught the smell of diesel fuel and dead fish. Bile stung her throat like acid and she fought hard to hold down the rising nausea.

A strong gust caught the *Island Spirit* full on its starboard side. She stumbled amongst the coiled ropes. A pair of strong hands steadied her.

'Are you okay, Mrs Reece-Carlton?'

She stared up into the concerned face and friendly dark eyes of Father Edward Collymore.

'I'll be okay,' she mumbled. She clutched the priest's arm as the boat rolled alarmingly in the opposite direction, and smiled faintly to herself.

Ever the perfectionist, Stephen had left precise instructions in his will.

The burial at sea must be at dawn and approximately ten miles out from the north point of the island, where the Caribbean meets the southern Atlantic.

Christina looked across to the eastern horizon as the skipper cut the engines. She gripped the gaudily painted side of the boat as it bobbed in sickening motion to and fro. Slowly the sea before her lit up as though floodlit, the top of the sun's glowing golden orb just visible above the rolling waves.

Dawn comes quickly in the Caribbean. Thick fingers of brilliant light punctured the darkness and suddenly the entire sky was filled with a bright-blue dazzling glow.

'Now,' Christina said to Father Collymore, who nodded and squeezed her hand.

He turned to the wheelhouse and said: 'It's time', signalling to a long metal box lying in the stern.

The skipper nodded his grizzled head and went below. A few seconds later he reappeared with five brawny fishermen dressed in faded T-shirts and surf shorts or ragged cut-off jeans.

They all nodded silently to Christina and the priest as they made their way to the stern and lined up three on either side of the lead-lined coffin which contained the mortal remains of Stephen Reece-Carlton.

Father Collymore took up position at the head of the coffin with Christina by his side.

'Stephen Reece-Carlton,' he began in his deep, sonorous voice, 'lived an exciting and eventful life. His departure, so premature and unexpected, will be sadly mourned. His last wish was to be buried at daybreak in the sea he had grown to love – the Caribbean – which laps the shores of our beloved Barbados, the island Stephen Reece-Carlton had made his second home.'

Christina stared at the coffin. Again, the wan smile touched the corners of her mouth. Trust Stephen to have dreamed up such a bizarre burial for himself. He had never conformed before, so why start now? Always larger than life . . . The smile left her lips and she felt the familiar pricking at the back of her eyes. Her husband wasn't larger than life. Not any more.

Her gaze clouded with tears as she heard the priest begin to recite Stephen's favourite psalm.

'The Lord is my shepherd, I shall not want, he makes me down to lie . . .' She longed for the whole dreadful ordeal to be over.

It was, soon enough. As Father Collymore finished, six pairs of muscular arms lifted the coffin. For a moment they held it poised as the priest murmured the final words, then they let go. It hit the side of the boat with a dull thud before plunging beneath the yawning Caribbean sea.

Christina stared dully at the place where the coffin had disappeared. Sun glinted on the water and a shoal of flying-fish flew over the place where Stephen Reece-Carlton had finally been laid to rest.

She felt the engines surge and the boat turned south and headed for home.

With Father Collymore standing silently by her side, Christina turned her eyes to the sky. To the north, a cloudless horizon stretched as far as the eye could see. It promised to be another perfect day in paradise.

She wrapped her arms around herself for comfort, listening to the swish of the waves lapping against the sides of the boat. A kaleidoscope of recollections filled her mind.

Stephen had always loved the sea. The first time he had taken her deep-sea fishing he had caught an 120-pound king-fish. She had been terrified. In her mind's eye she could see his teasing face and hear his laughter, as clearly as if it had happened yesterday. It was ten years ago. Probably more, she mused.

Then there was the wonderful holiday they had taken with friends on a small sailing ketch in the Grenadines. Long, lazy days spent snorkelling and swimming in the Tobago Keys. Bright starlit nights filled with love . . .

A sudden surge as a trawler ploughed into the swell brought her out of her reverie. She turned and looked back over the stern towards the place in the implacable sea where Stephen now lay.

'Death by misadventure,' the coroner had said, and his verdict had been final. But Christina was not convinced.

Stephen had trodden the hard path to immense wealth and power; a path which had become littered with routed

9

opponents and embittered rivals. One of them might have sought revenge, decided to arrange his premature departure.

Christina recalled Stephen's last conversation with her, only hours before his death.

'Remember, Christina, when you live as close to the edge as I do, there's always the risk of falling off. Or of being pushed. Take care, my darling, I may not always be around to protect you.'

She had thought it a strange thing to say at the time. She had not understood what he was driving at. Now, perhaps she did. When it was too late.

She shivered and turned to face the shore. They were close to land. Past the vast turquoise semi-circle of Brighton Beach she could see the bustling harbour and low stone buildings of the island's capital, Bridgetown.

'Don't worry,' Christina whispered, 'I'll take care of myself. I had a good teacher, the best there ever was – Stephen Reece-Carlton.'

21 SEPTEMBER 1993, NEW YORK

He wasn't going to catch her; not this time. Her legs torn and bleeding, Christina brushed through the sharp, brittle cane-stems as flying cockroaches buzzed and whistled past her head. The island sun in the cloudless sky was merciless, scorching her shoulders and arms whilst the rushing blood pounded in her ears.

Suddenly, the cane field cleared to a wide expanse of dry scrubland across which she saw the old abandoned plantation house. The breath sobbed in her throat as she ran towards it.

The crumbling coral-stone steps leading up to the front door looked scarcely able to take her weight. She stepped up them cautiously, glancing behind her. There was no one there. She had lost him.

'Thank God,' she gasped as she pushed open the heavy wooden door with its peeling paint. Inside the house it was cool. She stood for a few moments, adjusting her eyes to the gloom as her rasping breath echoed around what she gradually came to see was a vast, domed hallway dominated by a broad, sweeping stone staircase to her left.

She stopped at the landing, her expression a mixture of fear and fascination. She could hear something. It echoed faintly around the vast, empty house: a hushed, repetitive scraping sound, sinister yet strangely familiar. As if in a trance she walked slowly towards the noise. It was coming from one of the bedrooms. She tried the doors as she moved along the landing. They were all locked, except one – the door to the room whence came the ghostly sound. She opened the door and edged into the bedroom. Then she smiled.

Crossing the room she leaned over the old-fashioned gramophone and lifted the stuck needle. The record crackled slightly as she replaced it in the groove and Mozart's *Symphony No. 41* erupted around her.

It was loud, so loud that she did not hear the sound of manic laughter coming from the man who had appeared behind her. She heard nothing but the music until he was upon her.

She whirled round as he grabbed her arm.

He was wearing a crude voodoo mask. It covered his face, but she could see his eyes, cold and unblinking. Dead green eyes. The man's laughter turned into a high-pitched shrieking which shook his body. She tried to struggle but it was no good, he was too strong. Yet, strangely, she was not afraid.

He reminded her of one of the grotesque laughing men she had seen at fairgrounds when she was a child. Somehow he wasn't real. Yet he was real; so were his actions.

He began unbuttoning her blouse. She watched him as if from a distance, impassively, knowing that it was useless to resist. He bared first one breast and then the other. She cried out as he squeezed one nipple viciously. His laughter had subsided; he smiled at her pain and seemed almost peaceful.

He moved his hands up over her breasts towards her neck. She stiffened as the fingers closed around her throat. Now she was afraid. Rigid with fear she waited for him to tighten his hands. Then she saw the ring: the tricoloured band of gold that she had given Stephen on their wedding night. And it was then that she began to scream . . .

'No, Stephen, no, please.'

Christina woke up shouting, drenched in perspiration and knotted in a tangle of silk sheets. Shaking uncontrollably, she sat up and tried to calm herself as her overloaded mind began to distinguish dream from reality. She was not on the island, she reminded herself, but in New York for a meeting with Kingsleigh Klein, Stephen's lawyer. After a few moments she reached across and switched on the bedside light. It was 3.15. She leaned back against her damp and crumpled pillow and took a deep breath. It was the same nightmare she'd had for the past ten nights, since returning from Stephen's burial at sea to the familiarity of the apartment in New York's prestigious Sutton Place.

She ran a shaky hand through her dishevelled hair. Tonight, she thought, of all nights she had needed a good seven hours' sleep. She contemplated taking a sleeping-pill but thought better of it. It would make her groggy in the morning, and she couldn't afford that. Not tomorrow at the meeting which Kingsleigh Klein had unexpectedly called to 'discuss the disposition' of Stephen's Platinum Resorts shares. Christina had been surprised that this had not been covered in his will, but at the time it had been read to her by an overawed young associate from Bascombe and Partners on Barbados she had been too stunned and disorientated by grief to ask any questions. All she knew was that Stephen had left a great deal of money – many millions more than she had dreamed possible – in outright legacy to herself and in trust for their son Adam and Stephen's daughter from his first marriage, Victoria.

She shivered, though this time it wasn't the bad dream that caused her uneasiness. It was the cold breath of reality.

She knew that there was going to be conflict. In the weeks and months ahead the wolves would be after her, snarling and snapping, eager for blood. She had always hated the deviousness and brutality of high-powered business. It frightened her. Yet later that morning she was to be pitched right into the middle of it, thrown into the arena to fight it out with Antonio Cellini and the stepchild who had always hated her.

At least with Antonio it would be purely business. With Victoria it would be personal. It always had been. Like Christina she had expectations of Stephen's Platinum Resorts Inc. shares. After all, like Christina she had been much loved by him.

Though unlike me, Christina thought, as she made herself more comfortable against the pillows, she was also completely spoiled and indulged by Stephen.

She shook her head ruefully. She had never been able to make it work with Victoria. From the very beginning, at their first meeting, Christina had seen something in those lovely eyes that did not belong in a child. She had tried to win Victoria over, to become friends with the beautiful child who had fast become a beguiling young woman, but she had failed. Her efforts over the years had been constantly rejected; now the gap between them was filled with distrust and resentment.

It was, she supposed, the classic stepmother–

stepdaughter relationship. With Stephen in the middle.

Despite his acuteness in business he had never been able to see how treacherous his own daughter could be. He had showered her with material possessions; her trust funds and the country properties she would inherit in England made her worth tens of millions of pounds. And with her looks and brains she was bound to acquire herself a fabulously wealthy husband.

But it wasn't enough, not for Victoria. Platinum Resorts Inc. remained, a monument to Stephen's vision and legendary flair. Tomorrow the disposition of his holding in the company was to be made clear.

Tomorrow, at the lawyer's meeting, Victoria was certain to make her move.

Robert Leyton awoke with a colossal hangover.

Delicately he eased himself out of the bed, careful not to jolt his sore and aching head.

Behind the bathroom door was a full-length mirror. Robert squinted at his reflection. He looked like death. The muscles of his stocky, gone-to-seed body were slack and his face was drawn and haggard, eyelids drooping heavily over his dark eyes.

'Getting old, my son,' he told himself in the mirror.

His hand shook as he slowly and painfully shaved the dark stubble off his chin, careful not to nick himself. He didn't want shaving cuts on his face today, not with a meeting with that smart lawyer coming up. Besides, as Victoria's chief trustee he owed it to her to put up a good appearance. He must do his best for Stephen's daughter. His old friend and partner would have expected no less.

He lit a cigarette with a hand that trembled slightly and inhaled, letting the smoke curl lazily away from his thin lips as he gazed out of the window at the driving rain. Thirty-two floors below him it was washing some of the surface filth off the streets of the city. He hated New York;

had never been able to understand why Stephen had loved it so much.

But then, there was much about his former partner he had never understood.

Staring sightlessly out of the window, he drew smoke deep into his lungs and recalled Stephen's words to him the day before he died. His voice on the telephone had been cold and deadly serious.

'Robert, you must promise me something. It's very important. If anything happens to me in the next few days I want you to go to Zurich, to see Nicolas Wagner. He has a letter in his possession. It's to do with Platinum Resorts . . .' – the company Stephen had founded without Robert's participation – 'He'll know what to do if you tell him it's time. He'll contact Klein first. It's all arranged.'

Robert had expressed surprise. He had never known Stephen be so mysterious. 'But why?' he had asked.

'Because you're the only one I can trust to do it.'

'Do what?'

'Stop that bastard Cellini getting his hands on Platinum Resorts! He'll do anything to gain control, anything. It's up to you to stop him.'

Robert had shivered. He doubted if there was anyone who could stop Antonio Cellini getting what he wanted. Except a man like Stephen.

'Have I your word, Robert?' Stephen's voice had been low and urgent. 'You'll pull out all the stops?' It had been a demand.

Though mystified, he had agreed. 'Yes, of course, Stephen. You know I will. Anything you say. But come on, why so serious? You're as fit as a fiddle. Nothing's going to happen to you.'

'I know that,' the voice at the other end of the telephone had snapped back. 'It's merely a precaution. You know me. Better safe than sorry.'

They were Stephen's last words to him.

The following day Christina had phoned and broken the fatal news in a distant, choking voice.

Victor, the butler, had found Stephen's body at the foot of the stairs in their Barbados home, Crystal Springs House. His neck was broken.

The island coroner had ruled that it was death by misadventure. Robert had difficulty accepting the verdict, but kept his own counsel. It surely could not have been coincidence that Stephen had set in motion those complicated and highly secret arrangements 'in case of' his own death?

He turned from the rain-splattered window and savagely screwed his cigarette out in an ashtray. What, he wondered for the hundredth time, had Stephen got himself mixed up in?

After the fortieth length, Antonio Cellini pulled himself effortlessly out of the heated water and padded across the marble tiles to a towel draped on a chair at the side of the dark-blue-tiled swimming-pool.

He moved on the ground as he had in the water: effortlessly and with an animal grace. Standing at six one and weighing 180 pounds, he had the body of a man of thirty. Which, he considered, wasn't bad when next birthday he would be fifty-three.

Wrapping himself in the towel, he looked across the grounds of the Southampton colonial-style mansion he had finally bought from his parents-in-law. He never tired of the sense of pride that view gave him; it represented everything he had ever wanted, everything he had worked for and achieved.

A flash of blonde hair appeared at a bedroom window but was gone before he could lift a hand to wave. He wondered why Susanna was up so early. It was unusual.

He jogged barefoot up the well-manicured lawns and through the open french windows. He was surprised to see his wife sitting fully dressed at the head of the polished dining-table in the elegant, pale-green morning room. She was spreading butter sparingly over a wafer-thin slice of toast.

'Good morning, Susanna,' he said brightly. 'Up so early? To what do I owe this pleasure?'

She ignored his question. 'Antonio,' she demanded with barely controlled irritation, 'how many times do I have to ask you? After you have been swimming, please come in through the kitchen. You are dripping all over the Aubusson.'

Her blue eyes were cold and full of disapproval.

He was tempted to tell her acidly that the faded, thread-bare rug he was soaking had cost *him* several thousand dollars. That if he wanted to stand on it, wet or otherwise, he would. And that furthermore, if there was one thing he had learned in his long years of association with a tight-ass like Stephen Reece-Carlton, it was that it was vulgar to use anything but the generic: 'the car', not 'the Mercedes'; 'champagne', not 'Dom Perignon'; 'the rug', not the goddamned 'Aubusson'! He caught his own chain of thought and smiled ironically. Well, what do you know? Some of Stephen's class had finally rubbed off. Too bad it had to be after his death. He wondered if he ought to correct the supposedly classy woman he had married. But he thought better of it. He didn't want another argument, not this morning. This morning he had more important things on his mind.

'You haven't answered my question,' he continued, glancing at the Louis XV clock, yet another of Susanna's expensive antiques. 'Why aren't you still in bed? You're never up at this time in the morning.'

'I have an appointment with Clifford Norton about the party next month. He goes on vacation this afternoon. This morning is the only time he could make.' Her mouth nipped at a corner of the toast and she chewed it slowly

17

and delicately. He grimaced. It irritated him the way she ate like a bird.

'Not another party, Susanna,' he moaned. 'I'm sick of your constant parties. All those phoney people descending on us like a cloud of locusts. Give me a break. Haven't we done our quota of entertaining for this year?'

She gave him another icy stare but said nothing. He grabbed a warm croissant from a plate on the table and bit into it as he walked out of the room, leaving a trail of crumbs behind him. He bounded up the wide staircase two at a time and almost collided with a maid. She was new, dark-skinned and attractive, and he smiled at her. He didn't bother to learn their names any more, they changed so often.

He padded through Susanna's bedroom suite, which interconnected with his own. He hated the fact that they had separate rooms. He missed waking up next to her.

It has been wonderful, once: to be aroused by the musky remnants of her expensive perfume, to touch the silky strands of her wayward hair, to caress with eager fingers the fine golden hair of her bush. But it hadn't lasted long. He had realized early in their marriage, after a few cold and indifferent submissions, that Susanna loathed sex in the morning.

And that had been the beginning of their growing apart; the start of what had eventually led to separate bedrooms. It had never excited him to have his women acquiescent. He wanted them eager for it, hungry enough to match his own appetite. His mind strayed to the good-looking maid he had encountered on the stairs. She had possibilities, he thought, and felt his penis stirring into life.

He shook his head vigorously, shaking off thoughts of sex, then smiled to himself. The prospect of a fight always made him horny, and today at the meeting he expected there to be a bloody battle. It was important to keep his mind on business.

Christina, he was certain, could be persuaded to stay out. She had Adam to look after now. Victoria, though, was going to need some careful handling. She always did . . .

He showered and dressed in a sombre Armani suit, a blue shirt and silk paisley tie, then ran a comb lightly through his hair which, except for the distinguished wings of grey at the temples, was as thick and dark as it had always been.

He smiled at himself in the mirror, showing a set of even white teeth. He felt good: alert and exhilarated, his veins pumping with adrenalin, anticipating the battle.

He was sure he would win. Now, at last, he would gain control of Stephen Reece-Carlton's business empire. His grin widened at the prospect – and at the thought that his triumph would have Stephen Reece-Carlton turning in his grave.

Victoria surveyed herself in the full-length wardrobe mirror of room 263 of the Plaza Hotel.

She saw a slender, stern-faced young woman whose braided blue Chanel suit matched her eyes to perfection. She had pinned her long, black hair into a chignon in order to emphasize the exquisite heart-shaped diamond pendant glittering at her throat.

Tenderly, she touched the brilliant, six-carat stone and recalled the words that had been written in Stephen's open, scrawling handwriting on the card accompanying it:

When you wear this I'll never be far away.
  Your ever adoring father.

She felt the tears spring into her eyes and gripped the edge of the dressing-table, fighting to stay in control. He had given her the necklace only days before he had died. It had been his last gift.

She fought back the tears. They threatened to mess up her mascara and she hadn't time to start on her make-up again.

'Come on, Vicky,' she said softly to herself. 'You're Daddy's girl. Do what he always told you to do. Come out fighting.'

She smiled bravely at her reflection, pushing a wisp of stray hair out of her eyes, but inside she felt her heart breaking with the pain of his loss. She missed him so much. He had gone so suddenly, too soon for her to have learned all that he had to teach her: about winning people over, making them feel good, while all the time he was manipulating them for his own ends. About continued success and how not to grow complacent. Most of all about power.

Victoria was twenty-one, rich and beautiful. In his will her father had left money in trust for her until she was twenty-five, more than enough to buy her anything she wanted. But none of that was enough. She wanted power.

Now that her father was dead she saw herself as his natural successor. She had inherited much of his wealth, his good looks and his business acumen. She had also inherited his determination. And it was with that, the iron will she had seen him use so often, that she intended to wrest control of the one thing he had not left her – complete control of Platinum Resorts. Or rather – had not left her yet, she reminded herself. Today's meeting was to determine the reassignment of her father's shares. Antonio had been asked to attend, but she couldn't believe that Stephen Reece-Carlton would have been so weak as to make the sentimental gesture of giving away shares to a business partner. No, Antonio's presence was a mere formality, as was that of her trustee, Robert Leyton. Dear old Uncle Bob. Yet another man she could twist around her finger. Which left Christina.

There was a fierce stabbing pain in the palm of her

20

hands. Victoria looked down in surprise as blood seeped slowly down one wrist. At just the thought of her stepmother she had clenched her fists so tightly that her long nails had drawn blood. Maybe it was an omen? For the first time since her father's death, Victoria smiled.

The rain had turned Madison Avenue into a blocked artery of horn-sounding yellow cabs, all going nowhere.

Antonio peered past his driver's head at the immovable jam of vehicles stretching as far into the distance as he could see, then consulted his watch. He turned to stare at the pedestrians scurrying along the sidewalk. No matter how fraught and bad-tempered they were, he thought, at least they were going somewhere. He decided to join them. He might get a little wet, but that would be better than being a half-hour late.

He arrived at the New York offices of Platinum Resorts Inc. damp and agitated. It had been a struggle among the pedestrians on the wet sidewalks. He was fifteen minutes late.

'The traffic on Madison was hell,' he announced by way of an apology as he walked into the huge room that had been Stephen's office. The others seated around the polished American cedar boardroom table looked up. No one smiled.

'It was bad for all of us, Mr Cellini,' Kingsleigh Klein grated patronizingly. 'But, as you see, the rest of us made it for the appointed time.'

Antonio hid his irritation for the arrogant Kingsleigh Klein, who had been Stephen's choice of lawyer for himself and the company. Klein had always made it obvious he disliked Cellini. The feeling was mutual, and when he had control, Antonio reflected as he smiled ingratiatingly and sat down next to Victoria, one of his first moves would be to get rid of him.

He glanced at Christina sitting opposite and noticed

the dark rings around her hazel eyes, made all the more prominent by the exhausted pallor of her face. He nodded briefly to Robert Leyton. So who was the third man, neat and smooth and prissy-looking, wearing gold-rimmed half-glasses that made him look like a college professor?

'Now that we are all finally here . . .' – Klein glanced at him again – 'perhaps we can begin? We have a lot to get through. Ladies and gentlemen, may I present Herr Nicolas Wagner who has joined us today from Zurich? Like myself, Herr Wagner is a lawyer. Stephen Reece-Carlton consulted him a few months ago.'

Klein looked as if he had swallowed something sour, Antonio was pleased to see, but Wagner seemed to be out of the same mould: boring, precise and fond of the sound of his own voice.

'Before his death,' Nicolas Wagner began, 'Stephen Reece-Carlton left an important document with me. His instructions were that this document was to be opened not less than one week after his burial.' He produced a large brown manila envelope which he placed on the table in front of him. The room was silent.

Wagner paused for a moment before he went on: 'This document is to be opened and read to all of those present here today by Mr Leyton.'

The lawyer slid the envelope across the polished table to Robert, who proceeded to open it. Antonio, watching through narrowed eyes, noticed that his hands were shaking.

Inside the envelope was a sheet of white foolscap covered in Stephen's untidy scrawl.

Robert's voice cracked slightly as he began to read. He stopped, cleared his throat, and began again.

'Earlier this year I felt compelled to write this letter in case I met with an untimely death. The building of Platinum Resorts Inc. has been for me a wonderful and challenging experience. I believe that the hotels are a testament to all the effort and time put into making them what I consider to be perfect retreats.

'I have no regrets. It has been a labour of love. I wish to leave Christina and Victoria 24 per cent of the company each in the hope that, now that I am dead, they may settle their differences and unite to prevent Antonio Cellini gaining control of Platinum Hotels.

'That is something I do not wish to happen.'

There was a concerted gasp from everyone around the table as they shot Antonio embarrassed looks. His eyes smouldered and he reddened slightly, but he made no comment as Robert continued.

'Without me there to prevent it, I am afraid Antonio will drag the company down.'

At this he finally exploded. Everyone jumped as he smashed his clenched fist onto the table's polished surface, rattling the glasses and upsetting Victoria's cup. Coffee spilled onto her new Chanel suit. She frantically dabbed at the seeping brown stain with a tissue, then glared at him ferociously.

'I suppose it's too much to expect an apology?'

'For Chrissake, shut up!' he barked at her. 'I'll buy you a dozen designer suits.'

Robert looked up from the letter. He was tempted to smile. Cellini had always made him feel inadequate, and now he was enjoying the chance to observe the Italian's discomfiture. 'May I continue?' he enquired with a trace of smug satisfaction.

'Yeah, you can continue,' snarled Antonio, 'but don't expect me to hang around here if there's gonna be much more of this crap. Just cut out all the amateur dramatics and get to the point.'

His voice became even more angry. 'Christ, this is just typical of Stephen! That sonofabitch loved to play power games with people and even now he's dead he's still stringing us along. All we want to know is, who's holding the

23

remainder of the shares? When we know that we can get down to the real business.'

Robert had never been on the receiving end of Antonio Cellini's legendary temper and wasn't about to change that now. He became conciliatory. 'There's not much more.'

'Then get on with it,' snapped Antonio. Robert cleared his throat and continued.

'Several years ago, for reasons I choose not to disclose, I was forced to part with a substantial proportion of my company. The shareholder, my half-brother Edward Harrington, who holds 28 per cent of Platinum Resorts, has always preferred to remain anonymous and let me act in his best interests but, in the event of my death, I am certain he will make himself known to you.

'I must warn you that my half-brother is not to be trusted, not under any circumstances, and I am absolutely opposed to his becoming involved in any way with the running of Platinum Resorts.

'You must always be on your guard against this man. As the other shareholders in the company, you must try to get rid of him in any way you can. Buy him out, but get rid of him. This is vitally important.

'This is my last wish and I entrust you, particularly Christina and Victoria, with the task of carrying it out.

'I would like to think that Platinum Resorts will enter the next decade with the same vigour and style that have made it the phenomenal success that it is today.

'Thank you, Christina, for putting up with my obsession and loving me in spite of everything.

'Finally, I wish all of you everything I would have wished for myself. Especially longevity.

'Take care, and *bonne chance*.'

The sight of Stephen's signature, still bold and authoritative while his body was now at the mercy of the sea, caused Robert's voice to falter.

For a while there was a silence in the room, broken

only by the soft patter of raindrops on the window panes.

Then Victoria's voice cut crisply into the silence. 'This is quite incredible, you know. Daddy and Uncle Edward never got on, barely saw each other. They were only half-brothers in any case. There is absolutely no reason I can think of why my father should leave Edward Harrington a controlling interest in his company.'

The Swiss lawyer glanced at her sympathetically. 'I appreciate this has come as a shock to you, Miss Reece-Carlton, but your father's instructions were crystal-clear. It seems that, for whatever reason, Mr Reece-Carlton intended Edward Harrington to benefit.'

'For whatever reason,' thought Christina. A lawyerly euphemism if ever she'd heard one. Like Victoria, she could think of no reason why Stephen should have left Edward a stake in the company he had loved. Why, she could remember him refusing his half-brother the loan of a few hundred pounds once. And now to leave him all this? It didn't make sense.

'But why all the goddamned secrecy?' Antonio exploded. 'So far as I knew, Stephen wouldn't give his fag brother the time of day. I just don't believe he could do this! I mean, legally, didn't he have to notify me? We were partners, for Chrissake.'

Herr Wagner shuddered delicately at the choice of words, but hastened to assure them: 'Mr Reece-Carlton acted quite properly. On his instructions I formed an off-shore company and issued 28 per cent of the registered stock to Mr Harrington. An entirely legal manoeuvre, of course.'

Antonio snorted. 'Legal, perhaps, but something here stinks. I'm not letting Harrington get his fat little pinkies on my company!'

Christina chose that moment to intervene. 'Don't you mean *our* company?'

For once, Victoria agreed with her. 'Yes. By my

reckoning we three are equal partners, Antonio, dear, holding 24 per cent each.'

Kingsleigh Klein broke in: 'That's certainly the current position, but aren't you forgetting Stephen's express wish that his half-brother should not be allowed to take part in the running of the company?' He looked at Nicolas Wagner, who nodded slightly. 'And I'm not breaking any professional confidences if I tell you that Mr Harrington himself has no intention of becoming involved in the running of Platinum Resorts. I believe you have been talking with him, Herr Wagner?'

The Swiss lawyer allowed himself a careful smile. 'While delighted by his brother's generosity, Mr Harrington made it quite plain to me that he does not see business as his forte. He wishes to sell his holding and has instructed me to act on his behalf. Naturally I would approach the other stockholders first.'

'Now you're talking language I understand. How much does this bozo want, and how soon can you arrange a transfer to me?' rasped Antonio.

Christina felt her temples throb with suppressed annoyance. The man was impossible. 'Hang on a minute, Antonio. There's more than one guest at this party,' she reminded him.

So far she had taken a back seat in this discussion. The news of the bequest to Edward had both shocked and surprised her – it seemed such an uncharacteristic move for Stephen to make. But now Antonio's arrogant presumption had got through to her, and she was determined to challenge him. He had no automatic right to those shares. No more than herself or, God forbid, Victoria.

'Herr Wagner, I take it you would be equally happy to dispose of the shares to any of the existing shareholders?'

He inclined his head. 'That is so. Mr Reece-Carlton foresaw there might be some – how shall I say? – healthy competition, and I have considered how best to handle it.

I presume you will all three be bidding for Mr Harrington's holding?'

He was looking specifically at Victoria who murmured, 'Naturally.' Christina's heart sank. Her stepdaughter was twenty-one, had never held down a job or even completed her studies. Yet, with all the arrogance she had inherited from her father, she seemed quite convinced that she could step into his shoes.

'I think, my dear, as your trustee . . .' Robert Leyton began to bluster.

Victoria turned huge blue-grey eyes directly on him. 'Uncle Robert, I know this is what my father would want. Obviously I need your consent to proceed, but you won't withhold it, will you? After all, I am my father's daughter.'

He shrugged and glanced slightly shamefacedly at Christina. She was not surprised. Father or daughter, Robert Leyton never could refuse a Reece-Carlton.

'Then, with Mr Leyton acting on your behalf as trustee, I will accept a bid from you,' Nicolas Wagner told Victoria. 'I think the simplest and quickest way of handling this is to take sealed bids from all of you for outright control of Mr Harrington's holding. I suggest we reconvene here in this office in one week's time. That should give you all the chance to review your affairs and give me your best offer.'

Antonio was far from happy with this suggestion. 'Now hold on a minute. Christina, Vicky, come on!' His tone was heavily condescending. 'It doesn't have to come to this, surely? Competing like enemies after all the ties there've been between our two families.' He put one bronzed hand on his heart. 'If I promise, on the memory of my dead mother, to run the company just exactly as Stephen would have liked, can't we just forget this competition shit? I mean, surely you do realize how much money I've got behind me? This is just a lawyer's way of beefing up his fixer's fee.'

27

It was such a phoney act it was almost laughable, Christina thought. But before she could reject the suggestion, Victoria was replying, her remarkable eyes flashing a stormy blue-grey light.

'No, Antonio, I'm sorry, but I just don't believe you'd run Platinum Resorts the way Daddy would have wanted. Thanks for the offer, but I think I'll take my chance in the bidding.'

'Me too,' said Christina. 'Stephen left his family more than well provided for. It was obviously his way of giving us a chance to keep control of Platinum Resorts.'

Victoria gave her a cold, contemptuous stare. 'Less of the "us", please. No matter what Daddy might have wished in his letter, I'm acting purely for myself in this. If my bid's successful, Christina, you're out. As far as I'm concerned you were never more than an interloper in this family.'

Christina drew in her breath. More than ten years of it, and yet Victoria's venomous hatred still had the power to cut her like a knife. Such a depth of ill-feeling, just because Christina had had the temerity to become Stephen Reece-Carlton's second wife.

Stephen, she prayed silently, show me what to do. I miss you so. Why did you push us all into this crazy competition? Was it just to prove how well you had taught us?

Or perhaps it was for another purpose altogether?

Oblivious to the others, wrapped in her own private thoughts, Christina leaned back in her chair and closed her eyes to hide the stinging tears that threatened. Perhaps, by taking part in this battle for control of Platinum Resorts, she could find the answers to the questions that haunted her night and day. Why had Stephen died? Who had entered their house in Barbados and pushed him to his death – for that it had been murder all along she was suddenly in no doubt at all.

Yet the man she had met eleven years before had been

kind and generous, rich in more than monetary terms. How could she ever have dreamed it would one day come to this? One company and three contenders equally determined to wrest control. A regular scorpion's nest after such golden beginnings . . .

Chapter One

1982

'I declare the Westside Shopping and Leisure Centre officially open.' Chris Gowan, the soap star from *Coronation Street*, smiled broadly at the flashing press cameras.

'Thank you all for coming today.' He had to shout above the deafening applause generated by thousands of eager, noisy shoppers gathered outside the huge new shopping mall on the outskirts of Manchester.

Six young model girls dressed in Wild West theme costumes and armed with a stack of promotional brochures walked towards the small rostrum where Chris was standing. Their appearance was greeted by loud whistles and jeers from a group of crested and tattooed punks pushing precariously close to the platform.

'These beautiful girls will be mingling amongst you today . . .' Chris held up his hand for quiet as the youths shouted in unison: 'Get 'em off.'

'Later, lads, later.' Chris grinned, and the punk rockers roared their approval. 'The girls are laden with lots of free goodies for all of you.' He paused before going on to say, 'Westside Leisure Centre has something for everyone, and we are offering free gifts today and all of next week. Don't forget to enter our free prize draw and you could be the lucky winner of a holiday for two in Majorca.'

This announcement caused another wave of whooping and yelling.

'I do hope you will all enjoy shopping at Westside Leisure Centre.'

Chris Gowan stepped down from the small rostrum to join the six models, all wide, gleaming smiles, posed bodies and pouting lips directed at the press and local television cameras. He stood very close to one particular chestnut-haired girl, obviously appreciating the view over her low-cut boned bodice.

'Do you mind?' she hissed.

He winked and laughed. 'No. Do you?'

Christina O'Neill remembered that he was the visiting celebrity and she was just one of the glamorous bodies recruited for the punters to ogle at during the opening ceremony. With a smile fixed firmly in place she moved off through the crowd, handing out brochures.

'Can I interest you in one, sir?' she asked a grinning, shaven-headed spectator, and instantly realized her mistake.

'D'you hear that, lads?' he asked his mates. 'She fancies me. Yeah, come on, darlin'. I'd fancy one with you any day.'

Christina was about to tell him to get lost when he hooked his finger through the bright-red garter she was wearing and twanged it so hard against her leg that she jumped and dropped the pile of brochures she was holding. They scattered at her feet, some of them sliding across the ground.

Christina glared at him before bending down to retrieve the brochures.

'I get so sick of men like you,' she said angrily, as she rose to her feet and found herself staring, not at the leering youngster, but at a man in a beautifully cut dark-grey chalk-stripe suit. His thick brown hair was brushed away from a high forehead. She caught a hint of the subtle, tangy cologne he wore. Without knowing exactly how, she realized it was a very expensive one.

'I'm sorry.' She felt her face flush. 'I wasn't talking to you. I was about to tell that creep . . .' – she pointed

towards the punk, laughing and joking with his gang –
'. . . exactly what I thought of him.'

She sighed and added, 'Men!'

'Not all of us are like that, you know.'

Christina looked directly into his pale-green eyes.

'I'm beginning to wonder. So far I've had the misfortune of meeting too many of that variety.' She smiled wryly and added, 'I'm afraid it's an occupational hazard.'

He glanced at the scanty saloon-girl's outfit that accentuated her narrow waist and exposed most of her long, shapely legs, and nodded.

'I can understand why.'

'I must be mad, getting dressed up like this for a measly twenty-five pounds a day, but a gal's got to eat.' Her laughter held a hint of mischief, and he thought again that she was more than just another pretty girl.

'At least I've met one gentleman.' She smiled at him under downturned lashes as he handed her the brochures she had dropped. It seemed he was about to speak to her again when an older, slightly corpulent man approached, looking very agitated. She recognized Robert Leyton, one of the mall's developers, who had contacted the agency to hire girls for the opening.

'Stephen, there you are! Charles Naylor is waiting in the hospitality lounge. He's scheduled to tee off at two and would like to see you before he goes.'

'Mustn't keep the man from his golf,' Christina's rescuer commented, then, before Robert could steer him away, he said, 'By the way, I didn't catch your name?'

Robert glared in their direction. 'Stephen, Charles won't wait much longer.'

He ignored the impatient voice and smiled at her, showing even white teeth.

'My name's Christina.' She paused. 'Christina O'Neill.'

'I'll see you later, Miss Christina O'Neill.' His tone was emphatic.

'Come on,' Robert shouted, walking ahead.

Christina watched the two men walk away before being tapped on the shoulder by the tattooed arm of the punk rocker who insisted on showing her his fascinating assortment of chains attached to various parts of his anatomy. He took a dozen free offers and asked her out for a drink, much to the amusement of his motley crew of friends, who collapsed into shrieks of laughter when she refused the date.

She spent the next six hours giving away hundreds of free special-offer coupons, chatting to pensioners about the cost of living, placating fraught babies, fending off the unwelcome advances of gangs of unemployed youths, and being battered by an assortment of baby buggies, prams, and huge shopping bags.

'A free gift of six bags of sugar, three jars of coffee and four boxes of tea with every purchase of food over £50 in Tesco.

'A record voucher with every two LPs bought at Virgin Mega Store.

'Two for the price of one with every purchase of an exotic new fragrance from Estee Lauder.

'A holiday for two in Majorca in the Westside bumper holiday draw.'

Christina's voice had lost all its sparkle and her throat and head ached as she repeated the list of free offers for the final time and handed out the last of her brochures.

It was seven o'clock and the last few stragglers were leaving the shopping centre. 'Thank God that's over,' Christina said to Janine, a girl she knew vaguely from the same model agency, as they walked into the staff-room.

Janine sighed. 'It's bloody slave labour. I wish someone had warned me modelling was going to be like this.'

She took out a packet of cigarettes and handed one to Christina.

34

'No thanks, I don't smoke, but at this rate I think I might have to soon.'

They both sat down on a narrow wooden bench. Christina eased her aching feet out of the high-heeled black patent-leather shoes and wiggled her swollen toes.

'Look at the state of me,' she sighed, peeling the snagged black fish-net stockings down her slim legs and pointing to a large, sticky stain on her gaudy red-lace basque where a child had pressed a melting ice-lolly.

'Whoever said modelling was glamorous ought to be shot,' she commented.

Janine, clad in G-string panties with a stetson obscuring part of her face, was trying to pull a cowboy boot off one of her bruised feet. She nodded and replied through a haze of cigarette smoke.

'It's glamorous, Christina, when – or should I say if – you get into one of the big agencies in London. My friend Sharon works for Models One. She's just finished a big calendar shoot with Patrick Lichfield. She went to the Caribbean for three weeks, came back really tanned and got signed up three days later to do another big tropical location shoot for *Cosmo*.'

Janine looked down at her distorted feet and then back at Christina.

'Now that's what I call glamorous modelling.'

Christina nodded and sighed. 'I must admit I've thought about going to London lots of times, and if I have to do many more jobs like this I'll be on the next train.'

Janine pushed the stetson to the back of her head and took a long drag on her cigarette, staring at Christina's even profile.

'You should go. You're definitely pretty enough.'

Christina was about to accept the compliment when the girl went on, 'I'm stuck here in Manchester whether I like it or not – that is, until my little boy gets older. At least

35

here I can rely on my mum to look after him, and whatever I earn helps.'

Christina watched Janine stand up and pull on faded 501s and a blue chambray shirt.

'How old is your son?' Christina asked, and began to pull her own clothes out of a small leather grip.

'Eighteen months.' Janine hesitated before continuing, 'He's only got me, you see. I don't even know where his father is.' She shrugged, a resigned look on her pretty face. Picking up a shabby canvas bag, she said brightly, 'Hope to see you around some time. I'm sure I will.' She smiled warmly and her big brown eyes twinkled. 'But take my advice and get yourself up to London. That's where the real money and glamour are.'

'Maybe I will,' Christina replied, and waved as she left. She finished dressing, thinking about what the other girl had said. Perhaps it was time for a change, to try her luck in London? What had she to lose after all?

It was a few minutes after eight and raining heavily when Christina arrived at her small flat in West Didsbury, five miles south of Manchester city centre.

'Susie, I'm home,' she called as she turned the key in the front door and stepped into the narrow hall of the terraced house's ground-floor flat. There was no reply. A few moments later she remembered that her flatmate was going out with Nick, her boyfriend, that night.

Christina was pleased to be alone. She was dog-tired and relieved not to have to listen to Susie's incessant chatter. She walked into the tiny kitchen, planning to go to bed early with a large glass of white wine, a giant bag of Golden Wonder crisps, and Yuki, her Siamese cat, hopefully to be in a deep sleep before Susie and Nick could arrive back and keep her awake with their noisy lovemaking.

'Shit.' She slammed the fridge door shut angrily.

'Thanks, Susie,' she muttered, thinking how typical it was of her flatmate and the obnoxious Nick to drink the last drop of Christina's Frascati.

She poured herself a large gin instead, filled the tumbler with warm tonic, and managed to find half an ice-cube under an out-of-date packet of frozen peas.

Christina picked up her cat, and carrying her under one arm, the gin and tonic in the other hand, and the bag of crisps held between her teeth, padded towards her bedroom.

There was a message sellotaped to her bedroom door, penned in Susie's almost illegible scrawl.

Kate Mason from your agency rang. She asked if she could give a Mr Stephen Reece-Carlton your telephone number. He was trying to reach you urgently.

If he is the same Reece-Carlton I think he is, you've snared a big one, Chrissy!

Don't wait up for me. Nick has been away for a week and is as horny as hell – had to do it before we left the house, so God knows what time I'll emerge in the morning!

Sleep tight.

Susie.

'Stephen Reece-Carlton?' Christina said the name out loud. 'Where have I heard that name before?' she asked herself, and searched her memory whilst peeling off her clothes and hanging them carefully in the small fitted wardrobe.

She lay on top of the bed in a big baggy nightshirt and took a deep gulp of her gin and tonic. Yuki crept across the bedspread and snuggled close to her. Christina tickled the cat's tummy, enjoying the softness of her warm coat.

It was then she remembered where she had seen the name before. Stephen Reece-Carlton was co-owner with

Robert Leyton of the Westside Shopping Centre – his name had been mentioned in the *Manchester Evening News* a couple of weeks ago. Stephen . . . she remembered Robert Leyton's behaviour towards the man she had been talking to at the mall. They had obviously been business associates. Pale-green eyes, a strong determined jaw . . . So *that* was Stephen Reece-Carlton!

Maybe this time she would let Kate pass on her number, something she had automatically refused on every occasion before now.

'Christina, you must go out with him. You're mad if you don't,' Susie said between mouthfuls of cornflakes.

'Why must I just because he calls my agency and asks for my private number?'

'Then he calls you ten minutes after he gets the number and asks you out. If that's not keen, what is?' Susie cut in.

'I don't even know the man. Why should I go out with a complete stranger?' Christina said, and took a sip of tea from a Snoopy mug she was holding.

Susie scooped up the last of her cornflakes and pointed the spoon in her direction.

'He's filthy, stinking rich, that's why.'

Christina raised her clear brown eyes. 'I might have known that would be your reaction. For God's sake, Susie, is that all you can think about? The size of their wallet?'

Susie pulled a face, considering. 'The size of their dick?'

Christina burst out laughing in spite of herself.

'I could get lucky, Susie. He might be blessed in both departments.'

'Then, my girl, you've hit the jackpot. Go on, call him back and tell him you'll see him.'

'I've already told him I'm busy next Thursday. I promised to go to Robin's party and that was the only night Stephen could make it. He lives in London and only comes up here occasionally.'

38

Christina looked at Susie, who shook her head in disgust. 'Robin Hargreaves is the biggest wimp in the entire county – possibly the whole country! Come on, Christina.'

She agreed with Susie and her voice was lame when she said, 'But I've promised Robin. He'd be so disappointed.'

Susie ignored her. Standing up from the tiny kitchen table, she walked to the sink and filled the kettle with water to make a fresh cup of tea. She caught sight of herself in a small mirror stuck on the front of the fridge door and groaned.

'God, I look like death warmed up. That Nick is insatiable. In fact, I've decided the man's an animal.' She giggled, and Christina smiled.

'I must say I have seen you looking better, but you're crazy about him, so don't complain.'

Susie nodded. 'But he's broke and I get sick of always having to take him out.' She paused. 'Now, if I had your looks and the opportunity to go out with a big fat fish like Reece-Carlton, I'd be there with my boots blacked and my pussy powdered.'

'Susie!' Christina pretended to look shocked before saying, 'I will call him back, I promise, but not today. I'm sure Mr Reece-Carlton can have plenty of girls at the snap of his fingers, so it won't hurt to play hard to get.'

Susie winked. 'Good girl. But whatever you do, don't keep him waiting too long. Let's be fair – Robin Hargreaves will wait forever, but I doubt Stephen Reece-Carlton will do the same.'

'Good morning. Metropole Leisure. How can I help you?'

Christina's heart began racing as soon as she heard the receptionist's voice.

'Mr Reece-Carlton, please.' She made her voice sound crisp and businesslike.

'Mr Reece-Carlton is in a meeting,' the impersonal voice informed her. 'If you wish to leave a message I can transfer you to his secretary.'

Christina was about to say she would call back when the secretary's voice came on the line.

'Good morning, Rachael Newton speaking. How can I help you?'

This voice sounded older and kinder. Christina felt more at ease.

'I would like to speak to Mr Reece-Carlton, please.'

'I'm afraid he's in a meeting. Can I help you with anything?'

Christina paused, deliberating as to whether to leave a message or not, when the secretary said, 'Oh, Mr Reece-Carlton has just walked out of the meeting and will be able to speak to you now. Please hold.'

Christina was holding the receiver with one clammy hand whilst doodling on a message pad with the other. She was suddenly gripped by an overwhelming urge to put the telephone down when she heard him say, 'Hello, this is Stephen Reece-Carlton.'

His voice sounded deeper than she remembered from their brief meeting at the shopping mall and even briefer telephone conversation two days after that.

'Good morning, this is Christina O'Neill.'

There was a short pause which seemed interminable, and she thought for one terrible minute that he had forgotten who she was.

'Sorry, Christina. Can you hold for one minute? My private line is ringing.' He did not wait for her to reply, and she held the silent receiver for a few minutes more before Stephen's voice returned, bright and enthusiastic now.

'How are you?' He seemed genuinely pleased to hear from her. She felt encouraged.

'I'm fine, thanks, and you?'

'Busy as usual, but delighted you rang. I'm planning to come up to Manchester on Thursday as I said, and the offer still stands. I'd love to take you out to dinner if you can make it.'

'I did have a date, as I told you when you rang, but the party has been cancelled,' she lied. 'So the answer's yes, I'd really like to go out for dinner with you.'

'You don't sound sure about that, Christina.' Stephen had detected the hesitation in her voice.

She forced herself to sound more self-confident. She wanted to see him again, but wasn't used to such a high-powered approach. Packed schedule, private line, deferential secretary – she had a sneaking suspicion that Stephen Reece-Carlton was out of her league.

'Of course I'm sure,' she forced herself to say lightly. 'I wouldn't be calling you otherwise, would I.'

He laughed. 'That's true. Okay, Miss O'Neill, we've got a date. I don't know where you live but I'll be staying at the Midland Hotel on St Peter's Square, so if you give me your address . . .'

She interrupted. 'We could meet at the Midland. I'll be working in town that day so that would suit me fine. Say 7.30 in the bar, if that's okay with you?'

'Perfect,' he said. 'Till Thursday, then, Christina. I'll look forward to it. Bye for now.'

He rang off as she was saying goodbye.

She replaced the receiver, pleased that her heart had stopped racing and excited now about her forthcoming date.

'Finished?' her agent, Kate Mason, asked as she walked into the small, cluttered office where Christina had been using the telephone. She walked towards her desk, a large envelope in her elegant, manicured hands.

'Yes thanks, Kate. I'll pay you for the call. It was urgent and couldn't wait until I got home.'

'No problem, be my guest.' Kate detected a slight

nervousness in Christina's voice. 'Are you okay?' she enquired.

'Yes, I'm fine.' Christina nodded, and her long, glossy chestnut hair fell in thick waves across one cheek. She looped it back and looked across the desk.

'You're going to be pleased with these.' Kate held up the envelope. 'These, young lady, are fantastic.'

She moved a stack of other photographs and papers to one side and laid out the composite sheets before Christina, who stared at the forty or fifty small images through a hand lens, barely recognizing herself.

The photographer had caught a sensual yet innocent quality in her perfect oval face.

'Look at that shot. If we can't sell that to one of the glossies, I'll eat my hat.'

Kate pointed with a long, red-painted fingernail to the white cross marking an image of Christina wearing a black full-length silk jersey-dress by Bill Gibb. The photograph had been shot in a misty dawn light against the backdrop of the Pennine Chain. Her hair was loosely caught up in a diamante pin, and stray locks tumbled down to play about her face and shoulders.

'They don't look like me at all,' Christina gasped. 'I look like a wanton young gypsy girl.'

Kate tapped the sheet. 'They do look like you, but in a different guise. Like I said, they're fantastic.' She sounded excited. 'Colin is a bloody expensive photographer but he's worth every penny. These could make you a fortune.'

The light in Kate Mason's eyes suddenly reminded Christina of a similar expression she had seen so often shining in her father's, before he had killed himself chasing impossible dreams.

'Are you sure you're okay?' Kate looked at her expression, baffled. 'I thought you'd be pleased. This shoot is the best I've seen for years.'

Christina stared at the composite sheet.

'I am pleased, believe me, Kate. Sorry, I was miles away. Colin promised he'd destroy that one.'

Kate looked at the photograph showing Christina clad in nothing but tiny black panties, her hand covering one breast whilst she pointed an accusing finger at the camera. Her head was thrown back and she was laughing.

'On the contrary, Christina, Colin has already told me he's sold that one to *Penthouse*.' Kate's voice was deadly serious.

Christina looked shocked. Before she could speak, Kate burst out laughing. 'Only joking! But don't write the girlie magazines off, they pay bloody good money.'

Christina shook her head. 'No thanks, I'd be far better off working in Tesco.'

Several heads turned as Christina walked into the foyer of the Midland Hotel.

She had dressed carefully for her dinner date with Stephen Reece-Carlton. Fifty pounds drawn out of the bank and twenty borrowed from Susie had bought her a mid-calf-length dress and jacket in a dark emerald-green jersey wool. She had chosen black suede shoes and carried a matching suede clutch-bag. Her mane of hair had been blow-dried by Anthony at Headlines and fell past her shoulders in glossy soft waves.

She wore fake diamond stud earrings and a delicate antique watch which had been her grandmother's.

'Christina!' She heard her name called as she walked through the hotel reception heading for the bar.

She turned, an anticipatory smile lighting her face, expecting to see Stephen Reece-Carlton. Instead she was surprised to see Martin Ward waving to her from the reception area. He was a prominent figure in the city, having been signed recently by Manchester United as their great white hope of a goal-scorer for the eighties. She waved back and watched him excuse himself from the two people he was talking to and walk over to where she was standing in the lift lobby.

'Christina, how are you? Long time no see.' A wide smile lit up his boyishly handsome face. She laughed.

'The last time I saw you, Martin Ward, you were so drunk I don't think you could see or hear anything.'

He hung his head in mock shame, and she noticed how his longish blond hair curled slightly in at the nape of his neck.

'I do remember some things about that evening. You were wearing red and I was wearing black.' He looked at her with amusement in his grey-green eyes.

She laughed. 'I never wear red with this hair.' She lifted a strand. 'And to be honest, I can't remember what you were wearing.'

She glanced at her watch. It was 7.45; she was late. He noticed.

'Got a date?'

'Yes, I have, and I'm late. Lovely to see you. Oh, by the way, how's Carol?'

Martin pulled a face.

'Carol has progressed to pastures greener. She met a man with more money than sense who is at this moment indulging her every fantasy.' He winked. 'Well, not every fantasy – you know Carol! –but she seems to be having fun.'

'Sorry to rush, Martin, but I really do have to go.'

'It seems like every time we meet we're either in a hurry or with other people. How about we change that pattern and I take you out for a meal?'

Christina nodded. 'I'd like that. You've got my number – call me.'

'The club is organizing a big dinner-dance in a couple of weeks' time, so if you can get the ball-gown and tiara out of wraps, I'd love you to be my guest.'

'I would like Christina to be *my* guest this evening, if

possible.' Both Christina and Martin turned at the sound of the voice.

'Stephen.' Christina looked flustered. 'Sorry, I met an old friend.'

'Not so much of the old!' Martin smiled with the confidence of a young man who has found fame and fortune in his early twenties. Stephen did not. An awkward silence followed, broken by Christina's bright voice saying, 'Stephen Reece-Carlton – Martin Ward.'

'Pleased to meet you,' Stephen said, his voice curt.

'Likewise,' Martin said, equally abruptly, and he turned to Christina with a smile. 'Hope to see you soon. Take care.'

He walked back to join his friends. Stephen glanced at his watch.

'I think we'd better push straight off. I made a reservation for 8.30.'

'Where?'

'A surprise,' he replied, and took her gently by the arm, steering her towards the hotel entrance.

A uniformed doorman held open the door of a dark-blue Mercedes coupé, and Christina noticed that Stephen gave him a pound-note tip.

They drove south out of Manchester.

'How long have you been modelling?' Stephen asked after they had been driving for about five minutes.

'For almost a year, since I left school with bad A-level grades. I met a woman called Kate Mason at a friend's party. She's the top agent in Manchester and suggested I should become a model. I got work very quickly and easily, and as you probably know, the money when you're working regularly is pretty good.'

Stephen detected a flat note in her voice. 'You don't sound very enthusiastic.'

'I'm not, really. I get so many boring jobs to do I sometimes feel I'm wasting my time.'

45

'Like opening shopping centres?'

She laughed. 'I'm afraid standing for ten hours in a busy shopping centre is not exactly the stuff of modelling dreams.'

'I know that, but like you said on Saturday, a gal has to eat.'

'I wish I could eat a little better sometimes,' she said, and glanced at his firm profile.

'Well, Miss O'Neill, I can guarantee you are going to eat well tonight.'

'Where are we going? Please tell.' Stephen thought she sounded like an excited schoolgirl.

He looked at the speedometer. 'Ten more miles and all will be revealed.'

Fifteen minutes later they drove into the picture-postcard village of Prestbury, and pulled into the car park of the Legh Arms.

Christina let out a whoop. 'The Legh Arms! I've always wanted to come here. Wait until I tell Susie. She's going to be so green.'

'Who's Susie?' Stephen asked.

'My flatmate. She once said to me we would have to save up for a year to come to the Legh Arms.'

Stephen was pleased. He jumped out of the car and helped her out. Christina walked into the smart restaurant, head held high and face glowing with excitement.

She was oblivious to the admiring stares from other diners as she swept past, but Stephen noticed.

The tables were laid with pink cloths and silver cutlery. Stephen ordered a bottle of Dom Perignon.

'I hope you like champagne?' he asked, after the waiter had left. She was tempted to say no just to see his reaction, but thought better of it. 'I love champagne,' she said, and added, 'When I can get it.'

Her experience actually amounted to a lukewarm glass

which had been served with great pomp and ceremony at a cousin's wedding, but there was no need to make herself appear gauche, was there?

Christina had never heard of half of the dishes on the big menu she was given, and decided to play safe and have whatever Stephen had to start and Sole Bonne Femme as a main course, a dish she had had at the same wedding. It seemed more sophisticated than ordering a plain steak.

The waiter arrived to take their order.

'Christina, what would you like to start,' Stephen asked.

'I'm not quite sure yet; you choose,' she answered from behind the large menu card.

'I would like avocado and prawns to start, please,' Stephen said, and paused. 'And to follow, Steak Diane.'

'How would you like it cooked, sir?' the waiter asked.

'Medium.'

'And madam?' The man waited, pen poised.

'I think I will take avocado and prawns as well, please, and Sole Bonne Femme to follow.'

The champagne arrived and Christina drank two glasses in quick succession. She had eaten very little that day, so by the time the avocado arrived she was feeling light-headed. She stared at the dark-green fruit on her plate, covered with prawns and a Marie Rose sauce.

'*Bon appétit*,' Stephen said, and pushed his spoon into the centre of his pear.

Christina did the same, and scooped up a big piece of avocado which she placed in her mouth. It tasted bitter and waxy and she was tempted to spit it out. But Stephen was watching her, a slightly bemused expression on his face. She swallowed without chewing and almost choked. A spluttering sound came out of her throat, followed by a violent fit of coughing.

'You'll have to excuse me.' She stood up. 'I'm sorry. Something must have gone down the wrong way.'

Stephen stood up, concerned. 'Are you okay?' Her face was scarlet and two spots of Marie Rose sauce stained the collar of her dress.

'I'm fine, really. I'll be back in a few minutes.'

She rushed into the ladies' room and began rubbing the unsightly stains off her dress, talking to herself in the mirror. 'You idiot! Why did you order something you didn't know? You've made a fool of yourself now.'

She returned a few minutes later, quite composed, and noticed the way Stephen rose from his seat as she sat down. Christina had never before been out with anyone who had such impeccable manners.

'Okay now.'

He looked concerned. Her avocado had disappeared and in its place was a tiny crystal glass containing something white and frozen.

'What's this?'

'It's lemon sorbet to refresh your palate. I can get the avocado back if you like?'

'No thanks,' she said quickly, and took a mouthful of the cool, refreshing sorbet. 'Mmm, delicious.' She paused and then looked across the table at Stephen. She could read nothing in his expression.

'I have a confession to make,' Christina said, and took another scoop of her sorbet.

Stephen took a sip of champagne and looked at her over the rim of his glass.

'You hate avocado?' he said, and chuckled as she blushed.

'How did you guess?'

'Not difficult if you'd seen the expression on your face when you took the first mouthful!'

'To tell the truth I've never heard of it until tonight, and I don't think I'll be having it again in a hurry.'

'It's an acquired taste,' Stephen said, and lifted his champagne glass. 'Like good wine.'

'I'll drink to that.' Christina raised her own glass and touched his.

'To acquired taste,' she said.

'And to the money to acquire it,' he replied.

The Steak Diane and Sole Bonne Femme were perfection, as were the Chablis Grand Cru and the Belgian truffles and liqueurs served after dinner, Christina having declared herself too full for anything else.

'I think they'd like us to go, don't you?' she whispered to Stephen after her second Cointreau.

They were the only people remaining in the restaurant apart from two waiters hovering conspicuously behind their table. It was after twelve when Stephen paid the bill and they left.

'Be careful.' He grabbed her arm and saved her from falling as she tripped on a deep step at the front door.

She giggled. 'I'm afraid I've had a little too much to drink.'

'I think we both have, but my capacity is probably larger than yours, that's all.'

He opened the passenger door for her and she slipped into the seat. Her skirt rode up to her knees and he stared at her long, slim legs for a moment before slamming the door. He walked round the car and eased himself into the driving-seat.

'So tell me about yourself? I know so little about you. We seem to have spent the entire evening talking about me and my business.'

'There isn't much to tell, really. I was born in County Cork in Ireland and came to live in England at eighteen months old. We lived in several different parts of the country. My father was, as my mother put it, a dreamer, always chasing rainbows.' Christina stopped speaking and Stephen glanced at her.

'What is it?'

'I lost my father two years ago – I was only seventeen.

49

It was a bitter blow. I adored him, you see. I know now he was a hopeless romantic who found his dreams in the bottom of too many whisky bottles, but he was everything to me. After he died I was unable to concentrate. I flunked my exams. My mother went back to Ireland to be close to her sister and her three squabbling offspring, and I stayed on in Manchester and started work for Kate Mason. I accepted a job a week ago to open the Westside Shopping Mall, and now here we are.'

Christina's voice was light, but with a sidelong glance he saw how sad she looked. He had a strong urge to stop the car and take her in his arms. They travelled on in silence for a few minutes before she said, 'And what about you? You've talked about your office blocks and the shopping centres and car parks you build, the interesting places you go to and people you meet, but what about your real life? Age, where you live . . .' She paused. 'And who with.'

Christina looked at Stephen, but his face was a mask of concentration. It had begun to rain, and he was driving carefully on the narrow country lanes.

'I'm thirty-four, born in the north-east, left in my early twenties to seek fame and fortune in the south. My father's dead. My mother and half-brother still live in South Shields. I work too hard, don't play hard enough. I have a country house in Sussex and a central-London flat. No steady girlfriends. That's about it, really; not a lot to tell.'

She sensed he did not want to open up any further to her.

'Just answer one question – are you married?'

'I was, but she died.'

Christina looked straight ahead. 'I'm sorry.' Trust her to open her big mouth and put her foot in it!

'I have had a wonderful evening; I can't thank you enough,' Christina said as Stephen pulled the car up in front of the little terraced house.

He turned off the ignition.

'The feeling is entirely mutual. I'd love to do it again sometime.'

She was about to invite him in for coffee when he jumped out of the car and ran around to the passenger door to help her alight. She decided not to do as he probably expected.

'You've got my number; call me next time you're in town.'

'Goodnight, Christina.' He leaned forward and pecked her on the cheek. She turned her face towards his and returned the kiss, lightly brushing his lips with her own.

'Goodnight, Stephen, and thanks again for a memorable evening.' She paused for a moment before saying, 'If I never see you again, at least I can tell everyone I've been to the Legh Arms and drank Dom Perignon.' She started to walk away.

'You will be seeing me again, Christina, I promise,' he said softly in the deserted street.

The following morning Christina awoke with a splitting headache. She staggered to the bathroom, almost bumping into her flatmate coming out.

Susie looked at Christina's pale face and narrowed eyes. 'You don't look too good this morning. Good night, was it?'

Christina groaned, holding her head in both hands.

'Too good. Do you have any aspirin?'

'Hang on a tick, I'll get you a couple. Go back to bed and I'll bring them to you. It's only seven o'clock.'

'Thanks, Sue, you're a pal.'

Christina shuffled back into her bed. The thundering in her temples increased as she lay down.

Susie appeared a few minutes later with two paracetamol, a large glass of water, and a cup of weak tea. 'Come on, sit up. This will put you right.'

Christina did as she was told and threw the tablets down her throat, swallowing them with two deep gulps of water.

Susie propped three pillows behind Christina's head and handed her the mug of tea.

'So how was it?'

She couldn't wait for Christina's head to ease; she had to know now. 'Where did you go?'

'The Legh Arms,' Christina mumbled over the top of the mug.

'You jammy thing!' Susie sat on the edge of the bed, her eyes wide and excited.

'Nick would have to sell his old MGB to afford to wine and dine me in the Legh Arms.' Her voice was resigned. 'So when are you going to see him again?'

Christina shrugged her shoulders and downed the last drop of tea.

'He said he would call me.'

'When?' Susie demanded.

'How should I know? He might never call. He's a busy guy, got property developments going on all over the place.'

'What kind of car did he have?'

'A Mercedes,' Christina replied, her voice impatient. 'What difference does that make?'

Susie grimaced. 'You try going out in a sports car that leaks most of the time, feels like you're in a wind tunnel and if you're not careful your foot drops through the passenger floor . . . believe me, it makes a hell of a lot of difference.

'So what did you have to eat?'

Christina moaned. 'I think I had more to drink than I had to eat.' She slid down the bed and pulled the covers over her face.

'I can see you don't want my company, Miss O'Neill.'

Christina's head moved up and down under the covers.

'Okay, I know when I'm not wanted. I'll see you later.

Don't forget I'm going to Paul Colville's party tonight and you promised to lend me your black dress.'

Christina's head moved in the affirmative, and Susie left the room, switching off the light before she left.

Christina went back to sleep, to be woken four hours later by the telephone ringing.

She reached the phone located in the hall on its final ring.

'Christina! At last!' It was Kate Mason's husky voice.

'Yes, sorry, Kate. I overslept. Had a late night.'

'Model girls should not have late nights; they need their beauty sleep,' said Kate in her best schoolma'am's tone.

Christina felt like telling her to shut up, but Kate continued talking. 'I've got some great news for you, Christina. A big photographic shoot in two weeks' time for an American glossy. Five days' work for a big fat fee of £400!'

'That's great.' Christina could hardly believe what Kate was saying. Five days' work at a rate far higher than usual.

'The shoot is in London with a top photographer, so no more late nights for you, young lady. I'll see you later if you stop by the office. I've got a couple of small jobs for you this week.'

'What are they?' Christina asked.

'One is for the Milk Marketing Board and the other for a small old-fashioned lingerie house. They want a nasty cross-over bra and big knicker advert.'

'They both sound like a bundle of fun.'

'As I keep reminding you, Christina, they're your bread and butter.'

'I know, I know.' She looked at the hall clock. 'I'll see you about 2.30, okay? I've got a couple of things to pick up before I come into town.'

'No later,' Kate informed her. 'I've a meeting at three. See you, then. Bye.'

Christina walked back to her bedroom, thinking about

the photographic shoot and Stephen's words to her on parting last night.

Perhaps, Mr Reece-Carlton, she thought, I may be able to buy my own champagne in the not too distant future.

Susie was arranging twenty-four long-stemmed red roses in a water jug when Christina came home later that day.

'They arrived just as I did.' Susie pointed to the flowers, sighed, and said in an affected voice, 'I can't begin to imagine who they are from.'

She held out a small white greetings card. Christina tore it open.

'I had a marvellous evening – thanks for your company,' she read aloud.

'Smoothie, smoothie!' Susie yelled.

'You're only jealous,' Christina commented, and drew out one red rose. Holding it to her nose, she inhaled deeply.

'By the way, I got a fantastic job offered to me today. Five days' work in London for £400.'

'Wow!' Susie grabbed her friend's hands and squeezed them tight. 'That's great. Perhaps you'll be able to pay me back the eighty quid you owe me? I'm a bit short this month.'

Christina bit her lip. 'I'm sorry, Sue, but you know how it is in this game – always waiting so long for your money.'

She looked in concern at Susie's round, amiable face and bright-blue eyes.

'I'll pay you back with interest this time, I promise.'

Susie winked. 'I was only joking. Anyway, you know me. As I've always said, a friend in need is a pest – and you are the best pest I've ever had.'

Christina laughed and drew her arms around the small, plump girl.

'And you, Susan Philips, are the funniest, kindest and best friend I have ever known.'

'I'll drink to that,' Susie said, and produced a bottle of sparkling wine from the fridge. 'Not quite Dom Perignon, Chrissy, but it's all we've got, and if we drink enough it will have the same effect.'

Chapter Two

'Just one more shot, Christina . . . Good . . . Drop your left shoulder, moisten those lips. Come on, now, sultry eyes, mouth slightly open – wonderful! More teeth, wide eyes, left hand on leg. Imagine you're in bed with Robert Redford.'

She pulled a long face.

'Well, whoever turns you on, darling,' the photographer urged. 'Come on, baby, think sensual. You're making love to the man of your dreams. He's an Adonis, he's fantastic in bed. Imagine him caressing you.'

Christina imagined what she would actually like – a long hot bath, then, dressed in furry slippers and cosy bathrobe, a large gin and tonic in her hand, to curl up in front of a TV movie. It worked.

Max Raynor shouted: '*Bellissima*, Christina. Hold it like that. Don't move.'

The camera clicked furiously before he raised his head. 'Wonderful stuff. You're a gem.'

He looked at her, draped across an antique French day-bed. 'That's it, baby. We can wrap it up now.'

She relaxed and let her head drop onto the back of the padded chaise.

'I've got some great shots. You've worked really hard. Thanks.'

He stretched his lean frame and walked across his studio towards an assortment of transparencies scattered in disarray across a huge desk. 'Mmm, very nice,' he commented as he flicked through them, his trained eye picking out the best images at a glance.

He rummaged in a drawer under his desk and, producing a small tobacco tin and cigarette papers, began to roll a joint.

Christina massaged the back of her neck and said, 'Kate should have warned me I was going to be working with a slave-driving maniac who I now know has a reputation for overworking his models and sacking those who can't stand the pace.'

Max was one of the top photographers in Europe and could afford to be choosy.

With a dismissive shrug of his narrow shoulders, he said, 'A lot of girls are lazy. If they want to work with me, that's exactly what they have to be prepared to do. Work.'

He handed her the joint.

Christina shook her head. 'No thanks, I don't, but I'd love a glass of wine.'

'One glass of plonk coming up.'

Max poured a tumbler full of cheap red wine and handed it to Christina, who screwed up her small nose when she tasted the bitter Chianti.

He noticed her grimace and shook his head. 'Not good, eh?'

'I have had better.' She took another sip and added, 'I have had worse as well.'

He joined her on the sofa, 'So, Miss O'Neill.' Max eased his thin body close to hers, crossing his legs – a habit she detested in men. 'You're leaving me to rush back to darkest Manchester tonight? I can't for the life of me understand why when you could stay at my place. The bed is clean, and I know a very chic little Italian restaurant I think you'd love.'

Max inhaled the marijuana deep into his lungs and closed his deep-set dark-blue eyes.

Christina was very tired. She was also acutely

disappointed. Stephen had been in France all week but had promised to get back for the weekend. A brusque telephone call earlier that day from his secretary had informed her that Mr Reece-Carlton was delayed in Paris and would call her on his return tomorrow morning.

'Thanks for the offer, Max, but I've got to get back to Manchester. I have someone waiting for me.'

She fervently wished it were true.

'Woe is me.' Max pulled a long face. 'Is there no way I can tempt you?' He paused and then said, 'How about the promise of the front cover of *Vogue* next month?'

Christina stood up wearily. Every muscle in her body ached. She walked to the back of the studio and picked up her overnight bag.

'Just going to get changed. I won't be long.'

Max waved, a faraway expression on his face.

Christina squeezed into the tiny bathroom and peeled off the black-velvet boned bodice and long handkerchief chiffon skirt she was wearing. She then took off a heavy gold chain, earrings and assorted bangles, placing them carefully into a jewellery box.

Dressed in her own pale-blue leather trouser-suit and boots, she walked back into the studio, the clothes draped over one arm and the jewellery box in her other hand.

'Where do you want me to leave this stuff, Max?'

He ignored her question and took one last drag of the joint before grinding it into a cracked saucer.

Christina watched him run grubby hands across his groin.

'Bloody good dope,' he said. 'I feel so fucking randy. Are you sure I can't persuade you to stay?'

She shook her head.

'Sorry, Max, I've got to.get back to Manchester.'

She dropped the clothes and box onto a small chair next to her, eager now to leave. Stephen had let her down. She wanted to get home and sleep for a week.

Max stood up and crossed the few feet that separated them. Taking both her hands in his he said, 'Don't take any notice of me. I'm just a little stoned; it always makes me horny. Anyway, I fancy you like mad.'

The blush that spread over Christina's face seemed to encourage him, and he tried to pull her closer.

She backed off and chose her words carefully.

'Really, Max, I'm very tired. And, like I said, someone's waiting.'

'Okay, okay, I get the message.' He dropped her hands. 'It's been great working with you. I've been in this game a long time and believe me when I say you have a lot of potential.' His voice was sincere as he leaned forward and pecked her on the cheek.

'Thanks, Max, I really appreciate that,' Christina said.

'Off you go, then.'

He steered her towards the door, and patted her gently on the bottom.

'Back to the sticks, baby. Bye bye.'

She let herself out of the studio in Elm Park Mews into a warm, dusky evening. Fading sunlight glinted on the windows of the pretty, shuttered houses, where gaily coloured flowers spilled in profusion from window boxes and an assortment of terracotta and stone pots.

She recognized the number-plate, SRC 20, as the dark-blue Mercedes turned the corner into the mews.

Christina waved furiously, and was unable to stop a wide smile from transforming her face as the car pulled to a halt next to her and Stephen jumped out.

The exhaustion she had felt only moments previously evaporated, to be replaced by a feeling of euphoria when he ran towards her.

'I'm so pleased I caught you.' Stephen raked his fingers through dishevelled dark-brown hair. 'I've driven like a maniac from Heathrow to get here. I finished in Paris quicker than I thought and literally raced out to Charles de Gaulle. The flight took off moments after I boarded. Then I ran through Heathrow, and had a real up-and-downer with the customs boys who stopped me. The traffic was dreadful on the M4 . . . I really didn't think I'd make it.'

He stopped for breath, and Christina said, 'I was on my way back to Manchester. Your secretary left a message to say you were delayed.'

'Excuse me, is that your car?' an irritated voice intervened. 'I can't get out.'

'Sorry,' Stephen said to the irate driver, and, picking up Christina's bag, he led her to his car, which was double-parked. He backed quickly up the narrow mews.

'I've rung the studio three times in the last two days. The phone either rings continuously or else some dimwit of a girl answers and seems incapable of taking a message coherently.'

'We've been out on location for two days and the girl you are referring to is Max's assistant, Pippa, a complete air-head.'

Stephen stole a swift sideways glance at Christina, feeling ridiculously pleased to see her.

Her face was flushed and her eyes were bright with anticipation. She caught his glance and a surge of excitement passed between them.

'Fancy something to eat?' he suggested.

'I'm absolutely starved. I haven't had a good meal for five days. Max seems to live on sandwiches and take-away Chinese and Indian.'

'Okay. What sort of food?'

'I really don't mind. As my father used to say, I could eat a scabby horse between two mattresses.'

Stephen chuckled. 'I've got just the place, and it's only round the corner. Fingers crossed it's not fully booked.'

Christina lifted both her hands and crossed two sets of

fingers. Stephen turned the car into Roland Gardens and pulled up outside Blake's Hotel.

'You jump out while I try to park,' he said.

Christina did as she was told, and walked up three deep stone steps into what resembled a very chic London town-house. Entering the small reception area, she felt as if she was in a private home, and stood awkwardly next to the discreet reception desk manned by a trendy young man.

'Can I help you?' he asked pleasantly.

'I'm waiting for someone, actually,' she replied in a small voice, and turned as she heard the young man say, 'Mr Reece-Carlton, how are you?'

'I'm fine, Rupert. And you?'

'Overworked, underpaid, and busy,' he replied, and then added, 'So what's new?'

Stephen led Christina to the head of a narrow open-tread staircase, calling to Rupert before they descended, 'See you soon. Take care.'

'You obviously come here often,' Christina said before she reached the bottom of the steep stairs.

'I used to stay here a lot before I bought a place in London.'

'Monsieur Reece-Carlton, long time no see.' The head waiter came forward.

'I'm afraid I don't have a reservation, Philippe.' Stephen's voice was apologetic.

The small man glanced at his reservations list and his watch. It was 8.30.

'I can give you a table now, but I'm afraid you will have to vacate it by 10.30. I have an after-theatre reservation.' He looked at Stephen. 'Is that okay?'

'That's fine by me.' Stephen stood back to allow Christina to follow the head waiter to their table, which was located in the far corner of the small restaurant.

'Aperitifs, I presume?' Philippe asked as they sat down.

'I would like a large glass of Perrier, please, with lots of ice and lemon,' Christina said.

Stephen ordered a glass of champagne.

'What a fantastic place.' She looked around the dimly lit restaurant, fascinated.

There were long-stemmed white lilies spilling out of several tall glass vases and unusual feathery tulips in the palest shade of pink on every table.

The dark, narrow bar was packed with smartly dressed people, and Frank Sinatra's voice crooned in the background. Their drinks arrived along with the menus.

Christina, determined not to make a fool of herself again, asked, 'Can you advise me what to have, Stephen? You must know the menu pretty well by now.'

'It does change, but there are some firm favourites.' He glanced at the carte.

'Why don't you try the soup followed by fish? It's always very good here.'

Christina took his advice.

The food was delicious. She ate most of her cream of leek soup with two chunks of crusty granary bread, all of the baked fish with tomato sauce, and polished off her portion of potatoes dauphinoise and most of Stephen's. They drank vintage champagne followed by a Château Petrus.

It was almost 10.30 when Stephen suggested they have a nightcap in the small, deep-seated area located off the restaurant. Christina was a little tipsy as she sank into the soft Oriental cushions. Stephen joined her.

Brandy and chocolates arrived a few moments later.

'You must try one of these chocolates. They're out of this world.'

He pointed to the tiny dish of very thin, flat, dark chocolates. She nodded, and he was about to pick up the dish to hand her one when she leaned forward, her wide mouth slightly open. In a teasing voice she said, 'You give me one, please.'

He picked up a sweet and very slowly placed it in her mouth. She licked his fingertips before he withdrew them, then her own lips.

She looked into Stephen's pale-green gaze, and neither of them spoke for a couple of moments until Christina said, 'Absolutely delicious. May I have another one?'

He grinned. 'The same way?'

'Yes, please.'

He placed the chocolate in her mouth, only this time traced her slightly parted lips with one finger whilst she chewed, slowly and deliberately.

His fingertips trailed down her neck and brushed lightly across her shoulders.

Christina shuddered.

'Do you want to go now?' Stephen's voice was thick when he whispered in her ear.

'I thought you'd never ask.'

They left the restaurant ten minutes later and drove to his flat in Kensington. Neither of them spoke much during the fifteen-minute drive. They were both absorbed in their own thoughts.

Stephen's flat, though not as big as she had expected, was exquisitely furnished.

'It looks like something out of a glossy magazine,' she commented on entering the big open-plan living-room, dominated by two enormous, deep-cushioned beige sofas, covered in piles of assorted cushions.

A two-inch-thick glass-topped coffee table housed stacks of glossy magazines and books, plus framed photographs and a beautiful antique dish containing pot pourri.

'Have a seat.' Stephen indicated the sofa. 'Drink?'

'I think I've had enough to drink.'

'A final nightcap,' he said, opening a bottle of champagne.

'Okay, you twisted my arm.' Christina took off her

63

jacket and draped it over a delicately carved occasional chair.

'You have wonderful taste.' She sank into the luxurious sofa, running her hand across the smooth surface of a silk cushion.

'Not guilty,' Stephen said, pouring two glasses of champagne. 'My wife was born with several silver spoons in her mouth and grew up surrounded by beautiful things. She became an interior designer. All this . . .' – he gestured casually – 'is her work.'

He joined her on the sofa, handing her a glass as he sat down.

Christina took a sip of champagne.

'Mmm, this is lovely.'

'Krug is the best in my opinion.'

Stephen sipped his champagne, and stared at her over the rim of the glass.

'Has anyone ever told you that you have beautiful eyes? Such an unusual colour.'

'Millions of randy young men.'

Stephen looked pensive. 'I thought as much,' he said, and began to rummage amongst the books on the coffee table, mumbling, 'I wonder where it is?'

'What are you looking for?' Christina enquired.

I'm looking for my *How to Seduce a Beautiful Young Woman* manual. I'm sure it's here somewhere.' He looked at her helplessly. 'You see, I'm lost without it.'

Christina giggled, a deep, throaty sound.

'How about I teach you, Mr Reece-Carlton, since you're such a novice?' She lowered her eyes shyly. 'I'm not exactly the voice of experience, but I'm sure we could learn as we went along.'

He placed his glass of champagne on the coffee table and slid along the sofa to where she was sitting.

'That sounds like a great idea to me. I'll be your willing pupil.'

'Lesson number one, you kiss me.'

Stephen leaned towards her and, cupping her chin in his hand, kissed the end of her nose.

She closed her eyes as the tip of his tongue very gently licked the outside of her lips, gently prising them open before his own lips covered hers and his tongue explored the inside of her mouth.

'Lesson number two,' Christina whispered, as he started to kiss her neck, 'you take off my blouse.'

'I'll do whatever you say.' He was clearly enjoying the game.

Stephen undid the tiny buttons down the front of Christina's shirt. It fell open to reveal a half-cup white-lace bra, barely containing her round breasts.

He ran his fingers across her bare stomach, then circled first one nipple then the other with the palm of his hand. Her nipples rose in response, and he unhooked her bra. He caressed one breast whilst exposing the other, which he fell upon, sucking and pulling her hard nipple into the soft folds of his mouth.

'Lesson number three,' she gasped, breathless, as he ran his tongue across her stomach, 'you take off my trousers.'

He kneeled at her feet and pulled both her boots off before unzipping her leather trousers and sliding them down her long, lightly freckled legs.

Christina squealed as she spotted her big toe poking through a pair of worn Mickey Mouse socks.

She looked at Stephen, who hadn't noticed. He was too busy staring at her tiny white-lace bikini-briefs and the thick triangle of dark-brown pubic hair just visible beneath. He pulled off her old socks and flung them over the top of the sofa, then ran his tongue slowly up the inside of her thigh and across the front of her panties, biting gently into the open lace.

He lifted her legs onto the sofa and laid her carefully on her back, putting a cushion under her head.

He was kissing her passionately now, his mouth hard and urgent.

'You're beautiful, Christina,' he told her between frenzied kisses.

She began to undo the buttons of his shirt.

'Lesson number four . . .'

'Lesson number four, Miss O'Neill, is I fuck you until you tell me to stop.'

'You're a very good pupil, Mr Reece-Carlton,' she said in a breathy voice.

He looked deeply into her half-closed eyes.

'I catch on quick, Miss O'Neill.'

The loud blare of a car horn woke Christina the following morning.

She sat up and stared at her surroundings, confused for a few moments, until she realized that she was in Stephen's bed in his flat in London.

She recalled their lovemaking of the previous evening and, with a satisfied grin on her face, sank back down into the deep feather pillows.

A few moments later she looked up as Stephen appeared at the door, dressed in a long navy-blue bathrobe and carrying a tray of scrambled eggs and smoked salmon, plus a jug of what looked like fizzy orange juice and two glasses.

'Good morning. Sleep well?'

'Like a log, but I always wake early whatever time I go to bed. I'm afraid I've got an inbuilt alarm clock. I crept out of bed like a mouse this morning so as not to disturb you.'

'What's that?' She pointed to the tray.

'This is breakfast in bed, Stephen Reece-Carlton-style. So come along, young lady, sit up. We're going to eat.'

He dropped his robe and she averted her eyes, suddenly embarrassed at the sight of Stephen's lean, muscular body.

He noticed her embarrassment and quickly slid into bed next to her, pulling the covers over his nakedness and placing the tray between them.

He handed her a fork and a napkin.

'Dig in. It's delicious.'

'What's the orange stuff in the eggs?' she asked, pushing her fork into the centre of the plate.

'It's smoked salmon.' He poured a glass of the fizzy orange mixture, saying, 'One Bucks Fizz coming up.'

'Bucks Fizz?' She raised her straight eyebrows and took the glass.

'Champagne and freshly squeezed orange juice.'

'This is a very decadent breakfast,' she said between sips of Bucks Fizz. 'You're spoiling me, Stephen.'

He looked at the napkin draped across her breasts, one pert nipple protruding.

'And why not?'

'Talking of spoiling . . .' Christina ran her fingers up the inside of his thigh. 'Why don't I try spoiling you a little in return?'

Stephen put the tray on the floor.

'Why not indeed?'

It was almost midday when they left Stephen's flat and walked to High Street Kensington where they hailed a cab to the West End.

They wandered hand in hand down Bond Street, idly window-shopping, with Christina chatting non-stop.

'What a fantastic dress.' She pointed to a black silk creation in the window of Yves St Laurent.

'It would look a lot better on you than on that skinny mannequin,' Stephen declared, and before she could say another word he pulled her towards the big glass entrance door. 'Come on, try it on.'

'No, Stephen, it will cost the earth. I can't afford Yves St Laurent,' she protested.

'But I can,' he remarked, and pushed her into the shop.

An elderly shop assistant dressed in a simple yet very chic Yves St Laurent shift dress came towards them.

'Can I help?' she asked, staring disdainfully at Christina, who was now acutely aware of her creased trousers and cheap blouson shirt.

'We're interested in the black dress in the window,' Stephen said.

The assistant beamed at him.

'Oh, yes, it's stunning.'

She glanced at Christina, weighing her up.

'Size ten, I would say.'

Christina held her head high and stared back aloofly. 'You're dead right.'

'Charlotte, check if we have a size ten in the black silk, please,' she snapped at a girl standing a few feet away.

Charlotte arrived a few minutes later with the black dress draped over her arm. She smiled warmly at them both and gestured to Christina. 'The changing-rooms are over here.'

She followed the young girl, throwing a wary look at Stephen as she passed.

The dress fitted perfectly.

It was made from pure silk chiffon, cut very low at the back, almost to her waist, and falling in soft tiers to the knee. Thick black satin ribbon edged the hem and formed a waist, accentuating Christina's own small waist.

Stephen let out a low whistle as she emerged from the changing-room.

'The dress was made for you,' the assistant gushed in her best sales voice.

Stephen dragged his eyes away from Christina, who looked much older and more sophisticated in the elegant dress. 'We'll take it,' he told the assistant, ignoring Christina's shocked expression.

She was about to say 'But you haven't even asked the price', then bit her tongue, thinking that the dress was probably more than the rental on her flat for a whole year. She knew which she would rather have.

'Go on, get changed.' Stephen pushed her back into the changing-room.

'How much is it?' she hissed.

'Don't worry about the price. You look beautiful in it.'

'But, Stephen . . .'

'Shush.' He placed two fingers gently across her mouth, then walked towards the counter, putting a gold American Express card in the hand of the beaming shop assistant.

'She looked stunning in it,' the woman was saying as Christina emerged from the dressing-room and dropped the dress on the counter next to Stephen.

Sheets of tissue paper encased it before it was placed carefully in a smart black monogrammed carrier bag and handed to Christina, who was still flustered as they walked out onto Bond Street.

'You really shouldn't have done that.'

She sounded upset. He was surprised. He'd expected her to be pleased.

'Why not?'

'Because I know it must have been very expensive, and . . . it's embarrassing.'

'I really thought you'd be delighted. It was done only with that intent.' He stared straight ahead.

Neither of them spoke for a few minutes until she broke the silence.

'It's a fantastic dress. Thank you very much, Stephen. But please, never ever think you can buy me.'

'What?' He rounded on her angrily, his own temper abating when he saw her beautiful dark-amber eyes flashing defiantly at him.

Christina, he was discovering, was very different to most of the girls he took out.

'I have no intention of buying you! Christina, I mean that. I'm not being conceited when I tell you there are lots of beautiful women I could have who would be more than willing to be bought.'

She did not reply, but realized he was right. It would not be difficult for a man in his position.

They walked on in silence.

'To be perfectly honest, Christina, I was so pleased to see you, and had such an amazing time with you last night, I simply wanted to please you. It's a long time since I've felt that way about anyone.'

He lifted two fingers in the air. 'Scout's honour.'

'I bet you were never a scout!'

'I was. A sea scout, actually, for three years.' He stopped walking and turned to face her.

'Truce, Miss O'Neill?'

'You're impossible,' she said, and then added, 'Truce, Mr Reece-Carlton.'

Stephen took her to San Lorenzo for lunch, where they ate pasta and drank her favourite dry Italian Frascati. They walked to Harrods after lunch, where Stephen bought some new underwear, and Christina spent more than she ever had before on a pair of black suede shoes to match her new dress.

They arrived back at the flat at five.

Stephen busied himself making tea in the small black and chrome kitchen whilst Christina wandered around looking at books and studying photographs in antique frames.

'Who is this beautiful child?' she asked.

She was holding a photograph of Stephen pictured with a dark-haired little girl as he walked into the living-room bearing a tray of tea and fruit cake.

He placed the tray on the coffee table and took the frame from her hands.

'Tea is served,' he said, and sat on the sofa, patting a place for her to sit next to him.

He stared at the photograph. 'This is Victoria when she was six years old.'

He said the child's name with fondness.

'Who's Victoria?' Christina poured the tea.

'She's my daughter.'

'Oh.' Christina sounded shocked. She splashed tea into the saucer, and onto the glass coffee table.

'Look what a mess I've made.' She began to mop up the spilt tea with a napkin.

'Victoria is nearly eleven years old now, and you're right when you say she's beautiful.'

'I wasn't aware you had a child. Why didn't you say before now?' Christina sipped her tea and looked closely at Stephen.

His eyes shifted from her probing gaze and his face adopted the same enigmatic expression she had noticed the last time she had questioned him about his family.

'I didn't think it necessary. Anyway, you never asked.' His voice was dismissive.

Christina was about to remind him that on their first date she had asked him about his family and he had told her then he had been married and his wife had died. Why had he not taken that opportunity to mention Victoria?

Stephen, perceptive as ever under scrutiny, sensed Christina's unease, and reassured her.

'I didn't tell you because I am someone who needs to get to know people before I can open up to them. It's that simple.' He took a sip of tea. 'Victoria lives in Sussex, in my country house, and rarely comes up to town. I have a housekeeper there, Mrs Barnes, who looks after her whilst I am away.

'I do try to spend as much time as possible with Vicky at weekends. She and I have become very close since her mother's unfortunate death.'

71

'How did your wife die, Stephen?' He hesitated, deep in thought for a few moments, then said, 'Barbara killed herself. An overdose of alcohol and barbiturates.'

He closed his eyes as if to blot out a painful memory. They were still closed when he continued.

'Barbara had a lot of problems, and I don't think I helped. She was constantly accusing me of working too hard and neglecting her. She was an extremely demanding woman.'

His eyes were open now but staring straight ahead, unblinking. His voice was very quiet and resigned when he said, 'I wasn't capable of giving her everything she needed.'

He directed his brooding gaze at Christina. There was no pain visible now, only resignation. He looked away and poured himself another cup of tea, more for a distraction than anything else.

'Well, we have something in common, Stephen,' Christina murmured softly. 'We've both lost loved ones in a tragic way.'

She pushed a cushion to one side and found his hand. He lifted it to his face and kissed her palm, then her fingertips, one by one.

The gesture sent a thrill through her entire body. She stared at his long, angular face, scrutinizing every one of his features individually so as to imprint them on her mind, never to forget his image.

It was that moment that she realized she was hopelessly in love with Stephen Reece-Carlton.

'Where on earth did you find her?'

Nigel Sinclair stood with Stephen whilst both men watched Christina dancing with a huge red-faced bear of a man, who was sweating profusely and spinning her to and fro in a pathetic attempt at rock and roll.

'In a shopping centre in Manchester, actually.' Stephen

looked at his host's bemused face. 'I've always maintained the prettiest girls in this country are from the North, and so unspoilt.'

Nigel dragged his eyes reluctantly from Christina, whose long legs were revealed every time her partner spun her round.

'Is she totally unspoilt, old chap?' He nudged Stephen, an insidious leer curling the corners of his full mouth. The inference was obvious.

'That's none of your business,' Stephen growled.

'Okay, Stephen, keep your shirt on.' He held up his hand. 'A chap likes to know these things, that's all.'

Nigel gave Stephen a chummy slap on the back. Jerry Lee Lewis's thumping piano in 'Great Balls of Fire' ended and Christina emerged from the conservatory, which was set up as a disco, to join Stephen and Nigel.

'Thank goodness the DJ changed the music. That guy was all set to rock and roll me to death.' She was breathless, a becoming glow suffused her entire face, and most of her hair had tumbled out of the neat chignon she had spent half an hour perfecting. Her eyes sparkled as she smiled at the two men.

Nigel was clearly captivated.

'How about catching your breath with me? I can only dance to slow ones.'

Stephen held out his hand, pulling her away from Nigel Sinclair's lascivious stares.

Christina took it, and they walked back towards the darkened conservatory where several entwined couples smooched to Barry White singing 'Just the Way You Are'.

'It's been a fantastic party. I haven't enjoyed myself so much in years.' Her voice bubbled with exuberance.

She could smell his Givenchy aftershave mingled with a lemon, soapy smell when she rested her head on his shoulder.

'I want to make love to you, Christina,' he whispered in her ear.

'Right at this moment?' she whispered back, and giggled.

'If it were possible, yes.' His voice grew lower.

Christina let her hand slide down his back. She moved her body level with his and pulled him gently against her.

'Stop it, Christina. I won't be able to walk off the dance-floor if you continue to do that.'

Standing on tiptoe, her eyes open in wide-eyed innocence, she kissed him lightly on the lips.

'I really don't know what you're talking about, Stephen.'

He pinched her rounded bottom and said, 'Let's go home to bed.'

'That's the best idea I've heard all evening.'

It was almost 1.30 a.m. when they said their goodbyes to Nigel and Penny Sinclair and left their beautiful white-stucco terraced house in Pelham Crescent. Christina sat close to Stephen in the back of the chauffeur-driven limousine he had hired for the evening.

'I can't start to tell you what a wonderful time I'm having, Stephen.' She sighed wistfully. 'Manchester seems a million miles away.'

The car pulled up outside Stephen's flat in Eldon Road and the driver jumped out and opened both doors.

'Thanks, Ray. I'll see you soon,' Stephen said, and put his arm around Christina to lead her through the wide, dimly lit hall to his ground-floor flat.

He was opening the door when she stepped back. 'I refuse to enter unless you carry me across the threshold.'

'Come on, Christina, it's after two; I'm tired.'

She stood her ground, challenging him.

He grinned. 'Okay. But be warned, we may not make it.' He lifted her and staggered. 'Christ! You're heavier than you look.' She kicked her legs up and down. 'You're just a weakling,' she teased, and they half fell into the entrance hall.

Stephen's legs buckled and he lost his balance as he kicked the door shut behind them.

Christina collapsed onto the Chinese washed rug in peals of laughter, dragging him down on top of her. He brushed a strand of wayward hair from her face and kissed her, gently at first, becoming hard and demanding as she said, 'Fuck me, Stephen. I want you now.'

He ripped her new dress and she stained his shirt with dark-red lipstick as they tore at each other's clothes in mutual eagerness to share each other's bodies.

Afterwards they gathered up their clothes, which were strewn around the wood-panelled hall.

Then, wearing her black lace panties on his head, Stephen chased her into his enormous marble shower, where they soaped each other in fits of giggles.

Later, dressed in one of Stephen's old shirts, her hair still damp and hanging loosely down her back, Christina joined him in the kitchen to make piles of cheese and tomato toasties which they ate greedily whilst propped up in bed on the soft feather pillows.

'Look, you're covered in crumbs.'

He pointed to the front of her shirt and picked at a couple of crumbs, deliberately stroking her breasts at the same time.

Wrapping one leg across his bare stomach, she rested her head on his shoulder. Closing her eyes, she murmured, 'I'll never forget this weekend as long as I live.'

He leaned forward and placed a kiss on her forehead.

'I hope there are going to be many more just like this.'

Christina looked up at the departures screen as they walked into Terminal 1 at Heathrow Airport. BA 294 to Manchester was boarding at gate number six.

'I'd better go.'

She shifted from one foot to the other, suddenly unsure of what to say to this man with whom she had been so intimate only a few hours before.

'You really shouldn't have paid for a flight. I could have got the train.' Her voice trailed off as she saw the slightly irritated look cross his face. She rushed on, still feeling awkward. 'Anyway, what can I say apart from what I've been saying all weekend? You must think I sound like a cracked record.'

'You don't have to say a thing, Christina. It's been a pleasure having you with me. Believe me when I say I haven't enjoyed myself so much in a very long time.' He took her hand. 'I mean that.'

'This is the final call for flight BA 294 to Manchester. Any remaining passengers please go immediately to gate six.'

'I'll call you later this evening,' he promised as they walked towards the gate.

'Goodbye, Christina. See you soon.'

It was more of a question than a statement.

'You'd better,' she said. 'I'll not forgive you otherwise.'

'You're going to miss your flight,' he said, glancing over her shoulder at a diminishing queue.

'I wish,' she sighed, and leaned forward to plant a kiss on his cheek.

'See you, and thanks again.' She ran down the ramp and placed her handbag on the conveyor, turning to wave to him before going through the security check. But Stephen had already gone.

Christina spent the entire fifty-minute flight pretending to be asleep to avoid being forced to participate in a boring conversation with a pharmaceuticals rep sitting next to her who was on his way to Manchester for a three-day sales conference.

Her mind travelled back over the last week, cataloguing the events of the last forty-eight hours so as not to forget one single moment, especially Stephen's passionate yet sensitive lovemaking.

It was 7.30 p.m. when the plane touched down at Manchester's Ringway Airport in a heavy rain-storm.

She thought with dismay of her dingy flat which desperately needed a coat of paint that she could not afford.

It was Sunday night, so Susie's big bras and panties would be dripping above the bath. There would be no food in the fridge because Susie always went to her mother's for lunch and then out to the cinema with her boyfriend in the evening.

As Christina waited, cold and shivering, in a long, straggly queue for a taxi to take her to West Didsbury, she made a silent vow. She would leave Manchester as soon as she could, with or without Stephen Reece-Carlton.

Chapter Three

The electronic gates swung open and her car swept up a long drive, past a two-acre paddock. A thoroughbred bay pony was being led towards a small fenced ménage by a dark-haired young girl who waved and smiled at Stephen as they drove past.

Christina gazed up out of the window at a tunnel of elm and sycamore branches almost touching overhead. A light breeze stirred the leaves to reveal patches of blue sky. The driveway narrowed suddenly, and they drove past a high dry-stone wall with bright-pink and dark-lavender rhododendron planted under it.

Christina gasped as the part black-and-white-timbered seventeenth-century manor house came into view. Its many mullioned windows glimmered in thick shafts of sunlight filtered through the leaves of an enormous oak tree which stood before the house.

Stephen stopped the car in front of a heavy carved oak door with a highly polished solid brass knocker in its centre. Christina stepped out and stood absolutely still, awestruck. She looked up at the crest carved into the stone above the door. There was a date below: 1626.

Christina was speechless. She had never seen such a beautiful house.

'Lovely, isn't it?' Stephen commented, opening the boot of the car to take out their bags.

'Lovely is inadequate,' she replied, and watched as the front door opened and a stocky little woman stepped out onto the worn doorstep, a Cocker spaniel racing past her legs and almost knocking her flying in its eagerness to get to Stephen.

'Mr Reece-Carlton, welcome.' The woman smiled, and tiny dark-brown eyes almost disappeared into her dough-like face. Stephen patted the excited, barking dog and smiled at his housekeeper.

'Dorothy, I'd like to introduce Christina O'Neill.'

She took one step forward and held out her hand. 'Hello, Dorothy. I've heard a lot about you.'

The housekeeper in turn extended a plump, work-worn hand, her wary eyes taking in every inch of Christina, who was acutely aware of the scrutiny.

'Pleased to meet you.' Dorothy's lips were tight and her sharp voice indifferent. She turned her attention to Stephen, who was still trying to calm the boisterous spaniel.

'Come inside, Mr Reece-Carlton. I've got something very special for you.'

Stephen patted his flat stomach. 'Don't tell me, Dot. Cinnamon and apple tart with home-made ice-cream.'

Dorothy beamed. 'And fruit cake too. That's his favourite,' she commented to Christina as they all trooped into the large, square oak-panelled hall.

Christina heard her own heels clicking on the flagstone floor and was momentarily embarrassed in such grand surroundings, but Dorothy Barnes chatted on to Stephen, not seeming to notice her discomfiture. 'Good journey? How was the traffic? It's usually so bad on Friday afternoons.'

'It was okay. I picked Christina up at Gatwick and I think we made it before the real rush.'

Stephen dropped her bag at the foot of the stairs and they followed Dorothy into a big beamed kitchen.

'Sit yourselves down,' she ordered. 'Tea coming up.'

She bustled towards a bright-red Aga, where a kettle was already simmering.

Stephen and Christina sat at a long scrubbed-pine table, which was laid with a blue and white tea set. A big earthenware pot filled with fresh flowers stood in the centre.

Christina looked around the homely kitchen. Pots and pans hung from exposed beams in the low ceiling next to clumps of dried flowers and fresh herbs. Brightly coloured ceramic containers lined the Delft-tiled work-surfaces, and greetings cards, children's drawings and cookery books covered a thick stone mantelpiece above a deep fireplace blackened with age.

'This reminds me so much of the kitchen at home,' Christina commented.

'Really?' Dorothy's thin brows raised in disbelief.

'Though you could probably fit my kitchen into your pantry! I mean the atmosphere, really,' Christina said honestly.

The housekeeper's expression softened.

'This kitchen is an extension. Mr and Mrs Reece-Carlton built it a few years ago. It was a poky little thing before, half this size.'

She placed a teapot complete with a red woollen cosy onto the table, closely followed by rich, dark-brown fruit cake and a crumbly short-pastry apple tart baked golden-brown.

'Mmm, that looks delicious.' Stephen rubbed his hands together.

'Tuck in. I hope you're hungry because I've made wholemeal scones as well.'

Dorothy looked at Christina's tall, slender figure. 'You look like you could do with feeding up.'

'I eat like a horse, actually.' And as if to confirm her statement, Christina reached across the table and helped herself to a thick slice of fruit cake.

The telephone rang, and Stephen stood up. 'I'll get it. I'm expecting a call from Robert.'

Dorothy clicked her tongue and sighed as she wiped the top of the tiled work-surfaces.

'Always telephone calls during meals . . . infernal instruments! A damn nuisance if you ask me.'

'What's a damn nuisance?' The voice belonged to the pretty young girl who had padded into the kitchen in red-stockinged feet. Christina saw it was the girl from the paddock, Stephen's daughter presumably. She was dressed in beige jodhpurs and a white cotton jumper. Her long, dark hair was pulled back in a messy pony-tail, and her small, heart-shaped face was flushed from running.

'None of your business, Miss Nosey,' Dorothy chided, affection softening her tone.

'Where's Daddy?' the child asked, then looked from Dorothy to Christina, sitting at the breakfast table.

'Who are you?' She stared unsmilingly at the visitor with wide blue-grey eyes the colour of a stormy sea. Christina was about to tell the girl her name when Dorothy cut in, 'This is Christina. A friend of your father's, come to stay for the weekend.'

'Well, he never mentioned her to me!' the girl snapped, then turned at the sound of her father's voice.

'Please don't refer to our guest as "her", Victoria,' Stephen admonished gently. 'Where are your manners?'

Not waiting for her to reply, he continued, 'Christina, may I introduce my daughter, Victoria.'

She stood up and smiled as warmly as she could into the girl's pretty, scowling face.

'Pleased to meet you. Your father talks so much about you, I've been dying to meet you.'

It was the truth. After initially being slow to speak of his daughter, Stephen now mentioned her frequently - often as the reason why he could not leave Sussex. This weekend was an attempt to ease Christina into his home

81

routine. She wished she could feel it was going to be successful, but so far the signs were far from promising.

Victoria didn't smile but lowered her eyes and in a sullen voice said, 'Pleased to meet you.' It was obvious that she felt anything but.

Victoria turned her back on Christina. With a glorious smile transforming her face she stood on tiptoes to kiss her father's cheek, flinging her arms around his neck. 'It's so lovely to have you home with me, Daddy.' She took his hand. 'I have something very special to show you upstairs. Please come with me now.' Her voice was demanding.

'Can't it wait a moment, Vicky?' He glanced in Christina's direction. 'I was about to demolish some of Dorothy's wonderful apple pie.'

'No. You'll have to come at once or it will spoil. Please, Daddy,' the girl implored.

Stephen looked over Victoria's shoulder at Christina, his eyes apologetic.

'I'll be two minutes. Don't eat all the cake.'

She smiled. 'You'll have to be quick!'

'What about your cinnamon and apple pie, Mr Reece-Carlton? I haven't stood in this hot kitchen baking all day for it to go to waste,' the housekeeper shouted.

'Oh, shut up, Dossy. You know you love baking, whether it gets eaten or not,' Victoria shouted back.

'I'll spank your hide, you cheeky little monkey.' She pointed a chubby finger at Victoria, who dragged her father out of the kitchen without so much as a glance in Christina's direction.

'I'll eat it, don't worry,' Christina said, helping herself to a large slice of apple pie.

'Thank goodness someone will.' The housekeeper sat down next to her and poured herself a cup of tea, shuffling her ample bottom into a more comfortable position.

'How long have you worked here?' Christina asked.

'Too long, I think sometimes. Especially when that imp Victoria plays me up.'

She helped herself to a huge piece of fruit cake. 'I came to work here when my eldest, John, was fifteen. He's twenty-eight now.' She looked thoughtful. 'Nigh on thirteen years. Mr Reece-Carlton hasn't had the house all that time, mind you. There was the Naughton family before that. Americans they were, a funny lot, only came here a couple of times a year. And before them there was Lady Somerville, a lovely old lady. It was her who employed me originally. I'd only been here about six months when she upped and died. My old man used to joke and say it was my pea and ham soup that killed her off!

'Then, when Mr and Mrs Reece-Carlton bought the house in 1976, they asked me to stay on.'

She took a noisy gulp of tea and slopped a little onto her pinny. 'Mrs Reece-Carlton was a real lady, very generous too. It was so tragic.'

She stopped speaking abruptly and quickly stood up as she heard Stephen's voice in the hall, followed by girlish giggles.

Victoria raced into the kitchen. 'Daddy's promised to take me to the gymkhana tomorrow, Dossy, so could you make us a picnic lunch?'

'Of course I'll make a picnic, with all your favourites.' She fondly ruffled the top of Victoria's dark head then nudged her, eyes shifting to Christina sitting awkwardly at the table, watching the cosy scene.

'Would you like to come to the gymkhana?' Victoria asked, her tone flat and lacking any enthusiasm.

'As long as I can have egg sandwiches in my picnic.'

Victoria noticed the glance she exchanged with her father and her eyes narrowed. So they had already been on a picnic together? She wasn't sure she liked the sound of that.

Going to the fridge, she poured herself some orange

juice and then sat at the breakfast table, so close to her father that they looked glued together. Stephen edged away a little, feeling uncomfortable, but Victoria slid closer to him once more.

She glanced at Christina from under thick black lashes and announced, 'I wouldn't bother coming to the gymkhana if I were you.' She helped herself to apple pie then went on, 'Unless you absolutely love horses, you'll be bored to death.'

She turned to her father for confirmation. 'Won't she, Daddy?'

'I really think that's for me to decide, don't you?'

Christina forced her mouth into the semblance of a smile as she stared into Victoria's flinty gaze, aware for the first time of the strong resemblance to Stephen when he was deep in thought.

The girl continued staring at her whilst she ate her apple pie. 'It's up to you, but don't say I didn't warn you.'

'Victoria, if Christina would like to go to the gymkhana, she can. I personally think she would enjoy it.'

Victoria poked out her tongue at her father.

He tapped the end of it with his finger. 'Put that away. You don't know where it's been.'

She giggled and poked her tongue in and out rapidly whilst Stephen pretended to try and catch it.

Christina stood up. 'Sorry, but I must use the loo.' She glanced at Stephen.

He jumped up. 'I'll show you to your room.' He pulled Victoria's pony-tail as he passed the back of her chair. 'See you later, Miss Reece-Carlton.'

'I'm going down to the stables. Come and join me there,' she said.

'Thanks for the tea, Dorothy, it was lovely – especially the fruit cake. Just like my mother makes,' Christina called across to the housekeeper, who was taking a can of dog-food out of the pantry.

'My pleasure. I like folk who eat well and appreciate my food.'

They left the kitchen and Stephen picked up Christina's bag before leading the way up a wide, dark oak staircase.

She almost slipped twice on the highly polished stairs, and noticed that the uneven floor creaked with every other step as she followed Stephen past walls lined with paintings in ornate gilded frames.

He stopped at an arched, oak-panelled door which he flung open to reveal a medium-sized room with an elegant Regency four-poster.

The room was wallpapered in a yellow and blue flowered print, and the two colours in toning shades were reflected in the bedspread, curtains, cushions and upholstery.

There was a tiny beamed bathroom *en suite* with a white tub and a small antique sink. The towels were blue with lemon edging, and there were several pots and jars containing bath oils, soaps and cotton wool.

Christina emerged from the bathroom to find Stephen standing next to a small lead-paned window sill and looking out over the garden. It was planted in Old English formal style with smooth, green lawns divided by stone-flagged paths and neat hedges within which the richly stocked herbaceous borders burst with colour. It seemed to end at a high screen of neatly trimmed, spiralling topiary.

'What a magnificent garden,' she said. 'I've never seen anything quite like it, except in films.'

'This is only half of it. Come on, I'll give you the guided tour of the grounds. Put on some suitable shoes and follow me.'

He waited patiently whilst Christina unzipped her bag and found a pair of trainers which she quickly pulled onto her stockinged feet.

He took her hand and they left the house by the front

door, meeting Muffin, the spaniel, panting on the doorstep.

'Come on, Muffy,' Stephen called as they set off down the drive. Muffin slumped down in the warm porch and dropped his head on his paws, ready for a snooze.

'He must have been down at the stables with Victoria all day,' Stephen commented. 'He usually comes back exhausted.' They walked round the side of the house, down a set of old brick steps to a narrow path where they had to walk single-file. The path twisted through a vast rose garden where Old and New English Roses, floribundas, miniatures and hybrid teas blossomed in every shade from white and palest lemon to deepest pinks and crimsons. The garden was heavy with scent.

'There are over fifty different varieties in here. My wife had this garden planted specially. It was her pride and joy. She was a keen gardener,' Stephen said in a soft voice.

'What about you?' asked Christina.

'I'm afraid I haven't got green fingers; I love to see it looking beautiful, but I'd much rather pay someone to keep it that way.'

The path ended at a crumbling old summer-house where a white rambling rose swathed the black-beamed walls.

'Come on.' Stephen opened the door and Christina stepped inside. It was damp and musty-smelling.

'This was Victoria's den.' He pointed to a heap of dusty toys piled in one corner. Rubbing a small pane in one window with the flat of his hand, he beckoned to Christina. 'Look.'

With her nose almost touching the glass, she peered out onto an enclosed patio where flowering plants poked through old flagstones and honeysuckle and clematis crawled up pale stone walls. A small swimming-pool was set in the centre. It looked unused. Dead insects and leaves floated on the surface.

'Don't you use the pool?' Christina asked, staring at the stagnant water.

'I do occasionally, but Victoria never does. She's afraid of the water. She almost drowned when she was two years old and has never forgotten it.'

'I love swimming,' Christina said.

'Well, swim you shall. I'll get Jack the gardener to clean the pool out this afternoon, and if it's warm enough we can go swimming together in the morning.'

'How about skinny-dipping this evening?' she said mischievously.

'If we can manage it, I'm game.'

They left the summer-house and walked hand in hand through several acres of woodland, completing the tour of the twenty acres of grounds at the stables, where Victoria was grooming her bay gelding in the yard as they approached.

'Come and meet Mischief.' Stephen pulled a reluctant Christina towards the fourteen-hand pony. She thought the name might be apt and approached the animal warily.

Victoria continued grooming Mischief's tail as Christina cautiously stroked his mane.

'How long have you had her?'

'Daddy bought *him* for my tenth birthday as a surprise present. Didn't you, Daddy?'

Stephen nodded and smiled.

Victoria continued speaking just to him. 'Do you remember how you tied his tail and mane with lots of big red ribbons, and what fun we had that day? I'll never part with Mischief. Even when I get big I'll still keep him.'

Victoria finished grooming the horse's tail, and put the brush on a bench by her feet. 'Daddy always knows just what to buy me.'

She stood next to her father, watching Christina stroke the pony's neck.

Stephen smiled. 'I think he likes you, Christina.'

87

'This pony has good taste,' she said, and gave his neck a final pat.

Victoria left her father's side to stand in front of Mischief, saying, 'Come on, boy, back you go.' She pushed him back towards his stall, but he was enjoying the attention he was receiving from Christina and did not want to move.

'Back, boy!' Victoria slapped his hind quarters and Mischief bucked, landing heavily on Christina's foot. She screamed and pulled away from the beast, who rolled his eyes at the noise and movement. Victoria did not spare her a glance but concentrated on calming her pony.

'Are you okay, Christina?' Concerned, Stephen bent over and examined her rapidly swelling foot.

'She'll be fine, Daddy, really. What a fuss. It happens to me all the time.'

Victoria bolted the stable half-door and held out her hand to Mischief. In it were two Polo mints which the pony took and chomped with great relish.

'See you tomorrow, my darling Mischief,' she crooned. 'I hope you're going to win for me.' Then she turned to Christina. 'I really would think twice about coming to the gymkhana tomorrow. There'll be lots of horses there and you could get trodden on again.' Her voice was cold.

Stephen took Christina's arm and gave his daughter an angry glare. 'Have you no sympathy, Victoria? Can't you see Christina's hurt?'

'It's not my fault if she's not used to being around horses.'

A petulant look appeared on Victoria's face. She would have relented and said she was sorry, if only for her father's sake, but could not bring herself to speak as she watched him supporting Christina and tenderly sympathizing with her as she limped out of the stable-yard.

Victoria threw a spiteful look in Christina's direction and muttered under her breath, though loud enough for

88

them to hear, 'Stupid girl! She's just making a fuss to get attention.' Before her father could rebuke her she ran past them and up the small service drive across the top paddock. They saw her round the back of the house and vanish from sight.

'I'm sorry about her behaviour,' Stephen apologized as he helped Christina back to the house. 'She resents anyone in my life. That's why I never bring women down here. You're the first since Barbara's death.'

Christina winced in pain and thought: If this is the way Victoria's going to act, I'll probably be the last!

She would have liked to have said so, but held back.

'I'm sure she'll get used to me in time.'

She squeezed Stephen's arm as a sharp pain shot through her ankle. She was positive that Victoria had engineered her accident and sincerely hoped that the wilful child would get used to her soon. If not, she might not survive the weekend.

Within hours Christina's foot had swelled to the size of a small balloon, and Stephen insisted on calling in his local doctor, who suggested the possibility of a hair-line fracture. There was certainly a very severe sprain. He advised an X-ray first thing Monday morning. Meanwhile he strapped her foot and ankle and gave her pain-killers, recommending lots of rest with her feet up.

Stephen had planned to go to a local Italian restaurant for dinner, so had given Dorothy Barnes the night off.

Christina insisted he should still take Victoria.

'Really, Stephen, I'll be fine if you make me a cheese sandwich and leave me here in front of the telly.'

He hesitated. 'I really don't like to.'

They were sitting in the living-room in front of a deep inglenook fireplace.

'Would you like me to light the fire?' Stephen pointed to the grate which was ready laid with logs and newspaper neatly arranged on the black, charred iron. A dog-chewed wicker basket full of extra logs stood on the hearth next to a highly polished brass fender.

Christina shook her head. 'I'm warm enough, thanks.' She shifted herself into a more comfortable position on the royal-blue damask-covered three-seater sofa with its assortment of needlepoint cushions behind her back and neck. Her leg was resting on a small foot-stool.

'Anyway, you mustn't disappoint Victoria. She's looking forward to it.'

Christina watched Stephen's reaction carefully, thinking how attractive he looked in a navy-blue sports jacket and a mint-green shirt that almost matched the colour of his eyes.

She wanted him to say that Victoria could miss her treat for once, but was not at all surprised when he said, 'I'll be as quick as possible, I promise. We'll be a couple of hours at the most.'

He looked relieved as he said again, 'Are you sure you'll be okay?'

Victoria walked into the room and stood in front of the sofa, unable to disguise the satisfied smirk on her face.

'I'm really sorry about your foot, Christina. It's such a shame you can't come with us tonight. Mario makes the most fantastic lasagne.' She smiled sweetly at her father.

'My, my, you look very pretty. Is that a new jumper?'

Victoria had changed into a soft pink angora short-sleeved sweater with the head of a white Persian kitten appliquéd on the front. It was tucked into faded blue-denim jeans with silver studs on the pockets, and she wore pink socks and pale-pink ballerina shoes with bows on the front. Her thick, glossy hair hung loose, swinging down her back and shoulders, almost touching her elbows.

'Nanny bought this for me last time she came to stay. Don't you remember, Daddy?'

Stephen shrugged. 'You know me and clothes, poppet, I can never remember things like that.' He leaned towards her. 'Now you sit and chat to Christina while I make her a sandwich; then we can go.'

Stephen left the room and Victoria sat awkwardly on the very edge of the sofa.

Christina broke the silence.

'I realize you're used to having your father's exclusive attention, Victoria, and I really don't want to spoil anything for you.'

Immediately the child got up from the sofa and stood in front of her.

'That's good, because I'm not going to let you. Just stay away from us!' Christina was shocked at the harsh words and saw something in the eyes of the eleven-year-old that chilled her to the bone.

'I think I'll go and help Daddy now,' Victoria said, and ran out of the living-room before Christina had a chance to speak to her further.

Stephen returned ten minutes later with a big tray covered in a white lace tray-cloth. He placed it in Christina's lap with a flourish.

'Dinner *à la carte*.'

'Thank you.' She looked down at the tray on which he had laid cheese and tomato toasties, garnished with lettuce and delicately cut cucumber. A slice of apple tart sat next to a bottle of chilled Frascati, and a champagne tulip held a single pale-peach rose.

A small white envelope sat on top of the pile of sandwiches. Christina lifted it up, a question in her eyes.

'Read it later.' Stephen put his hand on her shoulder and bent forward. 'I won't be long, I promise.' He glanced at the open doorway where Victoria was standing, an impatient look marring her pretty face.

He planted a soft kiss on Christina's cheek.

'See you later.'

'Have fun,' she called, and heard Victoria shouting from the hall with glee: 'Don't worry, we will!'

The last sound she heard was Victoria's delighted giggling before the door slammed shut and she was left alone.

Christina had very little appetite but drank most of the wine.

Then she remembered the little card Stephen had left for her.

Remember the last time we had cheese and tomato sandwiches?
I'll never forget.
Love, S.

Christina sighed and thought about the wonderful time they had shared in London four weeks previously. Stephen was a very different man this weekend. She was dozing in front of an old black and white movie when Stephen and Victoria returned home by taxi two hours later. Christina could tell that Stephen had been drinking as he bounded into the living-room. She noticed two scarlet spots of colour standing out on his cheeks as he sat down next to her.

'How's the lovely injured Christina?'

'All the better for seeing you.' She touched his hot cheek and leaned forward to kiss him. He jumped up as if he had been stung as Victoria bounced into the room, cheeks ablaze with excited colour and eyes sparkling.

Christina groaned inwardly. Victoria did not look in the least bit tired.

'How about a game of Monopoly?' She began to rummage in an old oak chest, pulling out an assortment of board games.

Stephen looked at the Victorian carriage clock on the carved mantelpiece and said, not firmly enough in Christina's opinion, 'I think it's bedtime.'

Victoria pouted. 'It's only ten o'clock. I don't usually go to bed until eleven on weekends.'

She held the Monopoly box in front of Stephen's face. 'One quick game, please.'

'Monopoly is not quick, Vicky, it takes hours,' he sighed.

'I don't have to get up for school in the morning, Daddy. Please.'

Her big eyes pleaded with him.

'Would you like to play, Christina?' Stephen looked at her, his eyes imploring.

'It's best if we play at the big table in the dining-room. Christina would be uncomfortable there,' Victoria announced, pulling on his sleeve. 'Come on, Daddy. I can't wait to buy up all the Mayfair properties.'

Stephen gently extracted his arm. 'I think Christina should play. It's more fun with three.'

A defiant look entered Victoria's face, and Christina suspected she was about to throw a tantrum. She doubted she could stand it, so took the easy option, yawning deliberately and then stretching.

'I'm very tired, Stephen, so I think I will leave Monopoly this time. I was never very good anyway.'

She saw the look of delight in Victoria's eyes.

'Can you help me, Stephen?'

'Of course.' He leaned down and put one strong arm around her back and another under her legs, lifting her into his arms.

'You set up the board; I'll be down in a few minutes, Vicky,' he called.

'Okay, will do, but don't be too long,' she replied, not saying goodnight to Christina, who held onto Stephen's neck very tightly.

He helped her upstairs and lifted her onto the bed. 'I'll be fine now, Stephen. You go and play with Victoria.'

Christina tried to keep the resentment out of her voice, but he detected it.

93

'She is my only child, Christina, and I don't see as much of her as I'd like.'

Christina sighed. Victoria was just a little girl, and one who had lost her mother in tragic circumstances. What sort of man would Stephen be if he didn't put his daughter first, at least some of the time? 'I'm sorry. It's just I would have liked a little time with you alone. I'd been looking forward to this weekend so much.'

'I feel the same way, but it's difficult for me to refuse her anything. I'm over-compensating for the loss of her mother.'

He sat on the edge of the bed and held both her hands.

'Don't take any notice of me, I'm just feeling sorry for myself,' she said.

'I'll make it up to you later, as soon as I get Victoria to bed. You'll forget all about your foot, I promise.'

'And I promise to make you forget everything.' She touched the front of his trousers.

'I wish,' he said, and kissed her full on the mouth, his hand seeking her breast and gently tweaking her nipple between thumb and forefinger.

Christina was immediately aroused and wrapped her arms around his neck.

'Daddy, Daddy, the Monopoly's all set up. Do you want a cup of cocoa or a brandy?'

'I'd better go.' Stephen lifted his head and Christina nodded, letting her arms fall by her sides.

'See you later,' he said as he left the room.

'I may be asleep.'

'Don't worry, I'll wake you up!'

She undressed slowly and hopped into the bathroom where she brushed her teeth, combed her hair, and doused herself in perfume. Not wearing her customary bedshirt or pyjamas, she limped across the room and, holding onto one of the bedposts, hoisted herself into bed.

She lay awake for a long time anticipating Stephen's

94

lovemaking, and eventually fell asleep, trusting he would wake her up.

Raindrops pattering on the bedroom window and an excruciating pain in her ankle woke her at dawn the following morning.

She struggled to sit up and squinted at her wristwatch. It was ten past six and she was alone.

Christina got up and found the bottle of pain-killers the doctor had given her. She took two in a tumbler of icy-cold water and staggered back to bed, sleeping fitfully for the next three hours until Stephen came to her room with a breakfast tray.

'The top of the morning to you,' he said, mimicking an Irish accent, and set the tray on the bed.

'What happened to you last night?' she snapped, and pulled herself into a sitting position, rubbing her eyes. 'I stayed awake for ages waiting for you to come.'

'I played Monopoly for almost an hour like a good, dutiful father, then I tucked my daughter up in bed and tiptoed down here, intending to be a good, dutiful lover. But you . . .' – he pinched Christina's leg – '. . . were in sweet dreams.'

'I wouldn't have minded if you'd woken me up!'

'You looked so peaceful,' he grinned. 'Sorry.'

'Don't be.' She slid her legs out of bed. 'It's your loss as much as mine.'

'Come on, Christina, don't be like that. I'll make it up to you tonight.' His voice was flippant.

'Don't make promises you may not be able to keep, Stephen.' She began to limp to the bathroom. 'I must do my teeth before I can eat breakfast.'

He ran round the bed to help her. She refused his arm, saying, 'I can manage, Stephen. My foot's a lot better this morning.'

He watched her shapely naked bottom disappearing

95

into the bathroom and thought she had been right when she had said it was his loss.

'That's great. So do you think you'll be able to make the gymkhana?' he called after her.

'I'm sure I shall,' Christina shouted from the bathroom. I'll get to that bloody gymkhana if it kills me! she thought.

The gymkhana was crowded, cold and very, very wet.

Stephen tramped around the muddy field for hours under a vast umbrella, arm in arm with Victoria, whilst Christina, hating every moment, sat in the car becoming more and more morose.

Victoria won a rosette for second place and talked non-stop about horses for the hour-long journey back to Purley Hall. It was almost six o'clock when the car pulled into the drive, and Christina had a splitting headache. She took a further two pain-killers and excused herself to lie down.

Hobbling downstairs an hour later she found Stephen and Victoria curled up in front of a log fire watching a video. He looked up briefly. 'I'll be with you in a moment, Christina; this is a really exciting bit.'

Victoria's eyes did not leave the television screen.

She left them and walked towards the kitchen, where Dorothy was preparing a roast-beef dinner.

'We usually have Sunday lunch, but Mr Reece-Carlton has to go abroad tomorrow so we're having it tonight instead,' she informed Christina, who looked surprised.

Stephen had not told her he was going away – but then, she was slowly learning, there were lots of things Stephen did not tell her.

The smell of the meat roasting set hunger pangs gnawing at her stomach.

'Mmm, that smells wonderful.' She sat down heavily at the kitchen table. She would have loved a cup of tea but did not like to ask the rather formidable housekeeper to make her one.

'Well, I make a good roast even if I say so myself.' The housekeeper stuck out her ample chest. 'Mr Reece-Carlton says he's never tasted a better roast lunch anywhere.' She continued to heap praises on her own cooking whilst vigorously beating a batter mixture for Yorkshire pudding.

'How's your foot?' Dorothy enquired, but seemed indifferent to Christina's reply.

'A lot better, thanks.' She looked down at her swollen ankle, which was looking more like its normal size.

'You'll feel a whole lot better after you've had my roast dinner,' Dorothy assured her. Christina wished she would stop boasting about how good a cook she was, and just get on with it.

The housekeeper poured the batter mixture into a smoking oven-tin as Stephen came in to kneel down and survey several bottles of wine in a rack below the work-surface. He eventually pulled out a 1963 St Emilion which he opened and decanted.

'Twenty minutes for the Yorkshires,' Dorothy announced, and slammed the oven door tightly shut.

They ate their Yorkshire pudding separately as a starter, a custom Stephen's mother had faithfully followed. Christina didn't care how it was served; it tasted wonderful – light and crispy. The roast beef was done to perfection, and she had an extra helping of beef and golden roast potatoes with thick, rich gravy.

Victoria had spoken very little during the meal, much to Christina's surprise.

They were all eating enormous portions of plum crumble and cream when Stephen said, 'I thought your friend Caroline was coming to see you tonight?'

Victoria shook her head, and some of her hair fell into the dessert bowl. It was sticky with cream when she continued, 'She was, but I told her not to when I knew you were coming home for the weekend. You know how Caroline always spoils things.'

The girl pulled a face, and Christina thought how well Victoria knew about spoiling things.

Stephen poured the last drops of red wine from the decanter into his and Christina's glasses.

'I've got another James Bond video I thought we could watch together.'

Victoria was looking directly at her father as she spoke, deliberately excluding Christina. She glanced over Victoria's shoulder at a portrait of a very dark young woman. Her large grey-blue eyes stared back, heavy-lidded and mysterious.

'Is that your wife, Stephen?' she asked.

He turned. 'Yes, that's Barbara.'

'She was very attractive,' Christina commented.

'She was more than attractive – she was beautiful!' Victoria looked at the portrait then back at Christina. Her eyes were narrowed and her voice very quiet.

'No one could replace my mother. Not ever.'

Christina held Victoria's troubled eyes for a long time. They were both silent until Christina said, 'I don't think anyone would even try.'

She finished her dessert, though it stuck in her throat, and congratulated Dorothy, who seeped up the praise, a huge smile stretching from one ear to the other.

Christina hated old James Bond movies but was forced to watch *Goldfinger*, squashed at the far end of the sofa as Victoria lay full-length with her legs looped over her father's lap.

Christina was delighted when the child fell asleep halfway through the movie and Stephen carried her to bed.

'She's sound asleep.' He seemed relieved when he joined her on the sofa five minutes later with two glasses of Hine.

She took the brandy goblet from his outstretched hand, saying, 'You didn't tell me you were leaving tomorrow?'

He took a sip of brandy and sighed heavily.

'I'm sorry. That call from Robert Leyton last night was to confirm I had to go to Spain. I forgot to tell you after you hurt your foot.'

He raked his long fingers through his hair and rubbed the back of his neck. 'I'm afraid I have to catch the 11.30 plane from Gatwick to Malaga. We're trying to set up a leisure park in Spain and I must meet the planners on-site first thing Monday morning. It was the only available flight. I took the liberty of booking you a flight back to Manchester fifteen minutes after mine, if that's okay with you? I didn't think you'd want to stay down here without me.'

'No, thanks. With you gone, Victoria might eat me!'

'Oh, come on, Christina. She's not that bad.'

Christina suppressed the reply she'd have liked to have given. 'Only joking.' She pinched his leg. 'This is our last opportunity to be together. Let's stop wasting time.'

She lifted his dark-green cotton sweater and with her fingertips curled the fine hair of his stomach, which he pulled in with a sharp intake of breath. His head fell back onto the sofa as she began to undo the top button of his jeans. The zip slid down easily and Stephen moaned from deep within his throat as he felt her hand slip inside his boxer shorts. She leaned forward to kiss him – and jumped back in fright as a white figure loomed from behind the sofa.

'Daddy, I had a horrible nightmare! I couldn't get back to sleep; I was really afraid.'

Victoria, dressed in a long nightdress, walked round the sofa and stared at Stephen, who was frantically zipping up his jeans and pulling his sweater down.

'What are you doing?' She continued to stare wide-eyed. He pulled her quickly down beside him to cover his embarrassment, pushing stray hairs away from her brow and saying, 'Nothing, baby. Now tell Daddy all about the horrible nightmare and he'll make it better.'

Christina left Stephen and Victoria curled up on the sofa, engrossed in one another, and limped slowly to her room. She fell into bed angry and frustrated. There was no point in staying awake. She knew Stephen would never come to her while his daughter was under the same roof.

'Your daughter is impossible, Stephen. Surely you can see she's trying to jeopardize our relationship?'

Stephen looked across the table at Christina's flushed face.

'I really think you're over-reacting, as usual.' He sounded tired and exasperated.

'Over-reacting? Victoria feigns illness, so you instantly cancel a weekend in Spain with me. One which I have been looking forward to very much!'

'Keep your voice down,' he urged. They were seated in the bar of the Midland Hotel in Manchester, and Stephen could see several people staring in their direction. He leaned forward. 'Everyone is looking at us.'

'I don't care, Stephen,' she snapped.

'Well, I do, and as far as Victoria's illness is concerned, Doctor Montague thinks it may be some kind of virus. Can't risk it. What if she's seriously ill while I'm away?'

'Dorothy is with her. She knew about your trip to Spain a week ago. Don't you find it too much of a coincidence that Victoria takes ill the very day you and I are due to go away for a long weekend?'

'I'm sorry. I was looking forward to it as much as you.' He took another sip of his drink and emptied the glass. 'I can't go away next weekend; it's Vicky's school play and I've promised to be there, but we can go the weekend after that, Christina.'

'I don't know where I'll be in two weeks' time. As I've told you a million times, I have to spend some time in Ireland. My mother is *genuinely* very ill.'

'Well, we can go another weekend.' He paused. 'Soon.'

Stephen tried to take her hand but she pulled away.

'How about coming with me to France on Wednesday and Thursday of next week?'

He was trying desperately hard to make amends, but Christina was unforgiving.

'I'm working, remember? I do work for a living.'

'Who cares about some daft job for Manchester United football club? Cancel it.' His voice was dismissive. It made her suddenly furious.

'*I* care, Stephen. And I need the money.'

He turned away from her defiant expression and waved to a passing waiter. She shook her head as the man approached their table and Stephen ordered another large gin and tonic. 'Don't talk to me about needing money!' His voice had a cutting edge as he continued: 'I've offered you an allowance, and a beautiful flat in your own name. But you refuse to swallow your stupid pride and continue to live in squalor with that scatty flatmate who drives you nuts! You insist on taking degrading work and struggling to pay the bills when you could live in London close to me!'

The waiter came to their table. He jumped back as Christina shouted: 'No, no, no, Stephen! How many times do I have to tell you to stop trying to buy me?' The waiter placed Stephen's drink in front of him and backed away quickly.

She felt a tremor inside her when she encountered Stephen's narrow, unblinking gaze. She had never seen him look so cold or so remote from her.

'I'm not trying to buy you, merely trying to help you. Can't you see that? You are so stubborn and immature sometimes, Christina.'

He made an effort to control his voice, but there was no mistaking his mounting temper.

Christina stood up. She was visibly shaking and her legs did not feel capable of taking her weight.

'I may be both of those things but I am not stupid, nor am I blind. What I can see very clearly, Stephen, is that you want me on your terms and your terms only. Neatly tucked away in a cosy flat in London where you can come around whenever it suits you, far from any prying eyes – and of course your precious daughter!'

'That's just not true.' His voice shook with anger. Conversation ceased in the busy bar. Everyone was watching the scene.

'You know the situation as well as I do, Christina. You've known from the first weekend you spent at Purley Hall almost six months ago, but you just can't accept the fact. Victoria needs me.'

She stood up. He got to his feet and put a hand on her arm. 'I can only give you so much of my time, Christina. You must understand,' he implored.

She took a deep breath.

'I do understand, Stephen.' Her voice was resigned. 'You must go and catch your plane to London. You're right. Victoria wants you.'

Christina picked up the suitcase she had packed with such excitement that morning and gripped the handle firmly with trembling fingers. She was fighting hard to prevent the tears welling up in her eyes and blinked several times before she was able to say, 'I don't need you any more, Stephen. At least not like this.'

She turned and walked out of the Midland Hotel, hoping Stephen might run after her but knowing deep in her heart that he would not.

Christina squinted, trying hard to focus. She could have sworn Martin Ward had three heads as he came towards her. Thankfully they merged into one when he sat next to her.

'I've been looking for you for ages. Where on earth have you been?'

'Drinking. And I want another.'

'I really think you've had enough.' Martin gently prised the glass from her hand.

'I will decide when I have had enough.' She leaned forward to attract the barman's attention, and almost fell.

'Why don't we go back to my place?' Martin suggested, planning to give her coffee and perhaps something to eat in an effort to sober her up.

'Your place?' She glared at him. He was reminded of the little tabby kitten he'd rescued from the railway embankment as a child. Small-boned, saucer-eyed and spitting defiance. He realized she had mistaken his meaning.

'I really don't think you'd be much use to me in bed tonight, Christina,' he said as he caught her firmly in his arms. 'Come on, love, I'm taking you home.'

So much for using the club dance to show Christina how attractive he found her, Martin thought ruefully, as he steered her across the dance-floor. He hadn't been able to spend as much time with her as he'd hoped. The Chairman had been in an expansive mood, pressing forbidden cigars on him, and then there'd been the duty dances with players' wives and starstruck girlfriends. With his thick blond hair and broad-shouldered, tapering physique, Martin had caught the eye of any number of women tonight. But the one he wanted to attract, the one he found himself thinking of more and more these days, seemed to want him only as a shoulder to cry on.

He knew what was at the bottom of it, of course. A man, must be. Maybe the man he'd seen her with at the Midland that time?

103

Outside in his BMW Christina seemed to come to herself.

'I'm sorry, Martin. I feel so ashamed. I didn't show you up, did I?'

'Don't be, Christina. Everyone has too much sometimes. It's not the end of the world. Listen, I've made a fool of myself on more than one occasion and had to be carried home.'

She sniffed and blew her nose.

'I'd like to spend the night with you, Martin. I can't bear to go back to the flat.'

He stared straight ahead, both hands gripping the wheel. A car passed and his handsome profile was suddenly illuminated in the headlights.

'I'd love to sleep with you, Christina, and to be honest I've thought about little else since our date last week.' He thought carefully about his next words. 'But I don't want you on the rebound. You've had someone else on your mind tonight. I don't think you're ready for me or anyone till you've got him out of your system.'

Christina sniffed again and stared ahead, not speaking. They drove in silence for a few minutes until she spoke, very quietly. 'You're right, Martin, though not many men would be so understanding. Thank you. If you could take me home I'd be grateful.' He stopped his car in front of her flat.

'I'd like to see you again, Christina, and there may not be much time. As you know, I'm on the transfer list. If the deal with Tottenham goes through next week I'll be leaving Manchester.' He paused. 'I know you'd like to work in London . . .' He wanted to say 'We could go together', but his voice trailed off and he left the sentence unfinished.

Christina half smiled. 'I really hope you get it, Martin. I'm sure you will.'

She got out of the car. He was about to follow when she bent down and spoke through the open window.

'Don't get out, Martin. I'm fine now. Sorry about this evening.'

'No problem. Think about London, won't you, Christina? I'll call you in the morning.'

He waved and drove off. She watched the car until it was out of sight.

It was ironic, she thought. Half the girls in Manchester would give their eye-teeth to have an invitation like that from Martin Ward. Christina could see the attraction. He was good-looking, he was famous. But he wasn't for her. There was only one man she wanted.

She expected to hear Martin's voice when she picked up the telephone the following morning, but it was her sister instead.

'It's bad news, Christina. The doctors say Mam won't last the night.'

She stared at her own pale face and sunken eyes in the cracked mirror above the telephone.

'But – they said she had a few more months! God, Marie, I'd have cancelled my jobs if I'd realized.'

Her sister's voice cracked as she replied, 'Sure and Mam wouldn't hear of that. She was always so proud of you, Christina.'

She couldn't bear it. Her sister was talking as if Mam was in her coffin already.

'I'm on my way, Marie. I'll be with you just as soon as I can.'

The nausea Christina had felt the previous evening was nothing compared to the sea-sickness she suffered on the crossing from Liverpool to Dublin. She tried standing on deck where the biting wind blew into her face, and tried sitting down below, concentrating on anything rather than the coiling sensation of nausea which assailed her every few minutes. Nothing worked. Dublin was never such a welcome sight as when the ferry pulled into the harbour in a grey twilight.

Her sister's husband Ryan was waiting when Christina emerged from the customs hall, already feeling better after only ten minutes on dry land.

She waved as she spotted Ryan, then feared the worst as she saw his grim expression.

'Your Mam went two hours ago, Christina. I'm sorry.'

She stared at the big, ruddy face of Ryan Molloy in disbelief. 'Why, Ryan? She was only fifty-six.' Her voice was lost and infinitely pathetic. 'I want my mum, Ryan.'

'I'm sorry,' the big man said. 'I loved her too. But you wouldn't have wanted her to linger. Not the way she was at the end.' His eyes were full of unshed tears.

He opened his broad arms and Christina fell into them. The coarse material of his jacket scratched her face, but she felt nothing, numbed by an all-encompassing pain which engulfed her, a pain so intense it blotted out all other feeling. She would be twenty years old in three weeks' time and had never felt so utterly alone.

Chapter Four

The flight from Dublin to Manchester was delayed for two hours. The pilot made up a little time *en route* and the plane landed in Manchester Airport at 4.30 p.m. on a warm, breezy September afternoon.

Christina walked into the arrivals hall pushing a trolley and scanning the sea of strange faces, searching for Susie's familiar round, smiling one. She was nowhere to be seen, and Christina assumed that her friend had become tired of waiting and had gone home.

She pushed her trolley in the direction of the exit and the taxi-rank, stopping dead in her tracks when she heard her name being called.

'Christina!' She recognized the voice and knew it was him even before she turned round and found Stephen standing next to her.

They stared at each other in silence for a few seconds, Stephen thinking how pale and drawn she looked, and how much thinner she had become in the five weeks since he had seen her last.

'I'm so sorry about your mother.' His eyes held a mixture of sympathy and longing. 'It's good to see you, Christina.' His voice faltered. 'I – I missed you.'

She dropped her gaze and gripped the handle of the trolley.

'I missed you too. The last three weeks have been the hardest of my life, Stephen, but time's a great healer, don't they say? I suppose I'll get over it. I just feel so empty.'

She looked up at him again and he saw the chasm of loneliness in her hurt amber eyes. He wanted to take her in his arms right there and then, soothe away all the pain, help her to forget and make her feel whole again. But would she give him the chance after the way he'd behaved?

'I'm sorry I wasn't in touch earlier, but with you in Ireland . . .'

'It was only the last few weeks, Stephen. Why didn't you contact me before? When you didn't, I thought you didn't want to see me again.'

He put his hand under her chin and forced her to meet his eyes.

'I was pretty mad after we'd quarrelled, but that wasn't the reason. Besides, a lot of the things you said were true.'

Her eyes widened in astonishment. It sounded as though Stephen Reece-Carlton was climbing down. Was this a first?

He sighed deeply and slid his arms around her waist, pulling her close to him. She could no longer see his face, but there was tension in every line of his familiar body.

'I don't want to go into too much detail now, Christina, you've had enough on your plate recently, but there was some trouble at the South Shields site.'

'The car park you're building?'

'Yes. Our foreman there died in a fall. For some reason the police decided to poke their noses in – God knows why. It was an accident.'

'How horrible! The poor man. Did he have a family?'

'Yes, they've been taken care of, don't worry. Don't even think about it, Christina, please. I'm only mentioning it to explain why I didn't try to get in touch sooner. I had a lot to see to – the police, the inquest, the funeral. By the time I was able to ring you, Susie told me you'd gone to Ireland and why.

'I've been going mad trying to get your number there from her, but she said she wasn't sure you'd want to hear from me. It was all I could do to get your flight details from her. That's one loyal friend you've got there, Chrissy.'

'She is – and when I get home I'm going to murder her! Oh, Stephen, of course I wanted to hear from you. So much.' Her voice turned husky, and for a moment she thought she was going to cry.

'Christina, I have something I want to say to you, and it won't wait another minute.'

Stephen sounded profoundly serious. Oh, God, was he going to break it to her gently?

'Will you marry me?'

She gasped and stared at him in shocked silence.

'Am I hearing things,' she asked finally, 'or did you just ask me to marry you?'

'You're not hearing things.' He glanced down at the dirty concourse floor. 'If I wasn't wearing my most expensive suit, I might even get down on my hands and knees and do the job properly.'

Christina gave a watery smile.

'I insist.' She pointed to the floor. 'It's the only way.'

He pondered for a second.

'On one condition. If I can be guaranteed a yes?'

She shook her head. 'I have to think first.'

'You've got exactly one minute.'

He started to count down the seconds. She held up her hand when he reached twenty.

'Stop. That's my age.'

'When was your birthday?' he asked, surprised.

She glanced at her watch. 'Approximately four hours ago.'

'Happy birthday, my darling. I suppose I really must go down on my hands and knees now; that's if you are going to say yes?'

'I'm waiting, Mr Reece-Carlton,' she said, and watched as he bent his left leg, almost but not quite touching the floor. 'Further,' she urged, and Stephen sighed, dropping onto his knee. Passers-by stared and nudged each other.

'I hope you're not going to continue to be this bossy after you marry me?' he said plaintively.

She laughed for the first time in weeks.

'Christina O'Neill, will you marry me?' he asked solemnly.

An old lady lugging a wheeled suitcase nearby stopped and waited for the answer.

Christina held out her hands to him. Grasping them tightly, he rose to his feet.

'Yes, I will.' Her voice was tremulous and a rush of colour warmed her pale cheeks. 'And I'll try not to be so bossy, but I can't promise to change much.'

'I don't want you to change one bit.' He cupped her face in still shaking hands and said for the very first time: 'I love you, Miss O'Neill.'

'Snap, Mr Reece-Carlton.' She kissed him lightly on the mouth, tears falling softly from her half-closed eyes. It was the first time she had cried since her mother's death.

Stephen and Christina were married ten days later. They had both wanted a quiet wedding, and invited only a few close friends and family.

On the eve of their wedding, Stephen gave her a three-carat pear-shaped diamond engagement ring wrapped in a sheet of white foolscap paper containing an itinerary for their honeymoon in Barbados.

They exchanged vows and identical tricoloured wedding bands on a blustery September morning at Chelsea Register Office, witnessed by a small congregation including Susie, dressed in a hideous shocking-pink dress and clutching the arm of her boyfriend Nick, who wore his hair in a pony-tail, and looked uncomfortable in an ill-fitting suit.

Kate Mason surveyed the bride's elegant cream Bruce Oldfield suit from under the brim of her huge straw hat and calculated the fees she had lost on Christina's cancelled bookings.

Stephen's mother, a tall, stern woman in a worn and ancient Jaeger suit, sat ramrod straight and unmoved during the short ceremony, clinging on to Victoria's arm as if the girl were about to bolt.

Robert and Jane Leyton arrived late and talked in hushed whispers until the registrar coughed and shut them up with an irritated frown. Robert thought Stephen had gone completely mad, and had spent the last two weeks trying to talk his partner out of what he considered to be a rash and foolhardy decision.

Christina was oblivious to everyone but Stephen and herself. When she emerged onto the Town Hall steps, laughing and glowing with happiness and optimism, she saw only plain sailing ahead. This was one marriage that was going to work, she promised herself.

'Happy, Mrs Reece-Carlton?' Stephen touched her cheek and brushed back a strand of hair from her face.

Her eyes gleamed. 'I'm still pinching myself.'

She squeezed his hand and threw her small Victorian-style posy towards Susie's laughing face. Her friend stretched out to catch it, but Christina's aim was faulty. The posy winged through the air over Susie's head to land in Victoria's hands.

Christina watched in horror as the girl tore the flowers to shreds, scattering frail, crushed petals to the sudden chill wind.

She held her stepdaughter's challenging eyes for an instant, realizing in that split second that Victoria would never forgive her. Christina had committed the unforgivable sin – she had stolen her daddy.

*

The journey had been delightful. Nestling against Stephen in the first-class compartment of the British Airways jumbo jet, Christina avidly read the article in the in-flight magazine.

Barbados is a pear-shaped, coral jewel which slipped from the pendant of the Lesser Antilles and floated windward to come to rest in the Atlantic.

With a statue of Admiral Lord Nelson valiantly guarding the harbour entrance to the island's capital, Bridgetown, which also boasts its own Trafalgar Square, Barbados is often known as 'Little England.'

Visitors are quickly aware of the intrinsic British flavour to its narrow, leafy lanes, reminiscent of Cornwall, and its historic Georgian and Victorian architecture.

Here, a strong English colonial culture has been successfully grafted on to African roots, forming a unique Bajan society where 200,000 Barbadians live and work amidst miles of weaving sugar-cane fields interspersed with ruined windmills, stone churches and grand plantation houses glimpsed through thick clusters of alamanda and hibiscus.

Twenty-one miles long and fourteen wide, this is the island in the sun where English gentility meets Caribbean charm.

Christina looked up from the magazine, her eyes sparkling. 'How much longer before we get there?' she inquired excitedly.

'You've asked me that about twenty times in the past two hours.' Stephen smiled fondly at her childlike anticipation.

She stuck out her tongue at him playfully. 'You're exaggerating.'

He laughed and glanced at his watch. 'Another couple of hours, I'm afraid, before we land.'

*

The doors of the 747 opened to a surge of warm, balmy air. Christina and Stephen, blinking in the dazzling sun, walked stiffly down the aircraft steps. They were directed towards what looked like an old World War II aircraft hangar surrounded by arid wasteland and a few dusty and straggling palm trees.

They joined a long queue which eventually shuffled into a small, sectioned-off area reserved for immigration.

A uniformed officer stared at them with surly eyes before examining their entry forms and ponderously writing on them in red ink.

'Staying in Barbados long?' he asked.

'I wrote it on the form,' snapped Stephen, pointing to the appropriate part of the document. 'We're here for three weeks.'

The man continued his laboured writing. Stephen let out a sigh of exasperation and ran his fingers through his hair, already damp with perspiration in the humid atmosphere. 'We have been travelling for ten hours,' he announced angrily. 'Is there something wrong?'

'Nothing wrong, man, just doing my job.' The immigration officer did not look up from his desk. 'I need to see your return tickets.' He held out one large hand.

Again Stephen sighed in annoyance as Christina pulled the tickets from her handbag and handed them to the man, who took another age checking them minutely before waving them through.

'Thank God that's over,' she said.

'It isn't,' Stephen muttered, 'not yet.'

Suddenly they were surrounded by a crowd of young porters, all chattering clamorously. One young boy, taller than the rest, pushed his way to the front. He grinned broadly at them as he snatched up their bags and set off at a fast pace towards the customs desk, where a short, fat customs officer beckoned them over.

'We've nothing to declare,' Stephen told him curtly. 'We're here on holiday. We've never been to Barbados before and with the reception you're giving us, it isn't likely we'll come again!'

'Stephen, try to keep calm,' Christina whispered. Muttering under his breath about petty officialdom, he turned and walked away from the rickety table, leaving her to smile wanly at the glowering official.

After a long and thorough search, the man snapped their suitcases shut and motioned the porter to lift them onto his trolley. 'Have a good holiday in our beautiful Barbados,' he said automatically.

'We need it after coming through your bloody airport!' Stephen snapped.

'Just doing my job, man, just doing my job.'

Their lanky porter led them out of the ramshackle building into the heat and humidity of the late afternoon.

The taxi to the Royal Palm Hotel was a dilapidated 1954 Ford Zodiac driven by a gregarious, middle-aged Barbadian called Oscar, who did not stop talking and who, they decided, had missed his vocation as Minister for Tourism.

After a while Oscar's melodic but incessant commentary faded into the background as Christina, staring in fascination out of the car's open windows, found her preconceived notions of the island collapsing before her eyes.

She had always harboured an image of Barbados as being a series of chic hotels, decorously located close to vast, solitary, silvery beaches; of small, intimate malls of smart shops and expensive restaurants, peopled by a beautifully dressed, sophisticated clientèle.

Instead she saw a long succession of tiny, brightly painted wooden shacks – Oscar said they were called chattel houses – which looked almost like garden sheds, their inhabitants spilling out onto the verandas and the roadside in noisy, amiable, chattering profusion.

Everywhere there were children: playing barefoot in the wasteland, the narrow, unmade lanes between the tiny cluttered houses, even in the road. Oscar had to brake and sound his horn in every village they passed through.

The road they were on was bordered on both sides by dangerous trench-like gullies and pitted with deep potholes, though nothing about it seemed to disturb Oscar, who spent most of his time looking over his shoulder to talk to them. It seemed to Christina to be the most hazardous road she had ever driven on; the other drivers were even more erratic than Oscar, and there were animals all over the place: undernourished cats and dogs, young goats, crippled donkeys, tired ponies, even a few cows.

But then, when she got her first glimpse of the Caribbean at Paynes Bay, Christina realized that all the hazards of the journey had been worth it.

The sun was the colour of wild tangerines and was trailing long, golden streamers low across an indigo sky. The sea, reflecting the colours of the sky, was flat calm, as still as a glacier, its only movement the surf at the shoreline, gently folding onto a deserted beach of pale-cream sand.

Christina caught her breath. This was what she had imagined. She squeezed Stephen's hand.

'Beautiful, isn't it?' he whispered. She nodded and smiled but said nothing. There was nothing she could say; the scene was too beautiful for words.

A wide avenue of royal palms lined the entrance to their hotel, a rambling wooden building in the colonial style with faded white paint. Inside, it had wooden slatted floors, louvred jalousies, slowly sweeping paddle-fans and an assortment of faded furniture from the 1950s.

Crossing lawns broken by vivid clumps of oleander and poinsettia, they passed coconut-shaded pathways leading to the, low bougainvillaea-clad cottages. Their own was a delightful peak-roofed construction set amid sea grapes and palms.

The spacious sitting-room had a red clay-tiled floor and locally made rattan furniture, upholstered in bright-lemon and green local fabrics. A large bathroom and dressing area led off the main bedroom, and shuttered windows on all sides afforded gorgeous views and cool breezes.

A bottle of champagne rested invitingly in an ice-bucket next to a bowl of fresh tropical fruit.

Stephen popped the cork, poured two glasses and, handing one to Christina, led her by the hand onto the terrace. In front of them stretched a wide, mile-long sandy beach.

They clinked glasses and smiled at each other.

They moved to a low stone wall covered in bougainvillaea which bordered the terrace. Seating themselves, they drank their champagne in silence, staring at the view and listening to the low rumble of the surf.

Gently, Stephen leaned over and placed a soft kiss on Christina's neck. 'You are very beautiful, you know.'

'And so is this place,' she murmured in return. 'I'm very happy.'

He finished his champagne, smiled at her, and held out his hand. 'Let's shower together and then eat.'

She grinned at him impishly. 'If we shower together, we'll be very late for dinner.'

He laughed. 'I don't mind if you don't. So we eat late?' He stood up and shrugged. 'It's Caribbean time here.'

They walked inside hand in hand.

The thatched-roofed, open-sided restaurant was almost deserted when they got there. They were shown to a corner table with uninterrupted views of the sea, foam-flecked turquoise, dark and mysterious beyond.

'I feel ravenous,' Stephen exclaimed.

'And I feel wonderful,' she responded. They both laughed.

They ordered pumpkin soup, followed by pan-fried flying-fish with sweet potatoes and fresh, crisp salad.

It was almost midnight before they left the restaurant to walk back to their cottage. The gardens were beautifully floodlit and the lawns soft beneath their feet as they walked. They could smell the scents of the many flowering plants on the constant sea breezes.

'It's so beautiful here,' Christina sighed.

Silently Stephen pointed in the direction of a huge, floodlit frangipani tree where a tiny bird of paradise was flapping its luminous wings.

They arrived at the cottage, and Christina took one last look at the dark, calm Caribbean before following Stephen inside.

'Oh, look.' She picked up the pretty hibiscus flower from the pillow where the maid had left it and placed it behind her ear. Slowly she began to sway, imitating a Hawaiian dancer.

Stephen watched her from the side of the bed.

She saw his expression and giggled. She began to dance faster, intoxicated by a mixture of champagne and excitement.

'Come here.' His voice was deep and throaty.

She moved to him slowly and swayed into his arms. He could smell her musky perfume.

'I love you, Chrissy.' He kissed her on the throat.

'I love you too,' she whispered, and they fell onto the bed together, the hibiscus crushed beneath them.

He covered her face with kisses – her forehead, her nose, her cheeks, his burning lips leaving a trail of fire down her neck and across her throat. As passion mounted, he pulled the thin silk straps of her dress down over her shoulders, exposing her small, firm breasts and dark nipples, erect and firm from her own rising desire.

His hungry mouth slid down her body, covering her in hot, ravenous kisses as he pulled off her dress. Her honey-coloured skin shone in the warm glow of lamplight.

Slowly, she parted her legs and the soft, pink lips opened like a flower before him. The tip of his tongue found her. She moaned and began to writhe in ecstasy.

'Be patient,' he whispered. 'I want to make it last.'

She covered his shoulders and chest in greedy kisses. 'I'll try to be patient, Stephen' – her voice was low with desire – 'but I want you so much.'

They made love slowly and tenderly; it was almost dawn before they fell into an exhausted sleep. They were woken only a few hours later by the chorus of noisy birds and the ceaselessly pounding surf.

'What shall we do today, Chrissy?' It was the fifth morning of their holiday. They were sitting on the terrace, enjoying a breakfast of fresh mango, sweet, doughy bread rolls, and papaya jam.

'We'll do exactly what we did yesterday. And the day before, and the day before that. Take a walk on the beach, lie in the sun, swim, enjoy a pre-lunch planter's punch, and . . .' She ran her nails lightly along the inside of his thigh.

He laughed. His eyes looked paler than ever in his tanned face, but they were warm with love.

'I thought a change of scene might be in order today, so I've hired a car to take my beautiful wife on an island tour.'

She groaned. She had been looking forward to finishing the latest Ludlum and to topping up the deep, golden tan she was rapidly acquiring.

'Are you bored already, Mr Reece-Carlton? Do I detect a case of itchy feet?'

'Only the very slightest,' he admitted. 'It started this morning, on my left heel, but I'm afraid it will spread rapidly without treatment.'

She looked up at him pleadingly. 'Do we have to go?'

He turned towards the bungalow. 'Come on, Chrissy, where's your spirit of adventure? It won't kill you. You might actually enjoy it. And I promise to get you back straight after lunch.'

'You'd better,' she muttered, standing up.

They left the hotel a few minutes later. When Christina saw the car Stephen had hired she began to think the tour was not such a bad idea after all. It was a bright-yellow, open-topped mini-moke.

Stephen handed her a map as they climbed in. 'You're the navigator, so concentrate.'

She gave a mock salute. 'Yes, sir.'

'Right.' His voice was businesslike. 'First stop Codrington College, then Andromeda Gardens. Lunch at the Kingsley Club then back to the hotel via Crane Beach, the South Coast and Bridgetown.'

Leaning closer to her, he traced their route on the map from west to east. 'Okay, let's go.'

'How much will you bet me we don't get lost?' she asked as he started the car down the drive.

'With you navigating, my darling, that's a bet I'd be crazy to take.'

She pulled a face. 'Oh, ye of little faith. You watch, I'll make you eat your words.'

'I'd rather eat you.' He touched her bare, tanned leg.

She quivered and laughed. 'Is that all you think about?'

'You bet,' he growled, swiftly biting the side of her neck before pulling out onto the main road.

The navigation was perfect all day until, a few miles from the Royal Palm, Christina gave a wrong direction.

Stephen turned the car into a narrow, unmade road and swore as the mini-moke bounced into a deep pothole. 'Are you sure this is the right way, Chrissy?'

She was studying the map. 'I think,' she said uncertainly, 'that if we go down here, to the end, we'll meet up with the main coast road.'

Stephen stopped the car and peered over her shoulder at the map. 'I don't think this is the right road. We should have carried on at the last junction.' He began to reverse the car.

It was then he saw the house.

He spotted the gates first; they were impossible to miss. Tall, black and imposing, with an air of impregnability, they conveyed an uncompromising message – Keep Out.

Stephen stopped the car and got out. 'Look, Chrissy. There's an old house in there.'

They peered past the heavy, ornate wrought iron of the gates, black paint peeling into rust, towards a big, crumbling, coral-stone house, buried under a tangled mass of bougainvillaea.

Stephen rattled the rusty padlock impatiently. For a reason he did not understand he felt compelled to go inside. It was as if the house were calling him.

Christina exclaimed, 'Look, Stephen.' She was holding back a thicket of alamanda to expose a pitted brass plaque set into the coral-stone wall. Vigorously, he rubbed away grime. Slowly the faded copperplate script became legible. Crystal Springs, it read.

Stephen looked at Christina, and smiled.

'We've got to see this place. I don't know why, we just have to.'

Two days later the rusty padlock was finally prised open and Stephen and Christina followed a young Barbadian estate agent down a long, wide gravel drive. Curving gently past six huge royal palms, it led to the faded splendours of Crystal Springs.

The house was beautiful, even though the pale, golden hue of its coral-stone walls was almost impossible to detect under a mass of bougainvillaea and coral vine which were also entwined around its numerous verandas and peeling shutters.

Inside, the magnificent entrance hall's wide, curved stone walls rose towards a domed ceiling. To the left was a broad stone staircase; to the right, through a coral-stone archway, a partly covered inner courtyard, paved in black and white marble. The courtyard was shaded by half a dozen fan-shaped traveller's palms. At its centre was what had once been a circular lily pond, in the middle of which stood an old, neglected yet still handsome Italian fountain. The air was filled with the sound of hundreds of mosquitoes for whom the pond was now home.

Christina and Stephen followed the estate agent along a pathway, overgrown by dense clumps of pink and white hibiscus, to a large rectangular room with a coral-stone cornice and white walls. This, he told them, was the formal living-room. It had four sets of tall french casement windows opening on to a covered terrace which ran the full length of the house.

From there, the agent led them along a narrow covered walkway into a circular dining pagoda. Some vines had broken through and were infiltrating the walls and overgrowing the carved pine ceiling which, infested with termites, was pitted with deep holes.

Everywhere there was decay. Almost all the woodwork was infested with termites, and the place seemed to be home to a variety of creatures which scuttled, slithered or crept across the floors and into holes at their approach. The young estate agent seemed embarrassed, and explained that the house had not been lived in for more than twenty years. It had, he told them, been built in the thirties by a wealthy English aristocrat as his Caribbean retreat.

Christina could see that whoever had designed the house had had taste and style. Beyond the decay she could see the beauty; already she had visions of how she could restore Crystal Springs to its former glory.

After a while she left an intense and preoccupied

Stephen talking business with the estate agent and wandered into the grounds.

She had to fight her way through thick, clinging undergrowth, but finally emerged to find herself standing on a small, crescent-shaped beach which lay at the foot of a rocky inlet about three hundred feet from the house.

A tiny, silver-backed sand crab scurried across her foot, and she jumped. She watched it burrow frantically into the soft white sand before wandering to the water's edge, slipping off her shoes and allowing the warm, shallow water to eddy around her ankles. She felt sticky from her exertions in the undergrowth, and the slight sea breeze was cooling her skin.

She had no idea how long she stood there, half mesmerized by the beauty of the scene. Suddenly she heard her name being called.

'Christina!' Stephen's voice was coming from somewhere in the undergrowth. She squinted, scanning the thick, luxuriant vegetation, then smiled as he struggled into sight from a clump of mangroves.

'Where have you been? Look at the state of you,' she laughed, pulling twigs out of his hair.

He was panting slightly. 'It's a bloody jungle in there.' He took a deep breath. 'Well, what do you think, Chrissy? It's incredible, isn't it?'

She stared out to sea, to where the horizon met the cloudless, cobalt-blue sky. 'Yes,' she whispered.

It was a vivid scene, full of the exotic imagery of the travel brochures. Yet there was something else in the idyllic vista, something the travel brochures could never capture. Then it struck her. It was the light: a dazzling, radiant brilliance which defined every image with startling clarity, etching it indelibly in the memory.

'It's the most beautiful place I've ever seen.' Her voice was throaty with emotion.

'Would you like to live here?'

She turned and stared up at him, and for a long moment there was silence between them. She searched his face and knew what he was about to tell her.

'I've just bought it, Chrissy. The house, the land, the lot.' His voice, like his face, was filled with triumph.

Suddenly he let out a loud whoop and she jumped in surprise. 'It was a snip – a bloody bargain. I think they just wanted to get rid of the old place. Well, what do you think?'

It was all too much, like a dream. The man she adored and who she knew adored her was offering her the chance to live in paradise. She couldn't believe it was happening, not to her. She was enthralled by the scene; ecstatic over the prospect of living here. It was all so beautiful.

Speechlessly, she gazed at him. He was exultant, searching her face, waiting to hear what he wanted to hear. She smiled at him, her heart full of love. The old house, the beautiful grounds, Stephen's smile, the look of absolute triumph on his handsome face . . . No wonder her head was spinning with happiness.

'It's wonderful, darling. Absolutely wonderful.' She stared up at him. 'I do love you so. Thank you for buying Crystal Springs. It's all beautiful – the house, the grounds. And it has enormous potential. When I've finished with it you won't recognize it. It needs lots of new cane furniture and soft pastel fabrics, and we can clear a path to this cove so we can have barbecues and . . .'

'Now hold it right there, Chrissy.' Stephen's voice was crisp. 'We're going to have to do a lot more than just decorate the house and clear a few paths. And there isn't going to be a lot of time for barbecues. I've got plans for Crystal Springs.'

He paused for a moment, and when he spoke his voice was low and intense. 'I had the strongest intuition I've ever had in my life when we drove up to the gates a couple of days ago. It was like a vision . . . destiny . . . I don't know, call it what you will. But I *knew* what I had to do.' He grabbed her by the shoulders. 'Do you understand?'

She shook her head in bewilderment. His green eyes were on fire, dancing in the sparkling sunlight. 'I'm going to build a hotel.'

He let go of her and swept out his arm, encompassing the cove and the house. 'There are fifty acres of grounds. Plenty of room for me to build the best hotel on this island . . . the best hotel in the whole Caribbean! And I'm going to call it Crystal Springs . . . a Reece Resort.'

Somewhere, far back in the recesses of her mind, a warning note sounded. Her smile slipped slightly. 'A hotel? But I thought you were buying it as a holiday home for us?'

He threw back his head and laughed. 'There won't be any time for holidays, Chrissy. We'll be too busy building the best, most luxurious hotel you've ever seen. And this one will be only the beginning.'

The fiery light which Christina had seen in Stephen's eyes burned bright and intense for the rest of their holiday. He was like a man possessed. What had been an idyllic honeymoon was instantly transformed into frenzied days of transatlantic calls to lawyers and agents, and nights of manic planning and replanning.

Christina had known him for almost a year, yet now she wondered if she was living with a complete stranger. She had learned early that Stephen was a complex character, and unpredictable. But what she was witnessing, what she was caught up in, was a new and slightly frightening dimension to his personality. She had never known him be so driven; so obsessed with a single idea.

Unbelievably, she was pleased when their last day on the island dawned and they boarded the 747 that night for home.

*

After a few glasses of champagne and a sleeping-pill, Stephen slept like a baby, but Christina was glad to have eight hours' uninterrupted peace.

Her thoughts dwelt on the events of the past three weeks. If she had not agreed to go with Stephen on the tour of the island, would he have found Crystal Springs anyway? What if she had not misread the map, if they had not taken the wrong turning? What then? She shook her head. There were too many imponderables.

She had to stop thinking about the past and concentrate on the future. Crystal Springs was heaven on earth. It was beautiful, idyllic, and she loved it. But the uncertainties she had felt standing in that small cove, the small shadow of doubt, had grown larger and blacker with each passing day.

When she had agreed to marry Stephen, she had envisaged that the pattern of their lives would stay roughly the same. She would move into Purley Hall, which she already loved, and make a life for herself there while Stephen continued with his building and development schemes countrywide. She'd foreseen some problems ahead – notably with Victoria – but, confident of Stephen's love for her, nothing she couldn't handle.

Now, at a stroke, he'd changed the future for both of them – and without so much as consulting her first. The slight vibration of the huge aircraft as it flew east seemed somehow in tune with the quiver of apprehension she felt inside. She was setting out on an unknown journey, with no idea at all of what lay ahead.

With an hour to go before they landed, Stephen stirred and surfaced from sleep. Seeing the frown upon her face, he leaned across and smoothed it gently away with one finger.

'What's up, Chrissy? Don't you want to go home?'

She stared at him blankly. 'That's just it. I don't know where home is any more. It used to be Manchester. Then

I thought it'd be Purley Hall. Now it's Crystal Springs on an island I barely know except as a tourist. I think I'm scared, Stephen.'

'You – scared? The girl I first saw facing down a six-foot gorilla with fists like hams? Darling, what in the world is there for you to be afraid of?'

He was relaxed and smiling, his attention wholly focussed on her for the first time in days, she realized. In the warmth of his smile, the familiar green glow of his eyes, she relaxed.

'I suppose it is stupid, only it's different for you, Stephen. You've done this sort of thing so many times before – starting up new businesses, getting schemes off the ground.'

You've even been married before, she wanted to say.

He smiled tenderly at her. 'As a matter of fact, this is something I've *never* done before. I know absolutely nothing about the hotel business. I just know, I feel it here' – he pressed one clenched fist against his chest – 'that we're on the right track with Crystal Springs. But if you're convinced, Chrissy, you'd better say so and we'll call the whole scheme off right now before I start raising finance. Because I can't do it without you, you know.'

At the look of surprise on her face, he could not prevent himself from kissing her. 'I mean it. I say I know nothing about hotel-keeping from the business side, but I've stayed in enough of them to know what makes a truly successful hotel – and that's one where the owners' mark, their personality, is stamped on the place.

'I want Crystal Springs to be the best, Christina. Not a series of little boxes, a bland, soulless business. I want to offer people something more – luxury, yes, but also a dream, the feeling that Crystal Springs is theirs for the time they stay there.

'That's where you come in, Chrissy. One of the reasons I was drawn to you was your warmth. I'm a businessman and pretty hard-nosed, I suppose. For me the deal is it. Personality doesn't come into it. You're different. You're interested in people, genuinely like them, and it shows. People are drawn to you. You have an openness they respond to and it's not put on, a sort of charm you've acquired – it's you. I can't think of any better qualification for making a success of a hotel, can you?

'What do you say? Will you help me realize the dream? Shall we build Crystal Springs together?'

Christina smiled tremulously. She had been sure he loved her, but had never realized until now just how highly he valued her. An appeal like this was irresistible. Had he known it would be? It didn't matter.

'Of course I'll help, Stephen.'

The stewardess was surprised but resigned when they called for a bottle of champagne to be served with their breakfast. Some people just had to get their money's worth.

But to Christina, raising her glass to Stephen in the first-class compartment, it was much more than that. It was a pledge. Her thoughts of homelessness were forgotten now. Stephen was her home. So long as she was with him, she need never be lonely or afraid again.

Chapter Five

Christina was surprised to learn, on their return to Purley Hall, that Stephen's first task would be to raise finance for the development of Crystal Springs Hotel. To her he'd always seemed as rich as Croesus, but he laughingly told her that even he didn't have the sort of money the Crystal Springs project needed kicking around in his current account.

'Besides, Chrissy – first rule of business: never risk your own money when you can risk someone else's.'

She stared at him, suddenly uneasy.

'It isn't too risky, is it? You don't think we're going out on a limb here?'

'I am 100 per cent certain, sure and confident that we can make a go of it. Trust me, darling. I'm never wrong about these things.'

But his usual bankers were less easy to convince. After enduring a few weeks' waffling about 'third world location', 'absence of skilled labour force' and 'threatened downturn in the economy', Stephen lost patience.

'That's it!' he exclaimed, returning to Purley Hall late one afternoon after another inconclusive meeting with the bank's finance committee. 'Those fat-bellied, dim-witted merchant wankers have finally blown it. I'll give my pound of flesh to another bank – maybe two. I've enough collateral if I put up this place as well as my investments.'

Christina bit back her instinctive objection. Stephen

knew what he was doing, even if he was committing them to the hilt.

Besides, she had problems of her own to deal with. Victoria had welcomed her father home with open arms. Christina received only a dead-eyed stare and a blank refusal to look at the photographs she had taken or the gifts she had chosen for Victoria. So far, although she knew that Stephen was planning to build a hotel in Barbados, they had not told her of their plans to relocate there.

'Don't you think we should mention it soon, Stephen?' Christina asked one night, after Dorothy had served them a good if slightly odd dinner of home-made vegetable soup, toad in the hole with golden syrup – another Northern speciality – and pineapple sorbet. Victoria had gone upstairs to do her homework and Stephen and Christina were taking advantage of the fact to curl up together on the leather Chesterfield in the library.

'She's going to be really upset if we just suddenly up sticks and haul her out of school here, away from all her friends. And what about schools on the island? Do we know if there are any good ones?'

'Several excellent ones, I hear. A good education wouldn't be a problem in Barbados. But I've been thinking . . . I never thought I'd hear myself say this, but I'm beginning to wonder if boarding-school here might not be best for Vicky.'

Christina couldn't believe it either. When she'd tentatively suggested it once herself, feeling like the wicked stepmother, Stephen had gone through the roof. He had the grace to look a little sheepish as he continued, 'I met Caroline's mother when I picked Victoria up from the pony club the other day and she suggested something.

'Vicky and Caroline got quite thick while we were on honeymoon, apparently, and Virginia Colton seems to think the friendship's doing Caroline good. She's a rather quiet kid.'

Christina nodded, seeing a vivid mental picture of shy, scrawny Caroline completely overshadowed by her friend's vivid looks.

'The Coltons have been doing some research into schools. They want Caroline to go away at twelve like her brother did. Virginia says it made him so much more self-reliant. Anyway, she's found an excellent girls' boarding-school only sixty miles away. The teaching's reliable, but the big attraction so far as Caroline and Vicky are concerned are the riding facilities. The school has its own stables and girls can keep their ponies there, even train for a riding instructor's certificate as well as take GCEs.

'I couldn't bear to send her to one of those stuffy girls' penitentiaries, but this sounds something else. And she'd already have one friend if Caroline goes too. What do you think? Should we take a look at it?'

Christina was silently heaping blessings on Virginia Colton's head. 'Sounds ideal to me. Victoria could have the odd weekend at Caroline's, presumably, and fly out to us for end-of-term holidays.'

'Yes, or even half-term. They always get a week at least. I can't wait to show her Crystal Springs.'

'Maybe we should get it into shape first?' Christina suggested hastily. She felt very protective of the house already. Purley Hall and the London mews house, much though she loved them, bore Barbara's stamp. Crystal Springs was going to be the first home she made with Stephen, and she didn't care for the thought of her step-daughter turning up her nose at its present dilapidated state.

'Yes, that would be best,' Stephen agreed. 'We can always stay at the Royal Palm when she comes out in the meantime.'

But not, Christina noticed, all the time. Apparently it

was perfectly all right for her to rough it on a building-site, while Victoria was to be petted and cosseted at all times. Daddy's little girl . . .

She stifled the thought, which smacked of jealousy, when really she had no reason to be jealous. Stephen loved her and made it flatteringly plain how much he was relying on her. Besides, it was going to be tough on Victoria, poor kid, when her father told her he was sending her away to school. She was bound to look on it as a betrayal.

When Victoria was finally told, her screams of rage and desolation filled the house. Stephen emerged from her room white-faced.

'I'm not so sure this is a good idea after all,' he said weakly.

'Give it a few days,' Christina counselled. 'Maybe she'll start to come round to the idea. It's a great place, Stephen. I'd have loved it at her age.'

Whether it was the thought of having a friend at the school or the promise that she would not be parted from Mischief they did not discover, but unexpectedly Victoria did seem to adjust to the idea, at least when she was speaking to her father.

To her stepmother, however, she made her feelings quite clear. One morning she tracked Christina down to the newly cleaned and repaired swimming-pool. She was lying on an air-mattress in the water, topping up her Caribbean tan. She was hoping Stephen could find the finance for Crystal Springs soon, so that they could get started, when she heard her stepdaughter's voice, low and threatening, from the side of the pool.

'I want you to know it hasn't worked.'

Christina opened her eyes in alarm and squinted up at Victoria, silhouetted against the light. She looked taller suddenly, almost grown-up, her face so twisted with rage that it was almost unrecognizable.

'What hasn't worked?' Christina asked, puzzled.

'Your sneaky little plan to come between Daddy and me. Going on and on at him, persuading him to send me away.

'But it won't make a bit of difference in the long run. Even if I do go to this stinking school, I'll stay in touch with Daddy – write to him every day. And he'll write back – you'll see. I'll always be number one with him.'

Christina slid off the mattress and started to swim to the side. 'Now wait a minute, Victoria. We have to discuss this.'

Water lapped over the side of the pool and splashed across Victoria's feet. Her face drained of colour, she screamed: 'You did that on purpose! You know I'm terrified of water, and you deliberately splashed me! Daddy, Daddy – Christina's trying to drown me . . .'

She raced away through the gardens, intent on claiming all Stephen's attention, all his love. Christina sighed and decided to get dressed. Victoria had spoiled the pleasure of her swim, as she spoiled so many aspects of life at Purley Hall. Once more she found her thoughts slipping away from her present surroundings to the blue, blue Caribbean sea and sky, the place where her new life with Stephen would really begin.

Two weeks later Stephen told her that the finance for Crystal Springs was settled in principle. A wearying round of meetings with bankers and lawyers remained, and he'd been forced to adopt a course he had not initially foreseen. Robert Leyton was to take a 25 per cent stake in Crystal Springs, despite the fact that Stephen had originally planned to tackle this project alone.

'It was the only way I could swing it with the bank,' he told Christina. 'But I'll buy him out as soon as I can, don't worry. Crystal Springs is going to be our baby. Oh, Robert's all right when it comes to chatting up local councillors and having a jar with the union rep, but he'll never be a player on an international scale, and I don't want him cramping my style when it comes to the hotels. He thinks it'll stop at this one.'

It was the first she had heard that Stephen had plans for a hotel empire, and privately she thought he was being a bit ungrateful towards Robert, who had after all enabled the project to begin. But she had learned not to comment on Stephen's business dealings. He had a way of pointing out how ill informed she was which, while never aggressive, always made her feel cut down to size.

'Does this mean I can start putting together my wardrobe for Barbados?' she asked, changing the subject.

'Yes, you do that, Chrissy. You won't be needing anything too smart while the construction's going on, but you may as well stock up for later.'

The next day she went up to town and spent an exhausting few hours trawling Beauchamp Place and Sloane Street. She had intended to tour Bond Street and its off-shoots too, but decided that enough was enough. Loading her parcels into the sporty new Mercedes coupé – grey to complement Stephen's navy-blue model – she set off back to Sussex, arriving earlier than she'd anticipated.

She opened the heavy front door with difficulty, her hands full, and stood with her back against it to push it wide. As she did so she heard the sound of raised voices coming from Stephen's office.

'For Christ's sake, it's not very much! I didn't think you'd even miss a lousy few hundred pounds.'

'Hundreds, thousands, it's all the same. I'm telling you, Edward, not this time.'

The business meeting was obviously becoming heated, Christina decided – and was startled when she stepped into the dimly lit hall and collided with a man who was leaving in a hurry.

'You'll regret this, Stephen!' he called over his

shoulder, and cannoned into her, causing her to drop her parcels.

She had a brief impression of a slightly stocky, fair-haired man who wore his hair rather too long and his suit just too sharply cut. His eyes were green, she noticed, as he glared at her for a moment before pushing past her out of the door. She heard a car start up immediately, and the spray of gravel as it was driven fast down the drive.

Stephen emerged from his office, face slightly flushed and brows drawn tight.

'Who on earth was that?' she asked, bending to pick up her scattered parcels.

'Did he do that?' Stephen asked angrily as he helped her.

'Well, yes, but it was an accident . . .'

'Bloody typical!' he exclaimed. 'That's all my brother's fit for – barging in here where he's not welcome, whingeing for money, then barging out again when I won't give it to him. It's Mother's fault. She's too damn soft with him.'

'I didn't even know you had a brother,' she said, surprised. 'He wasn't at the wedding.'

'No, well, we see as little of each other as possible. And he's my half-brother, strictly speaking – Edward Harrington. My mother was married and divorced before she met my father. Harrington was a useless bastard, a gambler and worse – just like Edward.'

'Stephen, aren't you being a bit hard? He is family.'

'What do you know about it?' he said harshly. 'Just take it from me, Chrissy, Edward's bad news. He sponges off my mother shamelessly then leaves her in the lurch, taking off with yet another of his musclebound boyfriends.'

Christina thought she saw what lay at the root of Stephen's attitude.

'Edward's gay, then?'

'Yes, but you needn't think I'm so narrow-minded as to hold that against him on its own. Just take it from me, my half-brother's a nasty piece of work. Rotten to the core. If he ever turns up here again and I'm not in, shut the door on him, okay?'

'All right, Stephen.'

Nevertheless she was intrigued. Stephen had the power constantly to surprise her. A half-brother turning up out of the blue . . . How many other secrets did he have?

Privately she decided that if she ever got the chance to speak to Edward Harrington again she would do so. Maybe he could help her fathom some of the enigmas behind the mysterious man she had married.

Leaving Purley Hall was a tremendous wrench.

'Come home soon, won't you?' Mrs Barnes beseeched them. The day before, she had waved off Victoria, tears in her eyes.

Christina stepped forward and hugged the elderly housekeeper warmly.

'Take care, Barnesey,' she said. 'I'm going to miss you and your apple crumble.'

The countrywoman's lined face crinkled in disgust.

'You take care of Mr Reece-Carlton.' She glanced at Stephen, who was climbing into the Mercedes. 'Look after him, mind. And look after yourself.' She hugged Christina tightly. 'Take plenty of honey and lemon and lots of vitamin C to ward off all them foreign germs.'

Christina smiled through the thin film of tears in her eyes. 'Don't worry about me, Barnesey, I can take care of myself.'

They drove slowly down the long, sweeping drive.

It was early May, and the morning held a soft promise of warmth. Everywhere there was May blossom. The tennis balls she had forgotten to retrieve littered the tennis courts. Beyond the Hall's tall and intricately wrought iron gates, the countryside unfolded in a counterpane of green fields and budding hedgerows.

Christina turned in her seat and took one last look at the mellow Elizabethan façade. Mrs Barnes was still waving; Muffin was running in circles at her feet. Christina wondered how long it would be before she saw all this again.

Twelve and a half hours later their taxi bounced past the rusting gates of Crystal Springs.

'I thought someone was going to meet us here.' Christina's voice was weary as their taxi-driver lugged the suitcases up the crumbling steps and placed them inside the wide, hand-carved coral-stone portico.

Stephen grunted as he fished in his pocket and gave the grinning driver a ten-dollar tip. Concerned, she looked up at the big, brooding house. The sun was fast disappearing. Soon it would be dark.

They watched the taxi drive away.

Almost as soon as it had disappeared, a car turned past the gates and into the drive, raced past the royal palms, and slewed to a halt in a cloud of dust. A tall young man with an absurdly wide grin on his face got out. Christina recognized the estate agent who had first shown them around.

'Sorry I'm late, folks.' The grin broadened and grew yet more vapid. 'But you know how it is. Eastern Caribbean time. You'll get used to it.'

'I doubt that, Mr Garcia.' There was an edge to Stephen's voice.

Garcia produced a key and fiddled with the door lock. 'It opened okay this morning,' he told them. The grin seemed to be a permanent fixture. It took him some minutes to get the key to turn. Finally he pushed against the tall, heavy dark-mahogany double doors, which swung slowly open, scattering a pile of unopened mail across the dusty hall.

Garcia led the way into a drawing-room at the front of the house. He turned and caught sight of their expressions. For the first time the grin left his face. He looked uncomfortable, and his voice became hesitant. 'We've done the best we can to make it a home from home for you, but I expect there will be lots that you'll want to do yourselves.'

Christina looked around the sparsely furnished room. 'You can say that again,' she moaned. Wearily, she rested her arm on the back of the old, battered wicker chair. A fat lizard scurried across her wrist. She jumped.

'You needn't be afraid of lizards, Mrs Reece-Carlton, they won't harm you.' Garcia tried to be reassuring.

'I'm afraid of everything that crawls. Apart, that is, from Stephen when he wants something.'

Stephen laughed sharply, and Garcia's vacuous look returned.

'We've put some things in the fridge,' he said, and led them to a small kitchen at the back of the house. A stale smell hung in the air.

Christina opened the fridge, peered inside, and snorted at its meagre contents. Stephen stuck his head round the door to take a look.

'Well, George, you've done us proud.' His voice, heavy with sarcasm, turned sharp. 'When I was last here I deposited a considerable sum of money with you. You remember?'

George Garcia fidgeted with the edge of a dirty melamine kitchen table. 'Yes, Mr Carlton.'

'And I seem to remember telling you that I wanted you to spend that money on furnishing this place and stocking it with crockery and cutlery and bed-linen and a good supply of food. Especially food. Decent food.'

Stephen's face, as always when he was angry, was as white as chalk.

Garcia blinked and stuttered. 'M-my wife Kelly didn't

know what you liked to eat. She was going to pick up Mrs Reece-Carlton in the morning and take her to the local shops and then to all the furniture places. It was difficult for us to know your tastes and . . .'

'So why the hell didn't you say that in the first place? I'd have got someone else to do the job. Anyway, tomorrow morning, George, we'll go through the house and see how you've spent my money. Every penny of it.'

Garcia said nothing. He looked like a man who devoutly wished he was somewhere else.

Stephen turned away from him, and walked back into the drawing-room. By this time his anger had subsided; he was too tired for confrontation.

'Well, come on, George,' he ordered less irritably, 'make yourself useful and help carry the bags upstairs.'

They each took a couple of suitcases and struggled up the broad staircase. George led the way into the master bedroom suite, halfway along the landing. Night was falling fast and it was shadowy inside. He flicked a switch and the bedroom was suffused with a wan, yellow light.

On a threadbare rug stood an antique mahogany four-poster draped in faded gold damask. Close by was an even older armchair, its stuffing spilling out from rents in the fabric. It stood next to a set of wardrobes with pea-green paint peeling off their warped doors. Two deep cracks ran the full length of the high ceiling; where they joined in the centre, an ancient, tarnished brass chandelier hung precariously.

The room smelled of damp. Christina was desperate to throw open the windows and let in some fresh air.

'Bathroom *en suite*.' Garcia threw open the door with a flourish. The inane grin had returned.

In the centre of the huge room stood a large enamel bath. It was raised off the worn linoleum by heavy clam legs and covered in dark-yellow stains. A chrome showerhead, held by a single screw, hung drunkenly above it.

It was the second time that the expression on their faces wiped the smile off Garcia's face.

'Well,' he announced hurriedly, 'must be going.'

'Mustn't be late for dinner, eh, George?' Stephen's tone was sarcastic.

Looking at his watch, he spoke without thinking. 'Right. Kelly's got roast beef.' He looked up guiltily.

'Maybe you should call Kelly and tell her she's got guests for dinner,' Stephen said pointedly. 'With what you've left us in the fridge, there's a good chance we could starve.'

'I suppose I could call her,' the young man responded weakly. 'I'm sure she wouldn't mind.' He didn't sound at all convincing.

Stephen considered him for a few moments as he shuffled from foot to foot, eyes darting, looking for a way to escape. Then he smiled. He had taken pity on the young estate agent. It wasn't his fault he didn't match up to Stephen's exacting standards. Very few people did. At least not to begin with.

'Forget it, I'm only joking.'

A look of relief spread over George's face.

Stephen walked him down to the front door. 'Goodnight, George. I'll expect you and Kelly here at 8.30 sharp. Christina needs to go shopping and I need you to take me into town. Enjoy your dinner.'

Closing the heavy door on a relieved Garcia, he dashed into the kitchen and opened the fridge door. There were only a few items he had noted as important amongst the few supplies George had bought in: a few cans of Coke and a bottle of Mount Gay Rum, the island's national drink.

He scrabbled around in the cupboards to find two dusty tumblers which, after rinsing, he carried upstairs along with the bottle of golden rum and cans of Coke.

Christina had opened a pair of tall shutters and was standing on the deep semi-circular veranda of the master bedroom. She was looking out over a dense coconut grove, deep in shadow, towards the sea, which glittered occasionally in the light of the rising moon.

Stephen came up behind her. He handed her a glass. 'On our first night in our new home I think it fitting we drink the national brew.'

He handed her a tumbler and half filled it with the smooth, golden-coloured rum. After topping it up with Coke, he did the same for himself, then raised his glass to her. 'Cheers.'

'Cheers, my darling.' She took a gulp and choked. Coughing and spluttering, she cleared her throat. 'God, this is strong. A couple of these and I'd be anybody's.'

'Well, drink one and maybe you'll be mine.' He grinned mischievously at her.

She was, but not until they had enjoyed another lethal dose of rum and Coke and eaten a plateful of fried eggs and beans in the bare, dimly lit kitchen.

Afterwards, Stephen chased her up the staircase and into the bedroom. They were laughing as he dragged her jeans off and impatiently began to kiss her long, slim legs, but as his mouth moved up the inside of her thighs their laughter subsided. Soon Christina's giggles turned to soft moans of rapture as his wet, hungry tongue lingered enticingly at the rim of her silk panties. Eagerly, she pulled them to one side to allow him access to the dark softness of her sex. She cried out as he thrust himself deep within her, then arched her back wantonly as slowly he began to move.

For much of the night the old, slumbering house was kept awake; echoing to the sounds of their lustful, crazy lovemaking and the creaking of the ancient four-poster bed.

*

What little sleep Christina got was fitful, and when she awoke at five she felt completely dehydrated.

'Are you awake, Stephen?' She pinched him.

He grunted. 'I am now. What is it?' His voice was thick with sleep.

'I'm dying,' she moaned. 'I've got to have something to drink.'

Stephen snuggled into her. 'Go back to sleep,' he murmured. 'I'll get you a drink in a little while.'

She wriggled out of his arms. 'Okay, I'll go myself. I must have something.'

He groaned good-naturedly and rolled out of bed. 'All right, all right, I'll go. I think there's a can of Coke left in the fridge.'

He groped his way out of the dark bedroom and padded down the stairs. Suddenly she heard him shout, 'Bloody hell, what on earth . . . ?'

She sat bolt upright, leapt out of bed and rushed to the top of the stairs. 'Stephen, what's wrong?'

There was no response from the gloom below.

She crept cautiously down the stairs and into the drawing-room.

'Oh, God!' she screeched, and shrank back against the wall in horror.

Stephen was standing on a chair above a crawling, heaving mass of land crabs, their pincers held aloft as they scrambled on top of each other and ran sideways up the walls, only to drop like flies when they reached the ceiling.

Christina screamed wildly as a crab dropped onto her head and scratched and scrambled to get out of her hair. She knocked it to the ground with a shaking hand, and ran back upstairs sobbing, slamming the bedroom door behind her.

She was still shuddering when, a few minutes later, Stephen came into the room and took her in his arms. She hugged him close.

'I've never seen anything like that in my life,' he said in a strained voice. She could tell he was shaken too.

'And I for one don't ever want to see it again,' she mumbled through trembling lips, burying her face in his chest.

'Thank God they're harmless,' she heard him say.

She looked up. 'They may be harmless but we've got to get rid of them! Supposing they come upstairs?' She shuddered.

He shook his head. 'I doubt they could manage the stairs. Anyway, don't worry, darling, I'll call pest control first thing this morning.'

'Is there such a thing here?'

He shrugged. 'I expect there'll be something. After all, they are a pest – we can't be the only people who've been invaded.' He smiled at her. 'Don't worry, Chrissy, it's all over now.' He held her shuddering body tight.

'Worried? I'm not worried. I'm bloody petrified!'

Stephen fetched her a cup of tepid water from the bathroom and she lay down on top of the bed. She closed her eyes; there was a dull throbbing in her left temple. Stephen lay beside her. 'You'll feel better if you try to go back to sleep, Chrissy.'

They both tried without success. When, only minutes later, dawn came stealing beneath the bottom of the broken shutters, they gave up and decided to walk to the beach.

They crept down the stairs. Stephen had shut the drawing-room door and there were only a couple of crabs scuttling about in the kitchen.

Outside, the sun was dappling the leaves of the palms as they struggled through the dense vegetation to the beach. It was deserted save for one lone baby Hawksbill turtle struggling to find the sanctuary of the sea.

Christina lifted the small, harmless reptile in the palm of her hand and placed it carefully in the shallow water.

She watched with delight as its little flippers propelled it speedily out to sea.

She walked into the water until it was up to her waist, then allowed herself to float gently on its surface. The smooth movement of the sea, and the delicate light of the early morning sun filtering through her closed eyelids, helped ease her pounding head. Stephen, who was a strong swimmer, had swum a long way out from the shore.

'Come on, Christina,' he yelled, waving to her.

She pretended not to hear him, happy to drift carelessly in the shallow water.

She must have been floating for at least ten minutes when suddenly the water around her erupted.

She screamed.

It was Stephen.

'Don't, Stephen! No,' she squealed as he splashed her with great sweeps of water before grabbing her and pulling her under. He was laughing uproariously when she emerged, spluttering.

'Just you wait, I'll get you back.' She chased after him through the shallows. Stephen threw himself, panting and exhilarated from his energetic swim, onto the soft, ivory sand, and she dropped down beside him, laughing and shaking her wet hair vigorously. Her headache had disappeared completely.

'I feel marvellous. The water's wonderful,' Stephen said, grabbing a corner of the towel she was using and rubbing his thick, dark, glistening hair.

'It's fantastic,' she agreed, pulling the towel out of his grip. 'I think we should make this a daily ritual.'

'And I think that we should go skinny-dipping every evening,' he added, eyeing her lecherously.

'I'll think about it,' she replied coolly, then jumped up. 'Race you back to the house.'

She was away before he could reply. Her slighter build allowed her to get through the undergrowth more easily, and she reached the house well ahead of him. 'Sissy,' she laughed as he came racing up.

Christina made a breakfast of fresh orange juice, tea and toast; they ate on the terrace which stretched the full length of the house at the back. From where they sat they had an uninterrupted view of what must once have been one of the best coconut groves on the island, through which they caught glimpses of the glittering sea.

'Stephen, what's that tree there?' Christina pointed to a huge tree with brown and grey bark standing slightly apart from the grove. Its thin, twisted, gnarled branches, cascading profusely from its trunk, had rerooted themselves in the earth. The whole impression was of a giant fountain suddenly petrified in mid-flow and coloured by age. 'It's magnificent.'

He nodded. 'Yes, it is, and whatever else we do to this place, we'll make sure we preserve that tree.' She looked at him inquiringly. 'It's a fig tree,' he explained. '*Citrifolia ficus*, otherwise known as the Bearded Fig.'

She laughed. You never cease to amaze me. I didn't think you knew anything about trees.'

'I know about that one. The island is named after it.'

'Really?'

'Yes. When the first Portuguese explorers landed here in the sixteenth century there were hundreds of those trees lining the shore, looking just like that one there. From a distance they looked like old men's beards, so . . .' – he nodded at the tree – 'they called the place Los Barbades, the bearded ones.' He shrugged. 'Hence Barbados.'

Christina stared at it again. Now she'd heard Stephen's story, she could easily see why the Portuguese had likened the trees to big, bushy beards.

'That's fascinating. What else do you know about the island?' she asked animatedly.

He chuckled. 'You're not bored?'

'On the contrary. This place is going to be my home for

the foreseeable future; I want to know everything about it. Tell me more.'

'Well . . .' He paused and frowned slightly, trying to recollect what he knew. She gazed at his profile. For a change, the chiselled features of his long, angular face had softened. He concentrated on a Flamboyant tree a few yards from the terrace. Bursting with dense clusters of scarlet blossom, it looked like a big red umbrella.

'The first inhabitants were Arawak Indians who lived here peacefully for hundreds of years. They were conquered and assimilated by the Caribs, a fierce fighting tribe from South America who invaded the whole region. They, in turn, were conquered by the Portuguese.'

'And when did we arrive?'

'The British, commanded by Captain Henry Powell, landed in 1627 and pretty quickly colonized the island.'

'How do you know all this?' she asked, laughing quietly.

He turned to face her. Not for the first time she was captivated by his unusual eyes.

'I read – more than just the latest bestseller.'

She stared at him and felt her heart surge with love. Their eyes locked, and for a long moment nothing else in the world existed.

It was Stephen who broke the spell. He looked at his watch. 'George Garcia and his wife will be here soon; we'd better go.' He stood up.

Christina sighed. On the wooden balustrade of the terrace a lizard expertly caught a fly in its long tongue and swallowed it. She followed him into the house.

'Ugh!' she exclaimed, and jumped back onto the terrace, pointing in horror.

Stephen kicked the dead crab out onto the grass. 'I'm afraid you're going to have to get used to this kind of thing, Chrissy. You're in the West Indies now.'

She shuddered. 'Never. I'm never going to get used to this.'

She did, and much quicker than she would have imagined. She learned to live with it all, though she almost fainted the first time an enormous bat, flying over the terrace at dusk, brushed her face with its wings.

But she survived that, as she survived the flying cockroaches which flew through the open windows and landed on anything, or anyone, in their path; and the tree rats, the size of small cats, which raced across the window pelmets and the architraves to disappear into the roof arches. She learned to cope with the enormous frogs and toads, croaking and jumping on the terrace after a torrential rain-storm, and with the centipedes and millipedes crawling lazily inches from her feet. She even learned to cope with the massive black land crabs, or Swampys as they were called locally, which roamed the night with pincers the size of babies' arms and eerily crawled across the lights of the car when they drove out at night.

She got used to it mainly because she was so busy.

She and Stephen set to work on making Crystal Springs at least temporarily habitable. Within a week they had a squad of decorators who, armed with white emulsion, painted everything paintable – including themselves and a new pine desk.

George helped them acquire some new rattan and cane furniture and an assortment of bright Mexican rugs, and Christina scoured the antique shops with Kelly for old mahogany tables and decorative pieces.

One of the downstairs rooms was turned into Stephen's office. Upstairs, where apart from the master bedroom suite there were a further five bedrooms and three bathrooms, they created a spacious, self-contained flat. Along with the master bedroom and bathroom, there was a living-room, a dining-room, a pretty kitchen and guest bedroom.

In what seemed an incredibly short time, Crystal

Springs ceased to be a house and became their home. Christina knew that everything they had done was temporary; that she would have to wait until Stephen had fulfilled his ambition and built the hotel before she could really start on restoring the house and bringing it back to its former glory. Yet, even so, she felt that it was her first real home with him.

Now they had somewhere which was theirs alone; a home which, with its tall french windows running down each side of the house, was bathed in radiant sunlight from dawn till dusk; a home whose windows gave out on to glorious views of what would one day be beautiful, formal gardens sweeping down to royal palms and coconut groves beyond which lay the sparkling sea.

Kelly had found them a maid, a young local girl called Celia. Christina and Stephen soon warmed to her for, although her pace was slower than a snail's, she was always willing and she smiled a lot; a big, broad, open smile which made up for all her defects as a domestic.

Celia taught Christina how to bargain for vegetables in the market, and how to avoid paying the massively inflated prices for everything that the tourists paid.

Christina's driving on the local roads, pitted with potholes and frequently congested with animals, improved, though her language grew much worse. She also learned the art of banter with the local youths who hissed lecherously at any white female below the age of 100.

Gradually she became used to taking life at a much slower pace, although she still found herself functioning in top gear in comparison to the locals. Slowly she learned to accept her adopted country and its countrymen, and with great pleasure realized that they accepted her.

Stephen popped the cork high into the humid air and tried to catch the frothing champagne in Christina's glass. He laughed, and the lines of concentration that had been

147

etching his face over the past weeks slipped away. Christina laughed with him, noticing how much younger he looked when his face lost the intense expression which she called his business look.

It was almost dusk, and they were standing in the middle of a vast area of newly turned earth. It was the first day of work on the construction of Crystal Springs Hotel.

They had been on the island almost exactly three months.

'Well, Chrissy, so far so good.' He took a sip from his glass and looked at her over its rim.

'I want to tell you something. I'd better tell you now because it's quite likely either that I'll forget or that I won't have time in the next few months – I love you. Thank you for seeing me through all this.'

He indicated the mounds of warm, sandy earth and piles of coral-stone littering the area. The coral-stone blocks, quarried from the local coral beds, had soft hues of ivory and pink which at a distance made them look like confectionery or freshly baked meringue.

'I love you too, Stephen.' Christina sighed as she gazed around. 'Though we've a hell of a long way to go.'

He raised his glass and shouted across the desolate building-site: 'To Crystal Springs, and to all the luck in the world. We're going to need it,' he added in a quieter voice.

'To Crystal Springs,' Christina echoed softly, 'the best hotel in the Caribbean.'

'Come on.' Grabbing the champagne bottle he took her by the hand and led her along the path which the workmen had made through the undergrowth to the beach. He refilled her glass and together they sat in silence on the warm sand, drinking champagne and watching the great red orb of the sun sink majestically into the sea.

By the time they had finished the bottle, dark fingers of shadow were creeping along the beach. They stood up and retraced their steps towards the house, arm in arm.

'Stop, Stephen,' Christina cried. 'Look at the house. Don't you think it looks sort of sad in the darkness, almost foreboding? As if the old place is trying to tell us something.'

She shivered and he put his arms around her shoulders.

'That house is going to witness the building of the best hotel in the Caribbean, remember? I'm sure it's not sad about that. Anyway, look.'

He pointed to the dark sky, already filled with glittering stars. A full moon was sailing into sight, bathing the roof with what looked like a halo of incandescent light. 'See how it glows in the moonlight?'

'Yes, it looks wonderful.' She hugged him tightly.

'We're going to make you into a great hotel.' Stephen was addressing Crystal Springs.

'Yes, we are,' she agreed, 'the very best.'

Chapter Six

Paul Richardson had received a dawn summons from Stephen and arrived at Crystal Springs fifteen minutes later. One of the facts of Caribbean life that suited Stephen was the early hour at which people rose to start the day. Unfortunately an island working day needed to be swiftly curtailed once it grew hot. Stephen's never were.

He had asked Christina to attend this meeting too, saying he'd value her opinion on the revised pool plans which Paul was bringing in. She found herself praying that this batch would be more to his liking than the last.

Paul looked surprised to receive a wide smile of welcome from Stephen when he entered the office. Recovering quickly, he smiled in return and extended his hand. Stephen took it, saying, 'Don't look so astonished, Paul. I can smile – when people give me something to smile about.'

Paul shrugged. Caught off-guard, he blushed slightly, blinked his hazy blue eyes, and looked away in embarrassment. Christina felt sorry for him. Stephen liked to be able to wrong-foot the people who worked for him and was a master at taking them off-guard.

'You look tired, Paul.' It was a statement, nothing more. Stephen's voice held no concern, she noted.

'I am. I've been up all night working on these.'

Paul pulled out a roll of plans from the black plastic tube he was carrying. He laid them out on Stephen's desk and did his best to smooth them flat.

Christina found herself remembering the way the promising young architect had first come into their lives. After paying fruitless calls on the local architects whom George Garcia had recommended, Stephen had suggested they all go for a drink at the Reef Bar. He needed to let off steam, and it was impossible for the other people in the bar not to overhear.

'Do you know how many firms of bloody architects I've traipsed round to in the past two months? It's amazing. How the hell do such totally unimaginative, unoriginal idiots get to become architects in the first place? I don't know. I threw the last one's sketches across his office and told him: shoddy, unexciting, no thanks. I mean, I'm trying to build the kind of hotel people only dream about, and all those idiots can come up with are boring, square boxes!'

He slammed his drink onto the bar top, slopping the rum sour across the grubby pine surface. He didn't seem to notice, and continued, his voice rising even more: 'I believe when people come here on vacation they come to escape the perpetual grey in their lives for a short space of time. I want to offer them light, colour, romance, and to stimulate their imaginations. I want to capture a little bit of their hearts with the kind of simple pleasure and beauty this island has to offer . . .' He paused and took another shot of his drink. 'So that when they return to their mundane, repetitive jobs and stress-filled existences they retain an image of Crystal Springs and long to return. I bloody well can't achieve that by sticking them in dull concrete abortions! I mean, is it too much to ask? Eh, George? Is it *too* much? Well, what do *you* think?'

'No, it's not too much to ask,' a young man said from behind Garcia. He looked over the estate agent's shoulder at the surprised face of the Englishman. 'Excuse me for interrupting, but I couldn't help overhearing your conversation. My name's Paul Richardson, and I believe I'm just the man you're looking for.'

He was very young – only newly qualified in Britain before he'd decided he'd had enough of the climate, grey and defeatist, and come to the West Indies to try his luck – but Stephen had admired his chutzpah and Christina the laid-back island style he'd adopted. He dressed in baggy shorts and Hawaiian print shirts, but there was nothing relaxed about his working methods. Paul Richardson was the first person they'd met on the island who was prepared to work as long and as hard as they did.

Stephen had first asked for a design for an open-air bar. Paul delighted them with plans and perspectives for an irregularly shaped weatherboard construction cleverly built around a venerable tamarind tree, using its branches as an informal canopy to shade the seats below.

Since then, Stephen and Paul had discussed, argued, and occasionally fought their way through plans, revised plans and revisions of revisions until a design for the accommodation and service blocks had finally been agreed.

Most of the coconut palms had been cleared from the twenty-acre site, and the dense vegetation had been cut back to deepen the crescent-shaped beach where the six low-level Mediterranean accommodation blocks were to be built, each housing twenty rooms, varying in size and design but all with huge covered terraces overhanging the beach with uninterrupted sea views. A pathway led from the rooms through the gardens and past a hand-carved stone fountain to the reception and administration building, built around a central courtyard of white marble and hand-painted tiles.

Stephen had suggested a lily pond and miniature fountain in the centre of the courtyard, and they had copied the one from Crystal Springs House on a grander scale. Clustered around the courtyard were the four boutiques, hospitality desk and concierge.

High, curved, hand-carved doors led from the reception

area to the conference room and residents' sitting-room, where afternoon tea would be served looking down across the gardens to the accompaniment of a grand piano.

A long covered walkway from the other side of the pool led to the fine dining restaurant and smaller, less formal coffee shop, both restaurants overlooking the sea. Located behind these buildings were the vast kitchen, store-rooms, housekeeping, laundry, staff rooms and car parking.

Stephen wanted the hotel to look as if it had always been there, part of the landscape, and Paul suggested a South American landscape architect, whom he had heard of. Apparently, Roberto Sabortini could transform a desert into a lush tropical garden.

Finally it was time to tackle the design of the hotel's talking-point – the vast fresh-water swimming-pool Stephen planned to construct to cater for guests who, having come thousands of miles to see the Caribbean, decided they didn't actually want to swim in it.

Stephen had turned down the first set of plans out of hand. Christina hoped they could be more encouraging about this version. Paul had been a real find so far, and she knew it would do his professional standing a lot of good if he could design the whole hotel complex.

'I've been looking forward to this,' Stephen announced with a kind of childish glee. Taking his magnifying glass from a desk drawer, he fell upon the plans and scrutinized each one intently without speaking. Paul watched him carefully, trying to read his expression, but it was guarded, non-committal.

Eventually he looked up and, when he spoke, his voice betrayed a mixture of disappointment and impatience. 'I don't like them, Paul. In fact, I positively *hate* the shape of the pool. I'd envisioned more movement, excitement – fantasy, even.'

He tossed the plans to one side. 'This pool looks like a

thousand others I've seen. I want Crystal Springs to be different – unusual, magnificent. Like nothing anyone has seen before.'

Paul sighed and shook his head. 'I don't think it looks like a million other pools at all,' he stated, an edge of impatience to his voice. He placed one of the plans in front of Stephen, who bluntly refused to look at it. Paul ignored the rebuff and turned to Christina instead, pointing to his drawing and explaining: 'I drew the pool as an oasis, surrounded by traveller's palms for maximum shade, and I thought the waterfall cascading through the coral-stone rock formation balanced it perfectly.'

Stephen paid little attention – he had already dismissed the plans and his only response was a shrug. 'I want more waterfalls and perhaps a bridge.'

Paul thought the concept too messy and said so. 'I really think if you make it too busy it becomes like Disneyland, and I'm sure that's not what you want for Crystal Springs.'

Christina waited for the explosion. Stephen never lost his temper with her, but with others . . .

When he spoke again, his tone was clipped. 'I want to create fantasy and originality, and to my mind that pool of yours conveys nothing but boredom. So it's back to the drawing-board, Paul, and I need those drawings like yesterday.'

Paul tried one last shot. 'You realize, of course, what you want is going to cost a hell of a lot more money . . .'

Stephen didn't let him continue. 'Let me worry about the dollars. *You* concentrate on interpreting my ideas, putting them onto paper and making them work.'

Not bothering to put the designs back into the black plastic cylinder, Paul stuffed them under his arm. Christina noticed that he looked grey with tiredness and handed him a plan he had missed.

She didn't offer her own opinion, not because she

thought Paul's design was necessarily as bad as Stephen claimed, but because she had a hunch that, in time, he could come up with something really sensational instead of merely pedestrian. Unlike Stephen, however, she felt that support and encouragement were the most effective methods of getting the best from people.

'They're putting down the foundations for the bar today, Paul,' she told him. 'The arboriculturalist is here to supervise and check that the tree's roots aren't damaged. It's going to be fantastic, really individual. Stephen thinks so too, don't you, darling?'

Stephen was already mentally tackling the next task in a crowded schedule, riffling through the papers on his desk. 'What? Oh, yeah, the bar. Great,' he agreed. 'So see you tomorrow, Paul. Same time, same place – with the pool of my dreams, I hope.'

Christina found herself devoutly hoping so too, for Paul's sake. When things were not going the way Stephen wanted them to, he could be very hard on people, she had learned.

The strident ringing of the telephone broke in on them. Stephen dismissed Paul with a wave and picked up the receiver. There was the familiar, discordant sound of the long-distance satellite and then Robert Leyton's voice, speaking from England.

'Stephen! At last. I think it would be easier to get an audience with the Pope than to speak to you these days.'

Stephen was about to answer when Robert went on: 'I've had a very agitated Michael Davis on the phone. It's urgent he speaks to you.'

Stephen rolled his eyes at Christina.

'Okay, Robert, I know exactly what it's all about. I'll speak to him and sort things out. By the way, how's the Manchester deal?'

They were both so caught up in developments at Crystal

Springs that it was sometimes hard for Christina to recall that Stephen still had a stake in a totally separate business empire in England – one that Robert seemed to be finding increasingly hard to administer in his partner's prolonged absence, though Stephen still kept a very firm grip on English events from Barbados.

'And how's the hotel progressing?' Robert enquired.

'Fine, just fine. Don't you worry about this side of things; just keep the home fires burning.'

'You know I'll always do that, Stephen – you can rely on me.'

This last was said with a kind of passionate zeal that was typical of Robert, and which sometimes grated on Stephen's nerves. Irritated, he cut him short.

'Got to rush now, Bob; want to catch the bank before they close. Speak to you soon. Bye.'

'Michael Davis is from the bank, isn't he?' Christina queried.

'Mmm, and a bit of a pain in the arse.'

Stephen knew what the bank wanted, and for once he was a bit short on answers. How could a typically British and pedantic banker even begin to understand what he was trying to achieve on a tiny Third World island, known only as a sugar-producer and an enclave for the very rich?

To his delight, Davis's secretary informed him in clipped tones that: 'Mr Davis has been called out urgently and will not be back in the office until Friday.' Stephen left a message, grateful for two days' grace.

'God save me from bank managers and accountants!' he said to Christina. 'If we'd listened to them do you think for one minute we'd have got this far by now?'

They stood at the long sash windows of his office and looked out across the building-site. There was little left that bore any resemblance to the original landscape in which Stephen and Christina had first holidayed.

The dense palm grove had been cleared and hundreds of casuarina trees chopped down and grubbed out. Sand had been shipped in to form a deeper and wider beach, to accommodate up to two hundred people. To Christina's thinking it was a mess, but seeing the faraway look in Stephen's eyes she knew he viewed it differently. He did not see the tons of scaffolding or concrete blocks, but instead manicured lawns interspersed with narrow paths winding through lush tropical planting. He heard a fountain play, and marvelled at white stucco terraces ablaze with a riot of assorted bougainvillaea whilst smartly uniformed staff served a wealthy and sophisticated clientèle.

She felt a surge of strength and optimism run through her. Thank goodness she had married a visionary like Stephen. Whatever it took, and however long, nothing and nobody was going to stop them making Crystal Springs Hotel a reality. Of course, she hadn't bargained for a hurricane.

'Ah tell you, mistress, got to take it easy. A big storm be coming.' Celia's big eyes nearly popped out of their sockets. 'Ol' man Gordy tol' me,' the maid imparted gravely.

'How does he know?' Christina asked, sounding dubious. She had heard nothing on the radio.

'He jus' knows; he have special power.' The maid looked over her shoulder then hissed into Christina's ear, 'Black magic power.'

'Don't be ridiculous, Celia. I hope you don't believe in stupid nonsense like that?'

They were standing on the front steps of Crystal Springs House.

'No, not me, mistress.' She shook her head vigorously. 'Hope he wrong. Las' time there was a big storm, we lost our house and six chickens so we have no fresh eggs.'

The girl seemed to be more concerned at the loss of the eggs than her home, Christina noticed.

'There's nothing to worry about, Celia, there isn't going to be a storm. Look at the sky.' It was a clear, bright blue without a cloud in sight.

Celia looked unconvinced as Christina left the house and got into her car to drive to Bridgetown.

Stephen had given her the task of co-ordinating the interiors for the hotel, following the design schemes he had commissioned from a well-known Paris-based designer. They had decided that they would save a lot of money doing their own purchasing and importing, and Christina wanted to make her own contribution to all the work on the hotel. She had her first meeting this morning with a textiles importer called Colin Weatherhead, who had promised to show her a range of fabrics he was positive she was going to love.

The journey into town took twice as long as it should. Christina crawled behind one of the gaudily painted island buses for most of the journey, waving at several giggling little girls, their pig-tailed hair bouncing on pristine white uniform blouses. Why were the schoolchildren here always so much smarter than in England? she wondered. She was late for her appointment, and parked her car on double yellow lines in a narrow lane, hoping she would not get a ticket.

She walked briskly through the teeming streets and alleyways which lay behind the main thoroughfares of Bridgetown.

Ancient women sat in darkened eighteenth- and nineteenth-century doorways, heads covered in kerchiefs or round-brimmed hats like up-ended pudding basins. Skinny old men stood around talking in groups, or counted up their change for a visit to the rum shop. Busy young mothers chivvied and scolded their children, balancing huge bags of shopping on their heads.

So busy was she observing the hustle and bustle of West Indian street life that Christina almost missed the small, pink-painted sign swinging above a shabby fretwork façade. A dark interior greeted her and she blinked, trying hard to focus on a handsome young brown-skinned man coming towards her.

'Good morning. You must be Christina Reece-Carlton. Welcome to Tropical Island Interiors.'

He was very tall. She had to stretch her neck to speak to him.

'And you must be Colin Weatherhead.'

'The one and only.' His dark-brown eyes twinkled.

'Coffee?' he offered, and pointed to a rickety cane chair. She accepted the coffee but refused the chair.

'So you're building a hotel down there at Crystal Springs? Lovely site for it, I must say. You new to the island?'

'Yes, we came here on honeymoon, and fell in love with Barbados and Crystal Springs. I thought it was going to be a holiday home, but my husband had different ideas.'

'Sometimes husbands have a bad habit of doing things like that,' he chuckled.

'I agree with you, Colin. Anyway, we're here for the indefinite future and I've been given the job of furnishing the hotel. It's a little daunting, to say the least.'

The coffee arrived. It tasted very black and bitter. Christina sweetened it with two spoonfuls of golden local cane sugar.

'Don't worry.' His voice was languid and carefree. 'I'm sure we can take all the worry out of furnishing the hotel for you. We have done several hotels all over the Caribbean and have a very good reputation.'

'Yes, I was recommended to you by our architect, Paul Richardson.'

Colin picked up his coffee and drank it at a gulp.

'I have worked with Paul a few times. You can rest assured, Mrs Reece-Carlton, I will do everything.'

'Please call me Christina.'

'As I was saying, Christina, I can assure you that Tropical Island Interiors will take all the worry and stress out of furnishing Crystal Springs Hotel.'

He sounded so convincing that Christina was reassured, and spent the next two hours sorting through hundreds of fabric samples, eventually choosing two co-ordinating Caribbean prints – a bold poinsettia pattern and a smaller toning design featuring hibiscus and humming-birds.

She left Colin's office promising to meet him again later that week and clutching her chosen samples. She started down the street, and noticed that there was some sort of commotion. People were frantically packing up fruit and vegetable stalls, pushing carts and animals into their homes; shutters were being banged tightly shut and everyone was shouting in loud, clattering voices.

Christina approached a young lad unloading crates of Cockspur golden rum on to the veranda of a tiny bar.

'What's going on? Why is everyone panicking?'

'Bad nasty storm coming, mistress, real bad nasty.'

Christina looked up at the sky which was an ominous navy blue. She ran, fighting her way through the packed lanes and not slowing up until she reached Fever Alley, where she had parked her car. Driving out of Bridgetown in congested traffic, she prayed she would get back to Crystal Springs before the storm broke.

Stephen was busy battening down all the shutters and doors with planks of wood and eight-inch nails when she arrived at Crystal Springs.

'I'm afraid it's on its way,' he shouted above the hammering as she jumped out of the car.

'What is?'

'A bloody hurricane! The worst they've had for years, apparently.'

'When?' Christina was ashen.

'Within the next eight hours, but the speed it's travelling it could be sooner.'

Suddenly she noticed an unusual calm. There was no movement at all: no stirring of leaves in the breeze, no fluttering of birds.

A frightening stillness had descended before the storm.

Stephen hammered the final nail into a plank which criss-crossed the front door and held out his hand to her to step through.

Celia's frightened face greeted her as Christina stepped inside. 'Ah tol' you, mistress, ol' Gordy right. Bad nasty storm coming.'

The killer hurricane hit Barbados at 145 miles per hour six hours later. Christina, Stephen and Celia huddled together in the master bedroom on the first floor, listening to the whirlwind hell-bent on destruction.

'It sounds like a wild animal.' Christina's hand shook as she sipped golden rum from the bottle and passed it to Stephen.

'I only hope and pray it doesn't do too much damage,' he said, and jumped as they all heard a high-pitched, deafening roar which shook the house, followed by the sound of wood splitting as the wind tore at the planks and ripped the front door off its hinges.

The screaming tempest whipped into the house, hurling furniture twenty feet into the air.

He put his arms around Christina, who was trembling. 'I'm scared, Stephen.'

He held her very close.

'So am I.'

They stayed like that for hours, hardly daring to move until the noise subsided and the hurricane passed, leaving a trail of devastation in its wake.

Stephen, Christina and Celia left the bedroom and walked cautiously downstairs in single file, horrified by the sight that greeted them.

Two uprooted palm trees blocked their way at the foot of the stairs. Stephen stood on the top trunk to help Christina and Celia climb down.

They picked their way through broken pieces of furniture, their feet crunching across splintered glass and wood. Electrical wires hung limply from gaping holes in the walls where light-fittings had been.

Christina kneeled down to pick up the handle of a cup. It was all that remained of a new bone-china tea set she had bought only last week.

'Oh, no!' Stephen shouted when they stepped outside onto the terrace. He dropped his head into his hands.

Torrential rain was quickly turning the building-site into a quagmire. Christina counted at least six golden palms and four royals uprooted on the ravaged site. She looked through a steely sheet of rain to where Stephen was pointing.

'All the coral-stone is ruined,' he said in despair.

Christina looked at tons of coral-stone blocks smashed to smithereens.

'Can't you get any more?'

'Yes, but when? I've waited weeks for this load. And at what cost?'

He stepped down from the terrace and walked against the driving rain towards the footings.

'Don' go out, mistress, it's not safe,' Celia called from the safety of the house as Christina ran after him.

'Come inside, Stephen, you'll get soaked!' Her voice was lost on the wind.

He was shouting at the storm, his voice choked and barely audible through the battering rain.

'I'll get the money from somewhere, and I'll get more coral-stone. This has set me back a few weeks, that's all.

It will take more than a bloody hurricane to stop me.'

The wind and rain ceased over the next two days, but giant waves of up to fifteen feet continued to batter the shoreline, flooding and wrecking many homes.

It was a week after the hurricane, and Stephen had been working non-stop, salvaging coral-stone and tiles from the debris. They had also lost part of the roof of the house, which he was trying to replace himself, as it was impossible to get anyone to do any work. All the construction workers were busy repairing their own properties.

It was almost dark when Christina walked to the centre of the building-site, where Stephen was sorting through piles of broken terracotta roof-tiles with sore and bleeding hands.

'Stephen, you really must rest or you'll kill yourself. It's ridiculous. Come into the house. Celia has managed to get fresh fish today and she's cooked it in spices, just how you like it.'

'I'll finish this and be right with you.' He didn't look up.

She sighed. It had been the same every day since the storm. He had worked from dawn until dusk without a break. His face and neck were burnt a dark-scarlet colour and patches had peeled, exposing bright-pink lesions underneath, but he seemed not to notice.

'Good news,' she said.

He looked up expectantly.

'We're getting the telephone back on today.'

'Great! I must call Robert and order some more hand-painted tiles from Spain. Most of that crate was destroyed.'

'While you're speaking to him, I suggest you ask him if he knows anyone in the building trade who would like to come out here to help you. It's far too much to handle on your own.'

'I can handle it, Christina. Don't worry.'

She glanced at his tired, drawn face.

'I'm sure you can, Stephen, but I can't. Promise me you'll think about getting some help, someone with experience who could organize all the day-to-day menial stuff that you're forced to do? It would take a lot of pressure off you, and free you up to do more important things.'

Christina knew she had struck the right businesslike chord as his expression changed from preoccupied to thoughtful.

'I'll think about it,' was all he said.

She wasn't at all surprised, though, when Stephen spoke to her after a long telephone conversation with Robert Leyton, later that evening.

'Remember what you said to me, Christina, about getting some help over here?'

She nodded and he went on, 'Well, chance would have it that a man called James Morris called Robert this morning. He's been made redundant and is desperate for work.'

'What does he do?'

'That's the whole point!' Stephen seemed pleased. 'He's a projects co-ordinator; been working for a big building company for years. We've used him in the past on a few projects. He's a good man and knows his stuff.'

'That's great. Have you offered him a job?'

'Not yet, but I've got Robert sounding him out. I don't want to appear too keen – his price might go up.'

Christina encouraged him.

'He could be a great asset to you, Stephen. Don't miss the chance.'

'I know.' Stephen touched the side of his nose with his index finger, a shrewd light entering his eyes. 'But I want him on my terms.'

Chapter Seven

'That's them.' Stephen nudged Christina, pointing to a couple walking out of the customs hall at Grantley Adams Airport. Any preconceived image she had of James and Elaine Morris was instantly forgotten when they walked towards her. James was much shorter than she had imagined, with thinning, poker-straight brown hair and a paunch.

Elaine, his wife, was much taller than him, with shoulder-length blonde hair and long legs carrying a well-rounded body.

They were both pale-faced, hot and dishevelled, and dressed in loose-fitting crumpled clothes.

James held out his hand to Stephen and said in a deep, confident voice, 'Good to see you, Stephen; you look well.'

'You look well yourself.' In fact James Morris looked very different from the last time he had seen him, two years previously.

'Good flight?' Stephen asked pleasantly, turning his head slightly to smile at Elaine, who was standing awkwardly next to her husband, gripping a scuffed vanity case.

'As good as could be expected. Too long, too cramped, but we're here safe and sound, that's the main thing.'

'And this must be Christina?' James's eyes lingered on her low T-shirt, the tanned bare legs beneath her white shorts. She took his hand. It was soft and clammy, and she was acutely aware of his dark, intent scrutiny.

'Pleased to meet you, Christina. Robert Leyton told me you were attractive but he understated.'

She blushed. 'I'm pleased to meet you, James. Welcome to Barbados.'

Elaine gave Stephen a tentative kiss on the cheek, leaving a red lipstick mark which he quickly rubbed off.

'The last time I saw you was at a launch party in 1979,' she giggled. 'I think I was a little bit tiddly.'

'I think we all were, Elaine.' He touched Christina's arm. 'Meet my wife.'

Elaine patted her straight blonde hair into place, wiping fuchsia lipstick off her teeth with her tongue before turning to Christina.

Stephen made the introduction, and the two very different women weighed each other up, exchanging hellos and forced smiles.

'Okay, let's go.' Stephen clapped his hands and picked up Elaine's grip, whilst a porter took the trolley loaded with three large suitcases and two carrier bags packed full of magazines, newspapers and duty-free goods.

Stephen strode ahead with the porter towards the car park, the others a few feet behind. James chatted to Christina.

'Is it always this hot?' He opened another button on his shirt, and she could see his thick, matted chest hair.

'It is very humid today, and no, it's not always this hot. When we came here on our honeymoon in the winter it was quite cool. Cool enough to wear a jacket at night.'

'I love the heat,' Elaine announced. 'I can't wait to bake in the sun.'

Christina looked at her pink-toned skin and said, 'You'll have to be very careful. The sun here is very strong – you can burn in an hour.'

'I never burn.' She turned to James. 'Do I?'

He didn't reply. They reached Stephen's jeep, where the porter was piling the bags into the back.

Stephen drove out of the airport, taking the south coast-road for a couple of miles before turning inland to cross the island heading west.

Elaine Morris stared out of the window in astonishment. 'Do people actually live in those huts?'

Her incredulous tone amused Christina, who remembered her own first impression of the local Bajan dwellings.

'Large families often live in just one room. As they get more money, or a new baby is born, they add what is called another roof, which basically means another room. Some of them are very pretty and cosy, and the majority have TV and a stereo system,' she explained.

'Watch out!' James shouted to Stephen, as an old man driving a decrepit mule and cart erupted from a narrow lane into the path of the jeep.

'Silly old fool! Why don't you watch where you're going? You could have killed us all,' James shouted out of the window.

The old man replied with a toothless grin, yelling in thickly accented Bajan: 'You man. back back.' He lashed his mule, which refused to move. He lashed it again violently until the animal stirred into an indolent amble.

'Is it always like this?' James asked ruefully, already regretting his decision to come to what appeared to him to be a backward, run-down, poverty-stricken island.

'Just wait until you try getting into Bridgetown for an early-morning appointment!' Stephen laughed. Christina joined in whilst James and Elaine looked helplessly at each other.

'Crystal Springs – A New Hotel Development'. The bold black lettering on the construction board shone in the car headlights when Stephen turned into the wide, potholed drive up to Crystal Springs House.

Clyde, the night watchman, stood to attention as they

alighted. Two big gold caps shone brightly in his wide, gap-toothed grin.

'Evenin', boss man. Evenin', mistress.' He touched his woolly hat. 'Celia say she jus' stepped out to step back.'

Christina raised her eyes to heaven. 'I told her to be here when we arrived. Where on earth has she gone, Clyde?'

'Don' know, mistress. She jus' said to tell you she jus' stepped out to step back.'

Both Elaine and James wondered what the old man, dressed in an assortment of ill-fitting clothes, was talking about.

'Can I help you with that, mistress?' Clyde held out a gnarled old hand to Elaine, who handed him her bag with a timid smile.

Clyde struggled with one heavy suitcase whilst James and Stephen carried the other two.

'Put Mr and Mrs Morris's bags in the guest room, please, Clyde,' Christina said. 'And since Celia is stepping out as usual, could you fix us drinks, Stephen? I'm sure Elaine and James could do with one.'

The men went into the kitchen to fix the drinks, and Christina led Elaine out onto the terrace. They both sat down in the deeply cushioned cane chairs and looked out over what was left of the original coconut grove, now a building-site.

A few remaining palm trees clad in white coral dust looked ghostly in the moonlight. Elaine turned to Christina. 'Do you enjoy living here?'

She considered the question for a few minutes before she replied, 'Barbados takes a bit of getting used to, but its good points far outweigh the bad. Yes, I do enjoy living here, but it's very different from England and, I must admit, there are times when I miss things back home so much I could literally grab the first plane out of here.'

'What is it you miss so much?' Elaine wanted to know.

'Oh, you know, just ordinary stuff like roast beef and Yorkshire pudding on Sundays, going to the local pub for a quick drink, wonderful shopping sprees in London . . .' Her voice trailed off and she looked wistful. Elaine thought how pretty she was.

'Well, I'm certainly not going to miss racing around Tesco on Friday nights and struggling to my car laden with bags. Nor will I miss that filthy pub at the end of our road where James insists on going most nights. They don't wash the glasses there; they blow on them. We lived in a high-rise apartment, so I won't miss that, and the only garden I ever get to see is my mum's when we go down there on Sundays sometimes. And we rarely have roast beef.'

Elaine laughed, a merry tinkling sound. 'And I certainly won't miss the miserable weather!'

Christina agreed.

'I lived in Manchester, and I must admit I don't miss the terminally grey days or the long winter nights.'

'I can't wait to see the house you've rented for us. Is it far from here?' Excitement lit Elaine's face. It had looked pale and puffy after her journey. Now, in the soft light from the house, it had a piquant quality. Christina warmed to her and was glad for the trouble she'd taken on the Morris's account.

'It's about two miles away. I chose it, so I hope you like it. It's a small cottage and I think it's very pretty. I'm really sorry you couldn't move in there tonight, but as usual everything here is delivered in what they charmingly refer to as Eastern Caribbean time – which means late!'

She sighed. 'I ordered beds for you weeks ago, and the company promised faithfully they'll be delivered tomorrow morning, but that doesn't mean a thing. It simply means they promise anything to get you off the phone, so keep your fingers crossed or you may be staying here more than one night.'

'I don't mind where I stay to be honest with you, Christina. I'm so pleased just to be here, I would sleep on a tent on the beach. In fact, forget the tent!'

Christina felt herself relaxing with Elaine, and was enjoying the company of another female for the first time in weeks.

They stopped chatting as Stephen and James came out onto the terrace, Stephen carrying a tray of drinks and James two bowls of nuts and crisps.

'Your usual, Elaine.' James handed his wife a large gin and tonic, while Stephen handed Christina a glass of champagne.

James raised his glass and looked at Stephen. 'I want to thank you for this opportunity and tell you I will do my very best for you.'

'You come highly recommended, James. I have no doubt you will do a good job, but things are run a little differently out here. I'll need to show you the ropes.'

'I learn fast.' He winked at Stephen.

'I'm sure you do,' Stephen said, and a look passed between the two men which Christina did not understand.

'Welcome to Barbados; I hope you'll be very happy here,' she said.

Stephen and James had left the house when Christina woke the following morning. She pulled on a plain black swimsuit and headed for the sea. She was surprised to see Elaine's head bobbing above the surface of the water when she reached the beach.

Elaine waved. 'Good morning.'

Christina waded out to join her.

'I can't believe how wonderful this water is.' Elaine lay on her back, kicking her white legs. 'So clear and warm. You must live in the water here, it's so fantastic.'

'We do.' Christina floated alongside her.

'Are there any sharks?' Elaine asked, her eyes widening. Christina shook her head. 'Never been any sign of them, but I never swim far out anyway.'

She ducked under the water and emerged, pushing her long hair away from her face.

'Come on, swim with me,' she offered.

Elaine refused. 'No, I'm fine here, really.'

'Okay, see you later.' Christina struck out across the aquamarine water and swam quickly out to sea.

Elaine watched her for a few minutes before paddling further into the shore, lying on the soft, creamy sand, letting the shallow water caress her feet and legs.

Christina joined her ten minutes later, and they both walked back up to the house, on a path overgrown with headily fragrant mimosa and low, sweeping bamboo. The early-morning sun dappled their exposed shoulders through swaying fish-tail palms.

Showered and dressed in long, loose-fitting cotton T-shirts, Elaine and Christina walked out onto the shaded terrace where Celia had laid a breakfast of freshly squeezed mango juice, cereals, sweet, doughy local bread rolls, banana bread, and coconut chopped into big, thick slices.

'Where is Mr Reece-Carlton?' Christina asked Celia as she appeared on the terrace carrying a tray of fresh tropical fruit and a teapot.

'He gone with de other man. He axed me to tell you not to wait.'

'Where did he go, Celia?'

'He don' say, mistress.' She set down the tray and scampered off.

'Well, we might as well eat. I don't know about you but I'm starving,' Christina said, moving towards the table.

Elaine followed her. 'Me too. I've been up since the crack of dawn.'

Christina and Elaine sat opposite each other across the circular marble-topped table.

'I think Stephen wanted James to see the site first thing

this morning before you took us down to the house,' Elaine said, and helped herself to a warm bun which she tore open, spreading it thickly with butter and lime jelly.

Two tiny yellow birds landed on the table and hopped towards the open sugar-bowl. Christina shooed them away with her hand.

'I'm really excited about seeing the house,' Elaine said in her fast, bubbly voice, periwinkle-blue eyes sparkling in anticipation.

'In fact, I'm so excited about everything, I think I only slept for a couple of hours.'

Christina ate cereal and drank three cups of tea. She helped herself to a slice of banana bread, which she was about to eat as Stephen and James wandered onto the terrace.

'Mmm, that looks good.' Stephen pinched half the slice from her plate.

'Stephen, you pig!' She tried to slap his hand and missed. Both men sat down at the table. Christina turned her attention to James, whose face was flushed from heat and exertion.

'Well, James, what do you think?'

He helped himself to a glass of mango juice before he replied. 'There's one hell of a lot of work to be done, but I'm sure we'll make it if we give those niggers a kick up the backside.'

Stephen cleared his throat.

'If I were you, James, I wouldn't call these people niggers – unless, of course, you want to end up in the Queen Elizabeth Hospital.'

Elaine blushed. 'I did tell you, James . . .'

'Well, what the hell else do you call them, for Christ's sake?'

He looked directly at Stephen, who lowered his voice and in a quiet but firm tone said, 'Barbadians are a proud and self-respecting people, and they deserve your respect

172

too. You call them by their names as you would anyone else. Is that clear?'

James dropped his eyes. 'Okay, Stephen, I understand. We're new boys in town, don't want to upset the locals, now, do we.' He poured himself a cup of tea.

'It's not quite like that either, James. "Nigger" is a despicable word.'

James held up his hand. 'It shall never cross my lips again.' He changed the subject. 'So when do we move into our new home? The sooner I get settled, the sooner I get to work.'

'If you've got beds, you can move in this morning,' Christina said, and glanced at her watch. It was almost nine o'clock. She finished her tea and stood up. 'I'll call the factory now to check.'

She came back out onto the terrace a few minutes later. 'You will have two single beds delivered at 10.30 this morning, and a king-sized in four days' time.'

'They should all have been delivered a week ago,' Stephen commented, shrugging his shoulders and adding with a wry smile, 'Welcome to de West Indies, man.'

After breakfast Stephen had work to do, so Christina took James and Elaine to the small rented cottage on Sunset Ridge.

'It's so pretty!' Elaine exclaimed, her delight evident as she entered the open-plan living- and dining-room decorated in a fresh lemon and blue fabric which Christina had chosen.

They dropped their suitcases and Christina opened the shutters. Sunlight flooded the room. She led them onto a small covered terrace running the full width of the house.

Brilliant pink bougainvillaea covered the old stone walls of the cottage, and lemon and white hibiscus stirred in a soft, warm breeze.

Elaine closed her eyes and breathed deeply, holding in the sweet scent of blossoming magnolia.

173

'I'm in heaven,' she murmured.

'I'm so pleased you like the cottage. I've been worried it would be too small for you.'

'It's perfect, and thank you so much for decorating.' Elaine clasped Christina's hands. 'I really appreciate it.'

Christina was delighted.

'Don't you think it's wonderful, James?'

Elaine turned to her husband, who was lighting a cigarette, letting the smoke curl from his thick lips.

'It's somewhere to hang my hat. You know how I feel about houses, Elaine. Bricks and mortar so far as I'm concerned. No point in getting attached.'

Christina thought how ungrateful he was, and turned her attention to Elaine, who was calling, 'I can see the sea, James, look!' She was on tiptoe, pointing in the direction of the coast.

'I've seen sea before.' James looked uninterested.

'Not the Caribbean,' she retorted.

'It's all the bloody same to me, so when you've finished acting like a six-year-old will you come and help me unpack?'

Christina was tempted to snap back at him in Elaine's defence, but bit her tongue. Stephen was constantly telling her to think before she spoke, particularly when it was none of her business.

'Ignore him.' Elaine dismissed her husband with a wave of her hand. 'He never enthuses about anything.'

'I'm sorry,' Christina said.

'Don't be. I'm used to it. Anyway, I know how to enjoy myself without old grumpy-boots.'

Elaine giggled, and her face lit up with a glorious smile. 'I love the cottage, I love the climate, and I think I'm going to love Barbados.'

Her infectious enthusiasm was such a contrast to James's indifference, Christina wondered what they could have in common.

'I'd better go and help him unpack or he'll bite my head off.' Elaine turned to walk into the house. Christina followed and stopped at the front door.

'I'll call for you after lunch, and we can go shopping for all the things I thought you'd like to choose for yourself.'

'Like what?' Elaine queried.

'You know, towels and bed-linen, personal stuff.'

'That's great, Christina. About two o'clock okay with you?'

'That's fine. See you then.' She began to walk down the path, turning to wave as Elaine shouted, 'Thanks for everything.'

Christina and Elaine went shopping in Bridgetown that afternoon. They bought white cotton sheets with lace borders and matching pillow-cases, blue towels with white alamandas appliquéd on one corner, a collection of decorative shells for Elaine's bathroom, and an assortment of locally made wicker baskets.

Elaine also insisted on buying herself a brightly patterned sarong and a hand-crafted chunky necklace to match.

'I think I'll die if I don't have a drink soon,' Elaine panted like a thirsty dog as they stepped out of Cave Shepard department store and began walking down Broad Street towards the car parked in Trafalgar Square.

Several young men hissed and whistled, much to Elaine's delight. She hissed and whistled back.

'Don't encourage them,' Christina warned. 'They'll follow us and we'll never get rid of them.'

Elaine chuckled. 'I wouldn't mind! Some of them are very good-looking.'

'Come on.' Christina dragged her across the road away from a group of lecherous young men who leered and shouted: 'Cheese on! Woman, you got great botsy. Come chat down here, sis.'

Elaine waved. 'What are they talking about? Sounds like a foreign language to me.'

'They've just said you've got a great backside – and from a West Indian that's the highest compliment you can have.'

Elaine yelled in surprise.

'My fat bum?'

'The bigger the better for West Indian men.'

'Well, I'd better start feeding myself up. When in Rome, as they say.'

She turned round, checked that the men were still watching her and, sticking her bottom out, sashayed to the car, chuckling at the chorus of loud wolf-whistles.

Christina was pleased to get her into the car without being mobbed, and drove quickly out of town and on to the coast-road. Long shadows of dusk slid across the darkening sky. A lone horse and rider were visible on the shore of Carlisle Bay, starkly silhouetted against the sun, a bright orange globe slowly descending into the calm, silver sea.

'It's so beautiful, just like in the travel brochures.' Elaine stared out of the car window, captivated by the peaceful scene. They drove on in silence, both wrapped in their own thoughts, until Christina pulled the car into the car park of the Reef Bar and jumped out.

'Come on, Elaine, happy hour. A rum sour before dinner?'

'I'm not sure about the rum sour, whatever that is, but a gin and tonic would go down very well.'

The two women walked into the busy beach bar, ordered drinks, and sat at a table overlooking the sea.

'Doesn't it get dark quickly?' Elaine looked up at the black, velvety sky studded with tiny, twinkling stars.

'Yes, very quickly in the Caribbean. One minute it's light, the next it's dark. It's the same with the rain. It can be torrential one moment and the sun shining brilliantly the next.'

The drinks arrived and Christina paid.

'I've got a strong feeling I'm going to be very happy here,' said Elaine, sipping her gin and tonic. 'I already feel as if I've lived here for months. I don't think I'm ever going back.'

'I really hope you will be, and that we can become friends.'

Christina missed the friendship she had shared with Susie, her flatmate. In some ways, Elaine reminded her of Susie: vivacious, funny, and easy-going.

'Become friends?' Elaine's smile was warm. 'We already are.'

Chapter Eight

The road across-country to Crane Beach wound through a sea of sugar cane in undulating waves ten foot high; passed old stone churches filled to capacity for Sunday-morning worship, the doors and windows wide open to emit the sounds of loud, harmonious rejoicing.

Elaine chatted incessantly on the journey, oblivious to James's entreaties to shut up, and Stephen's impatience when she insisted on stopping at every plantation house – 'Just to have a peek.'

Christina was interested too, and the two of them were in good spirits when Stephen drove into the dry, scrubby car park in front of the Crane Beach Hotel, which from that aspect seemed an unremarkable low-level with thirties undertones to the architecture. It would have been at home in Bournemouth or Scarborough or any one of a dozen British seaside resorts, Christina thought.

Stephen opened the back of the jeep and everyone was given something to carry. Christina took a picnic basket Celia had prepared that morning, containing bread rolls, fresh fruit, napkins, tablecloth, plastic cups and cutlery. Elaine was loaded down with towels, and bags full of swimwear and sun creams. Stephen carried the small portable barbecue and coals, whilst James brought up the rear with the ice-box full of food, wine and local Banks' beer.

Though the front aspect of the hotel was unremarkable, passing through it and along one of the glassed-in corridors, Christina was amazed by the sight she saw. The hotel was in fact situated on a rugged windswept bluff, 250 feet above the ferocious southern Atlantic. In the fierce noon-day sun the water stretched as far as the eye could see, in every shade of blue from palest turquoise to the deepest indigo of the horizon. The wind was fierce when they left the hotel by a side door, whipping their clothes and snatching at their hair. Christina could taste its salty tang and feel it settle stickily on her skin.

The path down to the beach was a precarious one, tiny steps hewn out of the sheer rock face. A dizzyingly long way below lay a long, deep arc of white-powder sand. They stood on the observation point to the right of the path.

'Look at that, James,' Elaine yelled like an excited little girl, pointing to where several young boys surfed the high, rolling waves, struggling to balance their wavering boards on the crest of translucent walls of fast-moving water.

'I'd rather not.' James looked paler than usual. He was terrified of heights. 'I think I'll put up here if you don't mind. Have a drink. I'll join you later for the barbecue.'

'Don't be such a spoilsport,' pouted Elaine. 'I'll hold your hand down the path.'

'Push me down it, more like,' he grunted, and turned away from the spectacular aerial view, feeling dizzy. 'I'll have a couple of drinks to give me Dutch courage, then I'll join you. Go on, I'll be fine.'

Stephen had already set off down the path.

'See you later, then,' Christina said. 'The bar is right behind you; I suggest a planter's punch. Ask for it with a kick and you'll fly down to the beach.'

He made a pathetic attempt at a smile.

While Elaine took the path ahead, singing 'Beautiful, beautiful Barbados, gem in de Caribbean sea', Christina followed her, noticing the changes in her friend since her arrival. Though still far from slender, her figure now looked pleasantly voluptuous rather than overblown. With a golden tan and her hair sun-bleached rather than bottle-blonde, she looked thoroughly acclimatized, and today had dressed island-style in a bright multi-coloured sarong hand-printed with tropical flowers.

'I can't wait to get into those waves,' she shouted over her shoulder as they made their way carefully down.

Christina had to yell at the top of her voice to be heard above the wind, her long hair whipping across her face.

'I hope you've got a swimsuit with strong straps – the sea sometimes takes bikini tops.'

'I haven't, but who cares?' Elaine chuckled as she reached the bottom of the cliff and jumped from a smooth, rounded boulder into the shallow water. 'Wow, it's really warm,' she said, and turned to help Christina with the picnic basket.

'What did you expect? The North Sea?'

Elaine laughed. 'Hardly, but not this warm.'

She paddled in the shallow water for a few moments before joining Stephen where he was setting up the barbecue in a shaded spot.

Christina struggled with the picnic basket, which now seemed very heavy.

'Oh, damn, James has the ice-box with all the drinks.' Elaine pulled a face.

'Stephen, darling . . .' Christina adopted her most coaxing tone of voice. He ignored her pleading.

'James is coming down in a little while, Christina. Give me a break; those steps are very steep.'

'Not for a big, strong boy like you,' she beseeched him.

'Go and have fun in the sea with Elaine for a while. If James hasn't come down by the time you get back, I promise to go and get you a drink, my darling, dearest, demanding wife.'

She pulled her long, plain white T-shirt over her head. Underneath she was wearing a simple black swimsuit with a high neck and wide shoulder-straps.

Stephen wrinkled his nose in disapproval. He liked her in minuscule bikinis or high-cut swimming costumes.

'Sexy it may not be, but safe it is,' she told him. 'I don't see why I should put on a show for the whole of Crane Beach.'

'Well, Elaine is.'

Stephen glanced at the skimpy string bikini digging into Elaine's pink flesh.

She didn't hear him. She was already running down the beach, calling: 'Come on, Christina', her voice all but drowned by the crashing waves.

Christina followed her eagerly, laughing as she showed her friend how to body-surf on the smaller waves, and then how to dive and tread water waiting for a really big wave. When Christina gave the signal, they both body-surfed for a few minutes before tumbling over and over as the strong current literally threw them onto the shore.

Christina heard Elaine's screams and laughs even above the deafening roar of the sea. She finally emerged from the water to see her friend with her bikini-top around her neck and the bottom dangling from one ankle.

Elaine scrambled to recover her bikini and fell over, laughing as the relentless waves pulled her under the water, time and time again.

Christina helped her, and eventually they managed to get the tiny bikini back into place.

'Want another go?'

Christina pushed her sand-filled hair out of her eyes. 'I think I could use a drink after that.'

'Come on, then. If lazy-bones Stephen can't be bothered to go and get the ice-box, I will.'

Elaine ran up the beach, Christina sauntering slowly behind. It was then that she noticed a tall blond man busy coaching some young local boys in football. Two makeshift goal-posts had been erected using assorted lengths of strapped sugar cane, and she could hear a lively dispute about the penalty rules.

She stood nearby and watched, bemused by the sight of Barbadians playing anything but their beloved cricket. There was something familiar about the way the man's long hair fell at the nape of his neck, and his posture as he knelt in front of a small boy who was stamping his foot and refusing to kick the ball.

Christina edged closer to get a better look, and instantly recognized his voice.

'Martin, is that you?'

He turned abruptly, almost losing his balance.

'Christina, I can't believe it.' Martin Ward got to his feet, dusting off sand, and they held each others' eyes for a few moments without speaking. Then Christina laughed nervously.

'Fancy seeing you here.'

'I could say exactly the same. After all, it's a long way from Manchester.' He stood up, sunlight glinting in his sun-bleached hair. Soft golden hairs glistened on his tall, strong body, which was tanned to a deep honey colour.

'Yes, it's a small world all right.' She held up her hand to shade her eyes against the fierce sun. 'So what brings you to Barbados?' Christina glanced at the young boys squabbling over the ball. 'Setting up a Barbados football team?' she laughed.

'I wish it was as simple as that. No, I'm here for a late convalescence. A very fortunate one.'

His hazel eyes dropped, and he pushed forward his right leg awkwardly. 'I had a slight accident a few months ago, wrote off my car and almost myself.'

'Oh, Martin, I'm so sorry.' Christina stared at the ugly, twisted scar running from his thigh to his kneecap, and the gnarled tangle of flesh and sinew where the surgeons had tried to rebuild his shattered kneecap.

'Not a pretty sight, is it?' He grimaced.

She lifted her eyes, which were full of unspoken sympathy.

'Like I said, I'm fortunate to be here, standing on this beautiful beach talking to you. It's taken me months of physio to learn to walk properly again, and I'm very grateful to all the people who helped me. When you've stared death in the face, everything after that is a bonus.' She nodded silently.

'And how about you, Christina? How come you're in Barbados? We lost touch after I moved down South. I've always regretted it.'

She glanced up the beach and saw Stephen and Elaine unpacking the hamper. 'Long story. I'm not sure we've got time.'

'I've got all the time in the world.'

'The brief version is, I live here,' she announced.

'You what?' He was incredulous.

'To cut a long story short, I married Stephen.'

'I see.' She pretended not to see the look of dismay on Martin's face and continued with her explanation.

'We came here on honeymoon, fell in love with the island. We bought a house, but Stephen being Stephen . . .'

She looked heavenward at this point, and Martin wondered what she meant.

'He's very entrepreneurial, and wasn't satisfied with just a holiday home, so we're now developing a new hotel which promises to be – and I quote Stephen now – "the best in the Caribbean".'

'Martin, you're supposed to be coaching the boys, not chatting up Mrs Reece-Carlton.'

The voice came from behind Martin. It was light and teasing but the message was clear. A freckle-faced brunette with a lush figure pressed herself very close to him, and placed one arm around his narrow waist.

'You know each other?' Martin looked from one woman to the other.

The newcomer spoke. 'No, not officially, but I believe you know my father, Roger Dyson? He's done some surveying work for your husband at Crystal Springs. Daddy is over there.' She pointed up the beach to a man and a woman barely visible under a big beach umbrella.

'I'm Louise Dyson.' She made no move to extend her hand but instead cast assessing eyes over Christina.

'Christina Reece-Carlton; pleased to meet you. Sorry I've kept Martin, but we're old friends from Manchester. It was such a surprise to see him on the beach like this.'

'A nice surprise, I hope?' he asked, apparently oblivious to Louise's pique.

'I am sorry to interrupt your cosy chat, Martin, but Daddy's dying to go up to the bar for a drink and we've promised to stop by Carolyn Roach's house later on.'

'Okay, Louise, I'll be right with you. By the way, the last thing Carolyn said to me last night was that her party was open-house and we could go any time.'

A vexed expression crossed Louise's pretty face.

Christina turned round, feeling uncomfortable. She could see Stephen, his back to her, placing food on the barbecue, and smoke curling into the clear air.

Elaine waved and shouted something Christina didn't catch. 'I've got to go, anyway; I think I'm probably holding up our barbecue.'

Louise slipped her hand into Martin's.

'He's made a marvellous recovery since he's been with us in Barbados. I've been looking after him, haven't I, Martin?' The possessive way she looked and spoke was not wasted on Christina.

'This holiday has been a godsend and couldn't have come at a better time. I have Louise to thank for that.' He squeezed her hand then let it drop.

'We're old friends as well; did Martin not tell you?' the girl pressed.

Christina shook her head.

'We go back to when I was a silly little girl of eleven with a schoolgirl crush on Martin. Our families have been friends for years.'

He looked slightly embarrassed and made no answering comment.

'It's really good to see you, Christina,' he said warmly. 'Perhaps we can get together sometime? Catch up on all your news.'

'And yours.' She glanced at his leg again. 'I'm so sorry about that.'

'Don't be; it's not that bad. I can't play football again but at least I'm alive.'

'I'd love to see you again, Martin. How long are you going to be in Barbados?'

'For a very long time, if I get my way,' Louise interrupted.

Christina thought it was time to go. Louise was obviously infatuated with Martin and resented the intrusion of an old girlfriend from England.

'Listen, call me at Crystal Springs, Martin, and we can catch a quick drink sometime. Roger Dyson has the number.'

Louise looked peeved and dragged at his arm.

'Come on, we really do have to go.'

He extracted his arm gently and stepped towards Christina.

'I'll call you.' It was a promise rather than the usual social pleasantry.

He'd always had the nicest smile, open and boyish, but she'd forgotten the way his hazel eyes sparkled with greenish lights, perhaps because she'd never seen him so tanned before.

'Bye, Martin. See you soon, I hope,' she called, and began to run up the beach.

'Come on, Christina. I've burnt half the food waiting for you,' Stephen snapped impatiently as she joined him by the smoking barbecue.

'Who was the hunk you were talking to?' asked Elaine.

'An old friend from Manchester, would you believe? His name's Martin Ward.'

Stephen's back stiffened. He handed her a hamburger but made no indication that he had ever met Martin.

'I went out with him a couple of times. He was a footballer, a fantastic player. He was transferred to London, I got married to Stephen, and we lost touch.'

Christina noticed the ice-box standing next to Elaine's feet. 'You got the drinks, then?'

'Yes, James brought them down, had a hot dog, and went back to the bar. He hates sitting on the beach; does nothing but moan.' Elaine opened the lid of the box. 'What would you like to drink?'

'A beer, thanks.'

Elaine handed her friend a bottle of Banks' and helped herself to a glass of wine.

'Quite a dish, your footballer. I wouldn't mind a bit of coaching from him!'

'I'm afraid coaching is all he can do these days. He had a very bad car accident a few months ago and shattered his kneecap. He's staying with the Dysons – they're old friends, apparently. Stephen knows Roger Dyson, don't you, Stephen?'

He grunted something unintelligible and poked a sausage savagely. It hissed and spat a spray of hot fat onto his bare stomach.

'Ouch!' he yelled, and rubbed his burning flesh.

Christina appeared oblivious as she continued to talk about Martin.

'Anyway, he's here to recuperate, a long holiday from what I can gather. I was really pleased to see him. He was always a lot of fun and made me laugh.'

'I bet he's having a lot of fun with Roger Dyson's daughter. Can't remember her name, I only met her once, but she's an attractive girl.' Stephen ate a hot dog in three big bites.

'Her name's Louise,' Christina volunteered, 'and from what I can gather she's madly in love with him.'

'Who wouldn't be?' Elaine sighed, and picked up a handful of sand, letting it pour slowly through her fingers.

Stephen glared at her. It was wasted – Elaine was busy watching Martin and Louise walk along the beach towards the steps back up to the hotel.

Martin waved but Louise averted her face, pretending not to see them.

Elaine and Christina both waved back.

'I think we should befriend Martin,' Elaine said, winking. 'I'm sure he could do with some fun female company.'

'I'm positive he has enough of that on this island,' Stephen bristled.

'A little more won't harm him,' Elaine persisted.

'For Christ's sake, Elaine, don't you think of anything else?' Stephen snapped angrily.

Christina turned on him. 'That's not fair, Stephen. Elaine was only being friendly. Anyway, I agree. Martin is a great guy and a lot of fun. Why can't we invite him out? What harm is there in that?'

Her eyes met his unflinchingly.

'Nothing whatsoever, Christina; you do whatever you wish.' Stephen's controlled voice disguised his true feelings, but Christina sensed his jealousy and changed the subject.

'Why don't we drag your errant husband out of the bar, Elaine, and go to the Kingsley Club for a drink?'

'Sounds like a great idea to me,' she agreed, glancing dubiously at Stephen who was throwing water onto the dying embers.

'Stephen, fancy the Kingsley Club?' Christina asked in a bubbly voice.

He nodded without looking up.

'I assume that's a yes,' she commented, and began to pile used plates and napkins into the picnic basket, saying, 'Come on, then. Let's pack up and head for Bathsheba, to drink the best rum punch in the Caribbean.'

The Kingsley Club overlooked the wild and rugged Bathsheba beach, where huge boulders rose majestically from the thundering Atlantic surf. Stephen parked in front of the old white-painted building, its starkness relieved by bright-green shutters.

He led the way, followed by an ebullient Christina and Elaine, with James sullenly bringing up the rear. They walked up the wide stone steps and into a small reception area. Local art was displayed on the walls, and fans swished overhead.

A few late-Sunday diners were finishing their lime pie and coconut ice-cream as the small party walked past the vast open dining-room and onto the deep enclosed veranda which was used as a bar.

Christina's feet slipped on the highly polished wooden floor as she flopped into an antique mahogany rocking-chair positioned in front of a big open window, affording uninterrupted views of the ocean and a cooling breeze from off the sea.

An old waitress, wearing a tattered turban and starched white apron, shuffled towards them.

'Yous all too late fer lunch, dat finished gone an hour ago,' she informed them in no uncertain terms.

'We've not come for lunch today. We're here to have your famous rum punch, and I could definitely use a portion of that fantastic coconut ice-cream, if there's any left?' Stephen asked hopefully.

'Me too,' Christina agreed.

Before Elaine could add that she would like some as well, the waitress shook her head.

'Dat all gone.' She looked cross. 'I'll be gettin' de rum punch.' She left them, muttering under her breath about coming in here and expecting ice-cream when lunch was over.

It was ten minutes before she returned at a snail's pace with four rum punches.

Stephen engaged James in construction talk while Christina and Elaine plotted a night out on Baxter's Row, exploring the late-night bars and restaurants where all the best calypsos were sung.

'Perhaps we could invite your friend Martin?' Elaine nudged Christina, who agreed.

'He's calling me soon, so I'll invite him along. I'm sure it's something he'd enjoy.'

Christina gave her husband a sidelong glance. He seemed intent on what James was saying, and was obviously not going to rise to her remark.

The drinks arrived. Elaine drained hers thirstily and made a loud sucking noise with her straw.

'What a racket!' James commented, and looked at her with disapproval. He then did exactly the same thing, spluttering and spraying the remains of his drink down his shirt. They all laughed. Even James joined in, much to everyone's surprise.

Christina could feel her head spinning after only one drink, and refused a second. Stephen declined also as he was driving, but James and Elaine put away two more and left the Kingsley Club staggering and in high spirits.

On the way home, Elaine sang some old favourites out of tune, and James insisted on a loud rendition of crude rugby songs.

Christina was pleased when the jeep pulled into Sunset Ridge and Elaine and James got out, waving and shouting 'thank you' as, arm in arm, they helped each other up the path and into Magnolia Cottage.

Stephen was very quiet for the remainder of the journey back to Crystal Springs.

'Are you okay?' Christina asked eventually.

'Yes, I'm fine. Why?'

'You're very quiet, that's all.'

'It's Elaine,' Stephen lied. 'She irritates me. When you two are together you act like schoolchildren.'

Christina rose to her friend's defence.

'She's fun and warm and amusing – in direct contrast to James. He's so boring.'

'Just because he's not frivolous and making jokes every five minutes doesn't make him boring!'

'Jokes? Does he even know what they are? I don't think the man has a sense of humour – how she lives with him is beyond me. Anyway, I really like Elaine and enjoy her company. I haven't many friends here.

'That's why I want to invite Martin Ward out with us. Not because I fancy him or anything like that, but because he's a friend from way back. I know you'll really like him when you get to know him.'

But Stephen made no reply, and it was impossible for her to tell what he was thinking behind his impassive face. He parked the car at the back of the house. They unloaded the picnic things together. While Christina helped Celia empty the basket in the kitchen, Stephen put the barbecue in the store-room at the back of the house. Christina went upstairs to her bedroom, peeled off her sticky, crumpled clothes, and jumped into a tepid shower. After a few minutes she padded back into the bedroom wrapped in a big fluffy towel.

It was late afternoon and the intense heat of the day was dying. As she wandered out onto the balcony there was very little breeze, and she looked over the tops of the royal palms towards a calm, softly undulating sea.

She flinched as Stephen laid his hands on her naked shoulders and planted a hungry kiss on the side of her neck, his fingers fumbling in the thick folds of the towel, seeking her breasts.

'Come on, Christina,' he whispered urgently.

He tugged at one end of the towel, but she held on tight, her body stiffening. 'I'm not in the mood, Stephen,' she said. He stepped away from her, and walked out of the room without another word.

Christina watched him leave the house and walk towards the beach before she went inside and dressed slowly, thinking about his reaction to her refusal to make love.

It was only the second time since they had been married that she had rebuffed him. He was in a strange mood and, rather than provoke him further, she decided to forget about it, determined not to mention it again.

Christina arranged dinner with Celia, then picked some mimosa and bright-lavender periwinkle flowers for the dining-table, which she was arranging when Stephen appeared at the french windows of the dining-room, looming out of the lengthening shadows as dusk turned quickly into night.

'Where have you been?' She was holding a delicate spray of mimosa to her face, inhaling the heady scent.

'I went for a walk down the beach. It was deserted and peaceful; I wanted to be alone.'

'Oh.' And she continued to adjust the flower arrangement. 'Dinner will be at eight o'clock if that's okay?' She waited for his reply, but Stephen had left the room and was going upstairs.

Celia served the cold cucumber soup hot, and burnt the steak even though Christina had told her numerous times that Stephen liked his steak rare.

He left most of his meal, and seemed uninterested in

any of the conversation she attempted, answering in monosyllables most of the time.

Christina gave up and was relieved when he announced that he was going to bed. She followed him half an hour later, pleased to find him already asleep when she crept into the bedroom.

That night she lay awake for a long time, thinking first of her father, recalling many happy childhood memories and wishing fervently, as she had so many times before, that he had not left her so soon.

Then her thoughts drifted to Stephen, the stubborn, unpredictable, complex man she had married. A shaft of moonlight slanted through the shutters, revealing his face looking oddly defenceless in sleep. Poor Stephen – she shouldn't have teased him by exaggerating her friendship with Martin the way she had. Martin was a warm, attractive man, but Stephen was her husband, the man to whom she intended to stay married.

It had taken Christina a long time to grow accustomed to the nocturnal sounds of the tropics, but she loved them now, and finally fell into a deep sleep, lulled by the incessant chirping of crickets, wind rustling the huge traveller's palm outside the bedroom window, and the Caribbean sea breaking gently on the shore.

Chapter Nine

Christina disliked Michael Stein on sight. It was one of her immediate, intuitive reactions which were rarely wrong.

Stephen had asked her to join him and the new general manager in his office that morning, and she had been eager to meet the young hotelier who came so highly qualified. On the face of it he was just what they needed: minor-public-school background, not over-academic but Lausanne-trained and with experience of the top hotel groups in England, Europe and the Far East.

She saw that Stein exuded confidence; it dripped from him like honey. With his thick, smoothly brushed wheaten-coloured hair and slate-grey eyes he was handsome too – and knew it.

'Mrs Reece-Carlton – delighted to make your acquaintance.'

His voice had the rounded vowels of a public-school education, and his well-cut, tropical-weight putty-coloured suit was worn with a Sea Island cotton shirt and an Hermès tie. It was all in startling contrast to Stephen in his mud-caked shorts, T-shirt and docksiders.

Christina found she was still staring as if mesmerized at Stein's confident smile. It was practised, wide and welcoming, consummately professional, revealing perfectly capped teeth and concealing everything about the man behind.

'Pleased to meet you,' she said, trying to sound sincere.

Stephen quickly put in, 'Yes, Michael, delighted to have you on board.'

'And I'm delighted to be here. I've always wanted to work in the Caribbean.' Michael Stein examined his well-manicured fingernails. 'I know it will be a challenge but new beginnings are so exciting, I always think.'

He looked at Christina from under thick, curly lashes. 'Building a new luxury hotel in Barbados is a risk, no doubt of that, but if anyone can pull if off, I'm sure Stephen can.'

'Well, thank you, that's what we think too.'

She caught Stephen's eye and held it for a second. What exactly did he see in this patronizing little squirt?

Oblivious, Michael Stein continued, obviously seeking to impress. 'I've opened several hotels worldwide. Bali was a nightmare. We had no furniture two days before we were due to open. Maui was a little better – at least the interior decorator finished, even if it was in the worst possible taste, but the Seychelles took the cake . . .' He chuckled at the recollection. 'We had a riot and the bloody natives burned part of the place down a week before it was due to open. Myself and half the management team piled into a speedboat and had literally to flee for our lives.'

He lit up a Gitane without pausing to ask if they objected, letting the smoke drift slowly from his wide mouth.

'How inconvenient,' Christina commented dryly.

'Oh, all in a day's work, but I must add that after that little fiasco I decided to join a more conventional hotel group and enjoyed the civilized calm of the Savoy for a while. But I soon grew bored. Two years of pandering to bloated businessmen and the *nouveau riche* did begin to pall on one.'

He flicked his cigarette ash rather messily towards the waste bin, there being no ashtray evident. Christina knew that this was because Stephen usually objected strongly to anyone smoking in his vicinity. Obviously he'd decided it was worth putting up with the foul-smelling smoke for the sake of picking Michael's experienced brain.

'So you decided to pioneer again?' Stephen prompted.

'Yes, the Far East beckoned. How could I resist the call of the Orient? The Mandarin Group offered me a package I couldn't refuse.'

'And while you were there, someone else offered you a "package" you couldn't refuse, I believe?'

Michael Stein looked into Stephen's blandly smiling face. If he was taken aback, he didn't show it.

'You do your research very thoroughly, Mr Reece-Carlton. I admire that, so I'll be straight with you. There was a period in my life when I enjoyed' – he paused – 'shall we say, chemical diversions? It's over now, and I give you my word it won't happen again.'

'If the Mandarin Group didn't believe that, why should I?'

'Ah, but if you didn't, why bother to confirm my appointment in writing and fly me out first-class? It was their loss, believe me, and they were the first to admit my work was never affected. They gave me a reference, after all. I put more bums in beds for them than any other general manager they've had.'

'Bums in beds? What a dreadful expression.' Christina screwed up her face in distaste.

'It's used all over the world – hotel trade jargon. How's occupancy? How many bums in beds?'

Michael shrugged nonchalantly.

'As I was saying, I'd pushed their occupancy rates up by 40 per cent by the time I left, and headed up a worldwide promotional campaign that got Mandarin more free press exposure than ever before. The marketing budget was halved in the eighteen months I was there.'

Stephen looked impressed.

'I need lots of bums in beds here at Crystal Springs, Michael, so the sooner we get moving on sales and promotion, the better.'

'Leave all that to me. I have a great friend and former colleague in New York who heads a chain of major travel operators, both trade and retail. If we link in with Gary and his organization we'll have no problem selling Crystal Springs.'

'Can we get him down here?' Stephen asked. 'I think he should see the property and the island.'

'I'll call and set up a visit a.s.a.p. He can advise us on the best brochure layouts, promotional photography, video or slide presentation – the whole package. Later, when we're nearer completion, you might like to offer a free trip to the agents he recommends – get them to pass on the news to their customers.

'And then of course you need the same set-up in Europe. As it happens I know a man in London who can handle the operation there for you.'

'Sounds great, Michael.' Stephen was looking pleased. 'You obviously know a lot of people in the trade.'

'I've made it my business to. And I've forgotten more about the hotel industry than most people learn in a lifetime. I'm sure I can be a great asset to you, Stephen. You won't regret employing me.'

'I'm sure I won't,' Stephen was saying. 'Now, is there anything we can do about airline tie-ins? I heard that . . .'

At that moment James Morris barged into the office without knocking, looking flustered.

'Immigration are outside, Stephen. They want to see you urgently. A man called Elvin Braithwaite – says it's important.'

'Oh, Jesus, that's all we need,' Stephen groaned.

Michael looked surprised. 'It's not about me, is it? I thought you said there'd be no problem if I came in on a six-month permit?'

'There shouldn't be – but this is the Caribbean,' Christina told him. 'Don't worry. We've had this all before. Stephen can sort it out.'

He had picked up the phone and was asking Celia to show their visitor up. James Morris glanced disdainfully at the new manager. Obviously eager to show how indispensable he himself was, James offered: 'Why don't you let me deal with this, Stephen? I can see you're busy. So long as you okay the pay-off, of course. What's a work permit worth here – a few hundred Eastern Caribbean and a bunch of bananas?'

He laughed at his own wit. No one else did.

Stephen looked white-lipped. 'James, I won't tell you again – this is not our country, we are merely permitted to be here by its citizens. So why don't you use your common sense and show them some respect? If you can't do that you're no good to me, okay?'

James's pudgy face turned a dull red. He looked down, embarrassed.

'Sure, Stephen. I just thought . . .'

'Well, do me a favour, James, and don't! It's not your strong point. Why don't you go and chase up those roofers for me? Oh, and James?'

'Yes?'

'Don't come in here again without knocking. Next time you might not find me in such a good temper.'

'Yes, sure, Stephen. I mean, no . . . right.'

Michael Stein's lip curled contemptuously at the undignified retreat. He stubbed out his cigarette, smoothed his already immaculate hair. He seemed quite content to sit back and let Stephen do the talking when Elvin Braithwaite, the island's Immigration chief, knocked and entered.

Braithwaite was at least six foot five, and broomstick-thin – all long, bony legs and arms in his immaculately starched shirt and knife-edged trousers.

'Well, Mr Carlton – ma'am,' he drawled with a nod to

Christina, 'it seems we got a lickle problem here. Mr Stein got de wrong sort of permit. He got de temp'ry permit which clears him to work for up to six month, but I hear you makin' him your general manager which got to last more than that, isn't it?'

Not necessarily, thought Christina. Stephen had a way of getting what he wanted from people and then moving rapidly on. Sometimes his single-minded ruthlessness upset her. In connection with Michael Stein she suspected it would not.

'Please, Mr Braithwaite, have a seat. Why don't we all move over here where we'll be more comfortable?'

Stephen manoeuvred them away from the formal office seating around his desk towards some more relaxed sofas and chairs grouped around a low table.

'It's a hot one, Mr Braithwaite,' he said. 'Can we offer you some refreshment? Chrissy, perhaps you could . . .'

He gestured towards the small wet bar installed in a corner of the room. Braithwaite looked disapprovingly at the rows of bottles.

'I never touch liquor on duty. But perhaps something soft, Mrs Carlton?'

Christina smiled. 'What about a lime squash?'

Braithwaite nodded regally.

'Great. Why don't you make us all one?' Stephen encouraged. While she busied herself squeezing fresh limes and adding local cane sugar and iced water, he began his pitch.

'We hope Mr Stein will be working for us long into the future and obviously in that case we would need to apply for another permit for him. But you and I both know that applying for a stay of more than six months takes time. Hence the initial short-stay application.'

Braithwaite accepted his glass of lime squash from Christina and waited until the others were served.

'I hear what you sayin', Mr Carlton, but regulations is

regulations. It seems we got a irregularity here – Mr Stein knows he goin' to be workin' here long-term but he apply for short-term only.'

Braithwaite shook his head sadly. 'Is a serious matter. Very, very serious.'

'Couldn't we just apply for a long-term permit for him now?' Christina suggested.

'Oh, no, ma'am. Then Mr Stein would have *two* permits and regulations don't like that. Don't like that at all.'

Stephen frowned at her.

'I'm sure there has to be some way round this, Mr Braithwaite. I remember how helpful you were in our own cases.'

'Helpful' was not the word Christina would have used, but Mr Braithwaite had grudgingly reached an accommodation with a local lawyer whom Stephen had retained to act for them. Danny Bascombe had done a good job for them, and Stephen had been impressed by his ability, she remembered.

The Immigration officer was looking gloomier by the minute.

'It pains me to say it, Mr Carlton, but I think Mr Stein is going to have to return to England and make a long-stay application through the 'propriate channels.'

Stephen's eyes flared angrily. Any moment now he would lose his temper.

'Well, that's up to you, Mr Braithwaite,' Christina intervened. 'But it's going to put an awful lot of island people to a lot of trouble, and it will mean many hundreds of them will have to wait even longer for jobs now.'

Braithwaite looked at her. 'How so?'

Christina crossed her fingers behind her back.

'Well, one of Mr Stein's first duties as general manager is to recruit the rest of the staff, and he's already set up some interviews locally. I'm sure you don't need me to explain the scale of our requirements here.'

Stephen caught the ball and started to run with it. 'Of course he's not the only one who could recruit staff. I suppose I could get around to it myself in time. But at the moment I'm so caught up with our construction problems I don't see myself having the time for months ahead. After all, we're talking literally hundreds of jobs here, most for people living on the island. Mr Stein would have been looking for chefs, receptionists, back-room staff, chambermaids, gardeners, laundry workers, bar staff, waiters . . .'

'Hol' it there.' Elvin Braithwaite fingered his chin thoughtfully. 'My sister's boy, Alfa, he workin' as a bus-boy at Sandy Lane. Why for he don' join the police don't axe me, but Alfa know better – he wan' a be a waiter.'

Michael Stein looked regretful. 'He sounds just the sort of keen, experienced youngster I would have been looking for. But as I shall be on the evening flight home . . .'

Mr Braithwaite held up his hand. 'Hol' strain, Mr Stein. Take it easy now. Who sayin' anythin' about England?'

It didn't seem the moment to remind him that he had. Stephen asked Christina for a splash of rum in his lime squash and Michael Stein followed suit. Christina left the open bottle on the table. Mr Braithwaite drained off his lime squash and added a couple of jiggers of rum to his empty glass. Another quarter of an hour or so and he was solving Michael's recruitment problems across the board, recommending a dozen good, reliable workers. Stephen and he agreed that in view of the value to the island of Crystal Springs' recruitment plans, the regulations would be waived this time and Michael Stein's long-term permit would be processed as quickly as possible.

'So long as you don' give me no trouble in the interim, Mr Stein,' said Braithwaite, getting to his feet.

'No fear of that. I shall be far too busy.'

Christina saw Elvin Braithwaite back to his car. She returned to the office in time to hear Michael drawl, 'Well,

I'm impressed. That could have been nasty. You know your stuff, Stephen.'

'Thanks,' her husband replied. 'Construction, property development, diplomacy . . . Hotel-keeping's double Dutch to me at the moment – but I catch on fast, Michael. You'd better remember that.'

There was no mention of the part she'd paid in talking Braithwaite round, Christina noticed. And she saw something else: Michael Stein's easy, laid-back manner had subtly altered. He looked different somehow, more alert and on guard.

'Thanks, Stephen. I'll bear that in mind,' he promised.

The following months were all too often a case of one step forward, two steps back. The delays and frustrating disappointments of trying to keep to an eighteen-month construction schedule in the Caribbean were beginning to tell on them all.

Stephen had ordered some sophisticated German industrial kitchen fittings from a supplier based in Venezuela, on the basis that it would be quicker to import from there than to have them shipped direct. Perhaps it would have been had the South American dealer not ignored his every letter, fax and telephone call requesting confirmation of delivery date. As Stephen had already laid out a substantial sum on placing the order, he was damned if he was going to write it off. James Morris was sent to settle the problem from the Venezuelan end – which left the rest of the site problems on Stephen's shoulders.

Christina was determined not to add to them, but was beginning to experience grave doubts of her own about Colin Weatherhead's reliability. She'd been back to the shop twice hoping to chase the progress of her textiles order. The small factory she'd approached to undertake the making of the curtains, cushions and loose covers told her they'd be ready to start in a few weeks' time, and even allowing for this wildly optimistic schedule, she felt she ought to know when to expect delivery of the fabrics.

But the first time she'd spoken to Colin he'd told her there was a hitch at the manufacturer's end, and the second time the shop had been closed. Despite leaving numerous messages with his assistant and wife, she still had not heard from him.

She approached Paul Richardson one day – after all, it was he who had recommended Colin. Paul was having a tough time himself supervising the contouring of the land around the three-tier pool Stephen had eventually commissioned. He seemed distracted when she asked him about Island Trading's reliability.

'Yeah, go to Colin, great guy,' he mumbled absently. 'No, goddammit! I said a gentle slope, not the north bloody face of the Eiger!'

Christina pulled at his arm to divert his attention. 'But that's what I'm saying. I've already been to Colin, placed my order, given him a deposit – and nothing's happening. You don't think he'd try and do a runner like the kitchen man, do you?'

Paul looked at her ruefully. 'Oh, God, Chrissy – sorry. I didn't realize you were so far along. There's something I should have said. Strictly no cash to Colin personally till the job's completed. Any deposit, pay it direct to the manufacturer concerned.'

Christina clutched the sides of her head. 'Oh, no, I can't bear it. I don't want to let Stephen down.'

'Easy, easy. It's not that bad. Colin's not a crook – just a bit too fond of the ganja, that's all. He's probably smoking his way through your deposit. When it's gone, he'll be back to work.'

'Well, thank you, Paul. Thanks a lot! That really puts my mind at rest,' she flashed angrily. 'This is the last time I employ someone on your recommendation.'

He looked pained. 'Christina, I know I've been here a

year longer than you but I'm sure you've worked these things out for yourself by now. If you want anything done around here, you *have* to do it yourself.'

'But, damn it, I'm paying Colin to do it!'

'No. You're paying him for *knowing* how to do it. He has the contacts – it's up to you to make sure he gets in touch with them. Look, here's his home address. My advice to you is to get yourself over there and kick ass. Stand over him while he makes those calls.'

Which was pretty well what she had to do. She found Colin asleep on a rattan lounger on the veranda of his cottage in Holetown. He hadn't shaved for a few days and a sickly smell clung to his clothes and hair. She resisted the temptation to do as Paul suggested and instead made him pot after pot of black coffee and then drove him to his shop in Bridgetown. After he'd placed the order, she then braved the dusty unmade roads to St Philip to deliver a second deposit, this time to the factory-owner personally. She had already told Colin very firmly that she did not expect to be billed for any handling charge from him in view of the money he had already had – which was in fact a smaller sum. To her amazement he took this like a lamb, and then had the effrontery to say that it had been a pleasure working with a businesswoman like her, and if there was anything else he could help her with, she only had to ask!

She decided to give him another chance, this time on her own terms. She put him on to researching the availability of marble vanity-unit tops and free-standing occasional tables. This time she insisted on negotiating direct with the manufacturer, but agreed to pay Colin a finder's fee of 5 per cent if the order came up to scratch. To her surprise and relief he came up trumps, and the next time Stephen checked her progress she was able to report that the furnishings were to standard and on time.

Someone else who seemed to have no difficulties keeping to schedule was Michael Stein – but then, as Stephen had begun to remark rather acidly, a major part of his job involved sitting on his arse under a convenient fan listening to the sound of his own voice. Michael had been hitting the phone, recruiting some key staff from hotels he'd worked in in the past. Others were hired locally. A core staff of assistant manager, guest services director, food and beverages manager, head chef and housekeeper had already been appointed and were on the payroll, helping with preparations for the hotel's opening. Stein and his staff had also filled, in principle, the several hundred other posts, but most of these members of staff would not take up their positions until three weeks before the hotel's grand opening, timed to tie in with a huge party which Stephen was throwing for island dignitaries and specially invited celebrities. Michael Stein had proved his worth yet again in sending off invitations to the party, offering a free week's holiday to various A-list showbiz and society figures. The outlay would be well worth while in terms of the publicity featuring all the hotel's celebrity guests.

Whenever Stephen asked him a question, he seemed to have the answer at his fingertips. Instead of reassuring Stephen, now working himself up to a fever pitch of nervous excitement with the launch date in view, Michael's superior manner had begun to grate.

Today Stephen was worried about the reception staff. They would be the paying customers' first impression of Crystal Springs. It was vital that they should be prompt and professional as well as easy on the eye.

Michael told him not to worry, it was all taken care of. The off-hand answer irritated Stephen.

'What do you mean, don't worry?' he stormed when Michael appeared to dismiss him. 'Can you tell me when we can begin to teach the totally inexperienced, gauche young ladies you've employed as receptionists, or do we just let them loose on our unsuspecting clients?'

Michael ignored Stephen's heavy sarcasm, a smug expression on his face. He blew Gitane smoke in his employer's direction. Stephen coughed irritably and wafted his hands.

'Do you have to?' He pointed at the cigarette. Michael looked from him to the offending cigarette and back again, then reluctantly stubbed it out.

'As you are fully aware, we have been promised delivery of all the office equipment on the fifth, two days from now. I have personally been down to the suppliers several times and checked, and there is no doubt we will have delivery. As for my bevy of beauties . . .' He glanced at his gold Rolex watch. 'At this present moment they are engaged in a fully comprehensive training course using the systems run by the local college, on which I took the liberty of enrolling them. I had no choice under the circumstances, and the fees won't exactly break the bank. Does that answer you?'

Stein's grey eyes mocked Stephen, who had enormous difficulty in controlling his desire to wipe the look of triumph from the manager's arrogant face. But control was one of Stephen's strong points. Instead, he smiled.

'Well done, Michael, but in future I would appreciate being informed of your decisions. It might avoid wasting precious time.'

Christina foresaw further difficulties ahead between her mercurial husband and the languid but oh-so-efficient general manager. But at least they didn't need to worry about any area that came under Michael Stein's remit. Which was more than could be said for Mr Gittings, the decorator.

With only two weeks to go they were down to the cosmetic touches. Andrew Hall, the head gardener, was supervising the planting of hundreds of flowering tropical shrubs, and a skilled island craftsman was painstakingly carving intricate flowers onto the coral-stone fountain which was the garden's focal point.

Christina had just received the last consignment of furniture, arriving in the nick of time to prevent it being dumped higgledy-piggledy in the reception hall. She had coaxed, cajoled and bribed the delivery boys to do what they had already been told to do – carry it to the relevant floor of the hotel. She was feeling pleased with her progress when she walked in on a typical scene on the terrace of room 216. Paul Richardson had assured Stephen that Percy Gittings was the best painter and decorator the island had to offer. All three men were looking up at a newly stained wallaba beam which supported the terrace room.

'Well, what do you think?' Paul asked Stephen, pointing up at the beam.

Stephen looked at the insipid light-beige stain and said what he thought. 'It looks bloody terrible.'

'What did you say?' Paul asked in astonishment. He couldn't believe his ears.

'You heard, and I have no intention of repeating myself.'

'But we agreed the colour of the stain weeks ago, don't you remember?' Paul's tone and expression showed his puzzlement. 'I even had a piece of the same wood specially stained for you.'

Stephen simply stood, hands on hips, looking up at the offending beam. 'Well,' he said tersely, 'I don't like it now I see it up there. I think it should be dark brown.'

'We don't have any dark-brown stain and there's no means of getting any. We've less than two weeks to do *all* the beams – there just isn't time to chop and change now!'

'Okay, Paul. Okay,' Stephen interjected, raising his hand. 'Calm down, for God's sake. We do it that colour for now, and after we get open and organized, we change to the colour of my choice.'

Christina could see that Paul wanted to scream that *this* colour had been his choice, but he bit back his retort, clenching his fists.

Meanwhile Mr Gittings' head was obviously beginning to spin from all this toing and froing. He dearly wished they would hurry up and tell him what to do. Stephen gave an absent-minded nod and hurried off to solve the next problem. Paul unclenched his fists and addressed the Barbadian.

'Okay, Gittings, carry on with this stain – and no slacking, mind. You've 180 of these buggers to do.'

'Yessir, Mr Richardson, sir!' He wielded his brush vigorously and continued to do so until Christina and Paul left. They waited ten minutes, Paul timing it exactly on his wristwatch, then crept back to find Gittings comfortably installed on a newly delivered double bed, beginning his lunch of two fresh fish cutters and half a bottle of five-star rum.

'I start on dat pole tomorrow,' he promised airily.

Two minutes later, after Paul had threatened the loss of the contract, he had picked up his brush again and, grumbling, got down to work. But at least Gittings, though slow and inclined to lengthy siestas, knew how to do his job. Some of the unskilled youngsters drafted in to help with the decorating did not. One morning they spotted a young apprentice singing loudly while cheerfully splashing paint liberally over himself and six freshly planted ceramic jardinières. He was in full melodic voice, singing the latest calypso, and did not hear Stephen's shouts of outrage.

At last there were just the external walls to be given a final coat of white paint. Stephen left Percy Gittings to supervise, and he and Christina walked down the drive towards the ocean-front rooms which were now ready for occupation.

They climbed the red clay-tiled steps, enjoying the panoramic sea views from each landing. The heavy pine door of room 301 stood ajar, numerals depicted in hand-painted tiles set flush with the white-stucco wall. Christina entered the hallway and switched on the ceiling fan. The teak paddles began to rotate, making little more than a whisper of sound as they gently scythed the warm air.

'Well, what do you think?' she asked proudly.

The large room, a deluxe double, was decorated in pale-pink fabrics that blended in with the white rattan furniture. Low travertine-marble occasional tables held specially logoed ashtrays and vases of fresh flowers picked from the garden. Cream-coloured stationery embossed with the hotel's name was provided in a dove-grey leather folder on top of a carved pine desk. The pristine white walls were relieved every few feet with original prints of tropical flowers, their colours toning perfectly with the Mexican rug and quilted comforter tucked over coral-coloured bed-linen.

'I was right about you,' Stephen said slowly. 'You've done a bloody good job on the interiors – and right on schedule too. I'm proud of you.'

Christina flushed with pleasure. Wife or not, she knew that Stephen never gave praise unless he thought it was due.

'Well, Colin was a terrific help once we'd thrashed out a few problems,' she said modestly.

'You worked hard, Christina. No need to pretend. Not too tired, I hope?'

She was exhausted but, buoyed up by his praise, replied, 'I feel marvellous.'

'That's good.'

He strode over to the door and stood looking down at the handle, shaking his head sadly. 'Uh, oh. Your first mistake, Chrissy. You've forgotten the "Do Not Disturb" signs.'

'I have not!' she replied angrily. 'They're due to-morrow.'

'Well, today we'll just have to rely on a good old-fashioned lock,' he said, beginning to take off his clothes. 'Have you ever heard of in-depth market research? In the interests of our future guests we're going to put this room's mattress to the test. Come on, you gorgeous creature.'

Later, lying in his arms, she said drowsily, 'Stephen, we're never going to make it.'

'What do you mean? This hotel's going to be . . .'

'No, not the hotel, stupid. The market research. Another 199 rooms to go and we open on Thursday!'

Chapter Ten

Christina heard Stephen get out of bed and creep into the bathroom, trying not to make a sound.

'I've been awake for over an hour,' she said, sitting on the edge of the bed, when he came back into the bedroom.

'I don't think I've even slept. My stomach feels like it's been kicked by hundreds of yobs wearing hob-nailed boots.'

He was dressed in old shorts and a baggy shirt. He sat down next to her and took her hand.

'Well, Chrissy, we made it.'

'I never had any doubts.' She squeezed his hand. It was very warm and clammy.

'Not even for one split second?' He smiled and she touched his cheek.

'Not once.'

Stephen stood up and flung open the shutters, stepping out onto the balcony. It was still dark. He looked across the sea: a faint glimmer of pale light was rising in the midnight-blue sky. Dawn would soon break.

He thought about the long hours, the continuous toil, the mistakes, the mishaps, the inefficiency and the constant battle to build what he now saw before him.

He knew he would do it all again, because as he looked across the manicured lawns, the buildings shrouded now in darkness but soon to be brilliant in the blazing sunlight, the scene embodied all his dreams. It had been worth every minute of the effort they had put into it.

Christina was dressed in shorts and a loose cotton shirt when he came back into the room.

'Fancy a last walk on the beach alone? Because from now on we'll be sharing it with our guests.'

She nodded and they left the house hand in hand and walked across the springy turf. They slipped through the restaurant, shrouded now in darkness, and picked their way through new tables and chairs, empty but soon to be packed with people.

They could almost hear the chink of glasses mixed with chatter and laughter.

A tiny patch of blue punctured the dark blanket of sky, and the sun peeped out from a corner of the horizon as they headed down the beach, not stopping until they reached a small rocky promontory shaded by bushy casuarinas.

The dawn light flooded the sky, now clear and translucent, broken by one long finger of the brightest orange Christina had ever seen. She felt certain that if she reached out she could touch it.

Stephen watched two fishermen, father and son he guessed, gathering their nets.

'Morning,' he greeted them. The older man smiled, showing crooked brown teeth, and said, 'Going to be a good day.'

'I hope so,' Stephen replied. 'I prayed last night it wouldn't rain. I think He may have heard me.'

He raised his eyes towards the clear sky. There wasn't a cloud in sight.

'I'm christening my grandson today.' The older man pointed to the younger who was loading tangled nets into the small, brightly painted fishing boat, *Island Spirit*. 'My first grandson. Lots of girls but this is the first boy.' He beamed and chuckled. 'Now the good Lord knows better than to rain on the new Sandiford baby's head.'

Stephen smiled at him and nodded his head slowly. 'We

too are having a christening today.' He put his arm around Christina's waist, and pulled her close to him. 'So perhaps we'll both be lucky.'

Robert and Jane Leyton and Stephen's mother were waiting impatiently in reception when Christina dashed in.

The women were seated straight-backed on the edge of two big cane armchairs, and Robert, his back turned, was looking out of a high arched window.

He touched his wife's arm and pointed down the lawn beyond a stone fountain to the six low-level stucco buildings radiant in their pristine whiteness.

'It's incredible, Robert; I had no idea it would be this beautiful.' Jane clutched her beige cardigan tightly in one hand while she searched for a tissue in her handbag with the other. Robert turned at the sound of Christina's voice.

'Oh, there you are. Sorry to keep you waiting but the bellman said he thought you'd all gone to your rooms.'

Christina's face was flushed from running, and her hair was tied back in a thick, glossy plait. She wore a short white cotton dress and flat sandals, her long legs tanned to a rich golden-brown. Robert thought she looked about sixteen.

Jane eyed her slim figure enviously, dreading the evening ahead, certain now that the old Frank Usher dress she had decided to squeeze herself into was going to look absurd.

'Jean, you look well.' Christina smiled at Stephen's mother.

'Well, I certainly don't feel it. I've had a horrible journey, squashed next to a big fat woman and her squabbling children. She insisted on telling me her entire life story, regardless of whether I wanted to listen or not.' Pulling a disgruntled face, Jean Reece-Carlton wiped her brow with a delicate embroidered handkerchief. 'Why I ever allowed

Stephen to talk me into coming here is beyond me. He knows I hate the heat.'

Christina looked around the white-marble reception hall. 'Where's Victoria? I thought she was coming with you.'

'She did, but raced off ages ago in search of Stephen. I assume she found him. You know how she is with her father.'

Christina caught Robert's sympathetic look.

'You don't have to tell me.'

'Victoria hasn't seen her father for months. She's talked about nothing else. Naturally she wants to see him.'

Jean's small, deep-set eyes glittered coldly. 'Christina, instead of just standing there, could you please show us to our rooms? I for one am dying of thirst and hot enough to boil over.'

Christina blushed, angry at being spoken to like a member of staff.

'You and me both,' Jane grumbled, standing up and smoothing her hands down the front of her creased navy and white pleated skirt.

Robert picked up the overflowing hand grip lying next to his feet. 'What shall we do with the luggage?' He glanced in the direction of the reception desk where four suitcases stood.

'I'll take care of it, don't worry,' Christina assured them, before leading them down four deep stone steps and along a pathway, past a bright wall of alamanda and hibiscus bushes camouflaging the car park.

They skirted the palm-fringed swimming-pool which appeared to have been hewn out of solid coral-stone, and crossed it by means of a wooden bridge suspended above two huge boulders.

Jane stared around her, incredulous. Flower-lined terraces descended in tiers to the three miles of white sand beach.

'It's amazing,' she said, as much to herself as anyone else, marvelling at the beauty surrounding her. With every step she seemed to be going deeper into another world.

Christina led them under an arched stone portico and through a labyrinth of white-stucco passageways opening onto vine-covered courtyards where tiny humming-birds fluttered through tall bamboo, and antique urns overflowed with red and pink angelica.

'Suite 106 for Mr and Mrs Leyton, the best in the house,' she announced, and turned the key in an intricate brass lock. She flung open the solid pine door, standing aside for Jane and Robert to enter.

They entered the elegant suite and Jane gasped, her mouth dropping open. 'It's beautiful, Christina. You've done a great job on the interiors.'

She was visibly pleased. 'Thanks a lot. It wasn't easy.'

Robert had seen the development in varying stages, and had assisted in shipping out tons of building materials, but it was four months since he had been to Barbados and a lot of progress had been made since then.

He sat down heavily on a two-seater sofa upholstered in the palest of pinks, and pulled off his shoes. Wriggling his toes with a sigh of relief, he looked out through the tall louvred doors to the deep marble terrace stretching the full length of the suite.

Jean Reece-Carlton strolled out onto the terrace to inspect it. Jane and Christina followed.

'Bobby, come out here,' Jane shouted to her husband, who reluctantly joined them. She was hanging over the wrought-iron balcony above the gardens, pointing to the pink and white marquees flapping gently in the breeze like grounded hot-air balloons. There were dozens of staff milling about, laden with trays of crisp white and pink table-linen and embossed silver-plated cutlery.

Jane turned to her husband, her plain face animated. 'The sweet smell of success, eh, Bobby?'

'We've done it.' Robert's smile was triumphant.

Christina wanted to remind him that he had only helped with the backing and that the real work had been done by Stephen and her, but she kept quiet and instead watched Jean Reece-Carlton as she turned away from a gloating Robert in disgust, muttering something under her breath.

It sounded like, 'Done something good in his life for once.'

Christina was amazed. It seemed an extraordinary attitude for the mother of someone as successful as Stephen.

'I'll take you to your room, Jean,' she offered.

Christina offered to carry her small bag but Jean refused. 'I'm quite capable. Go on, you lead the way.'

She pushed Christina none too gently towards the door. 'I'll see you two at the party, no doubt?' she said to Robert and Jane. She made it sound like a public execution, Christina thought.

Stephen had allotted a corner suite to his mother. It consisted of a bedroom with *en suite* bathroom, balcony, small sitting-room with breakfast bar, compact kitchen in pickled pine, and a large square terrace which served as an outdoor dining area, complete with round marble table and four chairs.

Jean Reece-Carlton made no comment when Christina showed her the suite. She was more interested in getting a glass of water from the mini-bar and enquiring if she could have a cup of tea.

'I thought perhaps Stephen's brother might have come to the party with you?' Christina commented.

She had asked Stephen a couple of weeks ago if Edward was coming and he had replied: 'Over my dead body.'

Jean stared at Christina without really seeing her. It was obvious that her mind was elsewhere.

'I think under the circumstances that would have been very unwise.'

'What circumstances?' she asked.

The older woman stood straight-backed and fixed Christina with a hard gaze, her face suddenly charged with barely suppressed anger.

'Edward is Stephen's half-brother; they've never been close. As different as chalk and cheese – and equally as disappointing to me,' she snapped.

'Stephen never talks about his family or his past.' Christina searched her mother-in-law's face for answers to all the unanswered questions.

Jean laughed, a cold and hollow sound.

'There are lots of things Stephen will never tell you, my dear. Believe me when I say that he has an unexpected side to him. I'm his mother, I should know.'

'I hate it, I hate it, I hate it!' Victoria's glossy black hair swung wildly about her shoulders as she stamped her feet in front of the mirror.

'This is just the most hateful dress I've ever seen,' she said to Christina.

'Well, it's the only one you've got, Victoria, so it will have to do.' Christina sighed. She needed one of Victoria's spiteful tirades about as much as she needed the pain in the head which she already had, thundering relentlessly at her temples.

'You liked the dress in England; you wouldn't have bought it otherwise.'

'I didn't buy it!' Victoria screamed. 'That horrible Virginia Colton bought it, or should I say made me buy it? When I tried it on in Harvey Nichols it looked all right, but now I see it out here I realize how stupid and childish it looks.' She pouted. 'I wanted something more grown-up.'

Christina didn't dare risk mentioning that at thirteen she was not yet grown-up. That would have sent her into another tantrum.

'The one I wanted was too expensive and unsuitable

according to bloody Virginia. I only wish Daddy could have seen me in the black lace dress. He'd have bought it at any cost.'

Christina was sure she was right, and had sent a cheque to Caroline's mother to safeguard against such an event. The last thing she needed tonight was Victoria swanning around looking like a juvenile *femme fatale*.

Victoria ripped the pale-blue cotton dress from her slim body and flung it and herself onto the ruffled bed.

'I'm not going to the opening. I'm not going. I look dreadful and I really wanted to look beautiful for Daddy, especially tonight.'

Christina felt like telling her she would look beautiful in a torn sack, but decided she was going to hear comments like that all her life. Instead she said quietly, and with more patience than she felt, 'Victoria, your father will not only be annoyed if you don't go to the party tonight, he'll also be extremely upset. And in his present state of mind, I for one would not enjoy being on the receiving end of his temper. If you want to be, go ahead, but don't expect any sympathy or back-up from me.'

She pressed her forefinger into her left temple to ease the escalating migraine that threatened.

Vicky's dark head rose from the bedspread. She didn't face Christina when she said through clenched teeth, 'I've never expected or received any help from you anyway, Christina.'

Bending down, she retrieved the discarded dress from where it lay crumpled on the floor on the other side of the bed.

'I'm going to get dressed now. I just want you to know that not only do I hate this dress, I hate you even more.'

Her vituperative comments fell on deaf ears. Christina turned and left the room without another word.

It was six o'clock, only one hour to go. She actually

wished it was six tomorrow morning and the party was over.

She walked slowly back to her room and looked at the dress lying ready across the bed.

She had been lucky to see it in *Vogue* and to find it available in Harrods. She had sent a cheque, and Harrods had despatched it by courier.

It was a gown for a fairy princess.

Yards and yards of fine cream chantilly lace draped over ivory silk cascaded in layers to her feet, sprinkled with dozens of tiny white pearls.

Stephen was late. She had expected him back before now. He ran into the room a few minutes later and began to tear off his crumpled clothes.

'Calm down,' she said, looking at his angry face.

'Calm down? How the hell can I calm down when that fucking idiot of a chef has got the entire kitchen staff making canapés when they should be preparing the buffet? The man's mad.'

Stephen stopped to breathe.

'No, on second thoughts, he's not – he's West Indian.'

He jumped into the shower and felt a little better when he got out a few seconds later.

He walked into the bedroom and began to dress. Fumbling with his black tie, he swore in frustration.

'Christina, help.' She came into the bedroom on his third plea.

'I can't tie the damn thing; I'm all fingers and thumbs. I can't find my cuff-links either, and we've less than twenty minutes to go!'

'I know where your cuff-links are; I've got them in my jewellery box. Come on, let's do this bow-tie first.'

She stepped forward, and Stephen stood impatiently shifting his weight from one foot to the other whilst she struggled to fasten his bow-tie.

She managed eventually and patted it in place. 'There you are; you look great.' She stepped back and waited for him to comment on her dress.

He didn't. Instead, he looked deep into her amber eyes and squeezed her hand far too tightly, saying, 'We did it, Chrissy. We did it.' His voice shook with emotion.

He led her out of the bedroom and onto the terrace where Victoria was waiting.

She had piled her long hair into a sleek chignon, and tiny wisps escaped across her brow and to the nape of her neck. A wonderful smile lit her entire face as her father approached. It was a smile for him alone. Eyes the colour of gathering storm-clouds did not leave his face.

Christina stood back, feeling isolated and excluded, as Stephen planted a kiss on his daughter's forehead.

'You look lovely,' he said. 'Young, fresh, and very beautiful.' Christina noticed the triumphant look on Victoria's face as he stepped back.

'One glass of champagne, and then we must get down there.' He took a bottle from the ice-bucket. For once he allowed the cork to fly high into the air. Victoria squealed in delight as Stephen caught the erupting bubbles in three tall tulip glasses. He held his aloft. His other hand he held out to Christina. The cream lace of her dress rustled softly as she moved towards him, the pearl and diamond earrings he had bought her gleaming against the dark honey tone of her neck.

'Here's to Crystal Springs, the most beautiful hotel I have ever seen. And here's to my wife who looks more stunning tonight than ever before.'

He smiled lovingly at Victoria. 'And to you, Vicky. It's so good to have you here at last. Never forget, darling, this is your home too, just as much as Purley Hall.

'Come on, drink up! We've 600 guests to greet tonight.'

*

The black Daimler stopped under a brilliantly lit *porte cochère*, and Jonathon Alleyne, the Prime Minister, stepped out, closely followed by his wife Susan.

They stood together and posed for the press, Alleyne relaxed and smiling, a tall, angular man who carried himself with natural elegance. Christina noticed his unusual dark-green eyes and smooth *café au lait* skin.

His wife Susan was as short as he was tall, and looked uncomfortable in an emerald-green satin dress held on both shoulders by huge satin bows which flapped like startled birds in the breeze.

Stephen greeted his guest of honour. 'Good evening, Mr Prime Minister. May I introduce my wife Christina, and my daughter Victoria?'

Christina shook the Prime Minister's hand. He held her eyes for a split second, and she found his gaze disconcerting.

Their guests were assembling in the open-air piazza below. Alleyne stepped onto a specially constructed rostrum and cut a pink and white ribbon to release a profusion of pink and white fresh hibiscus petals onto the crowd who exclaimed and applauded.

'I declare Crystal Springs Hotel officially open – and wish her every success,' the Prime Minister announced loudly.

There was a burst of cheering, and black-coated waiters surged forward bearing trays of champagne. Everywhere glasses were raised and toasts were drunk: 'To Crystal Springs.'

Stephen and Christina led the PM and his wife down a flight of white marble steps and across the piazza to the marquee on the lawn. Their path was lit by concealed footlights.

They passed the fountain, which still lay in darkness, having beaten Stephen and the team of electricians he had had working until minutes before the guests' arrival – the one and only thing that was not finished.

Susan Alleyne stopped on the narrow wooden bridge that spanned the swimming-pool.

'I've never seen anything so magnificent,' she said, and stared at the water cascading down the three-tier construction. The Crystal Springs logo in mosaic was illuminated beneath the water.

Christina had seen it every day for the past few months, but had to admit that tonight it looked especially magical.

'Did you design it, Stephen?' asked the PM.

'I'm afraid I can't take all the credit. It was a joint effort between Paul Richardson the architect and myself.'

They carried on into the marquee, where eight ten-foot-long buffet tables decorated with pale pink and white angelicas held dozens of silver tureens, filled to capacity with imported smoked salmon, lobster, and finely sliced fillet of beef in aspic. Huge honey-roasted hams and game-hens were displayed on stands and silver platters. There were six-foot ice carvings depicting a Caribbean artefact or symbol at the head of every table.

Christina grabbed a passing glass of champagne, knocking one of Susan Alleyne's enormous satin bows. She didn't appear to notice.

Christina hoped it wouldn't be too long before she could make her escape. She was eager to mingle with the other guests, but had been carefully primed by Stephen that morning to wait until they could politely leave the Prime Minister and his wife.

Stephen steered Jonathon Alleyne to his place, answering his probing questions as succinctly as possible.

The guests of honour were to be seated next to the Minister of Tourism and his wife, who were already there, and a man called Sebastian Aguilar and his stunning-looking Trinidadian girlfriend.

Stephen had told Christina that Aguilar was the offspring of a white Barbadian mother and a black Trinidadian. He had inherited an oil company in Port of Spain from his father, and had also branched out into the airline business, owning and operating several profitable inter-island routes. He and Jonathon Alleyne were close friends – some said business associates, though technically Alleyne could not be tied to any commercial ventures. They had attended Oxford together and frequently mixed socially.

Christina forced herself to compliment Rachael Mottely on her heavily pleated canary-yellow dress.

'You look lovely; what a beautiful dress.'

'I bought it in London especially for this evening.' She leaned forward, planting a sour-smelling kiss on Christina's cheek.

Sebastian Aguilar congratulated Stephen.

'You've done a fine job here. Wonderful place. It will bring lots of new faces to Barbados and hopefully set new standards.'

'I agree,' Jonathon Alleyne said. 'Barbados has been waiting for a hotel of this calibre for a very long time.'

'Thank you both. I think we're all working towards the same goal. We have to attract more people to the island, and I'm sure Crystal Springs is going to put Barbados right up there on top of the tourist destination list.'

Stephen signalled to Orson, the head waiter, who almost fell over himself to get to the Prime Minister. Stephen excused himself and Christina.

'I'm afraid I'll have to leave you now in Orson's very capable hands. We have to greet our other guests, so if you would please excuse us?'

'Thank you, Mr Reece-Carlton, for building such a beautiful hotel in my country. It's a credit to you and the island.'

Jonathon Alleyne's voice held only a trace of a Bajan lilt.

It was more redolent of English public school and Oxford, where he had studied law.

'I would very much like to have a meeting with you in the New Year, Stephen. Once you get sorted out down here, call my secretary and he'll set one up.'

'I'll do that,' Stephen said, pleased, and added, 'Thank you for coming.'

'Believe me, it's my pleasure.'

Sebastian Aguilar shook Stephen's hand, then took one of Christina's.

'It was wonderful meeting you,' he said, and she found herself staring into his mesmeric blue-eyed gaze. His good looks were almost sinister, she decided, and she shook hands formally before pulling away.

'I need a drink,' Stephen said when they were out of earshot. He ordered a large vodka and tonic from a passing waiter.

At the door to the marquee they exchanged greetings with scores of other guests, gradually making their way inside. There were congratulations and awed exclamations on every side. Christina saw her husband gradually relax and begin to enjoy himself, tapping his foot to the strains of a calypso floating towards them from the dance-floor on the piazza outside.

'Where's Victoria?' he asked.

'I don't know; I haven't seen her since the Prime Minister arrived.'

They didn't have to wait long to find out where she was. A few minutes later she appeared on the swimming-pool bridge, chatting coquettishly to a tall blond man. Clearly visible as an up-lighter caught it was the strong profile of Martin Ward, with the Dyson family a few steps behind.

Victoria came up to her father, clutched his arm, and looked up at him excitedly.

'Daddy, let me introduce you to my new friend, Martin.

'And this is the owner of Crystal Springs – my father,' she announced with childish pomp.

'I believe we've already met.' Stephen held out his hand – rather slowly, Christina thought.

'Yes, Midland Hotel, Manchester,' Martin reminded him, and shook hands firmly. 'I must compliment you on your hotel, Mr Reece-Carlton. You certainly know what you're doing.'

'That's why I married Christina.' Stephen turned his attention abruptly to Roger and Amy Dyson, hovering behind Martin's broad back.

'Martin, how are you?' Christina flung her arms around him and kissed him on the cheek.

'I'm fine, and you look beautiful,' he whispered in her ear, ignoring Stephen's irritated voice as he interrupted.

'Christina, Roger's speaking to you.'

She left Martin, promising to catch up with him later. He was immediately joined by Louise who pulled him towards the marquee. Christina knew it was none of her business – Martin was a free agent – but it disturbed her somehow to see him being so hotly pursued by a determined young woman.

She made small-talk with Amy and Roger Dyson and greeted about fifty more guests before excusing herself to go to the ladies' room where she met Elaine powdering her nose.

'You look lovely tonight,' she told her friend.

'Thanks to you.' Elaine adjusted a shoe-string strap on her shoulder and surveyed the long, loosely draped black jersey-dress in the mirror.

'Thanks for lending me this, Christina. Loads of people have complimented me, including one very important person.'

Christina raised her eyebrows. 'And who might that be?'

Elaine applied a layer of lip-gloss and replaced the tube in her matching clutch-bag.

'Only the Prime Minister's friend, the divine Sebastian Aguilar!'

Christina pulled a face. 'Not my type. Too full of himself.'

'Good-looking, though, don't you think?' Elaine patted her hair into place. 'The things I could do for him,' she sighed. 'Maybe I'll get the chance. He's asked me out.'

Christina looked shocked.

'When?'

'A few minutes ago. Oh, I see what you mean. His secretary's going to call with the arrangements, would you believe?'

'Well, I wouldn't get mixed up with him if I were you.' Christina looked concerned.

'Listen, don't worry about me, I'm a big girl now and can look after myself.' A hint of mischief came into her violet eyes. 'And let's face it, James is never going to know. He's far fonder of the bottle than he ever was of me.'

Christina watched her go, a worried frown knitting her brows. On her return to the party a few minutes later, she almost bumped into James, who placed his clammy hands on her bare shoulders and squeezed them.

'You look lovely tonight, as always.'

'Thanks.' She smiled and gently eased herself free.

James didn't seem disposed to take the hint. He continued to stare at her, his fleshy face filmed with perspiration, neck bulging above his tight collar.

Christina detested what she saw in his expression. She ignored his lecherous gaze and scanned the sea of faces for Stephen. Her eyes caught Martin Ward's, and she waved animatedly.

'Would you excuse me, please, James?' she said, and made her way over to Martin without looking back. She didn't see the grimace of annoyance cross his face at her desertion, but Martin did.

'Who's that ugly-looking customer?' he said when

Christina reached him. 'Didn't seem too pleased about something.'

'Didn't he?' she said, too glad to see that Louise was not in evidence to think about what Martin was saying. 'That's James Morris, Stephen's project liaison man.'

'You mean that's Elaine's husband – a bright, bubbly girl like her is married to *him*?'

He'd met Elaine on several trips around the island which Christina had arranged, including a hilarious afternoon when the three of them decided to try out the hotel's water sports and attempted to learn to water-ski after too many rum sours at the Reef Bar.

'Well, loosely speaking he is,' she said. 'And what about you, Martin? I've seen the way Louise looks at you, and Roger and Amy obviously approve. Could it be wedding-bells for you soon?'

'No way,' he said emphatically, and she could not deny the jolt of relief she felt on hearing this. 'Louise is keen, like you say, but I've always been completely honest with her. Marriage isn't on the cards.'

He paused for a moment and frowned when he spoke again. The words came out awkwardly. 'There was only ever one girl I seriously thought about asking – and some-one else beat me to it.'

Christina looked down, her heart pounding nervously. She twisted her diamond solitaire engagement ring as she replied.

'We hardly knew one another, Martin. We'd only had a few dates. You can't really mean that.'

He put his hand on her arm. 'But I do. I asked you to come to London with me, didn't I?'

She thought back. It had been such a confusing time for her – the quarrel with Stephen and her mother's death following so closely. But yes . . .

'I remember,' she said softly. 'It wasn't meant to be,

Martin. I married Stephen and we're very happy together.'

'Are you? I wonder.' He searched her eyes for a moment, then sighed and held up his hands in surrender.

'Okay, Mrs Happily Married Reece-Carlton. But you can't refuse me the pleasure of a dance – just one, for old times' sake?'

'I'd love to dance with you, Martin.'

He took her hand and led her to the open-air dance-floor just as the band slipped into the first of their slow numbers. Martin slid his arms around her and they danced without speaking, swaying together to the sweet, sad strains of 'Island Woman'.

As the song was ending, Christina raised her head from his shoulder where she had rested it while they danced – and found herself looking straight into the hard, intimidating gaze of Jean Reece-Carlton, who was being escorted around the floor by a martyred-looking Robert Leyton.

'Glad to see you're able to forget all your duties and enjoy yourself, dear,' she said. 'Don't worry about Victoria, will you? My granddaughter is safe at our table with Jane, and in a moment we're all going to watch the firework display.'

Her gaze shifted to Martin, then back again. 'Perhaps you'd better find Stephen – unless *you* want to see some fireworks, that is?'

Christina turned her back on her mother-in-law as the music ended.

'Thanks for the dance, Martin, but I'd better go. Stephen expects me to do the rounds tonight.'

'I understand. And I'm looking forward to Thursday, by the way.'

For a moment she couldn't think what he meant, then she remembered with dismay that she'd already asked him to join her and Elaine and a few of the island friends they'd made on the new power-boat Stephen had treated them to as the hotel neared completion. Louise, who worked as a nurse, was not able to come that afternoon, she remembered.

She took her leave and went in search of Stephen, pre-occupied by her thoughts. She hadn't realized that Martin's feelings ran so deep. So far as she'd been concerned they had been just friends. He'd helped her through a bad patch and she'd been grateful, but she'd never really considered him in any other light. There'd been Stephen.

And there still was, she told herself firmly. He would always come first. She'd have to show Martin that though they would always be friends, her first loyalty lay with her husband.

With a feeling of relief, she spotted him talking to a distinguished-looking Barbadian and his exotic female companion. She hurried over to join them.

'Christina, there you are. I've been looking everywhere for you. I want you to meet Danny Bascombe, able lawyer and aspiring politician. It was Danny who sorted out our Immigration, remember?' Stephen asked.

Christina liked Danny at once. His warm, dark-brown eyes twinkled in a square, handsome face, and he had what his father had always referred to as an honest demeanour. The touches of silver at his temples added to the impression of experience and trustworthiness.

'I'm really pleased to meet you. Stephen has talked about you a lot in the last few months,' she said.

'My reputation precedes me.' His voice was deep and melodic. 'And you, my dear, are every bit as attractive as Stephen described.'

Christina blushed.

Danny laughed, and put his arm around the beautiful young woman standing by his side.

'Meet Pauline, my wife.'

Christina could hardly recall meeting anyone as naturally beautiful as Pauline Bascombe.

She was swathed in a red silk dress that fitted where it touched. The narrow straps seemed barely able to hold her full bosom, which threatened to spill out of the boned bodice with every movement she made.

Christina was tall at five foot eight. Pauline towered above her, a statuesque six foot in her high ankle-strapped gold sandals. Her long, braided hair was pulled off her exquisite heart-shaped face. Christina stared, transfixed by her huge almond-shaped black eyes and long, thick lashes.

'Glad to meet you, Christina, and I want to say what a marvellous job you have done down here. Stephen has been telling us how much you have helped him.'

'Yes, you've worked miracles,' Danny cut in before Christina could reply. 'I am Barbadian, and I know how difficult it is to get anything done here.' He examined his hands for a moment as if embarrassed.

'My mother was a maid in Crystal Springs House for many years, and I used to come here sometimes as a child. I have lots of happy memories of the place and wish you every success with it.'

'Thank you,' she said, and looked over his shoulder to see the Leytons approach. Evidently they had escaped Jean and Victoria. Stephen called Robert over to meet Danny.

Their conversation ceased as the eloquent tones of Michael Stein carried towards them on the public address system.

'Welcome, Mr Prime Minister, Mrs Alleyne, distinguished guests, ladies and gentlemen, to Crystal Springs Hotel.

'I would like to thank Mr Alleyne, our guest of honour, for performing the opening ceremony, and thank you all for your presence here tonight, sharing the opening of this wonderful new resort.

'Now, would you please welcome your host and the driving force behind Crystal Springs – Mr Stephen Reece-Carlton.'

Stephen stepped up onto the rostrum vacated by Michael Stein. He looked nervous. Normally he hated making speeches, and liked to prepare one week in advance so that nothing could go wrong. Tonight he had dispensed with his usual practice. Tonight he was speaking from the heart.

'Almost two years ago I came here with my then very new wife on honeymoon. After only a few days we were both madly in love, not just with each other, but with this beautiful island in the sun and with Crystal Springs, which we found by accident.

'The day we saw the outstanding location of Crystal Springs House was the day I decided to develop my first hotel.

'I know it may sound corny, but it happens to be true. As we drove through the gates, and into a then crumbling, tired and faded property, I had the strongest sensation – call it a vision, call it what you like. I was smitten.

'I decided to build a major development. Not just a hotel. My vision was nothing so commonplace. I wanted a resort of beauty, charm and tranquillity; a haven to enchant all who stayed there.

'I believe at that time my wife Christina privately thought I was mad. Tonight I want to take the opportunity to thank her for her patience and support. I haven't been an easy man to live with for the past year. Thanks, Chrissy.

'I also want to thank all of my management team for their devotion and all the unpaid overtime.

'Last but by no means least I want to thank Paul Richardson, my architect. Come up here, Paul.'

Stephen put out his hand and a reluctant Paul Richardson, egged on by several friends, walked slowly forward.

As he did so, Stephen made a further announcement. 'Crystal Springs, as all of you here tonight can testify, is a triumph. I would like to add that it is only the first of many Platinum Hotels I intend to open throughout the world.'

Christina heard Robert Leyton's angry murmur: 'That's the first I've bloody heard about expanding the resorts!'

'Since when has Stephen ever consulted you about anything?' hissed Jane. 'You know he's a law unto himself. I warn you, Robert, put your foot down this time.'

Applause drowned out their voices, and Christina was unable to hear any more as Stephen dragged a protesting Paul Richardson up onto the narrow stage next to him.

'Paul and I have had our ups and downs, good days and bad in the last year, but I feel I must share tonight with him.

'I want to thank him for his patience, foresight, and ability to interpret my ideas, incorporate his own with them, and achieve what you see here tonight.

'I believe my dream has been realized. Ladies and gentlemen, I give you: Crystal Springs.'

Chapter Eleven

Christina heard the commotion as she walked up the steps from Crystal Springs House and into reception. Michael Stein was trying unsuccessfully to calm an irate customer who was arguing about his bill.

'I refuse to pay for shoddy service! My wife and I waited over an hour for our meal last night and it's been the same throughout our stay.'

The guest had a shock of wiry white hair and a fleshy, sun-scorched face. He was wearing a pale-blue safari-style jacket, belted at the last hole, short-sleeved to display the diamond-faced gold Rolex worn on one beefy wrist.

'I checked with Orson our head waiter, Mr Banville, and he swears you were served after fifteen minutes.' Michael Stein was adamant.

'He's lying!' the man shouted. 'All your staff are bloody liars.'

Guests passing by on their way to the boutiques were finding excuses to hang about and listen to the heated exchange. Christina did not like them to receive such a bad impression of Crystal Springs. Nor did she like hearing her staff referred to as liars.

'I am Mrs Reece-Carlton. I wonder if I could help?' She held out her hand politely.

In the two years they had been operating, Stephen had taught her never to lose her temper with the guests, however unreasonable, but to try to win them over.

Mr Banville looked surly and refused to shake her hand. 'This arrogant upstart here is accusing me of lying.'

Michael Stein opened his mouth to reply but at the last minute, ever the professional, bit back a pithy retort.

'I don't think he is, Mr Banville,' Christina said soothingly.

'That is *exactly* what he's doing. I've spent a fortune in this place and all I'm asking for is a reduction in the service charge.' He glared at Michael, defying him to defend the hotel once more.

Christina walked behind the reception desk and asked for a copy of Mr Banville's account. She picked up a pen and drew a line through the service charge, then handed the bill to the indignant guest. He glanced at it, then at Michael, with a gloating expression.

For Christina he was all smiles. 'Thank you for being so understanding, Mrs Reece-Carlton.'

'I'm only sorry you were not happy with our service. Hopefully when you return it will be much improved.'

'Don't worry, we'll be back.' He handed over a credit card to pay his bill.

Christina walked away, closely followed by Michael Stein.

'Before you go, would you step into my office?' he asked.

Not until the door was firmly closed behind them did Michael speak again.

'Why on earth did you do that, Christina? The man has been a thorn in our side since the day he arrived three weeks ago. He's a professional complainer – I've encountered hundreds of them in my time. They deliberately pick fault with everything in order to get a reduction on their bill. I've had Banville thoroughly checked out, and I know he's stayed at two other hotels on the island and done the same thing.' Michael sank into his chair, scowling. 'He'll be running back to his cow of a wife now and laughing about the way he conned the owner's wife.'

Christina paled. 'I had no idea . . .'

'That's obvious!' He paused and chose his words more carefully, conscious of her influence with Stephen.

'Look, Christina. I'm the general manager, your husband employed me, and because I have had enormous experience in running hotels, I would appreciate it if you would leave me to get on with my job.'

'I'm sorry, Michael. I didn't mean to undermine you. I was only doing what I thought was best for the hotel. Stephen's told me, if it comes to the crunch, the customer is always right.' She managed a wan smile. 'It seemed the only way to avoid a huge argument.'

Michael sighed.

'It's done now. But in future, Christina, before you make managerial decisions, would you check with me first, please?'

The phone rang, and she was grateful for the intrusion, leaving Michael deep in conversation with his travel-operator friend from New York who was organizing a big conference reservation. She went on to her meeting with a young local artist who showed her his portfolio. She was impressed, and agreed to let him exhibit some work in one of the long corridors leading from reception to the dining-room. She also commissioned him to paint Crystal Springs as a present for Stephen's birthday in six weeks' time.

Stephen was talking to a tall, elegantly dressed woman, who looked younger than she actually was, and her much older husband when she joined him for lunch in the beach bar.

It was obvious that the woman was very drunk. She was slurring her words and holding on to the bar-top for support. The old man gripped a walking-stick with one twisted, arthritic hand. His face held the grey tinge of the terminally sick.

'Christina, meet Mr and Mrs Hamilton. They're in the hotel business in America and love Crystal Springs so much they want to buy it.'

The woman barely acknowledged Christina, and continued talking to Stephen, thrusting her abundant cleavage closer to him with every word.

'I would jus' love to own a hotel in the Caribbean. Isn't that right, Joe?'

He grunted.

'There's something about the place, so – so . . .' She groped for the right word. 'So charismatic,' she slurred finally. 'Think about what I've said, Stephen. Perhaps if you don't want to sell we could take on a joint venture.' Mrs Hamilton wobbled precariously on her high heels, almost losing her balance.

Instinctively Stephen held out his arms to catch her, and she fell into them with a ridiculous girlish giggle.

'If she wants the hotel she can have it,' Joe piped up suddenly. 'Name your price, Steve. I'll have the money transferred within twenty-four hours.'

'The hotel's not for sale, Mr Hamilton, I've already told your wife that.'

'Everything's for sale,' said Joe Hamilton with a dismissive wave of his hand. 'Whatever she wants she gets.' The old man took his wife's arm. 'Come on, honey, I'm hungry. Let's eat.'

'I'll see you later.' Mrs Hamilton directed a deliberate, lascivious wink at Stephen then, trying to support her ailing husband, moved away, bumping into several tables before reaching her own.

'Amazing,' Christina said when they were out of earshot. 'I've heard of men buying their wives jewellery, cars, houses even – but a hotel, just because she happens to like it?'

'He's a billionaire, about to croak it. What else can he do with his money?'

'I could think of a million things. Whatever she's doing, she's doing it right.'

'Christina!' Stephen pretended to look shocked.

They sat at their favourite table overlooking a pond to one side, covered with clusters of red and white water-lilies in full bloom, and the sea on the other. Today it was rough and noisy.

The *plat du jour* of cream of ochra soup followed by fresh snapper served in a spicy sauce with christophene salad came highly recommended by Orson, who took their order. The food followed quickly, and they both ate the delicious fresh fish with relish, and were enjoying coffee and coconut-cream pie when Stephen was called to the telephone.

His face was paper-white when he came back to the table.

'Michael Stein has been attacked by a guest.'

'What happened?'

'I don't have all the details, but apparently he argued with a chap this morning about his bill and went along to his room later. The man threatened to kill him and pushed him off the balcony.'

'That's terrible.' Christina didn't need to ask the guest's name. She already knew.

'It's the Banvilles. They've been nothing but trouble since they arrived here. I must go and sort it out. Catch up with you later.'

He rushed out of the restaurant.

Christina finished her coffee, then walked back to the house. She rang James Morris as soon as she was in, pleased to locate him in his office. Since Stephen had appointed him to the permanent position of maintenance manager, he was often out on the property.

She was convinced he would have the latest news on Michael. James made it his personal business to know everyone else's.

'It's Christina, James. I thought you might know what's happened to Michael?'

He sounded pleased to tell her.

'They've taken him to Queen Elizabeth Hospital with a suspected broken leg and a few cuts and bruises. Serves him right for biting off more than he could chew . . . but then, he's always doing that.'

'How did it happen, James?'

'Well, from what I can gather, Mr Banville checked into the hotel three weeks ago and gave a Visa card for a credit reference. When he paid his bill after the argument this morning it was with Amex and authorization didn't come through.

'Michael went down to his room to sort it out, they argued, and Banville went berserk and pushed him off the balcony. Shame it wasn't the top floor.'

'I know you don't mean that, James.'

'Don't you believe it! Stein and I have a mutual loathing. The man's a smart-arse, too clever by bloody half!'

'So what's happened to Mr and Mrs Banville?'

'They've hot-footed it to the airport. Stephen's informed both the police and Immigration. They won't get off the island. Exciting stuff, eh? Never a dull moment running a hotel in the Caribbean.'

'I hope Michael will be okay.'

'I shouldn't worry about him, Christina. The Michael Steins of this world have nine lives. They always bounce back.'

'Thanks, James. See you soon.'

'Oh, before you go, can you call Elaine? She's been trying to get in touch with you for ages. She's at home all day.'

'Okay, James. I'll call her now. Bye.'

Christina dialled Elaine's number. It rang unanswered. She tried several times during the course of the afternoon, but received no reply. She eventually got through to her in the early evening.

'I've been trying to contact you all day. James gave me a message to say you'd be at home.'

Elaine dropped her voice to a whisper.

'I had intended to be, but I got a call from my special friend and spent the afternoon with him.'

'Is James there?' asked Christina.

'No, he's not home yet.'

'Well, why are you whispering?'

'I always feel sort of furtive and illicit after I've been with Sebastian.'

'That figures,' Christina retorted. 'It's been going on a long time, Elaine. It must be quite a strain.'

'It's worth every minute – though a little rough sometimes, if you know what I mean?'

'I don't, so spare me the details.' Christina changed the subject. 'How do you fancy playing tennis on Thursday? I've invited Martin Ward and another guy he's met who's here on holiday.'

'Well, with Martin's dodgy leg, and my backhand, we're sure to have an exciting game!' Elaine laughed. 'Okay, you're on, but do you think you could do something about Martin mooning all over you? I really thought I was going to throw up last week at Maximillian's. He stares at you in raptures. How Stephen doesn't lose his temper is beyond me.'

'I don't think Stephen's even noticed.'

'Don't underestimate him.'

'I don't, Elaine. He is my husband – something Martin is fully aware of too. We're just friends. Though the only thing Stephen seems to be interested in these days is Crystal Springs. I sometimes wonder if all this wifely loyalty's misplaced.'

'You must be joking! Stephen's mad about you.'

'Maybe you're right; I just wish he'd show it a bit more.

238

Anyway, I've got to go now. I can hear him coming in. See you Thursday; be good until then.'

'I'll try,' her friend said. Christina knew she wouldn't try too hard.

She replaced the receiver and joined Stephen, who was sitting on the terrace looking at the sea. Sitting down next to him, she asked, 'How's Michael?'

'His leg's broken in two places and he's badly bruised, but he'll be all right. It could have been worse – that maniac might have killed him.'

'Have they caught Mr Banville?'

'Yes, he's in custody now. We're pressing charges for grievous bodily harm.'

Celia arrived with a tray of tea and placed it on the table.

'A Mr Ward rang earlier, Mrs Carlton. Said it was all right for tennis on Thursday.'

Christina blushed and lowered her eyes.

'Thanks, Celia,' she mumbled, and began to pour the tea.

Stephen was angry; she knew the signs. He always clenched his jaw and a nerve jumped to the side of his left eye.

'I really think you're seeing too much of Martin Ward. This is a small island and tongues are beginning to wag. Remember, I have a certain position . . .'

Christina cut in, her eyes flashing: 'Is that all you're worried about – what the local establishment thinks? You know as well as I do, they only stop talking about you when you're six foot under.'

'That's not the point, Christina, and you know it.'

He had difficulty controlling his voice, and his face and neck reddened with anger. 'We have a status on the island which must be maintained.'

'Oh, come on, Stephen. Don't give me all that crap. You're jealous, admit it. And with absolutely no cause.'

He was about to deny her accusation when James Morris appeared in the garden beneath the balcony.

'Thank God you're here, Stephen. I thought you might still be down-town. That militant Forbes – you know, the one I warned you about last week – has called all the food and beverage staff out on strike!'

Stephen was on his feet instantly.

'Where are they now, James?'

'All in the staff-room. They haven't walked out yet; I begged them to stay put until you got there.'

'Come on, then, let's sort this out.'

Christina sighed and watched him go. Yet again the business of running the hotel had come between them when they had something important to sort out. So far as she was concerned, the friendship with Martin Ward was just that – a friendship. But she was guiltily aware that at least part of his reason for staying on the island so long and not returning to England was his hope of one day furthering their relationship. She'd given him no encouragement – their encounters had been on a light, friendly basis only – but she knew that he'd long since stopped seeing Louise, and there'd been only a couple of short-term girlfriends since. But Christina's hands were tied. She was not only married but trying to conceive a child by Stephen – though as yet she hadn't sat down with him and discussed her worries about her failure to become pregnant. Every time she mentioned babies and what it would be like to have their own one day, Stephen changed the subject or yet another crisis loomed which he had to dash off and deal with. Sometimes she wondered why they hired a general manager at all.

'That fucking militant bastard. Aston Forbes has got the staff so riled up they've walked out!' Stephen announced on his return two hours later.

'Oh no!' Christina was horrified. 'How many covers have we reserved for tonight?'

'About forty-six.'

'How about we do it?' she suggested. 'You, me, Elaine and Celia. All the preparations will have been made; I'm sure we could get by.'

'It might come to that. I've got James ringing around all the private houses on the island to rope in a few cooks who aren't working tonight. I've told him to offer them anything, so we might just manage for tonight.'

The phone rang and Stephen took it. James had managed to locate four local cooks and one unemployed chef.

Ten minutes before the first orders went into the kitchen the island had one of its frequent power cuts. Candles were brought to the tables and any mishaps in the food or service were blamed on the lack of power, which lasted for three hours. The guests thought it was romantic and had great fun picking their way through the candlelit restaurant. For once Stephen and Christina thanked God for the inefficient island infrastructure.

Stephen had a meeting with the shop steward the following morning at 8.30, and came back to the house afterwards shouting to Victor the butler for strong black coffee.

Christina was swimming in the pool. He sat on the edge talking to her.

'I've threatened to shut the hotel down before I'll give them the 12 per cent they're asking for. It's ludicrous! I think they'll settle for five eventually, but you never know with these situations – they may call my bluff.'

'When will you know?' Christina climbed the pool steps and he handed her a towel.

'I've given Forbes a deadline of two this afternoon.'

'I heard a rumour that James has been arguing with Aston Forbes a lot lately and generally getting everyone's back up. Apparently James has no idea how to handle staff and they all resent him,' she said, wrapping the towel around her shoulders.

'Who told you that?' Stephen wanted to know.

241

'It came from Michael Stein's secretary, Donna; you know how they all gossip.'

'Michael Stein hates James and I wouldn't be at all surprised if he hadn't started a rumour like that himself. I don't trust the man.'

'You trust James, then?'

'Yes, I do. He may not have Michael's sophistication and finesse, but I know exactly how to handle James. Michael's an entirely different animal. I'm not happy about the way Banville beat him up, but at least in his absence we'll be able to see how we manage without him around.'

Christina suspected that Michael had challenged Stephen's authority once too often. He would have to watch his step on his return. Stephen and he had worked closely for two years now, but there was no question of the men sharing a social relationship, as she and Stephen did with James and Elaine.

Stephen gave her a quick peck on the cheek and said, 'Must dash. I'll see you this evening for dinner.'

'What about lunch?'

'No time today – emergency management meeting.' She watched him go, realizing it was weeks since they had sat down for dinner together without an interruption, and over a week since they had made love.

She vowed to herself that tonight, strike or no strike, she would make him forget about Crystal Springs.

Stephen looked exhausted when he returned home at seven that evening and tossed the local newspaper and a back edition of an American gossip magazine into her lap.

Christina recognized film star Ross Milton and his mistress immediately, even though the photographs were very blurred. There was one of them caressing on the beach at Crystal Springs, and another of the glamorous couple wrapped around each other in the crystal-clear water of the hotel beach. The article began: 'Sun, sand and sex for Ross Milton on vacation at Crystal Springs Resort, Barbados. Deena Milton has left their Beverly Hills home and has started divorce proceedings.'

'The papparazzi must have taken shots from a boat,' Stephen commented. 'I can't say I blame them. She's a beautiful girl.'

'And his wife looks a real dragon.' Christina studied the photograph of Deena Milton leaving her house while glaring into the cameras. 'I liked him a lot. He wasn't a bit precious and starry like so many of them who come to stay at the hotel.'

'He'll no doubt be hit with a crippling alimony suit,' Stephen said. 'Apparently his wife has some hot-shot L.A. lawyer who intends to go for the jugular. I just hope the lovely Claudia was worth it.'

Christina picked up the local *National* newspaper and read an account of their labour-relations problems.

The article went on to say that staff employed in the tourist industry were getting a raw deal, and that the government should take a hard line and introduce new legislation on taxation for the hotel industry.

There were quotes from the Minister of Tourism and the Prime Minister.

'Forbes has stirred up a hornet's nest. He intends to get other unions to lobby the government for some sort of taxation to be levied on the hotel industry, which is all we need.'

Stephen raked his fingers through his hair in agitation.

'This government can't see the wood for the trees. They don't understand that tourism is the only way forward. Without it they're dead. Barbados can't survive on the sugar market alone, but try convincing them of that. It's like banging your head against a brick wall. I had this conversation with Danny Bascombe the other day. He understands and would be totally committed to tourism if he got into office.'

'Do you think he stands a chance, Stephen?'

'He does if he has the right people and financial backing behind him. The electorate will buy what they're shown is right, though persuading them costs a lot of bucks. But I like Danny Bascombe, and I believe he's right for the changing face of Barbados. I'm prepared to put my money where my mouth is.'

There was a strange look in Stephen's narrowed eyes. Christina had only encountered it once before when he was hell-bent on buying Crystal Springs. Now she was positive that if Stephen had anything to do with it, Danny Bascombe would become the next Prime Minister.

Stephen suggested a quiet dinner at the Lobster Pot, a small restaurant located on Gibbs Beach. It was casual and served freshly caught lobster shipped in from St Vincent. They went, but neither of them was particularly hungry. They left most of their lobster and salad, returning home shortly after nine.

Victor handed Stephen a note from James on their return home. He opened it with trepidation, bursting into relieved laughter after he had read it.

'Lady Nugent-Scott has been up to her tricks again. The duty manager had to drag her off the dance-floor during the cabaret show. She was trying to limbo under a flaming pole stark naked – encouraged by that crazy drunken husband of hers as usual.

'James says the guests loved it and applauded her, whooping and whistling.'

Christina grinned. 'Just another day in paradise. That woman's seventy if she's a day. I wonder if she carries on like that in London?'

'I doubt it. She's probably lived such a repressed life she goes berserk when she comes out to the West Indies. You know as well as I do, Christina, Barbados has a way of doing strange things to people.'

'I remember when we first came here on honeymoon it

did wonderful things to you, Stephen. You couldn't keep your hands off me then.'

Candlelight flickered through the clear glass of a hurricane lamp, softly illuminating her face. He saw the naked longing in her amber eyes and realized for the first time how much he had been neglecting her.

He cupped her face in his hands.

'How could I forget?' He kissed her, and she thrilled to the familiar hunger in his embrace.

He loosened two buttons on the shoulders of her fine cotton-shift dress, which fluttered to the floor. She stepped out of it, naked save for a tiny pair of white lace panties so small that they exposed white patches of skin, luminous against her golden tan.

'Let's go down to the sea.' he urged.

They walked to the edge of the tranquil water where Christina wrapped her long, slim legs around him, and they made love with the warm Caribbean lapping over them. Afterwards he chased her back to the house, her screams of delighted laughter filling his ears.

Once there, still damp from the sea and glistening in the moonlight, she offered herself to him again. They made love on the cool marble floor of the terrace, and much later went to bed and slept in each other's arms for the first time in months.

'There's definitely something wrong. I can smell a rat.'

Christina looked over Stephen's shoulder at the accounts, spread across his desk.

'I don't understand. You say there are discrepancies in the reservations and room rates. How come?'

'Let me explain. At the beginning of last season we prepared our profit and loss accounts. I did the entire spread with Michael and the accountants. It was based on achieving a realistic occupancy target at rates that vary according to season. But according to these figures there's been some jiggery-pokery with the room rates. We've been selling our wholesaler shoulder rates when we could easily have achieved high-season. The same applies here – look.' He indicated a period at the end of April, beginning of May.

'For some reason rooms were discounted from low-season rate to the point where we were virtually giving them away in a definite shoulder season. We had 80 per cent occupancy over the entire year, yet we're about 25 per cent down on budget for those occupancy figures.'

He studied the list of figures, highlighting one in particular. 'You see this entry for $800,000 US? That's the gross amount received from Travel Enterprise in New York who operated all the conference reservations last year. It's at least 30 per cent down on anticipated revenue from conference lettings.'

Christina handed him a cup of coffee and sat down opposite. His face was a mask of concentration.

'I intend to find out just why we're selling room rates to Travel Enterprise for less than they are worth,' he said slowly. 'Michael will no doubt say he had to discount them out to achieve the occupancy in the shoulder period, but I don't know how he can explain doing the same in high season.'

Stephen pressed the intercom switch.

'Michael, can you come to my office immediately.' He paused. 'I don't care if the Prince of Wales is coming to see you! I want you here, right now.' He spoke to the financial controller too.

'Theo, can you come to my office straight away? Thanks.

'This may go on for some time, Christina, and could get very complicated. I'm sorry, I'll have to go through the refurbishing budgets with you later.'

Christina stood up. She was wearing a long white cotton skirt, flat shoes, and hand-knit cotton top in pale pink. He thought how fresh she looked.

'See you later, then. Call me when you get through; I'll be in my office.'

She met Michael outside Stephen's office. Six months after his leg had been broken, he still walked with a perceptible limp, and this morning he looked harassed.

'What can be so important that it couldn't wait? I've the head of the Board of Tourism coming to see me in five minutes.'

Christina shrugged. 'He's de boss man.'

Michael scowled and burst into Stephen's office without knocking.

Christina went to her own office, which was located on the first floor of the reception building. Though small, it had wonderful views across the gardens and fountain from a tall sash window which took up most of one wall.

The day was extremely hot with no breeze, and she was grateful for the air-conditioning.

She had bought a pretty pine desk, and had scoured the antique shops until she found the perfect eighteenth-century light-mahogany chair to go with it. The walls were covered in original pictures by several well-known Caribbean artists.

She insisted on fresh flowers every day placed next to a photograph of Stephen and herself at the opening night of Crystal Springs. She stared at it now, hardly able to believe that it was two and a half years since it had been taken. So much had happened since then. The hotel was now firmly established as a first-class resort destination. Fashion editors had used it as an exotic background to collections of fabulous clothes. Travel and feature writers from all over the world had stayed in Crystal Springs, going back to their desks to write for the most part glowing reports. It had been described as an exclusive enclave for the rich and privileged, an escapist's paradise, a tropical slice of heaven on earth . . . and so the praise went on.

Christina sighed, thinking of all the hard work and commitment, and the toll that building and operating Crystal Springs had taken on their marriage.

A knock on the door broke her reverie. It was Todney, Stephen's secretary, in her new uniform – a pale-blue sleeveless cotton seersucker dress with a wide, scooped neckline and crisp white collar. Stephen liked even the back-room staff to wear uniform, believing it gave them a more professional look and approach.

'You look lovely, Todney. I like the new uniform.'

The girl blushed and adjusted the collar of the dress slightly.

'I'm not sure about this.'

'It looks fine to me,' Christina said, dismissing the subject instantly. She knew from experience that if she started a conversation with the girls about anything other than business, it could go on for ever, and Christina did not have time to listen to Todney's domestic problems this morning.

'I'm busy making reservations for Mr Reece-Carlton's trip to Anguilla and St Maarten. I wondered if you could tell me how many nights he'll be staying in Anguilla? I've tried to speak to him but he's left strict instructions not to be disturbed.'

Christina flicked through her diary.

'He's going to Anguilla first. On the 18th, I believe. I know he has a meeting scheduled in St Maarten for the 20th, so I assume two nights will be fine. Make the reservation, Todney, and check back with him when he comes out of his meeting.'

'Thanks, Mrs Carlton. You know how Mr C. is. If I don't get it right.' The girl smiled nervously.

'I know, Todney, but you can always check with me first, and then you won't get it wrong,' Christina said, and smiled pleasantly, putting the young girl instantly at ease.

'I'll do that, Mrs C, I really will.'

When she had gone Christina thumbed through her diary, glancing at cancelled events and big gaps where Stephen had been away. So many nights when she had been left alone. Too many, she thought.

A pile of mail sat on her desk waiting to be opened. There were a couple of invoices for fabric, a request from a boutique in Bridgetown to stage a fashion show at the hotel, and an invitation from Martin Ward and his business partner, Bobby Stoute, to a cocktail party to launch their new sports superstore in Christchurch.

The invitation was for the 19th.

She was pleased that Martin was doing so well. When he had decided to stay in Barbados he had bought a tiny but pretty house in St Philip with his insurance money and savings, and opened a small shop selling surf-boards and scuba gear. He had rapidly expanded into importing sportswear and equipment from all over the world, and he and Bobby Stoute had enterprisingly approached several hotels on the island for sales outlets on their premises. They had not contacted Crystal Springs.

Christina hadn't seen Martin for about six months, since Stephen had made it plain how much he objected even to a friendship between them. It wasn't worth the arguments with her husband, she'd reasoned.

But this was different – a public event that would be attended by all the island big-wigs. It was perfectly natural that the Reece-Carltons, owners of the island's premier resort, should be invited to attend. And it was just bad luck that Stephen was scheduled to be away that night.

Christina pencilled the party into her diary. She was looking forward to it – and to seeing Martin again.

Chapter Twelve

A persistent ringing roused Christina from a pleasant dream. Half asleep, she fumbled for the instrument and dropped the receiver. A voice was speaking urgently: 'Hello? Hello, Christina?' as she retrieved it.

'Hello,' she said sleepily.

'Christina, this is Danny Bascombe. I need to speak to Stephen urgently.'

'I'm sorry, Danny, Stephen and James left very early this morning for Antigua to look at a site there. They'll be back late this evening. Anything I can do to help?'

She sat up, suppressing a yawn and rubbing her eyes.

'Is there any way I can contact Stephen?' He sounded worried.

'Is there something wrong, Danny?'

'I'm afraid so. Michael Stein has been arrested for possession of drugs. He's to appear before the magistrates today.'

Christina sat bolt upright, fully awake now.

'When did this happen?'

'In the early hours of this morning. Apparently they found cocaine hidden in his mattress.'

She gasped and slid out of bed.

'Where is he now?'

'In custody, in Glendairy Prison.'

'Oh, shit, Danny. Have you any idea what will happen to him?'

'In the worst scenario, he'll be sentenced to stand trial

and could go to jail. If he pleads guilty and begs for the mercy of the court, he may get off with a fine and deportation. I intend to advise him to plead guilty, yet he swears he's innocent.'

Christina was already thinking about who she could ring who could contact Stephen. They knew several people who lived in Antigua.

'I'll try and get a message to him, Danny; leave it with me. I'll get back to you as soon as I can.'

'I'm in court this morning, so leave a message with my secretary. Also, I'd make arrangements with your assistant manager to cover for Michael long-term. One thing's certain; he won't be returning to Crystal Springs. Ever.'

Christina replaced the telephone, deep in thought. She recalled her first meeting with Michael Stein, when he had admitted to possessing drugs in the Far East. How stupid to jeopardize his career again.

The next hour was taken up with rearranging assistant and duty managers' rotas and trying without success to locate Stephen, who was looking at a remote beach-front site miles from English Harbour, where the estate agents were located. Danny called her at two that afternoon.

'Michael Stein pleaded guilty and has been fined 2000 Barbados dollars. He's to be deported tonight on the British Airways flight to London. He's asked if you could pack some things from his house and bring the suitcase down to Immigration at Grantley Adams Airport at 7.30 this evening.'

'Of course. Tell him I'll be there.'

'Thanks, Christina. Sorry to be the bearer of such bad tidings, but these things happen. There are other managers. I'm sure Stephen will find someone very quickly.'

'Yes, I'm sure he will.'

'Oh, by the way, tell him I'll be free for the meeting on Tuesday of next week and that I'm looking forward to it.'

'Will do, Danny. Thanks for all your help.'

Christina located Norica Cummings, the housekeeper, who let her into the house within the hotel grounds that Michael Stein had occupied. Together they packed his clothes and personal belongings into one large suitcase and a leather grip.

Christina left Stephen a message before driving out to the airport to make her delivery. The roads were busy. The journey took her over an hour, and it was another fifteen minutes before she found where Michael was being held. No one seemed to have any idea. She eventually located an Immigration officer who led her through several corridors until they reached a locked red-painted door at the back of the airport building.

The hollow sounds of doors banging and footsteps receding echoed in her ears as she stepped inside the sparsely furnished room. There was one chair and a narrow desk riddled with graffiti and burn marks. A dishevelled Michael Stein was leaning against a faded sign scribbled on the peeling wall. It read:

Never trouble trouble till trouble trouble you
Trouble tree don't bear no blossom

Christina smiled at the irony of the old West Indian proverb.

'I'm glad to see someone's happy.' He was unshaven, and dark shadows ringed his eyes.

'I'm really sorry about what's happened, Michael.'

Christina kept her voice low, glancing at the glass partition to the right of where he stood. There was supposed to be someone guarding the prisoner, but she couldn't see anyone.

'Your husband wanted rid of me – it's that simple, Christina. My time here was up, so he made sure I got a one-way ticket out.'

She looked shocked and opened her mouth to protest. 'Stephen would never . . .'

He held up his hand, his grey eyes full of contempt. 'Please, Christina, spare me the innocent, unsuspecting wife act. I really don't have the stomach for it. You must know you're married to a crook.'

'I think I'd better go, Michael.'

'I think so too.' He lit a cigarette and blew smoke in her direction. Her throat dried. Suddenly gripped by a feeling of panic, she wanted to run out of the small room.

'Will you give Stephen a message from me?'

She nodded silently.

'Tell him to go fuck himself!'

The vituperative tone of voice was like a whiplash. Christina backed away from Michael, whose handsome face was twisted and distorted by hatred.

He didn't move. He dragged on his cigarette in a languid fashion, letting the smoke curl slowly from his mouth as he added slowly, 'Tell Stephen I'm a patient man with a long memory. You see, revenge, dearest Christina, is the sweetest taste of all.'

She rang a bell to be let out again and left him without a backward glance. When she reached the car, she realized she was shaking. She had barely recognized their cool, urbane general manager in the seedy, vengeful man who had made such wild accusations. There couldn't be any truth in them, she told herself. Stephen would never do anything mean or underhand.

'Mr Reece-Carlton is home, mistress,' Victor told her when she reached Crystal Springs House. She breathed a sigh of relief, and ran through to the living-room where she could hear Stephen's voice.

He was talking to James, and stopped abruptly when she came into the room. He jumped up and kissed her on the cheek.

Holding her at arm's length, he said, 'You look terrible, Christina. Whatever is the matter?'

'I've just been with Michael Stein in Immigration. You know he's been deported, I suppose?'

'Yes, Danny just called me. I'm not too surprised. After all, Michael has been involved with drugs before.'

Stephen seemed unperturbed, and she felt stupid for allowing the scene at the airport to upset her so much. 'A brandy for my wife,' Stephen called to Victor. 'Come and sit down, Christina. You're shaking. Tell me what's wrong.'

He led her gently to the sofa and sat down with her, holding her hand.

'I had to take Michael's stuff out to the airport. It upset me, that's all. Forget it, I'm all right now.' The butler came in and handed her a glass of cognac. She took a couple of sips.

'What did he say, Chrissy? If that bastard upset you, I'll go after him personally!'

'I don't want to talk about it at the moment, Stephen, if you don't mind.' She gave James a sidelong glance. Stephen got the message and indicated with his eyes for James to leave.

'I think we can finish this tomorrow in the office.' Both men stood up.

'That's fine with me, Stephen. I'm dog-tired.'

'You did a good job today. Nice work, James.'

'No problem, Stephen. I can quite honestly say it was a pleasure.'

Both men smiled and said their goodbyes. Stephen rejoined Christina on the sofa. She was already feeling the restorative effects of the brandy. He put his arm around her shoulders affectionately and stroked the back of her neck, running his fingers through her long hair.

'Feeling better, baby?'

'A little.'

'Why don't I take you out for a nice dinner this evening? How about your favourite, Mario's?'

'I'm not hungry, Stephen.' She leaned back in the sofa, studying his face.

'You seem very unconcerned about losing Michael. Aren't you worried the press will have a field-day with this one?'

'The press will never know; James is sorting that out. Several people have been whispering in my ear lately about Michael's drug-taking; I knew it would come to a head sooner or later.'

'Would James have been one of those people, by any chance?' Christina watched him closely.

'I rely on him for information. I'd never find out about a lot of things that go on at the hotel without him around. I know you don't like him, but he has his uses.'

'I can't stand him! He's always sneaking around, just where you least expect to find him.'

'We're not running a kiddies' tea party here, Christina. There are always enemies in the camp, and by sheer luck we've managed to get rid of one.'

'What do you mean, enemies?'

'Michael was cooking the books. He was selling Gary Druer from Travel Enterprise rooms at rock-bottom rates, and Gary was retailing them to the client for top whack, trading on our reputation. He and Michael were splitting the profits.'

'Did he admit that?'

Stephen shook his head.

'No, he hotly denied it, but he would, wouldn't he? It was all there in black and white. Michael had a nice fiddle going, and he's been at it for over a year now. He'll have a healthy bank account somewhere, full of our money.'

Christina suddenly felt very tired and completely disillusioned. It had been a long day.

'Michael was in a vicious mood at the airport. He intimated that you had him framed.'

'You don't honestly believe I'd do anything like that, do you, Chrissy?'

She shook her head, as if to shake away the doubts. 'No, it was just something Michael said . . .'

'What?'

'He said to tell you he was a patient man with a long memory, and that revenge is the sweetest taste of all.'

Stephen laughed.

'Well, I hope it sustains him on his long journey into obscurity, because I intend to make sure Michael Stein never works in the travel industry again.'

Stephen called all the heads of departments to a meeting the following morning, informing them of Michael's departure and the appointment of James Morris as acting general manager. He stressed that this would be temporary whilst he looked for a replacement.

Christina knew nothing of this decision until she overheard Peter Thomas, the duty manager, chatting to the food and beverage executive later that morning.

'I don't know how long I'll last here with Mr Morris as general manager.'

She thought she was hearing things, and was about to track down Stephen to confirm the appointment when Edward Harrington, his half-brother, walked into reception. She was stunned. Stephen had not mentioned he was coming to Barbados.

Christina approached him at the reception desk where he stood.

'Mr Edward Harrington, I believe?'

'Yes, I am, and to what do I owe this pleasure?'

He was wearing a floral shirt, tucked into tight jeans. The zip gaped open an inch at his waist, which was cinched in far too tightly by a fake crocodile belt. He carried a man's handbag in burgundy leather, and wore flat slip-on sandals with no socks.

'I'm Christina Reece-Carlton, Stephen's wife.' She smiled at him. 'Welcome to Crystal Springs. Stephen didn't tell me you were coming.'

'No, darling, he has no idea. I didn't know myself until yesterday. There was no time to contact him, so I came on the off-chance. I'm so pleased he's here.'

'You're lucky to catch him. He's away such a lot these days, trying to develop more hotels.'

'He's a little beaver is our Stephen. Always was, always will be.'

She noticed the way he looked constantly about him, observing the marble-floored entrance hall, the smartly uniformed staff, and the guests in their casual resort-wear and serious jewellery.

Christina asked the receptionist to ring upstairs to Stephen's office. Edward placed a hand on her arm.

'Don't tell him I'm here. It will be a wonderful surprise.'

Christina wasn't sure her husband would agree. Edward grinned, showing lots of gum and small, slanting teeth. The receptionist informed them that Mr Reece-Carlton was in his office on the telephone.

'Come on then, Edward, I'll show you the way. Then I can share the wonderful surprise as well.'

'I'm in your hands, Christina. What a surprise he's going to get.' The sunlight from an open window shone into his eyes, and she noticed that they were exactly the same shade of green as Stephen's, and just as opaque.

She burst into her husband's office saying: 'Surprise, surprise. Look who's come to see you.'

Edward was standing behind her. As he stepped to one side, Christina had a clear view of Stephen's face in an unguarded moment. A look of complete shock registered first, closely followed by raw anger.

'Stephen, don't tell me you're not pleased to see your big brother. Shame on you.' Edward chuckled. He didn't seem in the least put-out by the hostile reception.

Stephen ignored him and turned to Christina. She felt suddenly uncomfortable, unsure of what she should do or say next.

'Would you mind leaving us, Christina? I have some family matters I'd like to discuss with Edward alone.'

'Of course, Stephen.' She took a step back and said, 'I'll see you later, Edward.'

'If I have anything to do with it, fair lady, you most certainly will.' He lifted her hand and kissed it. '*Au revoir*.'

She grinned and left the two men alone. James came running up the stairs as she came out of the office. He leaned against the wall, his doughy face sweating profusely.

'Where to in such a hurry, Mr Morris, our new general manager?'

'A temporary position, Christina.' He flicked a tiny piece of cotton off the sleeve of her dress. She recoiled. She could see by his self-satisfied expression that he intended to make himself a fixture, and somehow, despite her friendship with Elaine, the thought of having to work closely with James on a day-to-day basis made Christina's flesh crawl.

'I must see Stephen. It's urgent,' he said.

'Everybody's always racing around this hotel wanting to see Stephen urgently! He's with his half-brother Edward, and I don't think he wants to be disturbed.'

She automatically crossed her arms across her chest, a habit she had adopted whenever she spoke to James. Too often she had caught him looking at her breasts.

'I didn't know he had a half-brother.'

'Well, between you and me, I think he'd rather forget about Edward. I think he's a bit of an embarrassment to the family.'

James poked his head around the door of the office adjacent to Stephen's.

'Where's Todney?'

Christina looked at her watch. 'I think she's usually at lunch from twelve till one.'

'Well, I've a few notes to make. I'll sit in her office and maybe catch Stephen when he finishes.'

Christina left him in Todney's office with a gnawing suspicion that he was up to something. He was obviously curious to see Stephen's relative, and she mentally chided herself for revealing the state of things between Stephen and his half-brother. It really was none of James Morris's business.

That evening she expected Edward to join them for dinner at the house. Stephen made lame excuses, saying Edward was jet-lagged and preferred to stay in his room. Christina saw Edward about the hotel for the next few days. He was always friendly enough, but seemed fully occupied with the bevy of young beach-boys who seemed to swarm around him. Christina decided he looked happy enough and left him to enjoy himself. It was not until she noticed a bill on Todney's desk, to be authorized by Stephen as complimentary, that she knew his half-brother had checked out of the hotel without so much as saying goodbye to her.

When she thought about it later, something about the visit left her feeling uneasy. Why did Stephen have to be so secretive and aloof in his dealings with all his family, with the exception of Victoria?

Christina recognized the American couple taking photographs next to the fountain as she and Stephen walked back to their offices after lunch. She had seen them around the hotel for the last five days.

The blonde woman was always elegantly dressed and absolutely immaculate, even when she came off the beach, her hair neatly pinned up in a French pleat or out of sight under a chic floppy straw hat.

The man was tall and thick-set, with swarthy skin tanned to a deep brown. He had thick black hair and clear, penetrating navy-blue eyes. Today he wore fashionable baggy Italian shorts in a khaki colour and a white short-sleeved cotton shirt.

Christina thought he had attractive Latin looks. He was obviously besotted with his wife and was constantly photographing her. Christina guessed they were on honeymoon.

The blonde struck a pose and fixed a tight smile on her immaculately made-up face. The man continued clicking his camera. Stephen looked at him to see if it was convenient to pass.

'We don't want to spoil your picture,' he joked.

The man smiled, revealing perfect white teeth.

'If you don't mind, I'm sure Susanna would love a shot with the owner of the hotel.'

She patted the place next to her on the lip of the stone fountain.

'That would please me very much.' It was said in such a way that it was difficult to refuse, and Stephen felt obliged to sit next to her, smiling awkwardly into the camera, whilst Christina looked on, unable to prevent a suspicion that the whole scene had been orchestrated by the two Americans.

'Hold it right there – that's great.' The camera clicked several times.

'Thank you so much, Mr Reece-Carlton.' He held out his hand. 'Antonio Lorenzo Cellini.' Again the brilliant smile.

His wife held out her own slim, manicured hand.

'Susanna Cellini – so pleased to meet you. I must say your hotel is wonderful. I can't remember ever feeling so relaxed.'

'You're on honeymoon, baby. You're supposed to feel relaxed.'

Susanna's thin mouth parted slightly, and she ran her tongue over glossy red lips.

'I really didn't want to come here; I've had some awful experiences in the Caribbean.'

Christina cringed as Susanna pronounced it the American way.

'You know – bad service, animosity.' She lowered her voice. 'In Jamaica once I really feared for my life.'

'We have very little trouble like that here. Barbadians are a warm, hospitable people,' Christina said.

'My wife, Christina.' Stephen introduced her. The Cellinis both nodded and smiled.

'I persuaded Susanna to come here. It was the best wedding present I could have given her.'

Antonio slipped a muscular arm around his wife's waist. Christina saw her stiffen and after a moment step away.

'I'm delighted you're enjoying Crystal Springs. We're always pleased to hear good reports.'

Antonio said quickly: 'Are there any bad ones?'

'Well, you know the saying: "You can't please all of the people all of the time, just some of the people some of the time." We strive to please some of the people all of the time.'

Stephen bestowed on them his best hospitality smile. Desperate to escape the clientspeak, Christina said, 'I've a meeting in ten minutes, so I must dash.'

Thankfully, Stephen took her cue.

'Yes, we must get back to the office. Nice to have met you both.'

'Before you dash off, we'd love to invite you both out to dinner.'

Christina groaned inwardly, dreading another boring evening with people they had nothing in common with. She hoped Stephen would refuse.

'We're really very busy at the moment, but give me a

ring tomorrow in my office and we'll try and make a date,'
he said feebly, hoping his lack of enthusiasm might act as
a deterrent.

Antonio Cellini would not be put off so easily. He
seemed determined to ingratiate himself with Stephen.

'I'm sure you can manage one evening; if not for dinner,
then drinks. Or lunch even.' He raised his eyebrows. 'You
can't tell me you're constantly busy?'

'Well, not exactly.' Stephen hesitated, and Christina
thought how pushy Cellini was.

'I'll call you tomorrow and hopefully get to see you in
your office. If that's okay with you, Stephen? I have
a very exciting proposition that might be of interest to
you.'

Stephen's ears pricked at the mention of business.
Antonio fished in his back pocket and handed him a card.
Stephen read it, noticing the address in midtown Man-
hattan.

'Do you ever get up to New York?' asked Antonio.

'Occasionally, but every time I go it's either too hot or
too bloody cold.'

Susanna adjusted her tortoiseshell-framed sunglasses.
'You must come up in the fall; it's beautiful. I lived in
New England before we were married, and in September
and October it's just divine.'

Christina disliked her nasal drawl, and said for the final
time, 'Well, nice to have met you both. I really must go
now.'

'Me too,' Stephen added.

Antonio held out his hand.

'I think you've done a great job here. And don't forget
– I'd like to come and talk to you soon.'

Stephen shook the strong, powerful hand which gripped
his firmly. 'Call me tomorrow, okay?'

'You're on, Steve,' said Antonio, and turned back to
Susanna, a satisfied smile on his handsome face.

'Don't invite them to dinner, Stephen,' said Christina when he caught up with her. 'I warn you, if you do I'll never forgive you.'

The butler walked into the garden where Christina was reading in the shade of a white tulip tree.

'Mistress, sorry to disturb you, but Mr C. is on the phone for you.'

She didn't look up from her book. 'Ask him if I can call him back. This is a really exciting bit.'

'He say it important, mistress.' Victor had no intention of telling the boss-man his wife wouldn't speak to him.

She sighed and dropped her book, exasperated.

It was cool in the circular coral-stone study overlooking the courtyard. She idly watched a tame yellow warbler hopping back and forth across the window sill as Victor put the call through. She heard the excitement in Stephen's voice as soon as he began to speak.

'I can't believe it, Chrissy! You know that American guy Antonio we met yesterday? He's just left my office after discussing investing in the Bahamas site. I've given him all the figures. He's taken them away, promising to get back to me in a couple of days. You realize what this means? If I can get this equity investment, I'm on my way to my next hotel. And I can buy back Robert's 25 per cent of this place – you know I don't like him having a foot in the door here.'

'That's fantastic.' She tried to sound enthusiastic.

'You don't sound very excited, Chrissy?'

'It's just that you've been close so many times in the past and the deal has fallen through. And Robert isn't so bad, is he? He's looking after the UK end and there are worse people to be in partnership with.'

'Yeah, you're right, I suppose. Cellini may not be able to come up with the goods. Who knows? No deal is certain until the signatures are on the dotted line and the money comes through. Anyway, I've invited them for dinner this evening, if that's okay?'

She groaned.

'Stephen, we promised to go to Danny and Pauline's for drinks and then on to the Bagatelle.'

'I know, but I've called Danny and he understands. Come on, Christina, this is very important to me.'

She ached to remind him of all the wasted evenings with prospective investors: the long, boring meals with pompous bankers and their dull, provincial wives.

'It always important to you, Stephen. All you think about is bloody business and I'm sick of it.'

Silence followed. She could hear him take a deep breath.

'I'm not in business for the good of my health. You knew how I was when you married me, and everything I do is as much for you as for me. Come on, Chrissy, we're a team.'

'Are we, Stephen? I used to believe that, but I'm not so sure any more.' She bit the side of her lip, something she did unconsciously when she was upset or nervous.

'I don't know how you can say that, Christina. I share everything with you.'

'Do you? I wonder sometimes. Anyway, this is neither the time nor the place to discuss it. What time for dinner?'

'That's my girl. About seven for drinks, and 7.30 for dinner. Apparently Susanna likes to eat early.'

'That's fine. I'll organize it now. Anything you fancy in particular?'

'I'll leave it to you.'

'Okay, Stephen. See you later.' Her voice was flat.

'Chrissy, I do love you, you must never doubt that.'

'I love you too, Stephen,' she said, tempted to add: But I need more of you. I'm sick to death of sharing you with your business.

It would have to wait for a more opportune time, she

decided, and replaced the receiver. A cool breeze drifted through the open window, carrying with it the sound of water trickling softly from the old stone fountain they'd painstakingly renovated in the inner courtyard.

Her mind drifted back to the first day they'd seen Crystal Springs. It seemed a lifetime away.

The dinner table was laden with Baccarat crystal and freshly polished silver. In the centre of the table a huge Lalique vase held Christina's favourite flowers, the pale-lemon cup of gold. She watched Victor place two tall, white, tapered candles under delicate, hand-cut, antique glass hurricane covers, and carefully fold starched Irish linen napkins monogrammed with the initials C.S.

It was 6.30, and Christina was putting tiny pink and white sugared almonds into a glass bowl when Stephen walked along the covered terrace from the dining pagoda.

He didn't even say hello, merely demanded, 'Give Victor a shout, Christina. I could use a strong vodka and tonic.'

'Yessir.' Standing to attention, she gave him a mock salute. It was done to antagonize, not to amuse.

He frowned. 'What's wrong with you these days, Chrissy?'

'So you've noticed, at long last?' Stephen looked mystified as she went on, 'When was the last time you really listened to anything I had to say unless it was about business? When, Stephen?'

'I try to make time, Chrissy, I really do, but there's never enough.'

'That's the trouble. You don't have enough time for me any more. You can't fit me into your busy schedule. I've forgotten the last time we really enjoyed ourselves together and sat down to a meal uninterrupted by telephone calls.'

She looked away, afraid she was going to break down.

'Come on, Christina, it's not that bad.' Stephen reached out to touch her, a question in his eyes. 'Is it?'

She turned away as Victor announced the arrival of their guests. They both greeted the Cellinis with practised charm and ease.

Antonio looked fit and handsome. He had acquired a deep mahogany tan which accentuated his deep-blue eyes.

Susanna wore a black silk strapless dress. Her narrow shoulders and long, slim neck had barely seen the sun, and gleamed white and translucent against the dark fabric; her small-featured, impassive face was made up to salon standard.

Antonio smelt of lemons mixed with spice when he leaned forward and kissed Christina's cheek. Susanna held out a thin, freckled hand, and parted heavily glossed lips in what Christina assumed to be a smile.

'You've got a real nice place here,' Antonio commented appreciatively, nodding his head in approval. 'Mmmm, real nice.'

'Thank you.' Stephen accepted the compliment and led them out onto the terrace, asking as he did so, 'What would you like to drink?'

'I'll have champagne. That's if you've got Premier Jouet pink or Cristal?' Susanna was quietly assertive. 'Otherwise I'm happy with dry white wine.'

'Any preference in that direction?' Christina asked pointedly. They were entertaining in their own home, not a restaurant.

'Only the best for the little lady.' Antonio glanced with pride at his wife, who was flicking her long, straight blonde hair over her shoulder.

Victor served ice-cold Cristal from a silver Georgian cooler, and for once Christina felt a thrill of pride in her possessions. Not that Susanna Cellini – or Belford-Cellini as she apparently preferred to be known – would be impressed, but neither could she be disparaging.

They sat in high-backed cane chairs on the terrace overlooking the sea. The horizon was a dark terracotta colour, the top of the dying sun just visible for a few seconds before it dropped out of sight and the sky doused the remaining light like a heavy black blanket.

'This is the most amazing place,' Susanna said, accepting her glass of champagne from Victor's outstretched hand. 'Just the most wonderful hotel I've ever stayed in.'

'And she's been to the best,' Antonio chipped in.

'In fact, I can't wait to return.'

This produced an answering smile from her husband.

'Whenever you want, honey, just say the word.'

Antonio winked in Stephen's direction. 'Do you mind if I look over the place? I'm fascinated by the architecture.' His ebullient enthusiasm won Stephen over.

'I'd be delighted to show you around.'

'Susanna, want a peek?' Antonio asked.

'I'm fine, Toni.' She gestured for him to go with an indifferent wave of her hand. She had seen and lived in lots of houses far superior to this one, it implied. 'I'll stay and chat to Christina.'

'So when do you go back to New York?' Christina feigned interest.

'Oh, don't remind me.' Susanna pulled a long face. 'Four days' time, and I've got a big charity function to attend the night I get back. It's going to be such a rush, I can't tell you. I'll have to get Roberto, my hairdresser, and his manicurist to virtually meet me off the plane.'

She laughed, a tinny, hollow sound.

Christina took a big gulp of champagne, and wondered what on earth she was going to find to talk about all evening with this woman.

She needn't have worried.

Antonio and Stephen dominated the conversation while they all ate delicious avocado and salmon mousse, fresh dolphin in lime sauce, and mango crêpes.

267

'What kind of fish is this?' Susanna examined the moist white fish with her fork.

'It's dolphin, but not of the flipper variety,' Christina replied. 'It looks exactly like a dolphin, with a flat head and smooth black skin – hence the name.' Christina noticed that Susanna played with her food, moving it around the plate before leaving most of it.

Afterwards they drank coffee on the terrace, Antonio admiring the garden and pointing out to Susanna a cannonball tree, its cream- and pink-coloured blossoms softly illuminated in the light from a carefully concealed spotlight.

Christina was tired, and felt relieved when at 10.30 the Cellinis decided to leave.

'We get so very tired here in the islands.' Susanna faked a yawn.

'She gets tired. I'm raring to go as soon as we get to bed.' Antonio pinched Susanna on her bony backside. She grimaced.

'It's the island air, Toni, it exhausts me.'

'Well, exhausted or not, you won't be getting much sleep for the next four days. Come on, baby, like I keep telling you, it's our honeymoon.'

She squealed, protesting as he bear-hugged her, ruffling the perfectly set hair and smudging her red lipstick.

'Antonio, for goodness' sake, control yourself. You've obviously had too much to drink again.' She pushed him away, smoothing her dress with short, irritated movements.

'She loves it, really,' Antonio hissed behind his hand. Christina suspected he was a little drunk.

'We've had a great evening. Thanks very much, both of you. Great food, Chrissy, you really can cook.'

'I doubt whether Christina did the cooking, darling,' Susanna drawled.

'As a matter of fact, I did do some. Stephen prefers my

268

cooking, so for dinner parties I always go to the kitchen and help. It's not a chore, I really enjoy it.'

She smiled as sweetly as she could.

'The only thing Susanna can make for dinner is a reservation!'

Antonio roared at his own humour, joined by Christina and Stephen, while his wife stood silent. Christina noticed her face, and thought it was time for goodnights, before Antonio added something he might really be sorry for. She secretly nudged Stephen, who said, 'Well, I'm dead beat. Bed beckons. It was our pleasure seeing you this evening.'

'Yes, lovely to have met you both. Enjoy the rest of your stay,' Christina added.

'Thank you for a wonderful evening. I'm sorry about Antonio's behaviour, but he's always like this when he's had a couple of drinks.'

'Don't apologize; he's only having fun.' Christina winked at him. Antonio returned it with a broad smile.

'Goodnight, and thanks again.' He took his wife's hand, and they walked off, lost within seconds in the velvet darkness.

Propped up in bed ten minutes later, Stephen said, 'So what do you think of Antonio?'

Christina had anticipated this question. The Cellinis had been invited partly for her scrutiny. Stephen had often told her he respected her judgement.

'I think he's a tough, shrewd character who desperately wants to buy prestige. He's married to someone so socially and culturally removed from him she might as well be a foreigner.'

'You're right, Christina. They're from totally opposite sides of the tracks. She's old money and as snooty as they come, while he's the typical self-made second-generation Italian who wants to buy himself a piece of class.'

269

Christina wriggled her toes and found Stephen's feet with her own.

'He appears to have lots of money – probably why Susanna married him. I think he sees in you and the hotel industry the opportunity to be part of a glamorous, high-profile business, and one his hard-faced wife would approve of. I'd imagine his taste and originality are in his backside.'

'Who cares? I need his money, nothing more.'

'Now it's my turn for question-time.' Christina looked straight ahead. 'What do you think of a man who neglects his wife?'

Stephen had drunk a lot of champagne, and red wine. He felt expansive and full of well-being. The last thing he wanted was an argument.

'I think a man who neglects his wife should be given lots of lashes, man.'

'I'm not joking, Stephen.'

'Okay, Chrissy, I'm sorry.' He stroked her arm. 'I know I don't give you enough of my time, but you get all I've got to give, if that's any consolation.'

Her voice was shaking a little as she put the important question to him.

'And what if it's not enough?'

Stephen broke the silence after minutes that felt like an hour.

'Okay, Chrissy, you asked for it.' He grabbed her and pulled her close. 'I love my business, I love the hotel, and I love you. That's it. There's no more.'

'In that order?' she challenged.

He didn't rise to it; simply carried on with what he had to say.

'If you think I'm going to make huge sacrifices for you, forget it, Christina. I married you thinking you were like me. I can't stand the demands you make on me sometimes.'

His words stung. She pushed him away from her.

'I'm sorry, Christina, but that's the way it is.'

She wanted to say that she was sorry too, but tears choked her and she was unable to speak.

Chapter Thirteen

The following morning, Stephen awoke with Antonio Cellini on his mind. He couldn't ignore his gut instinct, which had never failed him yet.

He felt sure he could sweet-talk Antonio and get the 25 per cent equity he needed to put the new deal to bed. It was the biggest of his life. Just thinking about it aroused such passion in him it was scary: $75 million from the bank, $25 million from Antonio, and he, Stephen Reece-Carlton, could develop his own small island in the Bahamas, with a marina, golf course and casino.

As he showered and got dressed, he wondered what Antonio Cellini would want in return for his equity investment. Somehow Stephen had a sneaking suspicion that the American would be no pushover.

Susanna Cellini was looking in the window of the ladies' boutique when Stephen and Christina walked through the lobby just after noon. She waved to them, and they strolled across the white marble floor to join her.

Antonio appeared from the shop a moment later, carrying a small package which he presented to his wife.

Susanna thanked him sweetly, standing on tiptoe to plant a kiss on his forehead.

'You deserve it. You've put up with me for the last ten days.'

Antonio turned his attention to Stephen and Christina. 'So glad you could make lunch today.'

'We're on the Pan Am flight this afternoon,' Susanna explained, and pulled a long face.

'All good things have got to come to an end,' said Stephen.

'But why, that's what I want to know,' Susanna wailed. She was dressed in navy and white, her ivory skin slightly tanned and for once minus make-up. Her long, straight hair was tied back in a bow, and she looked younger and more approachable.

'You look great, Susanna.' Stephen's compliment was genuine.

She thanked him and smiled, delighted.

'It's this place. I've had the vacation of a lifetime. Crystal Springs is going to be *the* resort name on the tip of every socialite tongue from Boston to New York this winter, I'll make sure of that.'

'Want a job in PR, Mrs Cellini?' Christina joked, before Stephen guided them out of the lobby and down a path past a row of mahogany trees separated by bright thickets of hibiscus.

'Your gardens are stunning, Stephen. You could charge to come round here,' Antonio commented.

'I've got a man called Roberto Sabortini to thank for that. He's a Brazilian, and designs landscape with such an eye you'd swear Mother Nature was his partner.'

The Golden Palm restaurant was quiet, and they were shown to Stephen's own table. This particular part of the hotel never failed to delight him. It was in his opinion a piece of architectural magic, suspended twenty feet above sea level. Clusters of tall, willowy bamboos rose out of ten pale-pink marble planters and almost touched the high triple-domed ceiling. Six wide archways opened on to the sea, affording all diners uninterrupted views of the shimmering Caribbean and the powder beach below.

'Oh, look at that beautiful bird!' Susanna pointed to their left, and they all watched a humming-bird perform fluttering water sports in the spray from a sixteenth-century fountain almost hidden in a discreet courtyard setting of creeping plants and old hand-painted tiles – the kind of secret place usually found behind old stone walls in Florence or Seville.

Stephen and Susanna ordered lobster salad, Christina a club sandwich, and Antonio his last cheeseburger. 'I reckon it's the best burger I've ever had outside the US.'

'You shouldn't be eating them at all. You've put weight on in the last ten days.' Susanna nipped the side of his stomach.

Antonio chuckled and addressed Stephen. 'We've had an amazing vacation. I won't bore you with all the usual shit that you must hear every day of the week . . . how absolutely wonderful it all is, blah blah blah, and the clichéd "Any time you're in New York" line.'

The food arrived, halting the conversation. Antonio devoured half of his burger in one bite, whilst Susanna took a tiny morsel of lobster.

'This is delicious.' She chewed slowly. 'Are the lobsters local?'

'We import them from St Vincent,' Stephen said. 'They're good, but not quite up to Maine standard.'

'Well, Antonio, have you thought any more about the deal I've offered?'

The American tried hard to look non-committal, but Stephen could detect the thread of eagerness underlying his words.

'Well, I'm interested . . .'

Antonio laced more ketchup onto the remaining burger and picked up a French fry.

'I want to talk, money talk, and I'd like you to come up to New York next week to meet with my financial boys, if that's okay with you?'

It was in the bag. He had his finance, he could feel it.

'That's great, just great.' Stephen beamed, unable to disguise his own delight.

Antonio put out his hand, 'My town, next week it is, then . . . partner.'

Christina felt guilty. It was weeks since she'd seen Elaine, and she hadn't even asked her how she felt about James being given the general managership, albeit only temporarily as yet. She knew it would keep him away from home even more than usual, and wondered what Elaine thought about that. If her affair with Sebastian Aguilar was still going on, presumably she'd be delighted.

She rang her friend and arranged to meet her early that evening.

The Reef Bar was packed when Christina arrived at ten past six. She saw Elaine as soon as she walked up the planked wooden steps to the bar, and noticed as she drew closer that her friend was already tipsy. She had an unkempt air about her, too. Her blonde hair looked unbrushed, and she was wearing a scruffy old T-shirt and a sarong skirt patterned with an hibiscus print.

'Hi, Chris,' Elaine slurred, and patted a bar stool next to hers. 'What do you want to drink?' She gave an unfocused grin.

'I'll have a lime-squash sour – no syrup, thanks,' Christina ordered, and climbed onto the stool. She turned to her friend. 'So how are you? Haven't seen you around for a while.' Elaine looked down at her glass of rum and ginger, frowning. Something serious was coming, Christina could sense it.

'I'm pregnant, Chrissy – about two months.' Christina took Elaine's hand in hers. She ignored the curious stares directed at them.

'Is that all? Having a baby isn't so bad, you know.'

Elaine seized her wrist. 'You've got to help me, Christina. I'm desperate.' Her eyes were wide and panic-

275

stricken. It was obvious she'd reached breaking-point.

Christina ordered two more rums – she could see they were going to need them – and asked the bartender if they could go somewhere quieter. He carried two chairs and a table over to a dark corner where they could talk more freely.

'I'm in a bit of a mess,' Elaine sighed, calmer now. 'I'm sorry to dump all this on you, Chris, but there was no one else I could turn to. I had the result this afternoon, but I've known for a few weeks, really. Oh, God, how bloody stupid can you get?'

'Calm down,' Christina told her, trying to disguise her own shock and concern. 'I take it all this is because James is not the father?'

'Him?' Elaine's pretty face twisted in contempt. 'He hasn't been near me in months. It's not *me* he's interested in.

'On the rare occasion he bothers to leave that damn hotel – sorry, but you know what I mean – he just wants to drink himself into a stupor. If he hadn't been such a lousy husband I might not have got myself in so deep . . .'

'Deep into what?' Christina probed, certain now that Elaine was worried about more than just impending motherhood.

She looked down at the table-top, her expression a curious mixture of pride and shame. 'You know about Sebastian, and you must have guessed it was pretty serious between us to have lasted more than two years. To begin with I got such a kick from it all. I never knew in advance when the next meeting would be. He always says he's a busy man, unable to predict his schedule, but really it's all part of the game.'

She twisted her hands fiercely.

'All part of what game?' Christina looked puzzled.

'Oh, Chris, you're such an innocent. Married to the first man who asked you, and I bet you've never even thought

276

of being unfaithful, even with that hunk Martin hanging around.'

'I couldn't do that to Stephen,' she said, uneasily conscious that Elaine had too high an opinion of her. She'd definitely thought about Martin, wondered what it would be like . . .

She forced her thoughts back to Elaine, who was carrying on with her story.

'. . . and it was so *exciting*, like something you read about, you know, but you never dream it could happen to you. I'd get a phone call from his secretary and then a limousine would be waiting for me down the lane. Sebastian's driver would deliver me to him. At first we'd meet in hotels. All sorts of people owe him favours, you'd be surprised. But it all got too public. There were times when we needed more privacy . . .'

'I should think there were! You're a married woman, Elaine, and Sebastian's very well known – a friend of the PM's. It all sounds pretty dangerous to me.'

Elaine lowered her eyes. 'I don't mean just covering our tracks, though we have to do that of course. It was what he was doing to me – what we were doing together.'

Christina's mouth felt dry. She remembered her friend saying something on the phone: 'It gets a bit rough' . . . something like that.

'Go on.'

'Sebastian believes in living life to the full. Just having sex isn't enough for him. He thinks you can only appreciate its full pleasure after feeling pain.'

Christina felt more and more uncomfortable. What Elaine was saying was bizarre, out of her experience.

'He sounds a real bully to me,' she said.

'You still don't understand,' her friend replied sadly. 'Oh, sometimes it goes too far – although I've always said he mustn't leave any marks that are too obvious. James

277

may be a drunken sod, but he's not a stupid one!'

'But Sebastian isn't a monster, please don't think that. He hasn't done anything to me that I didn't agree to . . want. Enjoy, even.'

'I don't believe it,' Christina said faintly. 'You can't *enjoy* having pain inflicted on you. No one would.'

Elaine's face, which had pleaded for her understanding, became closed and withdrawn. 'Like I said, it goes too far sometimes,' she said brusquely. 'In fact, the last few times, if I'm honest. I've been covering myself up and praying James wouldn't notice. But you'll just have to take my word for it. When we first got together it was so good between us. James never did anything for me that way, Chrissy, never once. Sebastian was the best lover I've ever had, and when he wanted to start this stuff – well, I thought, what the hell?

'I know I've shocked you – I've shocked myself, over and over again. But I thought it was worth it, until this happened. I can't have the baby, you do see that, don't you? I'll have to have an abortion.'

'Yes, I see,' Christina said, stunned. How ironic that while she dreamed of becoming pregnant and bearing a child, her friend could think only of getting rid of hers.

'Will you lend me the money?' asked Elaine, shame-faced. 'I could ask Sebastian but I'd rather he didn't know. I'm not sure how he'd take it.'

It was amazing the way she seemed to put his thoughts and feelings above her own, Christina reflected.

'If you're sure, Elaine?'

'I am. I'll tell James I'm going back home to see my mother. Say she had a win on the bingo and sent me my fare – God knows she'd never have the money else. There's any number of private places in London. I can be in and out the same day.'

Christina suppressed a shudder. It was a child's life they were talking about, after all. Elaine seemed to know instinctively what she was thinking. Her voice was unsteady, but she tried to smile.

'It's the only way, believe me. And it won't happen again, Chris. I'm going to tell Sebastian before I leave that we'll have to cool things. He didn't do anything I didn't agree to, but we were getting into deep water, I see that now. I think it would be best all round to end it.'

That was something, at least, Christina thought.

'Don't worry, Elaine. You've got your money. I can get you a couple of thousand, no trouble. You'll want cash, I presume? Give me a few days and I'll do it when Stephen goes to New York.'

A look of relief transformed her friend's worn face. 'Oh, Chrissy, thank you. I don't know what I'd have done without you.'

The Pan Am flight to New York was scheduled to leave at 11.30 a.m. Christina had offered to drive Stephen to the airport, but he had refused her offer in favour of James Morris's, saying they had a lot to talk about.

The day was heavily overcast, with drizzle threatening, as Stephen and Christina stepped out of Crystal Springs House. James was waiting in the parked car. He looked away as Stephen slid his arms around Christina, pulling her against him as they said goodbye.

'Take care, Stephen, safe flight.' Her upturned face was close to his. He could see the fine sprinkling of golden freckles on her nose and cheekbones.

'You could have come with me, you know,' he reminded her.

'I know that, but when we go away I don't want it to be for business – I want to have you all to myself.' She slapped him gently on his flat stomach, thinking how attractive he looked in the pure-white cotton shirt and khaki cotton slacks he wore for the flight. His hair had grown long and curled attractively at the nape of his neck.

He must have read her thoughts. 'I'll try and grab a haircut while I'm up in civilization.'

'No, don't you dare, I like it like that.'

'Well, just a bit.' He held up his forefinger and thumb.

She nodded doubtfully, and he leaned closer to kiss her. Her full mouth quivered slightly at his touch.

'You take care, Chrissy. Be good,' he whispered in her ear, and added, 'Remember, I love you.'

'I love you too, Stephen.'

He released her and walked to the parked car. 'Bye, baby, see you next week – I'll ring you tomorrow,' he called.

Christina waved and waited on the step until the car was out of sight, then turned back to the house. She felt strange, elated, set free almost. She felt rather guilty at the thought, then told herself she was being ridiculous. Stephen didn't expect her to mope around while he was away on business. There was nothing wrong with enjoying her own interests and social activities – including Martin Ward's party in a few days' time.

Christina had arranged to meet Pauline Bascombe for lunch to discuss a forthcoming charity event for children in need which Crystal Springs had agreed to sponsor. Pauline had made a reservation at the Waterside Café in Bridgetown for 12.30.

Christina did her daily fifty lengths of the swimming-pool, showered, and called in at her office to check her mail before leaving the hotel at ten minutes to twelve to drive to Bridgetown.

She turned up the volume of the calypso tape Elaine had given her and sang at the top of her voice, thinking about whether to have a formal dinner party for the charity night, as Pauline suggested, or a more casual fancy-dress party on Halloween, which was what she would prefer.

Stuck behind an open truck full of jeering young boys

for several miles, she seized the first opportunity to over-take as the truck signalled to turn left. Checking her rear-view mirror, she accelerated and moved into the centre of the road, not noticing the dark-grey jeep pulling out in front of the truck. She slammed on her brakes and horn simultaneously as the jeep swerved to miss her, careering off the road and crashing into the gully alongside.

'Oh, shit,' Christina swore, and ground her car to a standstill.

She jumped out and ran the few feet to where a man was struggling out of his jeep, which had tipped onto one side with the two left wheels suspended above the open gully. Even from the back he looked familiar.

'Martin, is that you?'

He turned at the sound of her voice, anger ebbing away as he saw who it was.

'Christina!'

'How's your jeep?'

He jumped across the gully and looked under the car. 'Seems okay. If I can get it back onto the road in one piece, I think it will survive.'

Several people had gathered around the accident, and all were chattering in fast Bajan-speak.

'Dat's a bad nasty job you got there. You needin' ol' man Boysey, he fixin' anyting,' a young boy with wide eyes and a wider grin informed Martin.

'Where is he, then?' Martin asked.

'He live up de gap next to mah house. He got cars and stuff there – he fixin' all de cars in the whole gap.'

Martin handed the boy a dollar bill.

'Will you go and ask him if he'll come and fix my jeep?'

The boy snatched the note and ran off up the hill, shout-ing: 'Ol' man Boysey, ol' man Boysey!'

'I'm really sorry, Martin.' Christina touched the side of his jeep and jumped away as it began to rock.

'If this is what it takes to get to see you, I'll put up with it. But just be careful you don't injure me next time.'

He ran his fingers through his hair and smiled at her.

'How are you, anyway? Long time no see.'

'I'm fine, and you?'

'All the better for nearly running into you.'

She tried not to blush, but could feel the heat creeping into her face.

'I have to rush, Martin. I've a lunch date with Pauline Bascombe at 12.30 – it's almost that now.'

'I haven't seen you for months, Christina. You drive me off the road into a gully, and now you're dashing off!'

She looked uncomfortable and glanced at her watch.

'What can I say?'

'You can say: "I'll make it up to you, Martin. I promise to come out for a drink or dinner, even a game of tennis with you."' She knew she ought not to agree, but she felt guilty about the accident, and surely a public meeting couldn't hurt?

'Tennis this evening, 6.30, my place. Can you make it?'

'I've been practising my serve for weeks. You're going to be in a lot of trouble later.'

He laughed, and she realized how much she had missed seeing him.

'You're all talk, Martin! Now I really must dash.'

She glanced in the wing mirror as she pulled her car into the road. The young boy was running down the road towards Martin with a posse of four helpers close behind.

Christina did not reach the Waterside Café until fifteen minutes after one, panting, agitated and apologetic.

'Don't worry, this is the West Indies. Everyone is always late,' said Pauline, unconcerned.

'I'm afraid I'm still very English and get in a terrible state if I'm late for an appointment. It was unavoidable this morning. I drove Martin Ward off the road.'

'Well, there are easier ways of meeting people,' Pauline said, and signalled to a passing waiter. 'Drink?'

Christina pushed her long hair off her face. 'I'd love a beer, I'm so hot.'

They ordered two Banks'.

'Martin Ward is the flavour of the month at the moment,' Pauline commented. 'Every hot-blooded female under sixty on the island wants to climb into his pants. You have to admit, Christina, he's a dish.' She lowered her voice to a throaty drawl. 'That golden tan, sunstreaked hair, and rippling body. Can't say I haven't thought about it myself on occasion.'

Her eyes levelled appraisingly at Christina, who flushed at the mention of Martin's name and buried her face behind the menu.

After deciding to have her favourite crab-cakes, Christina sat back in the uncomfortable rattan chair, admiring Pauline's Batik printed dress. It was made of a fine gossamer fabric that clung to her smooth, flawless skin. Heavy gold chains were coiled around her long neck, and chunky gold earrings swung from her pierced ears.

'Your hair looks amazing,' said Christina.

It was the first time she had seen Pauline's hair unbraided, and she couldn't believe the abundant black mane hanging in wild, tangled curls past her shoulders.

They both ordered crab-cakes with salad and hot-pepper sauce, accompanied by a bottle of dry white wine.

'How's Danny?' Christina asked between bites of crab-cake.

'Danny is as always too busy, too motivated, too ambitious. In a nutshell, too English.'

Pauline's wide, full mouth turned up at the corners. A languid smile on her face, she pushed the plate to one side and leaned forward. Christina could smell her musky perfume.

'I'm sure we share the same problem. Sometimes I think my husband is a driven man.'

'Stephen's exactly the same. I'm beginning to wonder, if I had a cardboard cut-out made of myself and stuck that in front of him, whether he'd even notice.'

Pauline looked up, fixing her huge, dark, liquid eyes on a tall man who had entered the restaurant. He waved and she smiled, then returned her gaze to Christina.

'Are we ever satisfied, I wonder? I married Danny because I was madly in love and wanted to share my life with him. I gave up a promising career in advertising in England and came back to Barbados with him. I now find myself, after four years of marriage, still madly in love, but sharing less and less of his life.'

'We're in exactly the same boat. I have been married three and a half years, and the last year has been very difficult. Stephen has been away so much, and is so obsessed with building another hotel, we eat, sleep and drink it.'

Christina flicked back her long hair and concentrated on Pauline, who seemed for the first time to want to confide in her.

'Danny, as you know, is hell-bent on a political career. I'm not sure if you're aware of it, but he is from a very poor background. As a result, he has a social conscience which is way out of proportion, all based on guilt and of no practical use whatsoever.' She paused and refilled her glass with wine before going on.

'He listens to me about as much as he listened to his mother – in one ear and out the other.'

'Stephen's determined to open a hotel chain and listens to me about the same amount.'

The two women smiled at each other, so different yet sharing a common bond.

It was almost three o'clock when Christina left Pauline after agreeing to meet for lunch once a week. They had finished the wine and talked about almost everything but the charity that had been the purpose of the lunch. They vowed to sort that out when they next met, and Christina felt she had made a friend and ally in Pauline Bascombe.

There were several messages for her when she arrived back at the hotel, and she worked at her desk until six before walking back to the house through the gathering dusk.

Martin arrived for tennis while she was changing upstairs. She heard his car in the drive, and called down to Victor to offer him a drink while he waited.

The match on the floodlit court was no match. It was over in less than an hour with Christina winning in straight sets. Martin conceded defeat gallantly.

'Well done, Christina. All that expensive coaching I've been having, and yet I'm still no match for you. Are you sure you're not related to that other Chris? I think her name's something like Evert.'

She chuckled and poked him gently in the ribs with the handle of her racquet.

'Well, I do play several times a week, and to be honest you're not that difficult to beat.'

They walked side by side down a moonlit path leading to Crystal Springs House.

'You can't send a beaten man home without a drink.' Martin leaned against the door. 'I'll die of thirst after all that effort.'

'I think I owe you more than one drink after this morning. Come on in.' They walked into the hall, and both jumped when Clyde the night watchman spoke from the shadows behind them.

'Evenin', mistress.' He stood stiffly to attention. 'Clyde your guard and protector here.'

'Oh, you startled me!'

Christina breathed a heartfelt sigh of relief. Clyde wouldn't intentionally startle even a fly. He was old, infirm, and the most gentle man she had ever met. She only hoped she was never attacked and needed him as protector, as he so sweetly put it.

'I'm home safe and sound now,' she assured him. 'You can go and do your patrol. Goodnight.'

'Night, mistress. Now you sure you's all right? Lots of badminded folk around these days.'

Clyde eyed Martin suspiciously.

'I'm fine, really. Mr Ward is an old friend.'

She looked at Martin, who winked and reassured the old man.

'Believe me, I'll look after her.'

Clyde left with a toothless grin. 'Tha's okay, then. Ah's goin' on patrol now, jus' call fer Clyde if you needin' anythin' at all.' He shuffled out of the courtyard, his over-sized shoes flapping noisily on the stone floor.

Martin and Christina both chuckled. 'He means well,' she said fondly.

'I'm sure he does, but I doubt he could protect a minia-ture poodle,' Martin commented, thinking how very vul-nerable she was in this big house with only old Clyde to look after her.

'I know,' she agreed, 'but he came with the house. I've got a full security force as back-up at the hotel if I need them.'

She held out her hand to lead him through the court-yard, stopping at the fountain which was lit by soft moon-light. They watched a fat frog plop into the pond, its skinny back legs paddling frantically under a perfect white lily.

She had given Victor the night off, and got Martin a beer and herself a glass of juice from the fridge. Martin was standing at the furthermost edge of the terrace, look-ing over the gardens and down to the sea.

His eyes did not leave the view as he said, 'Did you ever think when you were living in that flat in Manchester that you would one day own all this?'

'No, not for a minute, Martin. I did know I would leave Manchester – I was determined to do that and never had any doubts that I would succeed – but Barbados . . . I don't think I dreamt that far.'

She handed him the beer and their fingers touched briefly. Christina sat on the low wall of the terrace and he sat next to her. Both lost in their own thoughts, neither spoke for several minutes, then they both spoke together.

'I've really . . .'

'Where's . . .'

'You first,' he said, grinning.

'I was about to say I've missed seeing you, Martin. I thought that this morning when I saw you again, and I want you to know I don't think we should leave it so long the next time.'

'That had nothing to do with me.' She touched his lips with her fingers.

'You must appreciate Stephen is jealous and kicks up a fuss every time I even suggest seeing you, but I don't intend to let that stop me in future. Life is too short.'

Martin took her hand in his.

'Life's very short, Christina, and I don't have to tell you again how I feel about you. Stephen neglects you, you've said so yourself. I won't make any demands on you, I promise. Just so long as I can see you.'

He lifted her hand to his mouth and kissed every one of her fingertips, his eyes, under golden, sun-kissed lashes, never leaving hers.

She made no attempt to stop him as he leaned forward to kiss her. Encouraged, he covered her mouth with his, and started to pull her shirt free of the waistband of her shorts, sliding his hands beneath to cup her breasts.

Christina made soft mewing sounds in the back of her throat. Martin's tongue slid into her mouth. She could feel his bare legs, covered in wiry golden hairs, brushing against hers as he moved closer to her, his heart thudding wildly.

'I want you, Christina, like I've never wanted any other

woman.' He held her by the shoulders with shaking hands.

It was impossible not to notice how aroused he had become, and she thought of all the women who would envy her for being in this situation. She felt reckless and more alive than she had for months, her own desire rising as his hungry mouth fell on her breasts like a starving child, and his eager hands tore at her clothes.

'Martin, calm down!' Christina pushed him gently away. 'You're hurting me.'

'I'm sorry,' he said. 'But look what you've done to me.'

'I noticed,' she said, reaching out to touch him – and pulling away as if she had been stung as the telephone rang inside the house.

'Ignore it.' He grabbed her hand. 'Please.'

Christina hesitated, holding his pleading gaze for an instant while the telephone rang and rang insistently, determined to be answered. She knew it was Stephen even before she picked it up.

'Hi, Chrissy baby, how are you?' His strong voice broke the spell.

'I'm fine, just fine. And you? How are things up there in the Big Apple?'

'It's wet and windy, and I'm bloody cold, but things seem to be progressing okay. I saw Antonio this afternoon, very briefly. He's set up a meeting for tomorrow with his financial boys, and I get the impression he's very keen, but it's all down to what he wants for the equity investment and how much I'm prepared to give him.'

'I'm sure you'll sort it out, Stephen.' Christina sat down in the small desk chair, her legs unsteady.

'Are you okay, Chris? You sound tired.'

'I've been racing around for most of the day. It's been very hot here. I think I'm just whacked.'

'Well, have a good night's sleep, because I want you to come up here tomorrow.'

'What?' she gasped. 'I can't . . .'

288

'It's very important,' he interrupted. 'Antonio and Susanna are having a big party at their house in the Hamptons. I want you to be here with me. I've made a reservation on the Pan Am flight in the morning, and there'll be a limo to pick you up at Kennedy. It's all organized. Anyway, you've never been to New York. You'll love it.'

'I've nothing to wear,' she faltered, thinking of her tropical wardrobe and one old warm suit she had worn to travel out from England.

'I will personally whisk you up Fifth and Madison tomorrow afternoon, and get you a dress to stun the Cellinis. We could stay a few extra days and make a holiday of it. What do you say, Chrissy?'

She turned at the sound of footsteps, expecting to see Martin, and was surprised when James Morris strode unannounced into her living-room. She was flustered, and tried unsuccessfully to push her shirt back into her shorts whilst speaking to Stephen and holding the phone.

'James has just arrived, Stephen.'

'Oh, good. He's got your itinerary and a set of photographs of the site in the Bahamas I need. If you could bring them up with you, Christina, that would be great.'

'Do I have a choice?' she asked, her voice heavy with sarcasm.

Stephen ignored that and went on to say, 'Okay, darling, I'll let you go. Sleep tight, and I'll look forward to seeing you tomorrow. Safe journey.'

'Bye, Stephen.' She hung up and joined James and Martin on the terrace. There was an awkward silence.

'Sorry to barge in on your cosy evening.' James looked from her to Martin, and back again.

'Hardly cosy,' she snapped, over-reacting. She could have bitten her tongue.

'We had a game of tennis and came back here for a drink, that's all.' Stop explaining, for goodness' sake, she

289

screamed to herself inwardly. It's none of his damn business what you do!

'Would you like a drink, James?' She forced her voice to sound polite and casual.

'No, I'm in a hurry,' he said, and handed her a brown manila envelope. She took it with slightly trembling hands.

'Photographs for Stephen and flight details for you. You're shaking, Christina.' He touched her fingers and searched her face with suspicious eyes. She held the envelope with both hands.

James was no fool. He could see by her awkward stance and darting eyes that she was acutely embarrassed. He would have liked to have stayed and pried further, but he had a list of figures to telex up to New York, and as usual Stephen wanted them instantly.

'I really must be going, Christina. Sorry I can't stay, but then you've already got company.'

'Martin was just leaving when Stephen rang, weren't you?'

'Yes, I've got a hot date with Linda Fields.'

James whistled. 'I wish I was in your shoes. Miss Barbados, and tipped to be Miss Eastern Caribbean – she's a stunner.'

Christina wondered if Martin really had a date, and suddenly felt cheated, guilty and annoyed, all at the same time.

Both men started to walk towards the door.

'Don't forget my opening night, Christina,' Martin said. 'It should be a great evening. We've organized a fashion show, and Spice are playing for us.'

'I don't think I'll be able to make it. It looks like I'll be in New York.'

The disappointment on his face was so intense she wanted to hug him and kiss it away.

'Elaine and I can make it, Martin. Thanks for the invite.

Elaine's really looking forward to it. She says everyone is talking about the new store.'

Martin hardly heard James. 'Yeah, great – look forward to seeing you there,' he said absently.

James pointed to the brown envelope Christina still clutched in her hand. 'Don't, whatever you do, forget those photographs or your husband will go ape-shit. And, by the way, your ticket will be issued on departure. Have a good flight, and regards to Stephen. Goodnight, Christina – Martin.' James stepped outside and started to walk towards the hotel. Martin held back, and she waited until James was out of sight before she spoke.

'I'm sorry for what happened back there. I almost forgot for a moment that I'm married.'

'I'm not sorry about what happened, I'm just sorry about you being married. Christina . . .'

He came forward to kiss her and she pushed him gently away.

'No, Martin. I think you should go.'

A slight breeze ruffled his hair. He gazed at her, hurt and disappointment in his eyes.

'When will I see you again?'

'I really don't know, Martin. I'll call you.'

'Is that a promise, Chris, or will I have to wait another six months before I bump into you – literally?'

She sighed. 'No, it's a promise, Martin. I meant what I said earlier.'

'And I meant what I said. I want you, Chrissy. I'm just not sure how much longer I'm prepared to wait.'

He walked to his car and did not look back or glance in her direction as he drove quickly out of the drive.

Chapter Fourteen

Christina slept fitfully and rose the following morning at dawn. Stephen had said it was cold in New York, and she had searched the wardrobes the previous night, finding a couple of Stephen's woollen sweaters and a blazer she had forgotten she had. She packed the sweaters, underwear, a pair of trousers, and her old suit, plus a long black chiffon dress and a pair of black shoes, just in case the flight was delayed and she was unable to buy a new one.

She opened the bedroom shutters on a grey overcast morning. Low, ominous cloud draped the tops of the casuarina trees outside the window, and a heavy mist veiled the dark, flat sea.

She stood on tiptoe and looked towards the east coast. Thick cloud covered the sky as far as the eye could see – not a chink of blue or a whisper of wind. A bad storm was coming and could last for days.

Christina showered and dressed in jeans, a white long-sleeved cotton shirt, flat tan slip-ons, and a matching leather belt. She intended to carry her blazer.

Victor served her a light breakfast of orange juice, fresh fruit, and lemon tea on the bedroom terrace whilst Celia braided her long hair into a thick plait.

Mr Payne, the driver, came for her in the Daimler limousine at a few minutes after nine.

'We'll be back in a few days, Victor. Any problems, you know to contact Mr Morris.'

'No problem, mistress. I lookin' after everting fer you and de boss man.'

Victor stood to attention, and Christina had difficulty keeping a straight face. She expected him to salute at any moment. His chubby, attractive face, so often smiling, was solemn and resolute today.

'And you, Celia – I want you to clean out all the drawers and cupboards in the kitchen while I'm away. I found two dead cockroaches in a pan the other day.'

Celia bent her head in an affected, subservient fashion which always irritated Christina.

'And no excuses for not coming to work if it rains. I've bought you a lovely big umbrella so you won't get your head wet.'

Celia smiled, her square white teeth gleaming.

'Yes, mistress.'

Christina walked towards the car.

'See you next week,' she said as she sat in the back seat and Mr Payne closed the door.

Victor and Celia waved until she was out of sight.

'I have to make one quick call at Mrs Morris's house *en route*. Do you know where that is?' Christina said to Mr Payne as he drove sedately along Highway One.

'Yes, mistress. Mr and Mrs Morris live on Sunset Ridge in Magnolia Cottage.'

Christina was pleased to see James's car was not parked outside the cottage as Mr Payne pulled the limo to a halt before the small garden gate.

Elaine opened the door before Christina reached it. The sight of her friend stopped her dead in her tracks: she was dressed in a grubby kimono, her blonde hair falling unkempt and wild across her ashen face.

'What on earth's the matter, Elaine?' Christina stepped inside the house and held her at arm's length. Elaine stared at Christina from swollen eyes, red and puffy from crying.

'It's come to a head, that's all. It's over.'

Christina suspected that James had found out about her affair, and was about to ask her when Elaine loosened the belt of her robe. It slid from her naked body, falling in folds at her feet.

She stood perfectly still as Christina took in the full horror of her bruised and damaged flesh.

'Oh, Elaine!'

Christina reached out to touch her back, an angry patchwork of deep crimson lacerations and purple bruises. She stared at her buttocks covered in small red, open wounds, feeling sick with rage as she realized they were cigarette burns.

'My God, what kind of an animal beats a woman like this?' she exploded, her eyes not leaving Elaine's body. 'It's disgusting.'

Elaine dropped to her knees. Crouching, she frantically gathered the dressing-gown around her bare shoulders in a pathetic attempt to hide the shameful abuse.

'I have to get away; he might kill me the next time,' she mumbled. 'I must get away from him. I'm scared, Christina. So scared.'

She sat on the floor, a soft whimpering noise coming from her quivering mouth.

Christina knelt down and helped her to her feet. She opened her arms and Elaine fell into them, sobbing like a child. Christina held her close, careful not to hurt her, stroking her tangled hair.

'Tell me who did this terrible thing to you? Was it James? Did he find out?'

She lifted her head from Christina's shoulder and wiped her sleeve across her wet face.

Her voice became very quiet, and when she spoke again it was barely audible. 'I feel so ashamed. I thought he loved me. I never knew he could be like that.' She dropped her head onto her chest. 'I must get away,

294

Christina, as soon as possible,' she repeated. Her voice had changed rapidly from plaintive to desperate.

'I've got the money, Elaine.'

Christina fished in her bag and handed her an envelope.

Elaine took it and stared for a few moments without speaking.

'What can I say? Thank you seems inadequate.' She composed herself a little. Her eyes had lost their haunted look.

'I really must go now or I'll miss my plane,' said Christina. 'And you must go to see Dr Gilbert at once, Elaine. Those wounds could turn septic. Promise me you'll go?'

She nodded.

'And promise me something else – that you'll report him. I don't see why James should get away with this.'

Elaine's laughter scared her. It was so bitter and unlike her warm-hearted, fun-loving friend.

'Report James? Why should I do that? It wasn't my husband who did this – and can you honestly imagine me in court, baring the scars and telling them how the best friend of their beloved Prime Minister likes to get his rocks off!'

Christina recoiled. She was a stranger to violence, and finding her best friend caught up in something so sordid left a sour taste in her mouth.

Elaine laughed again and clutched the money to her.

'No, I couldn't go through with it. Besides, I wouldn't stand a chance. But with this I do.' She waved the brown envelope. 'I'm leaving Barbados as soon as possible, Christina, so I won't be here when you get back. But I'll call you and let you know how and where I am.'

Christina hugged her, kissing her on the cheek, Elaine's tears wetting her face.

'Good luck. Call me soon as you can.'

'I will. You're my best friend. I'll never forget what

you've done for me. I mean it, Chris – you've saved my life.'

Rain pattered on the tinted windows of the Lincoln stretched limousine as it purred across the 59th Street Bridge towards the Long Island Expressway and onward to Southampton, where Susanna and Antonio were hosting their party at the Belford family estate.

'We could forget about the Cellinis' party and have one in here – it's big enough.' Christina looked around the plush interior of the huge car. She fiddled with the TV controls and lifted the walnut top of the drinks cabinet to peer inside.

'Look at this – incredible.'

'You'd think you were about twelve instead of twenty-three,' grinned Stephen.

'I'm excited.' She sat closer to him and ran her fingernails up his leg. 'We could do anything in here and nobody would be able to see.'

Stephen placed his own hand on top of hers, tapping her knuckles. 'Maybe we will on the way back.'

'Lust in a limo.' Christina freed her hand and gave his leg a gentle squeeze. 'All you ever give me these days is promises.'

She turned her head to gaze out of the rain-spattered back window at the towering Manhattan skyline rapidly fading into the distance. Light glittered from thousands of windows like twinkling earthbound stars.

'This is an amazing city. I still haven't caught my breath since I got off the plane this afternoon.'

'Everyone's first time here is exciting. It's a city of such extremes it tends to provoke extreme reactions. People either love it or hate it.'

'I already love it,' she said.

He looked at her. 'I must say you look beautiful tonight. You remind me of the way you looked the first time I took

296

you to a party. Do you remember going to the Sinclairs' in London?'

She nodded. 'And do *you* remember you bought me that Yves St Laurent dress, and I was cross?'

He smiled in recollection.

'The only difference today is you didn't get cross when I insisted you buy the Valentino instead of the Ralph Lauren.'

She grinned. 'I still think you should have bought me both, a celebration for doing the deal with Antonio.'

Stephen looked out of the window, thinking about Antonio Cellini.

'He's a tough bastard, and drives a hard bargain. I had to give away more than I'd anticipated.'

'Why was that?'

'The banks have been pushing me to close the deal. They said last week if I didn't have the equity within twenty-one days, it was all off. Can you imagine trying to raise seventy-five million dollars cold before completing the land purchase in a month's time? I could have lost the lot. No, I had to tie Cellini in. It was the only way.'

She thought he was being a bit downbeat about things. Financing the Bahamas development was a considerable coup, she'd have thought.

'Why change the name to Platinum Hotels? What's wrong with Reece Resorts?' she wanted to know.

'Because I don't intend to give Antonio any shares in Crystal Springs. Reece Resorts is my company and it's going to stay that way.

'Antonio's equity investment gives him 24 per cent of the new company, Platinum Hotels Inc. It also gives him back interest only on his investment over two years, and then pays off his twenty-five million stake over five years in equal instalments.'

'Is that a good deal for Antonio?'

'Good? It's amazing! He gets his money back with

interest plus 24 per cent of an expanding company developing world-class hotels.'

Stephen sighed.

'He had me by the short and curlies, Chrissy. Without his money I couldn't have put the deal to bed.'

'Well, I hope now you've got his money, you'll spend more time putting *me* to bed.'

The strained expression left his face. 'What would I do without you, Chrissy?'

'You're not going to have to worry about that,' she said, pushing aside all thoughts of Martin and her promise to see more of him. 'Now put all that business to the back of your busy mind, Stephen; we've got a party to go to.'

Huntington Lodge, the Belford family estate, was set well back from the road behind high, imposing walls and wrought-iron gates. The sleek limo purred up the long, sweeping drive and pulled up in front of an ivy-clad, stone-built house with mullioned windows and huge, heavily carved oak doors. Edward Belford III had built the house in 1926, and Stephen estimated that it was now worth well in excess of twenty million dollars.

'Some place!' he said under his breath as they walked past a white-gloved butler and into a vast oak-panelled hall. An elaborately carved staircase swept down from a deep gallery past a long casement window draped in crimson damask.

'Darlings!'

They turned to see Susanna floating towards them, rustling in clouds of burgundy taffeta and smelling of Jean Patou perfume.

'So wonderful you could make our party.' She offered a pale, powdered cheek first to Christina and, rather more lingeringly, to Stephen. 'I haven't a clue where Toni is, but I'll get you drinks and we can go in search.' She snapped red-tipped fingers at a hovering waiter and asked what they would like to drink.

'I'll have a vodka and tonic,' Stephen said, 'and Chrissy will have a glass of champagne.'

'Any marque,' Christina said, smiling sweetly.

'A glass of Dom Perignon and a vodka and tonic, Charles,' Susanna commanded. She spoke in the tone of voice of one who had been accustomed to servants all her life. There was no way you could affect that, Christina thought wryly.

Susanna guided them into another huge room, filled with expensively dressed people, and waved to Antonio, who was talking to her father. They pushed through the throng and Jeffrey Belford held out his hand to Christina. 'Well, what a charming surprise Stephen has brought us tonight. No wonder he didn't want to leave you alone on that island, eh, Stephen?' The old man patted him on the shoulder. 'Just joking.'

Christina fought down a guilty reaction. She noticed that under wrinkled, drooping lids, Jeffrey Belford's piercing blue eyes were dancing.

After Antonio had greeted Christina warmly, Belford monopolized the conversation.

'I must say how delighted I am that you and Antonio here have done a deal,' he enthused. He leaned forward in a confiding manner.

'The boy's a hard worker but lacks style – do you know what I mean?'

Stephen knew exactly what he meant, but thought it in bad taste to say so with Antonio standing next to them.

Antonio saw the expression on Stephen's face and shrugged, his handsome face unabashed. 'Don't worry,' he said. 'I'm constantly being told by my wife I've got no class. But I've plenty of another commodity she doesn't turn her nose up at. More than one, in fact!'

He laughed, and Jeffrey Belford looked at him with undisguised distaste.

'Don't talk about my daughter like that!' the old man snapped.

'Ah, come on, Jeffrey – I was only joking.'

Belford promptly turned his back on Antonio and said to Stephen and Christina, 'Excuse me, please. I've just seen someone very important I *must* speak to.' He left them abruptly and began to make his way to the other side of the room.

'Puts us in our place, doesn't it?' said Stephen, amused.

Antonio watched his father-in-law go, his usual smile absent.

'Come on, I'll introduce you to some of my people,' he said.

Christina noticed how he stressed the word 'my'. She felt a momentary flash of sympathy for him – Jeffrey Belford was a cross for anyone to bear. Then she met some of Antonio's associates, and began to wonder for whom exactly she should feel sorry.

It was a clash of two different cultures at the Belfords' that night. Without exception, everyone Antonio introduced to them either worked for him or was married to someone who did. He seemed to have no social relationships at all, she noted. The women all wore brightly coloured designer clothes, gold instead of Susanna's diamonds, and seemed to hang on every word their husbands spoke. The men were uniformly smart and well presented, but their stylish suits lacked the Ivy League disdain for fashion displayed by Jeffrey Belford and his Southampton friends. There was something just a bit too careful and contrived about the way they looked and dressed and acted, she thought. Yes – acted was the right word. They seemed to be playing a part somehow, and tonight the watchword was 'respectability' – which begged the question, how did they behave the rest of the time?

One man seemed unwilling to play the part, even for one night. His tie was knotted too casually, displaying the undone top button of his shirt. He wore a tight grey suit of some shiny material, and dark glasses. On anyone else they would have seemed ridiculous in such surroundings. On Gino Santorini, as he was introduced to her, they seemed appropriate somehow. Christina found that she was glad she did not have to meet his eyes uncovered. Gino Santorini looked like a man who had seen a lot in his life, none of it pleasant.

In the car driving back to the city she was quiet and reflective. Stephen was exhausted after the past days. He'd closed his eyes and rested his head against the leather seat.

'Are you sure about this deal?' she asked suddenly.

He opened his eyes and sat up abruptly.

'It's signed and sealed, Chrissy. Sure I'm sure. As of yesterday, Antonio and I are the owners of Platinum Hotels Inc. – though not equal partners, I'm glad to say. Have you got any problems with that?'

She could see that he was ruffled by having his judgement called into question, but felt that she had to speak up about what she had seen.

'Antonio's business associates . . . they were all very charming, but I got the strong impression somehow that tonight they were playing a part. That this wasn't their normal lifestyle at all.'

Stephen's eyes narrowed. 'You mean they weren't all fourth-generation millionaires with estates in the Hamptons like that old fart Belford? I didn't know you were such a snob.'

'I'm not,' she replied, stung. 'But there was something off-key about tonight. I can't quite put my finger on it. Gino Santorini, maybe . . . he looked as if he'd stepped straight out of central casting for a bit part in *The God-father.*'

Stephen threw up his hands. 'Christ, I never knew you were so prejudiced. Just what are you saying, Chrissy?

That because Antonio and his friends are wealthy, self-made Italian-Americans they're automatically crooks?'

She noticed he didn't say the one word that immediately sprang to mind.

She felt embarrassed, put on the spot. After all, she had nothing tangible to go on, just an uneasy gut feeling. But Stephen would have checked Antonio out before going into business with him, she told herself. He always did when it was a big transaction.

'Just promise me you know what you're getting into?'

He gave her one of his most expressionless looks. 'I do, so stop worrying, will you? I brought you over here to help me celebrate, not to put a dampener on the whole deal.

'Come on, Chrissy. Don't look like that. Why don't you come over here? Now, what were you saying earlier about the things you could get up to in a limo . . . ?'

In the end they spent longer than they'd intended in New York: shopping, eating out, seeing the latest films and Broadway shows. They each had the most expensive haircut of their lives in a chic New York hair stylist's, and one day didn't leave their suite at the Pierre at all, but stayed in bed like honeymooners, ordering room service and having their meals served in the adjoining dining-room in between lovemaking.

Christina was so pleased to have Stephen paying her more attention that she pushed aside her doubts about Antonio. And when thoughts of Martin occasionally troubled her, she told herself firmly there was no need. She'd almost given in to him in a weak moment, when Stephen was neglecting her. Now he was neglecting her no longer, and if Martin were her true friend, as he persisted in saying, he'd understand and be glad for her, wouldn't he?

But she couldn't quite convince herself of that.

Chapter Fifteen

Stephen spotted the police car parked in front of the hotel as Mr Payne turned the limo into the drive.

'What on earth is going on, Christina?' he said, before jumping out of the car and running up the steps two at a time.

Christina followed close behind, and saw James Morris coming out of his office flanked by two police officers.

His crumpled clothes looked as if he had slept in them, and his bloodshot eyes were confused and disoriented.

She caught up with Stephen in time to hear him say, 'What's happened?'

'Elaine is dead.'

The words hit Christina with such force she reeled.

'What? That's impossible. She was . . .' She caught herself in time and stared at James.

'She was what, Christina?' he asked, in a dull, lifeless tone.

'She was fine when I left her last week. I can't believe it. How did it happen?'

Christina clung to Stephen's arm. He stroked her hand.

'She died from a lethal dose of barbiturates and alcohol poisoning.' James faltered. 'The maid found her this morning. The police have ruled out foul play; it looks like straightforward suicide. They've taken her away already. I had to go and identify her.'

'I'm so sorry, James,' Stephen said. 'I think you should go home and try and get some rest.' He called to Mr

Payne, who was loitering near the reception desk, trying to hear what was going on.

'Take Mr Morris home, Payne.'

Christina caught James by the arm as he walked past her. 'Why would Elaine kill herself?' She searched his blank face.

'I have no idea, Christina, but that's what she did.'

'No. It's not possible. She would never have killed herself.' She shook her head from side to side. 'She didn't kill herself, I know she didn't.'

Several people had stopped and were staring in her direction. Stephen put an arm around her shoulders.

'Give me one good reason why Elaine would kill herself, Stephen.'

'I really don't know, Christina, but I think I should take you home now. You're very upset.'

'Before you go, we would like a statement from you, Mrs Reece-Carlton, if you don't mind,' the taller of the two policemen said.

'Can't it wait, officer? You can see my wife is very distressed.'

'I'm fine, Stephen. I'd rather get it over and done with,' Christina insisted.

'Okay, let's go to my office,' he said, and led the policemen out of reception and upstairs.

'How well did you know Mrs Morris?' the policemen asked Christina, when they were all seated and the door was firmly shut.

'Very well. She was a close friend.'

'How well did she get on with her husband?'

'Okay, I think.' Christina's eyes were on Stephen.

'They appeared to get along as well as any married couple. You know, the usual ups and downs,' he interjected.

'I would like Mrs Reece-Carlton to answer the questions if you don't mind, sir. I will question you later.'

Stephen gave an irritated nod and said nothing.

'Stephen's right. They were an average sort of couple.'

Christina was praying that the policemen was not going to ask her about Elaine's extra-marital affair.

'It's just that the victim was found with lesions and scars on her body that resembled wounds, probably inflicted by a leather strap or belt, and small burn marks. Whoever had messed her up had done a pretty good job, and we assume it was because of this she committed suicide.'

He did not look up as he continued talking.

'Did Mrs Morris have any male friends outside of her marriage?'

It was the question Christina had dreaded. She decided to lie.

'I'm not sure. Elaine was very popular. She made friends easily. She had lots, both male and female.'

Christina hoped that she sounded convincing.

'Why are you so sure she didn't kill herself?' The police officer looked up from his notes for the first time. Christina thought hard about her reply.

'Because she was so optimistic. Whatever happened to her, she always used to say: As one door closes, another opens.' A sob caught in her throat and choked her words.

'Thank you, Mrs Reece-Carlton, that will be all for the moment.'

The policeman stood up and spoke to Stephen.

'You knew Mrs Morris as well as your wife, did you, sir?'

'I did. She was a fun-loving, light-hearted girl, more interested in parties and having a good time than anything else. It seems inconceivable she should kill herself.'

The police officer snapped his notebook shut and slid the pencil into his top pocket.

'Perhaps she didn't,' he said, and fixed his dark gaze on Christina.

'That will be all for now. We will be in touch.'

Stephen saw them out. When he returned to the office, Christina was staring out of the window overlooking the sea. A water-skier whipped past in a hazy blur. The haze cleared and Elaine's face appeared before her, vivid and animated. She was smiling and thanking Christina for saving her life.

She couldn't control her voice as she said: 'She was murdered, Stephen.'

'Don't be ridiculous! Who on earth would want to kill Elaine Morris?'

Christina rounded on her husband with blazing eyes.

'I'm telling you, she was murdered. And I know who did it!'

'Why did you not tell the police about your suspicions when they were here?'

'How could I tell them that they should question Sebastian Aguilar in connection with a murder? Everyone knows he's hand in glove with the PM.'

Stephen looked shocked.

'You're joking, of course?'

'I don't think it's a suitable time to joke.'

Christina sat down on the small sofa in the corner of the office. Her legs felt weak. Stephen sat next to her.

'She's been having an affair with Sebastian for more than two years. She met him at the opening night of Crystal Springs. A few weeks ago she asked me for a loan to go back to England for an abortion – it was his baby. I promised to lend her the money and took it to her on my way to catch the plane to New York. It was then she showed me . . .'

Christina felt a wave of nausea threaten. 'It was horrible, Stephen. He'd beaten her half to death when she broke with him, and she was very scared and planned to leave the island as soon as possible.'

Deep in thought, Stephen stared across the room to a framed photograph on the wall behind his desk. Taken during the hotel's opening night, it showed him standing next to a smiling Jonathon Alleyne cutting a ribbon to declare Crystal Springs open.

'You must realize you can't report any of what you have just told me.' He took her hands in his. 'I don't want you to get involved in something as sordid as this. And anyway, you only had Elaine's word for it. She could have been lying.'

'She wasn't lying, Stephen, and she didn't kill herself. I don't care what you say, I'm going to do something about it.'

'Believe me, Christina, it won't do any good. She was English, she liked drinking and parties, and they're bound to suspect she'd done drugs a couple of times.' He sighed, knowing he was right and that he would have to prevent Christina doing anything silly.

'Sebastian Aguilar is the Prime Minister's best friend and a half-Barbadian. You know as well as I do that this is a small, insular community. You don't stand a chance with your allegations. You've got no evidence; only hearsay from Elaine herself, who can't do much substantiating. It's your word against the whole Barbadian establishment – who probably wouldn't believe such allegations could be true. For God's sake, Christina, see sense.' He squeezed her hand. 'She's dead now; let her rest in peace.'

'Poor Elaine, she didn't deserve to die.'

Christina started to shake, and clutched the edge of her seat to disguise the fact.

'I agree, but she's dead now and you can't alter that.' Stephen wrapped his arms around her, holding her close. 'Please, please, my darling, don't get involved in this any further. Let sleeping dogs lie.'

'And let that bastard get off scot free, you mean?' Stephen was surprised to hear her swear. It was unusual.

'You have no choice, believe me.'

Christina could see that she was wasting her time trying to convince him.

'Perhaps you're right – it would be a waste of time, and what good would it do poor Elaine now?'

'That's my girl,' he said, and stroked her white face. 'I'm as sorry as you are about her death, but the last thing we all need right now is a scandal.'

Stephen helped her to her feet. 'Come on, I'll walk you home. I think you could do with some peace and quiet.'

Christina allowed herself to be cosseted and fussed over by Stephen and Celia, and played the game until he left to go back to the office a couple of hours later.

Stephen was wrong when he said she did not have a choice. She placed a call to Danny Bascombe.

'Hi, Danny, how are you? Christina Reece-Carlton here.'

'I'm fine, Christina, and how are you?'

'Not so good; I've just had some bad news. You remember Elaine Morris? Well, she was found dead this morning.'

'Oh, my God, how did it happen?' Danny sounded shocked.

'Suicide, they say, but I don't have all the details yet. She's the reason I'm calling. I need to see you. Would it be possible to come down to your office today?'

'Well, I'm very busy.' Danny hesitated.

'It's very important,' she pleaded.

'Does Stephen know you've contacted me?'

'No, Danny, and he's the last person I want to know.'

The line went quiet. She could sense the way his mind was turning.

'Please, I promise you, no obligation. Just a little advice.'

'Okay, Christina. I'll see you later today. About 6.30, okay?'

'Yes, that's fine. I'll see you then.'

It was very dark when Christina walked up the path to the office of Bascombe and Williams. The secretaries had gone home and the outer office was dimly lit.

She called softly, 'Is anyone home?' She was relieved to see Danny's square, handsome face, broken by a wide smile, appear at his office door.

'Come in, Christina, good to see you.' He held open the door, indicating a large brown leather chair which she sank into. He walked behind his desk and sat down opposite her.

'It's good to see you, Danny,' she said. 'Looking good as always.'

'Thank you. So, Christina, you want some advice?'

'Yes, but I must have your word that this is strictly between us two?'

She looked straight into his eyes. He nodded, and she decided she could trust him.

'I want to tell you about Elaine Morris, and then you can advise me what to do.'

Christina inhaled deeply and began to relate all she knew about Elaine. Danny looked grim-faced when she had finished talking.

'Well, that's quite a can of worms you've got there, Christina. Are you absolutely certain you want to open it?'

'I'm prepared to on one condition: that you act for me.'

Danny considered his promising political career and the prominent connections of the man they would be accusing, the lack of evidence, and the likely weight of opposition.

'Let me think about it, Christina. I promise I'll call you with a decision tomorrow. What will you do if I refuse?' he asked. 'And I must warn you that I probably will.'

'Confront the bastard myself!'

Danny looked worried. 'I really don't think our Mr Aguilar would appreciate that – nor Stephen, for that matter. Be careful, Christina. If you want my best advice I'd steer clear of the whole affair. You're walking on very thin ice.'

'That's what Stephen said.' She stood up, and he noticed the puffiness around her eyes and her washed-out pallor.

'I'm really sorry about Elaine, by the way.'

'Yes, it's tragic.'

Danny walked her out to the car park, dark and gloomy under a thick, black, moonless sky.

'Thanks for your time, Danny, and regards to Pauline.'

'I'll tell her you asked after her. Goodnight, Christina; I'll talk to you tomorrow, I promise.'

She waved as she pulled out of the drive, doubting very much that Danny would help her. It was too much to expect with his political career at stake.

In the event it didn't really matter. The following morning, news broke that Sebastian Aguilar's Jet Ranger helicopter had gone down in the sea between Trinidad and Barbados. Beside the pilot and Aguilar himself, it had contained only one passenger: Jonathon Alleyne, Prime Minister of Barbados.

The coroner's report declared that Elaine Morris had died by suicide. She was cremated, and a service was held at St James's Parish Church.

Mourners attending included her distraught mother and sister, who had flown out from England, and her husband, who kept a tight grip on himself throughout the entire proceedings.

Stephen shifted uneasily from foot to foot. He hated church services of any kind.

Paul Richardson and his wife Mandy seemed genuinely sad.

Christina was full of bitter resentment for her friend's young life, cut so tragically short.

Sebastian Aguilar was buried in his family's private plot on their Trinidad estate.

Jonathon Alleyne was buried in All Saints Catholic Church, Barbados, six days later, with all the pomp and ceremony afforded to a statesman. Mourners attended from all over the world, and the island was given a national holiday.

Stephen attended Jonathon Alleyne's funeral alone. He didn't listen to a word of the memorial service, totally engrossed as he was in planning a brilliant manifesto for Danny Bascombe's election campaign.

One month later Daniel Andrew Bascombe was nominated head of the Opposition party. Alleyne's deputy, Charles Payne, was serving as acting PM until the election, already scheduled for three months' time.

Stephen brought in a brilliant PR man from England to handle Danny's campaign. He was to be hailed as the new young professional Barbadian, the poor boy from St Lucy who, through diligence and hard work, won a scholarship to Oxford and law school, became a barrister, and returned to his home country to practise law and help the people.

The general consensus was that it was time for young blood to appeal to an electorate tired of old-style government.

Danny knew he had a good chance of winning, and felt a mixture of exhilaration and trepidation at the prospect of becoming, at forty-two, the youngest Prime Minister the island had ever had.

Christina and Stephen watched his first speech as Leader of the Opposition on prime-time television.

'Good evening, this is Terri Gale and *Caribbean Today*, coming to you live from Bridgetown, Barbados.

'Tonight we have in the studio the leader of the Opposition party, Mr Danny Bascombe. He is going to tell us why he thinks he'll make a better Prime Minister than Mr Charles Payne.'

Danny gave the camera his irresistible boyish grin.

'In response to the lovely Terri Gale, I'm sure she won't mind if I correct her on one point – I have never said I would make a better PM than Mr Payne, only that I think I would make a very different one.

'I believe this country needs reform. We are still shackled to the old colonial regime. Independence was won twenty years ago, yet you could be forgiven for thinking it happened only last week.

'We need new blood, fresh ideas, young, enthusiastic politicians who will take this country on into the eighties and nineties with optimism and vigour.

'I believe the way ahead depends on our most valuable commodity: tourism.

'We need to encourage overseas investment, build new hotels, boost the economy with foreign currency, attract tourists by offering them everything we take for granted on our beautiful island.

'They already come from all over the world, but we need more, many more. And more hotels, more advertising, more investment, because I intend to turn our visitors' currency into new schools and universities so our children can be educated to the sort of standard I enjoyed in England. That money will also be used to build new hospitals, equipped with the latest and best equipment, new homes for the poor, and centres for our old folk.

'I pledge myself to you, my people, each and every one of you – I, Danny Bascombe, the fieldworker's son from St Lucy, can offer you a better future. I will work every hour that God sends and do everything in my power to make Barbados, my country, a more prosperous and better place to live for one and all.'

Danny sat back, genuine tears filling his eyes.

'We wish you every success, Mr Bascombe, and I hope to interview you again during the campaign.'

'Brilliant.' Stephen switched off the television, a broad grin on his face. 'Well, what did you think?' he asked Christina enthusiastically.

'I thought he was fantastic,' she replied, still staring at

the blank screen. 'And do you want to know why?' She looked at Stephen. 'Because Danny genuinely wants to help people, and it comes across powerfully.'

'It certainly does, Chrissy, and they'll buy it. He has got so much, he'll have them eating out of his hand.' Stephen let out a triumphant whoop as if the battle was already won.

'Old ugly-face Charlie Payne doesn't stand a chance against our handsome young Danny Boy.'

'I must admit Charlie Payne isn't the most attractive of men,' she said. 'Danny will certainly pull in the female votes.'

He must have convinced some male voters too. Everyone, it seemed, loved and admired the handsome young Leader of the Opposition, who seemed to epitomise the prosperous, optimistic eighties. Danny won the election with a landslide victory. Cheering drowned out his televised victory speech, and Christina felt tears come to her eyes as she watched. There was no doubting Danny's sincerity or commitment.

She and Stephen were invited to attend the inaugural celebrations at Government House.

'Christina, we're ten minutes late already.' Stephen's voice was sharp as she fussed with the back of her dress. 'I don't think for one moment anyone will even notice that stupid bow on your dress – they'll be too busy looking at Mrs Bascombe's breasts.'

'Thanks a lot; you're a great comfort.' She grabbed a velvet bag and stole one last glance at her long black taffeta dress.

'Don't you think that lipstick's a bit bright?' he asked as they walked downstairs.

'No, I do not. If it's good enough for Paloma Picasso, it's good enough for me.'

He shrugged. 'Suit yourself.' He preferred her in soft coral shades that accentuated her auburn hair and golden tan. But he was pleased to see that she was wearing his birthday present to her. Diamonds twinkled at either side of her face, and he nodded approvingly.

'The earrings look lovely. In fact, *you* look lovely, Mrs Reece-Carlton . . . apart from the scarlet lips.'

There was a queue of cars waiting to turn into Government House when Stephen's Mercedes slowed behind a dark-blue Daimler and crawled through the imposing wrought-iron gates and into the drive. As they entered the high semi-circular hallway to join a mass of guests, a liveried footman offered them champagne from a huge silver salver. They entered the ante-hall, and joined the long queue of people waiting to be introduced to the new Prime Minister. Eventually they were announced, and moved forward into a large, ornately decorated ballroom.

Danny walked towards them, immaculate in a made-to-measure Savile Row dinner suit. He took Stephen's hand and shook it.

'Stephen, delighted you could make it.' His face wore the widest smile Christina had ever seen, but when he kissed her hello she noticed there were new lines of worry and strain around his expressive eyes.

'You made it, Danny. I knew you would. Never backed a loser yet.' Stephen clapped him on the shoulder.

'*We* made it, Stephen – I couldn't have done it without your backing. I won't forget how much you helped me.'

'Don't worry, Danny – I won't let you.' Stephen laughed, his humour tinged with intent.

Christina couldn't decipher the strange expression which crossed Danny's face as he turned away to welcome another guest. Wary, she decided. Surely not afraid? She must have been mistaken. Danny was obviously tired after the hard campaign.

Pauline was in front of her, holding out her hand, every muscle in her face and neck set tight as she smiled.

'How are you, Pauline?' said Christina, ignoring the

proffered hand and leaning forward to kiss her friend. 'You look like you've lost some weight.'

Indeed, Pauline's famous curves seemed depleted tonight. Her low-cut emerald-green dress hung off her.

'You try being a politician's wife for a few weeks and see what it does for you!'

Pauline had not only lost weight; she had lost some of her sparkle. There were dark circles beneath her eyes, and her skin had a grey pallor that not even make-up could conceal.

Stephen said lightly, 'You're still the sexiest lady here', and Christina was surprised to see the same closed expression on Pauline's face that she'd noticed on Danny's.

To cover the slight chill of the moment she said, 'I hope we can still have the occasional long, gossipy lunch now you're the PM's wife, Pauline? I'd miss them if we had to stop.'

'Well, of course we can,' she replied automatically. 'Only not for the next few weeks. I'm a bit tied up.'

'Of course; I understand. I'll wait for you to ring me when you have more time.'

She waited in vain. Though Pauline was outwardly friendly when they met at official functions, and Danny assiduously invited Stephen to serve on several committees and think-tanks charged with stepping up the island's tourism, something seemed to have gone out of Christina's friendship with Pauline.

'I can't understand it,' she told Stephen after a few months. 'Pauline and I were good friends for a while, yet now she's the Prime Minister's wife she's dropped me completely. Why do you think that is?'

He shrugged. 'I shouldn't worry about it. It's not a very nice thing to say, but she was probably just using you before – keeping in with you while Danny needed my help. Politics is like business: everyone's always looking for the pay-off.'

'And now Pauline's had hers, you mean? No, Stephen, it's not as cut and dried as that. I wish I knew what it was . . .'

'Let it go,' he advised. 'The Pauline Bascombes of this world know when to move on and so should you. In fact, I think we're both getting a bit stale. You enjoyed your time in New York, didn't you? If I can leave James in charge for a few weeks, what do you say to a trip to Europe, just the two of us? We're long overdue for a proper holiday. We could combine it with taking Vicky back after the summer holiday. What do you say?'

'I'd say thank you, Stephen,' she smiled. 'And not before time.'

Chapter Sixteen

It was one of those rare late-autumn days that are warm and very still. Weak sunlight filtered through a fine tracery of tumbling russet leaves. Chaffinches and thrushes sang in hedgerows, clinging to the last days of summer.

A slight breeze caught the mass of ivy covering the front of Purley Hall as Christina and Victoria alighted from the car. Christina experienced a resurgence of the same excitement and expectancy she had felt the first time Stephen had brought her here. Since they had moved to Barbados they had seen the house only occasionally, on brief visits to bring Victoria back to school.

Mrs Barnes came busily out onto the stone steps with an excited Muffin racing past her legs. A warm smile lit up her wrinkled face. Christina thought she had aged, and seemed robbed of her old energy and sparkle. Dorothy Barnes must have been well into her sixties.

Victoria ran to the housekeeper and hugged her. Dorothy stroked the top of Victoria's gleaming, dark head, then gently disengaged herself to greet Christina.

'Mrs Reece-Carlton, lovely to see you. And, my, you do look well. Brown as a berry.'

Christina held out her hand. She had never kissed Dorothy before, and doubted that the old housekeeper would like it if she did.

'I feel well . . . it's good to be back.'

'Lots of fresh air and some of old Barnesey's home cooking, and you'll feel even better.'

'If I start eating your wonderful food I'll be like the side of a house.' Christina patted her flat stomach.

'Now, I'll have none of that talk. I've had five in my own family and none of them ever got fat on my cooking.'

Dorothy directed the chauffeur into the hall with the luggage as Victoria ran upstairs with Muffin scrambling behind.

'I'm so sorry Mr Reece-Carlton couldn't come back with you. I was really looking forward to seeing him again. It's been a long time.'

Christina sighed. 'I'm sorry too, but he had to go up to the Bahamas urgently. He did try to put it off but it was impossible, so I decided to bring Victoria back and do some shopping before Stephen comes over, next week. I need to buy some new clothes for our trip to Italy.'

Christina's face lit up at the thought of her forthcoming holiday, and she chatted about how much she was looking forward to it as she followed the housekeeper into the warm kitchen.

'That'll be nice; I'm sure he needs the rest, but I was hoping you'd all be staying here for a while. I miss the old times – the weekend parties and that. It used to be lots of fun. Now there's only me and Muffin, two old crocks together.'

Dorothy took a copper kettle off the shelf and filled it with water, putting it on the hot-plate to boil. 'Sit yourself down there and I'll make a nice pot of tea.'

Christina sat at the breakfast table.

'I've made Victoria's favourite lunch – steak and kidney pie, and apple crumble and custard,' the housekeeper announced with a satisfied grin. 'I know you like it too.'

Christina didn't have the heart to tell her that after a transatlantic flight through the night the thought of steak and kidney pie was abhorrent.

Instead she said, 'Mmm, can't wait. It's been a long

318

time since I've had anything that even resembles your wonderful home-cooked pies.'

'I don't suppose them folks out there know how to cook proper food, do they?'

'Well, I must admit it's different,' Christina said. 'We eat lots of fish and salad.'

'I was just saying to Bill the gardener the other day, you and Mr Reece-Carlton have become so thin since you left England, him especially.'

'That's because he works too hard.'

'I can't believe that's the only reason. He worked hard when he lived here. The last missus was always complaining about the long hours he worked.'

Dorothy took the boiling kettle off the Aga plate and filled a big brown teapot. She joined Christina at the scrubbed-pine table where she had placed two Worcester mugs and a plateful of home-made shortbread.

'Just made those this morning. Go on, try them. Me and Bill will have to eat them all, else.'

'I'll try one.' Victoria came into the kitchen and pinched a biscuit. Snapping it in two she gave half to Muffin, who was begging on his hind legs.

Victoria had changed from jeans into beige jodhpurs that clung to her shapely, coltish legs, and a snugly fitting pale-lemon sweater which accentuated her firm young breasts. No longer a child, she was now a desirable young woman, and well aware of the fact.

'How many times have I told you, Victoria, not to feed that dog? He's always sniffing around me when you're gone; drives me mad.'

Victoria ignored Dorothy and ruffled Muffin's ears.

'I'm going down to the stables now.'

'Aren't you tired?' the housekeeper asked.

'No, I slept on the plane.' Victoria glanced under her lashes at Christina.

'She slept all the way back because she insisted on

having three glasses of champagne. They knocked her out.'

'I really don't know what all the fuss is about,' said Victoria loftily. 'Daddy always lets me have champagne on planes.'

Christina raised her eyebrows. 'I was merely concerned because I knew you had to go back to school tonight, and I didn't want you to have a horrible headache.'

She tried hard to keep the exasperation out of her voice. She had had a particularly nasty argument with Victoria on the flight, and didn't feel like another one now.

'Well, I've decided I'm not going back to school this evening.'

'What do you mean? You're expected back.'

'I've rung Caroline and she's going back first thing in the morning. If you ring the housemistress it will be all right, Mrs Colton says.'

Victoria ran out of the kitchen before Christina could reply, Muffin barking at her heels.

'See you later,' she called over her shoulder.

'I've got steak and kidney pie for lunch,' Dorothy shouted after her.

Christina ate a buttery shortbread biscuit which melted in her mouth, and drank the mug of steaming tea. It refreshed her a little, but she still felt tired to her bones. She hadn't slept a wink on the flight, kept awake by a man in front who had snored, and by Victoria shuffling and kicking for most of the night.

'So how have you been, Mrs Barnes? Are all your family well?'

'We've had a bit of bother with our Trevor, not being able to find work and all. He's took to drinking nights, and leaving Sally and the baby. I've tried to talk to him, but you know how these young 'uns are, won't listen . . . and then there's our Rosy. Got herself a smashing chap at long last; she's thirty-six next month . . .'

The ringing of the telephone broke into what promised to be a continuing saga.

'I'll get it,' said Dorothy, standing up. 'I'm expecting a call from the butcher.'

The poor woman was starved for company, Christina thought as Dorothy left the room.

'It's Mr Reece-Carlton on the phone,' Dorothy called from the hall.

Christina took the telephone from her.

'Hi, Stephen. Yes, darling, I'm fine, just tired. You know how it is after a long flight. How are things over there?'

'Okay, but it's just as well I came; there are a lot of decisions to be made. I won't bore you with them at the moment; tell you all about it when I see you.' He changed the subject. 'Mrs Barnes seems to be over the moon now she's got people to fuss over.'

'Yes, she's delighted. Already planning to fill me up with stodgy food.'

'Great! Got to dash into a meeting now, Christina. I'll see you next week, all being well.'

Stephen was in a rush, and she didn't like the sound of 'all being well'. She hoped everything would be okay, and that he would be able to join her soon.

'Take care, darling. Speak to you tomorrow. And give my regards to Paul.'

'Bye for now.'

She rang off and shouted through to the housekeeper, 'I'm going to have a bath.'

Dorothy came to the kitchen doorway.

'What did you say, dear?'

'I said I'm going to have a bath and relax for an hour. What time for lunch?'

'Is 1.30 okay? That gives you an hour and a half.'

'That's fine. See you later.'

'Now don't go unpacking your cases; I'll do that this afternoon whilst you're having a nap.'

Christina made her way up the wide oak staircase. On the landing, a huge bowl of red roses stood on top of a small Regency table. She leaned forward and touched a petal. The flowers smelt fresh. Mrs Barnes must have bought them specially; she knew how much Christina loved roses.

The door to the master bedroom was ajar. This was the one room in the house Christina had insisted on re-doing after her marriage to Stephen. She ran her hand across the king-sized bed covered in antique lace and touched the tapestry cushions piled high on the French Empire chaise-longue.

She wandered to the deep, mullioned bay window beyond which lay neatly manicured lawns and thickly planted borders. Far off in the distance the spire of St Andrew's church rose into a crisp ice-blue sky laced with wispy clouds. Christina embraced the familiarity, pleased to be back in England.

Dorothy brought her a cup of tea at seven the following morning. She placed it at the bedside, saying, 'Morning. It's not a good one, I'm afraid.'

She pulled back the heavy drapes on a wild and blustery day. A noisy wind tore through the trees, and an early shower had left the old oak tree outside the bedroom window dripping and bedraggled.

'Victoria's up, but I must warn you she's in a foul mood. She doesn't want to go back to school.'

'She never does, and she's always in a foul mood, with me at least. What's new?'

Christina sat up in bed. Her eyes felt leaden and she forced them open.

'I'll go and get the breakfast started, and then you can get on the road. Victoria has to be back in her house for ten o'clock, so she has just told me,' Dorothy said, and left the room.

Christina slid out of bed, showered, and dressed in casual slacks, a soft blue cashmere sweater and flat shoes. She walked downstairs and joined Dorothy in the kitchen where she was beating eggs in a deep mixing-bowl.

Victoria came in dressed in her dark-green school uniform.

'Good morning,' Christina said brightly from her place at the breakfast table.

'It's not a good morning! I have got to go back to that ghastly prison, remember?'

'I'm sure it's not that bad.'

'You try it!' Victoria sat down opposite her and helped herself to cereal and milk.

'It won't be for much longer,' Christina said, trying to cheer her up. 'Only two more years.'

Victoria swallowed a mouthful of cornflakes.

'Not if I get my way. I've already asked Daddy if I can leave after GCSEs and he said that he would think about it.'

That's less than a year, Christina realized.

'I thought your father wanted you to stay on? He hasn't said anything to me about you leaving.'

'He doesn't tell you everything, Christina.'

A spiteful light shone in Victoria's eyes. 'He would like me to stay on, I admit, but not if I'm unhappy. I've told him I hate it so much he's agreed to think about letting me leave.'

She set her jaw in exactly the same determined way as Stephen did when he wanted something, and Christina resigned herself to the fact that if Victoria wanted to leave school next year, she would do so by hook or by crook.

'Anyway, there's more than one way to catch the monkey,' Victoria giggled.

'What monkey?' asked the housekeeper, placing two platefuls of scrambled eggs on the table.

323

'It's a Bajan saying,' Christina explained. 'It means, if you can't get what you want one way, you try another.'

Victoria toyed with her scrambled eggs and stared at the autumn leaves fluttering past the window.

'If Daddy doesn't allow me to leave school, I'll find another way.'

Her young voice had taken on the hard edge that Christina was so used to hearing.

I'm sure you will, she thought. You're exactly like your father in that respect. If you want something badly enough, God help anyone who tries to stand in your way.

Christina tried three times to start a conversation on the journey to the school in Hampshire, without success. She was pleased when after half an hour Victoria closed her eyes and slept until the chauffeur pulled the Mercedes into the school gates. John unloaded Victoria's trunks and suitcases as Christina said goodbye to her on the steps of her school-house.

'Have a good term, Vicky; we'll see you at Christmas.'

'You might see me before.'

'What do you mean?' Christina suspected she was plotting something.

'If that old bag Miss Montague tells me off once more, I'll walk out of this place.'

'I really don't think your father would be very happy about that.'

'Daddy would understand. He always does,' Victoria snapped and, throwing a heavy bag bursting with books over her shoulder, she stepped into the house.

'Bye for now, Christina,' she waved. 'Try not to miss me too much.'

Christina opened her mouth to say goodbye as Victoria slammed the heavy door in her face.

Christina listened to music and dozed on the drive back from Hampshire to Sussex, pleased to be free of her step-

324

daughter's taunts, and planning a trip up to London within the next few days.

'What's that?' Christina asked, as Susie walked into the kitchen carrying a box.

'Flowers for the lady.' Her old friend, who had been delighted to be asked down to stay with Christina in London, handed her a long, slim cellophane box containing a white orchid. 'One of these days someone is going to send me flowers,' she said ruefully. 'Tell me, why is it I'm always receiving them for you?'

Christina didn't reply, but took the box. Turning it over, she searched for a card.

'No message?' She raised her eyes.

'The delivery boy said there was none. His instructions were to deliver to Mrs Reece-Carlton personally, so I said I was you.' Susie shrugged. 'It sure beats being Mrs George Williams.'

'Oh, come on, Sue, George isn't that bad!'

'No, he's worse. Still looking for the right job. The problem is there are plenty of right jobs, it's *him* that's wrong!'

Christina opened the box carefully and slid the orchid out.

'It's beautiful. It must be from Stephen. He knows how I love orchids.'

'Well, if he calls today let him mention it to you first, just in case you have a secret admirer,' Susie commented, and sat down at the breakfast table, pouring herself a cup of coffee.

Christina sat down next to her.

'Who besides my husband would send me an exotic tropical flower?'

Susie stuffed half a croissant in her mouth. Through the crumbs she said: 'Search me, but you never know. I met a guy at work a few months ago, a real ugly dumbo. I felt sorry for him and took time out to chat a few times. He sent me several anonymous sloppy cards before I found out it was him. George went berserk. I really didn't have a clue who they were from, so if it can happen to dull boring ol' me, *you* could have an army of admirers out there.'

Christina sipped her coffee, looking at the flower on the table beside her.

'I'm sure it's Stephen, trying to pacify me after our last argument. He promised he'd be here for the weekend, but now apparently he's got problems with the main contractors. He ordered them off the site, which means he has to go back out to tender and get a new firm started before he can safely leave.'

Susie buttered a slice of toast.

'I'm sorry Stephen can't get home, for your sake, Chris, but for mine it's a godsend. It's a real treat for me, coming up to town and staying in this beautiful place.' She looked around the elegantly decorated flat.

'Well, it's lovely to see you, Sue, and I'm pleased you could stay.' Christina sighed. 'We're supposed to be going to Italy this weekend, but if Stephen doesn't get this mess sorted out the trip will be cancelled – again. It's always the same, Sue; business seems to take priority over our personal life.'

'Don't complain! I see George's miserable face every day, and wish sometimes he'd go away for a very long time.' She thought for a moment. 'Actually, forever would be great.'

Christina looked at her friend's gloomy expression.

'Is it that bad?'

Susie nodded. 'I'm afraid so, but we're stuck with each other – for the time being, at least.' She patted her rounded stomach.

'When this little one arrives, I want him to have a father at home.'

'I don't blame you, Susie; it's no fun having a baby on your own.'

'What about you, Christina? No bambinos?'

Christina blushed slightly. 'I'd love a baby. I stopped taking the pill over a year ago, but as yet no luck.'

'Well, you've got loads of time, Chris. You're so young. I'm sure it will happen eventually.'

'I just wish Stephen would try a bit harder. He's either too busy or too bloody tired from being too busy.'

Susie laughed.

'My heart bleeds for you, Chris. It's tough at the top.'

Christina smiled and stood up. 'You're right there – it's bloody tough. Come on, then, let's get dressed. We've got some serious shopping to do.'

The following morning, at almost the same time as the previous day's delivery, a pink four-day hibiscus arrived.

Christina answered the door this time.

'Mrs Reece-Carlton?' the delivery man asked.

'Yes.' Christina held out her hand to take the box.

'There was a different lady yesterday,' he said, holding onto the package.

'That was my friend posing as me,' she said. 'And, by the way, can you tell me why there are no messages?'

'I've got no idea. Call the shop – they might be able to.' He handed over the box.

Christina called the florist, who explained that a man had ordered the flowers last week and had been very explicit: there were to be no messages.

Christina was positive it was Stephen. It was the sort of romantic thing he had done in the early days of their marriage. She hoped it was a prelude to their trip to Italy, and decided to wait until he got to London to thank him.

On Wednesday she received a ginger lily, and on Thursday a beautiful pale-pink frangipani.

Susie left to go back to Cheshire on Friday morning.

The two women hugged on the doorstep as a black cab waited to take Susie to the station.

'I've had a fantastic time, Chris. In fact, I'm dreading going back. Life's pretty dull under normal circumstances, but after this week it'll be bearable.'

'I'm sure you'll survive, Susie. You always do.' Christina kissed her cheek. 'Take care of yourself. It's been great seeing you again. I'd forgotten how much you make me laugh.'

She patted her friend's protruding bulge.

'Take care of my godchild, and don't forget – as soon as you give birth, call me. I want to be the first to know.'

'I'll call if I can find you, Chris. You could be anywhere in the world.'

'Call the English office and speak to Robert Leyton's secretary. She'll locate me.'

Christina carried Susie's bag to the taxi and opened the door for her to climb in. She hung out of the window.

'Thanks again, Chris, for everything. And tell Stephen from me to get trying for a baby as soon as he gets back!'

Christina chuckled. 'I won't forget. Love to George.'

Susie pulled a face. 'Don't remind me. Look after yourself and have a wonderful time in Italy.' She waved as the taxi pulled away. Christina stood on the pavement until Susie's cab was out of sight.

She spent the morning buying a few extra things she needed for the forthcoming holiday, and then went to the hairdresser in the afternoon. The telephone was ringing as she let herself into the flat. Dropping her parcels on the floor of the hall, she picked it up.

She could hear the long-distance bleep, and then Stephen's echoing voice.

'Christina, I have been trying to call you since lunch-time. I've got bad news, I'm afraid. I won't be home tomorrow. This thing with Mitchell Robards is taking a lot longer to sort out than I'd first anticipated. I'm really sorry.'

He sounded tired and his voice was flat.

'Oh, Stephen, no!' she wailed. 'Is there no one else who can take over? Can't you get James up for a few days to sort it out?'

'He's minding the shop in Barbados, and there's only me to sort it out. It's just one of those things, Christina. It's not the end of the world; we can go to Italy another time.'

'It *feels* like the end of the world to me. I've been looking forward to this holiday so much.'

'As usual you're over-reacting.' She could hear the irritation in his tone as he continued: 'I was looking forward to going away to Italy as much as you, Chrissy, but unlike you I understand that things happen sometimes to change the course of events. If I can accept that, why can't you?'

'Of course I can accept that circumstances change, Stephen,' she snapped. 'I understand why you can't make it. What I can't understand is why, unlike me, you don't seem particularly upset!'

She was angry. His whole attitude reeked of impatience, not the real sadness she felt.

'Oh, for God's sake, Christina, grow up! I've got some important business to sort out. We can go on holiday any time. I promise to take you away as soon as this mess is sorted out.'

'Forget it, Stephen. I don't want to go, now. And anyway, your promises are empty. You make them so lightly, I really can't trust you not to break them again.'

'I'm sorry, Christina. What more can I say?' He didn't sound sorry enough.

'There's nothing more to say. I'll cancel the flights and hotel reservations tomorrow.' She felt close to tears.

'I thought you might like to take a friend. Susie would love a trip like that,' he suggested, trying to cheer her up.

'No thanks, Stephen, I wanted to go with you.'

Neither of them spoke for a moment. When Stephen eventually broke the silence, she noticed that a hint of regret had entered his voice.

'I'll call you tomorrow, Chris.'

'I may not be here. Since you're not coming back I'll probably take up an invitation from the Websters to go for dinner at their house tomorrow night. I might even stop over. I'll speak to you at the beginning of next week.'

'Okay, Chris, have a good weekend. Bye for now.'

'Goodbye, Stephen,' she said as the line went dead. Her own eyes, full of sadness, stared back at her from the mirror above the telephone.

She jumped at the sound of the doorbell and picked up the entry phone.

'Delivery for Mrs Reece-Carlton,' a strange, tinny voice said. She opened the door to see an outstretched arm holding out a single red rose in a cellophane box. She poked her head round the door to see to whom the arm belonged.

'Delivery for Mrs Reece-Carlton.' Again the same affected voice.

'Martin!' she squealed, and took the box from his hand. He stepped in front of her and bowed.

'Your very own personal delivery boy.'

She held up the box. 'The flowers I've had all week – you?'

'Guilty,' he announced. 'Only difference is, this one has a message.'

She glanced at a tiny white envelope pinned to the top of the box.

'Come in,' she said, her voice a little shaky as she stepped to one side, allowing him to enter the hall.

She shut the door and, pulling the card from the envelope, read aloud: '"Darlin', I love you so bad, so very bad

. . . You have me goin' so mad, so mad. You sweeten me, girl, you sweeten me."'

Christina was smiling when she looked up from the card and into Martin's face.

'You remembered?'

'How could I forget your favourite Bajan song, or the times we've danced to it?'

She blushed and held out her free hand to him. 'Thank you.'

The pleasure she felt at seeing him illuminated her entire face, and Martin felt happy, elated and embarrassed all at the same time. He dropped his own face to hide his sudden shyness.

She led him into the drawing-room, asking if he wanted a drink.

'I'd love a glass of wine, please.'

She nodded. 'Wine coming up.' She walked into the kitchen, returning a few moments later with a tray containing two glasses of dry white wine and a small bowl of her favourite pistachio nuts.

'Wow! Some place you've got here, Christina.'

'It was Stephen's London pad before we were married. It's been let for a year, and to be quite honest with you, I think we'll put it on the market after Christmas; we just don't use it enough.'

She handed Martin a glass of wine and helped herself to the other. Sitting on the sofa, she indicated that he should sit next to her.

He was wearing a pair of faded blue jeans, a navy-blue wool sweater, and a soft leather jacket, which he took off and draped over a chair, before sitting down, careful to position his long legs in front of the delicate coffee table, nervous that he might break some priceless antique.

His face, still with its tan, looked healthy and infinitely attractive.

'How did you know I was here?' she asked.

'I rang the hotel, and James Morris told me you were here.' He sipped his wine and smiled, showing perfect white teeth.

'I rang to say goodbye, actually, Chris. I've left Barbados, for good. I've been thinking about it for a while now. I love the island, but after a while it starts to become claustrophobic. It served a great purpose for me, getting me back on my feet after the accident, but it was time to move on.'

'What about the business, Martin? I thought you were doing so well?'

'We were, but a few months ago I got offered an opportunity to work with an old friend of mine – an ex-footballer. He recently set up his own PR company dealing only with large football clubs. In just over a year he has more clients than he can handle on his own, and he asked me to join him. He's full of great ideas and enthusiasm, and to be honest with you, Chris, it feels good to be back. Bobby Stoute was more than happy to buy me out, my house was rented and up for renewal, so the only asset I had to sell was my jeep, which hasn't been the same since a young lady ran me off the road a few months ago.' He chuckled and pinched her leg playfully. 'So how long will you be staying in England?' he said casually, hoping she was going to say months.

'I'm not sure. We – that is, Stephen and I – were supposed to go to Italy tomorrow, but he's been delayed in the Bahamas and can't get back.'

Martin wanted to whoop with delight, but tried to make his voice sound indifferent. 'I'm really sorry about that.'

Christina burst out laughing.

'What are you laughing at?' He looked confused.

'I'm laughing because you are absolutely delighted Stephen can't get back. It's written all over your face.'

His deep laughter mingled with hers.

'You're right, I'm not sorry at all. In fact, I'm bloody ecstatic.'

She grabbed his hand and on impulse asked, 'What are you doing this weekend, Martin?'

'Something with you, I hope.'

She looked at her watch. It was almost six o'clock.

'How about Paris, right now?'

He jumped to his feet and held out his arms. 'What are we waiting for?'

They caught the 8.30 Air France flight from Heathrow and landed at Charles de Gaulle Airport in teeming rain an hour later. Thankfully it had stopped by the time the taxi dropped them in front of the Hôtel de Suède in the rue Vanneau.

The building had been a monastery in the seventeenth century, and all the bedrooms were housed in the original cloisters, set around a vine-covered cobbled courtyard.

They were shown to a small beamed room with an antique four-poster bed draped in faded gold tapestry. The same material had been used for lots of cushions piled on a shabby old chaise, which stood next to a small writing-desk and two pretty carved bergères.

'This is so beautiful,' Christina said, opening the tall casement windows and stepping out onto a tiny, crooked balcony.

Martin stood behind her, his hands on her shoulders.

'How ever did you discover it?' she asked, leaning over the wrought-iron balustrade and listening to the muted sounds of a small stone fountain in the courtyard below.

'Now that would be telling,' he whispered into her ear.

'Tell me.' She turned to face him.

'A friend of mine spent his honeymoon here and said it was the most romantic hotel he had ever stayed in.'

She kissed him softly.

'Thank goodness we could get a room. It's wonderful.'

She kissed him again, and he responded instantly. Christina pushed him gently back into the room.

'I don't know about you, but I'm starving. Can we go and get something to eat?'

Martin steered her towards the bed.

'Later. How about some room service now?'

'Food first, Martin. I need sustenance.' She ignored his downcast expression. 'This is my first trip to Paris, remember? I want to see as much as I can.'

He laughed at the childlike anticipation on her face. He loved her so much he could deny her nothing.

'Come on, then, let's go,' he said, picking up their coats from the bed and holding open the door for her.

A cool breeze blew across the street as they walked out of the hotel, and hazy moonlight clung to the rooftops of the quaint old buildings of St Germain des Prés.

Christina was excited by the vast profusion of bustling restaurants, and couldn't make up her mind where she wanted to eat. They stopped at several, reading the menus displayed outside and peeping into the darkened, busy interiors before arriving at one particularly crowded place.

'This one looks great,' Martin said, pushing her inside before she could change her mind.

They were shown to a corner table in the noisy bistro, decorated in dark, sombre colours enlivened with dozens of Impressionist prints and huge bowls of fresh flowers on every table.

'I'm starving now, Chris,' he said, looking at the *plats du jour* chalked up on a blackboard. He ordered terrine and *steak au poivre*. Christina ordered *escargots* and *boeuf bourgignon*, in what to him sounded like perfect French.

'I'm impressed. Where did you learn to speak French?'

'At school initially, and since we've had the hotel quite a few of the chefs have been French. I've picked up a bit that way.'

Martin ordered two glasses of champagne with *framboise* as an apéritif, and to follow a bottle of Gevrey Chambertin.

He picked up his glass and, looking deep into her eyes, said: 'To us.'

Christina dropped her gaze.

'To this weekend. Tell me about your new job. I'm dying to hear all about it.'

'It's fantastic,' he said with enthusiasm. 'Everything I could have hoped. I'm marketing and promotions manager for the old club. It's well paid and varied, and most important of all I'm back in football, the game I love, which makes me very happy.'

The food arrived then, and they both fell on it ravenously. Martin didn't speak again until he had finished his terrine.

'And what about you, Christina? Can you honestly say that you're happy?'

She considered his question. Happy? She wasn't sure any more. The feeling of completeness she had enjoyed at the beginning of her marriage seemed gradually to be eroding, slipping away from her. Sometimes it terrified her.

'I have what most people would consider a marvellous life, but I get very lonely. Stephen is so involved with the business, I think he forgets I'm there sometimes.'

'The man's a fool,' Martin said simply. 'He doesn't appreciate what he's got.'

She sipped her wine.

'You're wrong. I think he does, and I know he loves me, but it isn't enough just to tell me – I need more of his time. This last year he's been totally obsessed with his new project in the Bahamas. Our life has been impossible. We hardly see each other. Cancelling our holiday to Italy was the last straw.'

Martin considered his next question, unsure whether to

ask it or not. At last he said, 'Is that the only reason you're here, Chris, to punish Stephen?'

She looked into his handsome, square-jawed face; at the warm, dark-green eyes, and the generous mouth, always threatening to break into a wide, beaming smile.

'No, that's not the only reason. I'm here because I want to be with you.'

The undisguised joy her words produced was so evident that she wanted to reach across to touch him. He seemed to read her mind, and his hand crept across the table to clasp hers. She stroked his palm with her fingertip, suddenly and unexpectedly consumed with desire for him and anxious for the meal to be finished so that they could return to the hotel.

They strolled back through quiet, almost deserted streets, hand in hand, their feet echoing on the cobblestones as they walked through a walled garden to the front door of the hotel.

A bad-tempered night porter let them in, muttering under his breath. They ignored him and squeezed into the tiny lift, giggling as Christina pressed the wrong button and they descended to the basement.

Neither of them spoke as Martin locked the door of their room and turned on the light next to the bed.

He watched, his eyes never leaving her, as she slowly undid the buttons of her silk shirt, pulling it over her shoulders and letting it fall on the floor. She undid her skirt, which fell at her feet, and stepped out of it, standing in front of him wearing nothing but a pair of tiny white panties. His eyes roamed the entire length of her body, resting on the dark triangle which the lace could not conceal.

He could see that she was shaking slightly. Her full breasts rose and fell.

Christina ran her fingers down her body in long, sensuous strokes. Letting her hands stray to the top of her panties, she pulled them down, burying her fingers deep inside and caressing herself with slow, circular movements. After a few moments she held out one hand to Martin, who took it, licking each finger separately.

'You taste like nectar,' he said in a muffled voice, kneeling down in front of her. She shivered and moaned when his hot lips and tongue found how aroused she already was.

She kicked off her shoes as he carried her to the bed, laying her down like a precious piece of porcelain. She opened her legs and he stared long and hard before tearing off his clothes with frantic hands.

Naked, he crouched above her. She ran her fingers up and down his thick penis, marvelling at its size.

He entered her slowly. She was wet and eager and, winding her legs around his back, pulled him deep inside, calling his name.

'I'm home,' she heard him say before his mouth covered hers in hungry kisses, drowning her small cries as she reached a shuddering orgasm that went on and on.

A little later he withdrew from her gently, and she brought him to a final climax with her hand, watching mesmerized as his semen spurted out and spattered across her stomach.

She rubbed it into her breasts and stomach, whispering, 'This is supposed to be good for the skin.'

'Any time you want a treatment, call me.'

She laughed, and he licked and kissed her breasts and stomach, telling her over and over again that he loved her.

'I love you too, Martin,' she said, kissing the top of his blond, tousled head.

He held her face in his hands and kissed her bruised mouth. 'You've made me so happy tonight, Christina. I've thought about making love to you so many times, dreamt about how it would be.'

'Did it live up to expectations?' she asked, and pinched him as he pretended to look disappointed. 'No, it exceeded my wildest dreams,' he said finally. She chuckled, and he wrapped his arms around her waist, moulding her body against his.

'You're very beautiful, Christina,' he said, tempted to ask if their lovemaking had been good for her. He was horrified to hear her next words.

'That was the most terrible experience I have ever had and I never want to do it again!'

'Are you serious?' He sat up, resting his head on one elbow, gazing into her face. She burst out laughing at the disbelief in his expression.

'Martin, if you don't know that I had a wonderful time then you need your head examining!'

She kissed him on his open mouth and murmured sleepily, 'It was great and I love you.' She rested her head on his chest before drifting into a light sleep.

Martin lay awake thinking.

He listened to Christina's soft breathing, and gently eased his arm from behind her head before it went completely numb. Early in the morning he heard the sounds of bread being delivered, mingled with bird-song, and fell into a deep sleep as light began to peep through a narrow gap in the shutters.

Christina woke him at 10.30 with a soft kiss on the back of his neck.

They made love again, a sleepy, lazy arousal culminating in wild passion as both of them reached orgasm together.

Martin ordered croissants and *café au lait* as Christina ran a bath.

'Come on in with me,' she shouted from the steamy bathroom, chuckling as she pulled him into the hot tub.

Christina spent the next forty-eight hours on a self-induced delirious high. All thoughts of Stephen were pushed firmly aside as she lost herself in the fantasy, and in Martin.

It was a long time since she had had such crazy, spontaneous fun. She laughed until she cried when Martin tried to eat an *escargot* and it shot off his plate, landing at the feet of a particularly snooty waiter.

She had a fit of uncontrollable giggles in the Louvre when he made a suggestion as to why Mona Lisa was smiling, and kissed him passionately on the lips when he bought her a painting in Montmartre. They cruised up the Seine, joking with a boat-load of Japanese tourists who gabbled in high-pitched voices and took millions of photographs, and then ate steaming-hot crêpes from an outdoor vendor.

In spite of the howling wind they trudged up the Eiffel Tower, braving it for only five minutes before coming down, shivering, and racing to a tiny café to drink hot, creamy chocolate and eat delicious French pastries.

On their last night, Martin paid over the odds for two tickets to the late-night Crazy Horse Saloon revue show. Christina, wide-eyed and fascinated, watched a bevy of beautiful half-naked girls cavort in the smoky, sleazy club.

They made love frantically that night, unsure what the future might bring. Afterwards it was Christina's turn to lie awake, unable to sleep.

Thoughts of Stephen, which she had forced to the back of her mind, now haunted her and refused to be dispelled.

Tomorrow she had to go back to London and her real life; leave the fantasy behind in Paris. Should she tell her husband the truth? That she was in love with Martin Ward, as well as him?

All night the most important question of all whirled around her mind unanswered: did she want to leave Stephen for Martin?

She had made up her mind before she rose from the bed to fling back the shutters on a glorious morning. Sunlight flooded the room, catching Martin's blond head.

'Come on, lazy-bones. This is our last morning. Let's walk down to the river.'

'Later,' he muttered, his voice muffled as he pulled the bed-covers over his head to shut out the glare.

'Now!' She pulled them off, exposing his hard, lean body and erect penis.

'Let's have breakfast first.' He held out his arms to her. She was tempted, but stayed where she was.

'No, Martin, please. It's a fantastic day.'

'Okay, okay. Your wish is my command.' He rolled out of bed and then grabbed her around the waist, flinging her back onto the bed and jumping on top of her whilst she fought him, her fists pummelling his chest.

'No, Martin! No!' She was trying hard to resist and becoming aroused against her will as he found her nipple with his mouth, sucking it whilst his fingers teased her.

'Please stop,' she implored him. 'We need to talk – seriously. Let's go out, Martin. Please.'

They showered, dressed in jeans and big woolly jumpers, and strolled hand in hand through narrow alleyways. They passed a bustling street market, the smell of fresh fish mingling with newly baked baguettes, before reaching the Seine.

Martin put his arm around her shoulders, and they walked along the river-bank, casually watching passing boats and other walkers.

Christina leaned against the railing at the water's edge and watched a small tug go by.

'I don't think it would be wise for us to see each other again, after today.' She blurted out the words, afraid to look at him. She stared at the boat chugging slowly past, her body tense, holding her breath for Martin to speak.

'Why not?' He held her by the shoulders and turned her round to face him.

'Because we lead such different lives. It would be impossible.'

'So you've had your fling, your bit of fun? Exciting, was it? Did I live up to expectations?' His voice was charged with a suppressed rage.

'It's not like that, Martin – Stephen would never let me go.' She turned away from the sight of him, his face bleached of colour and tight with pain.

'It's okay. Christina. I understand. You run home to your husband and marital bliss. Don't dare to ask yourself why you needed me in the first place.' His harsh words bit into her like a freezing wind. 'Was I a good fuck, Chris? Did I break the monotony of marriage for a few days?' he continued relentlessly.

'Stop it, Martin! Stop it!' she screamed, and held her hands over her ears. 'I'm in love with you but I can't leave Stephen. You'd never understand. He needs me.'

'No, Christina, I don't understand. I think you are far too loyal to a man who needs you only second to his business. If that's what you want for the rest of your life, then go ahead.'

He turned away from the appeal in her eyes. If she was looking for forgiveness he was far too hurt to offer any.

'You're a coward. You haven't got the courage to leave Stephen, and you obviously don't need me. I really hope, Chris, that at some point in your life you'll need and love someone as much as I love and need you at this moment. Because only then will you realize what you've just thrown away. Goodbye. And don't worry – I won't bother you again.'

He turned and began to walk away. If he had punched her in the stomach the pain could not have been more intense. She buckled over, trying to call his name. Her throat tightened, and she was unable to utter a sound.

Motionless, she stood and watched his broad back until he was out of sight.

'*Ça va?*' An old Parisienne lady out walking her poodle looked at Christina's stricken face. She was oblivious to both the dog and the old woman.

'*Pomme, ici.*' The old lady picked up her dog and moved on. 'Coward?' Christina repeated Martin's accusation out loud. How could she begin to explain that she was destined to be with Stephen Reece-Carlton; had known that from the first time she'd met him. Only death could part them, she was sure of that. But that didn't make losing Martin any easier to bear.

The dark-blue sky was reflected in the waters of the Seine and turned into the colour of dirty steel.

She walked slowly back to the hotel, arriving just before it began to rain.

Martin had already left. He was catching an earlier flight to Manchester for a meeting with his old club; she was grateful not to have to see him at the airport.

Christina lay on the messy bed in the empty room, sad and guilt-ridden, brooding for over an hour until it was time to go.

She arrived back in London in the early afternoon. John, the chauffeur, picked her up at Heathrow and gave her a message from Stephen to call him as soon as possible. It was urgent, apparently.

It was always urgent with Stephen, she thought. That was about the only thing that was predictable about him. She didn't really want to speak to him that night, and was pleased when she did ring to find that he was in a meeting.

She spent a miserable night alone, drinking a bottle of white wine and ignoring the continuous ringing of the telephone. Afterwards she slept fitfully, her sleep broken by dreams of Martin and Stephen.

The next morning she rose early, and after breakfast

342

rang her travel agent to book a flight back to the West Indies. A place was found on the noon flight from Heathrow, and Christina spent the entire eight-hour journey trying to put thoughts of Martin out of her mind.

Chapter Seventeen

Christina was greeted by the sound of laughter when she walked into the courtyard of Crystal Springs House. She recognized Stephen's immediately, but the other? Surely it couldn't be . . . ?

But it was – Victoria, sitting on the arm of Stephen's chair, her arm draped casually about her father's shoulders while they obviously shared a joke. At this sight the crippling weight of depression which Christina had borne since parting from Martin felt almost too much to bear. After making the most difficult decision of her life, she'd been looking forward to some time alone with her husband.

'I thought you were coming out on Christmas Eve, Victoria?' she said, a touch of ice in her voice.

'And Daddy thought *you* were going to be in London this weekend. If you had, you'd have been there for Miss Montague's phone call – well, one of them – telling you how ill I'd been and asking you to bring me home early to recuperate.'

Victoria looked smugly triumphant as Christina coloured nervously.

'Oh – Susie wanted me to go up to Manchester for a party she and George were having. There were lots of old friends there, and I didn't really get the chance to . . .'

'I wish you had let me know,' said Stephen, a hint of reproach in his voice. 'I was worried when we couldn't trace you, and so was Dorothy. She said she hadn't heard from you in a week.'

Christina groaned inwardly. She could just imagine the agitated phone calls that must have been exchanged. Heaven only knew what conclusions had been drawn about her absence – the right ones, she supposed guiltily.

'And why didn't you let us know you were coming home today?' Stephen continued, looking perplexed. 'You know I'd have sent Mr Payne to meet the flight if you had.'

'That would have spoilt Christina's surprise, Daddy. She obviously likes to keep you guessing.'

Victoria's voice was laced with spite. Christina could tell she'd been looking forward to having him all to herself for even longer.

'Why don't you come upstairs?' Stephen asked. 'You need a cool shower and a stiff drink. I'll get Victor to bring you a vodka and tonic, shall I?'

'Just a lime squash would be fine, thanks.'

She climbed the stairs wearily, and sank into the mahogany-framed chaise-longue in the bedroom. Stephen appeared in the doorway and scrutinized her thoughtfully.

'Everything all right?' he asked eventually. 'You worried me, you know, taking off like that.'

'I know, I'm sorry. It won't happen again,' she said dully.

I'll never see Martin again, she thought, and tears filled her eyes. She averted her face from Stephen and went through to the bathroom. She was sure he had seen her distress, but he made no comment, leaving her to her shower and closing the bedroom door gently behind him.

She stayed there a long time, tears mingling with the water that streamed over her, soothing her tired body but doing nothing for the aching void that was her heart.

When she was cried out she held a flannel soaked in ice-cold water to her puffy eyelids until they were no longer red and sore. Afterwards she vigorously towelled dry her hair, applied a fine dusting of blusher to her pale cheeks, and sat staring at her reflection in the dressing-table mirror, making herself a promise. She had said no to Martin. Now she must put all thoughts of him aside and get on with her life with Stephen, which included trying to get along with Victoria. Thank goodness the Christmas holiday wasn't a long one, even if she had artfully managed to extend it with talk of her 'illness'. She certainly looked healthy enough.

With this resolve in mind, Christina left the bedroom to join the other two. She heard her stepdaughter's excited voice as she stepped out into the courtyard and walked over to them. They had moved to the small two-seater sofa now, Victoria sitting very close to Stephen with one leg sprawled across his lap.

'I'm so looking forward to living with you here, Daddy. We're going to have a lot of fun together, aren't we?'

Christina was visibly shocked. 'What did you say?' She looked directly into Victoria's grey-blue eyes which were wide and innocent as a kitten's.

'Oh, I forgot you didn't know, Christina. I've quit school altogether, and I'm going to live here with you and Daddy all the time now.'

Christina turned to Stephen. 'What do you know about this?'

'What Vicky told me when she arrived on Sunday,' he said with a shrug. 'If you'd been where we could contact you, you'd have heard it too. She's not happy at that school any more. It's too stodgy and old-fashioned for her.'

'And what about all your plans to go to college, Victoria?' Christina asked. 'What's happened to them?'

'Oh, I still intend to go. Daddy and I have already discussed it and made all the arrangements. I'm almost sixteen, after all. I can have a private tutor here for six months, and then college in America after that. Isn't it exciting?'

She threw her arms around her father's neck and buried her head in his shoulder. Stephen looked at Christina over the top of her head, his face imploring her to understand. Christina nodded slowly in response. It looked as if Stephen and Victoria had settled things to their own satisfaction, if not hers. At the moment she didn't feel like making an issue of it.

She stood up and walked to the edge of the terrace, where she parted a mass of white bougainvillaea to make enough space to be able to sit on the low retaining wall. She let her legs dangle over the side while she watched a tiny bird of paradise hover in front of a bright-scarlet ginger lily.

She jumped as Stephen placed his hands on her shoulders and leant forward to say softly in her left ear: 'She's young, Christina. Try to understand and make friends. For my sake.' He pushed her hair gently to one side and kissed her neck.

'I'll try, Stephen, I promise,' she murmured, and turned and kissed him full on the mouth. It was a deep, hungry kiss which surprised him. Despite his daughter's watchful presence, he responded by pulling her closer to him in a tight embrace.

Any promise Christina had made to herself or to Stephen was forgotten as she looked over his shoulder to see Victoria's beautiful face transformed into an ugly mask of undisguised hatred.

Crystal Springs glittered, dressed to kill in a dazzling array of Christmas decorations. Christina had been decorating for the last week, and was finishing the Christmas tree when Stephen walked into the drawing-room of Crystal Springs House at five o'clock on Christmas Eve.

'Be careful,' he warned, looking up as she wobbled

precariously on the top rung of a ladder, putting the final touches to the top with a big red star.

'Well, what do you think?' she asked breathlessly, still adjusting the decoration. He looked up and down the full length of the Christmas tree shimmering in red and gold finery, and whistled. 'It looks magnificent. Well done,' he shouted up at her. 'Now, please come down; you're making me nervous.'

He held the foot of the ladder as she climbed carefully down. She stepped from the last rung, flushed and full of excitement. She stood back and looked up at her handiwork, running her fingers through her hair and pulling out a piece of tinsel.

He laughed. 'Your face is covered in gold glitter – and grime!' He leaned forward and rubbed her cheek with his thumb. 'Impossible to get it off. You'll have to stay like that for the whole of Christmas! While you're decorating, here's another present to put under the tree.'

It had been carefully wrapped in gold foil and a pink three-day poinsettia was held in place on the top of the box with bright-red ribbon. He placed it in her hands, and Christina shook it, trying to guess the contents.

'You'll just have to wait until tomorrow,' said Stephen, smiling.

'Wait for what?' They both turned to see Victoria walking towards them. Christina held up the Christmas present.

'To see what your father has bought me.'

Victoria sneered, 'Oh, I already know – I chose it.' Her words stung, as they were intended to.

'That's not exactly true, Victoria,' Stephen cut in. 'You *helped* choose it.' He gave his daughter a warning look and turned his attention back to Christina, who suddenly felt flat, robbed of the warm anticipation of Christmas she had felt only moments earlier.

Stephen changed the subject. 'Come on, then, we'd

better go and get ready. The carol service starts in less than an hour.'

Victoria yawned and moaned. 'Do I have to sit through a boring old carol service?'

'I'm afraid you do, young lady. You know I like a family atmosphere for the guests at Christmas. So go and get ready or we'll be late.'

The choir finished their rendition of 'Once in Royal David's City'. Christina, visibly moved, watched one very small chorister of about eight years old step forward and hold up his carol sheet. His face looked angelic above the starched white ruff he wore. He sang 'Away in a Manger', his sweet, melodic voice breaking the stillness of the warm West Indian night.

She felt her throat swell with tears as he came to the end and stepped back to join the choir. They all burst into 'Hark the Herald Angels Sing', joined by the 250 guests who had gathered in the restaurant and were spilling out onto the terrace while they watched the carol service.

A guests' cocktail party followed, and after that a traditional West Indian Christmas Eve dinner consisting of deep-fried salt fish, roast turkey with spicy West Indian stuffing, and pumpkin fritters, sweet potatoes, couscous and yams. And for dessert – if anyone could manage it – sweet lime or coconut-cream pie served with rum and raisin ice-cream or mango mousse.

After dinner, limbo dancers, fire-eaters and pretty young Barbadian girls dressed in gaudy carnival costumes performed an unsophisticated but enjoyable cabaret for the closely packed audience. Filled with freely poured Christmas spirits, they applauded wildly.

At midnight the still air was filled with delighted cries as hundreds of multi-coloured balloons rained from a star-filled sky, each bearing the message: 'Happy Christmas from all at Crystal Springs'.

Stephen and Christina stood to one side of the

bandstand as the quartet began to play 'We Wish You a Merry Christmas'.

Afterwards he took her hand and led her to their table. Victoria was noticeable by her absence as Stephen poured two glasses of champagne and handed one to Christina. He raised his glass to her animated face and proposed a toast: 'To us, and the future of Crystal Springs.'

She took a sip of her champagne and looked into Stephen's pale eyes. He'd never questioned her again about her movements on the weekend during which he and Victoria's school had tried to trace her. A rush of love for him filled her, and she raised her glass and said, 'To us.'

Soon afterwards, James Morris came towards her, arms outstretched.

'Happy Christmas, Christina.' She flinched as he kissed her cheek wetly.

She could see that he was very drunk. His bow-tie was undone and lying across his left shoulder, and the front of his shirt was stained with spilt food and drink. He reeled forward in an attempt to kiss her again, this time on the mouth, but she anticipated it and deftly dodged him.

'So . . . Mrs Reece-Carlton's too good to kiss the likes of me, is she?' he slurred. 'Not too proud to offer her favours to others, though.'

'What do you mean by that?' she asked, watching him warily.

He tapped the side of his nose. 'You can't fool me, Christina. I've got eyes, you know, and you were so easy to read – both of you. A quiet drink together, you and that clapped-out glamour-boy, Ward? Pull the other one! You were panting for it, both of you. Shame I had to come in and spoil your little game, wasn't it?'

Christina closed her eyes for a second, sickened by the proximity of his sweating red face and whisky-laden breath.

'You'd better be careful,' she warned. 'Like I said at the time, I was having a quiet drink with a friend. Nothing wrong with that and you know it.'

He shook his head slowly. 'It's not what *I* think – it's what your doting husband Stephen Smartass Reece-Carlton thinks that really counts. Oh, yes, I could put the cat among the pigeons very nicely if I wanted to.

'You see, I ran into Bobby Stoute the other day. He told me about buying the rest of the business off your pretty boy and mentioned that Goldilocks was living it up in London on the proceeds. Funny the way he pitched up there at just the time you did, isn't it?'

Christina swallowed. 'You can make of it what you like. We happened to be there at the same time, but London's a big place. Tell Stephen if you want. He won't thank you for making malicious insinuations.'

James lowered his voice threateningly. 'No, he wouldn't. But for proof positive . . . ?

'I don't know if you've bothered to notice, Christina, but since Elaine died I've been seeing a lot of a certain travel agent – Pam, a most obliging young lady. I asked her to check out passenger flight-lists for me. She has contacts. And, hey presto – would you believe which two names turned up on a flight to Paris. Just when you had your "lost" weekend, too. Now I'd call that more than a coincidence, wouldn't you?'

She shuddered violently. James was Stephen's man, a toady with an eye to the main chance. God, how could Elaine ever have been married to a shit like this?

He had hold of her arm and was pulling her gradually closer as he spoke. 'Of course, Christina, he doesn't *have* to find out.'

But he did, she realized. There was no way she'd allow this poor excuse of a man ever to think he had a hold over her.

She shook herself free angrily. 'Stop right there, James,'

351

she warned in a voice that throbbed with rage. 'I don't want to hear your grubby little threats, and I don't care what you think you've got on me – Stephen knows it all. If you value your job and what little reputation you have left, you'll keep quiet, do you hear?'

She could see the doubt creep into his eyes, and played on it for all she was worth.

'I think you've had enough to drink,' she said firmly. 'Why don't you leave your assistant in charge? I'll make your excuses to Stephen and we'll forget we ever started this conversation, shall we?'

James seemed taken aback that she had seized the initiative. She couldn't believe he'd leave it for long, but if she could just hold him off for tonight, it would give her the opportunity she needed. It wasn't the Christmas present she'd have chosen for Stephen, but she knew that tonight she must tell him the truth. It would be too dangerous not to.

Once she'd decided to confess, she was impatient to get it over with, but Stephen seemed infuriatingly reluctant to leave the party while there were still guests there enjoying themselves. A pouting Victoria was sent to bed by him at one o'clock after disgracing herself by dancing way too close to the nineteen-year-old son of some regular guests. The boy looked embarrassed when an indignant Stephen warned them both to behave, but looking at her stepdaughter, in a low-cut, slinky red dress, wearing too much eye make-up and jewellery, Christina thought he could be forgiven for the mistake he'd made. Victoria looked his age at least, or even more.

It was three in the morning before she finally persuaded Stephen away from the hotel and back to the house. He looked exhausted, and she felt overwhelmed with guilt at the fresh burden she was about to place on him.

'I had an affair with Martin Ward,' she blurted out as Stephen began to pull off his tie. She rushed on, not daring to look up, 'I'm sorry, Stephen. I felt neglected, you see – you were always so engrossed in the hotels, and then when you cancelled our trip to Italy, Martin came along and we . . .'

There was a long pause. She expected reproaches, anger, a cold declaration that she should get out. She was not prepared for what he said.

'I know, Christina. There's no need to tell me any more. There was always something between you – an affinity, a sort of spark when you were together. That's why I asked you not to see him. But you did – while I was in New York and then in London.'

Christina stared at him in disbelief.

'Why didn't you say something?'

'Because I knew you would tell me eventually, one way or the other.'

'How do you feel about it, then – are you angry?' She still couldn't bring herself to look at him. He didn't sound angry, she realized. More resigned than anything.

She dared to look up then, and was amazed by what she saw. Her imperturbable, tough husband was fighting to control himself. He was trembling as he put his hands on her shoulders.

'Will you promise me it's over with him? That you've come back to me for good?'

She nodded mutely.

He hugged her to him. She could feel his heart beating frantically against her cheek.

'But things will have to change, Stephen. I came back because I love you and always will. What I don't like – what made me turn to Martin in the first place – is the way you've let the business come between us. You forced me away.'

She put her hand to his mouth when he started to speak.

'No, hear me out. This is important. I want us to be

together, but it has to be on equal terms from now on. Remember what you said to me when we first bought this place? I was scared I wouldn't be able to live up to the Reece-Carlton flair for business, but you convinced me I had a contribution to make too. You made me think you valued what I was, what I could do. And then you shut me out. It hurt, Stephen. I didn't deserve that.'

'I know. I let business take over sometimes. It doesn't mean you don't matter. You're the best part of me, Chrissy. Without you I'd be a different person – one that even *I* wouldn't like.'

It was the most open declaration she had ever had from him. They didn't make love that night, content just to fall asleep in each other's arms. Christina awoke at ten to find the bed beside her empty. She was about to get up and go in search of Stephen when he appeared carrying an envelope.

'Have you been up long?' she asked.

'No, and I'm coming back to bed right now. I just went to fetch your Christmas present.'

She looked at the envelope in surprise. 'But it's under the tree, isn't it?'

'Well, your new diamond bracelet is. This is something much more important. Open it.'

She took the envelope and pulled out the single sheet of paper it contained. She read it twice, convinced she was seeing things.

I, Stephen Reece-Carlton, hereby assign to my beloved wife, Christina Reece-Carlton, a joint interest in Crystal Springs Hotel, Barbados. She already has joint ownership of our home, Crystal Springs House, and all my heart.

'We'll have it drawn up legally straight after the holiday,' he promised, sitting on the side of the bed.

'Thank you,' she whispered, stroking his face. 'You can

354

trust me, you know. I'm yours now. Nothing will ever come between us again.'

And not even the announcement of her pregnancy, a few weeks later, managed to disturb their new-found closeness. They both knew, though neither of them ever mentioned it, that the baby could be either Stephen's or Martin's. There was no way of telling, for the moment, at least. But from the start Stephen welcomed the idea of a child, fussing over Christina and making gigantic efforts to cut down on work commitments for them both. He had not gone back on his Christmas Day promise, and she was now legally joint owner of the hotel, and just as involved as he was in the day-to-day running. She herself drew the line at becoming too involved in the Bahamas development – for the time being, at least. She owed it to the baby to take care of herself and not to overwork.

Her pregnancy passed in a kind of happy daze. She felt she had it all now: a happy marriage, a child on the way and, most important of all, the new love and understanding she shared with Stephen.

She thought of Martin occasionally – with fondness – and hoped he would find a new love soon. It was only a few weeks before the birth was due, when she was feeling fat and clumsy and longing for the pregnancy to be over, that she began to worry what it would be like if the child were born resembling Martin.

But when her son Adam arrived, early in September, the only likeness he bore was to her: the same red-brown hair, fine features, and eyes of baby blue which mysteriously turned to a clear light hazel when he was a few weeks old.

Stephen was touchingly pleased with the new arrival – so much so that an affronted Victoria announced that she'd decided to attend a fashionable crammer's in London. A suitable arrangement was reached for her to live with the family of a former schoolfriend, and Christina waved her off with a sigh of relief. To her surprise, the huge fees the crammer's demanded were money well spent. Victoria passed her GCSEs, took A-levels in French and Mathematics, and would eventually pass her American SATs and be offered a place at Brown University, Rhode Island.

But not even his clever daughter's achievements could compete with Stephen's love for and pride in Adam. He went everywhere with them. Stephen had decorated and equipped a lavish nursery for him at Crystal Springs House, but more often than not the baby could be found over at the hotel where Stephen delighted in introducing him to the guests as 'Adam, my son and heir'.

Chapter Eighteen

It was a brilliant day when the plane bringing Christina to the Bahamas touched down on Providence Island. She blinked and shaded her eyes with one hand as she climbed out of Stephen's new four-seater Cessna, steadying Adam in her arms with the other.

Stephen was waiting when they came out of the terminal. She almost fell into his arms. It was the first time they'd been apart for longer than a few days since her pregnancy and Adam's birth, but in the last few weeks things had hotted up on the Bahamas development, and he had been obliged to go over and trouble-shoot, leaving Christina in Barbados to recruit long-distance a nanny who would not object to their peripatetic lifestyle.

'How's Patricia working out?' Stephen asked after he had hugged Christina and kissed the baby.

'Absolutely fine. I've given her a few days off while you and I and Adam are reunited as a family, but she'll be over soon.

'She was working for Melody Lyon, the actress, before, so she's used to moving around, travelling from location to location and so on. She couldn't stand it in the end, though. Too many tantrums.'

Stephen looked alarmed.

'You mean she can't handle babies?'

'No – not the baby's; Melody's. Pat is the no-nonsense, down-to-earth, good, solid Welsh stock type. You'll like her, honestly. I'd never have hired someone I didn't trust. After all, she's going to have sole charge of Adam when the opening festivities start.'

'If there is an opening,' Stephen grunted.

'Why? What's gone wrong?'

'Tell you later,' he said, directing the porter to a waiting car and guiding Christina across the road.

The drive from the airport to Paradise Island was a scenic one, with glimpses of foaming surf and pastel-coloured shuttered houses. Flowers and shrubs spilled in profusion over low walls, but Stephen showed little interest and sat thoughtful and quiet.

Roads lined with ancient, overhanging, leafy trees soon gave way to condominiums and hotels dotted along Cable Beach before they reached historic Nassau, which was steeped in colonial charm. Christina glanced out of the cab window at bustling Bay Street lined with its assortment of shops and restaurants. It looked a peaceful, prosperous scene.

'You'd better tell me the worst,' she sighed.

Stephen brushed dust from the car seat with tense, agitated movements. 'The contractors are behind schedule, Paul Richardson is in bed with some strange virus, the general manager is panicking, and Antonio is driving me mad! Apart from that, everything's fine.'

'What is it you always said, Stephen, when we were battling to open Crystal Springs?' She nudged him.

'I know, I know – it'll be all right on the night.' He didn't sound confident, and gave her a tight, nervous smile. It was unlike him, she thought; things must be tough. She held his hand as they approached the toll-bridge that would take them across to Paradise Island.

The taxi-driver paid the toll and the old Plymouth trundled under an arched bridge above Prince George Dock. They passed hotels, condos and restaurants set in lavishly landscaped gardens, before turning off the road and down a long, freshly laid asphalt drive lined on both sides with swaying traveller's palms.

A flashing neon sign reading 'Crystal Springs Beach Club and Casino' was the first thing to meet their eyes as they stopped outside the impressive double-storey entrance to the new hotel. Stephen stared at it in horror.

'What on earth is that monstrosity?'

He jumped out of the taxi and bolted into the lobby. Christina soothed Adam, who was beginning to whimper, and followed. Antonio was there, deep in conversation with a lean, dark man she instantly recognized. He was shaking his head vigorously, knitting heavy, dark brows over the darkest of sunglasses.

'I'm telling you, Toni . . .' he was saying when Stephen interrupted.

'Where on earth did you get that sign from?'

A dark, stubbled face turned to him, frowning.

Antonio's eyes flickered heavenward.

'Excuse me, Gino,' he murmured, giving him a quick placating smile. 'Be right back.'

He walked towards Christina, ignoring Stephen.

'You make a lovely mamma,' he told her, kissing her on both cheeks. 'And this must be Adam? He's a beautiful boy; I know how proud of him Stephen is.'

'We both are,' she agreed, and for once felt that Antonio was perfectly sincere. He'd told her how much he himself was looking forward to starting a family, though somehow she couldn't see Susanna being as keen.

'Cut the soft soap, Antonio,' Stephen cut in brusquely.

She saw the Italian's dark eyes flicker at this open rudeness. But Stephen couldn't help himself. For him it was a matter of principle. He wouldn't back down.

'The sign – I want it down, like yesterday!' He slapped one palm to his brow. 'Neon! Where do you think we are – Las Vegas? This is *not* what Crystal Springs is all about, Antonio.'

'Calm down, Stephen. Come on, let's all sit down and get a drink and I'll explain why the sign has to stay.' He took Stephen's arm persuasively.

'I'll shut the whole fucking place down before I let a flashing sign stay! You can just forget it, Antonio. Anyway, you had no right to do it without consulting me. Did Paul know about this?'

'No he didn't, believe me.' They turned at the sound of Paul Richardson's voice behind them.

'What *is* all this shit you're handing me?' Antonio asked in an incredulous voice. 'One stupid neon sign – it's no big deal, for Chrissakes. Gino got it from the guy who's supplying the gaming equipment, and I for one like it. I think it should stay. It'll look great at night when people are coming to the casino.'

'We've never had neon at Crystal Springs,' Christina put in. 'If you are going to use our hotel's name, Antonio, don't you think you ought to honour its spirit? It's what attracted you to us in the first place, after all.'

She kept her voice low and reasonable, deliberately looking down at Adam as she spoke rather than taking up the adversarial stance which Stephen knew he ought not to adopt with the Italian but somehow could never avoid. It was not turning out to be a happy association.

'Hey, we gonna fall out over one lousy sign?' Antonio raised his arms and grinned at Gino Santorini, who looked as angry as Stephen.

'Not so long as it's down by tomorrow.'

And, while Christina smiled an apology, Stephen rudely turned his back on Antonio.

'How are you, Paul? You look knackered,' he said with real concern, studying the architect's drawn face. 'I thought you were supposed to stay in bed?'

'I was, to be honest, but I can't stay there just thinking about what needs to be done. Starting with tearing that bloody sign down!'

Paul looked over at Antonio, who had gone back into rapid conversation in Italian with a fiercely gesticulating Santorini. Once he turned to look at them, his shielded eyes looked like two black holes in his narrow face.

'I don't trust those two together,' said Paul. 'They're always plotting something or other.'

'Oh, come on,' Christina chided. 'It's no good getting into a "them and us" situation. We're in this together. Without Antonio's backing, none of this would have got off the ground. And he's going to give in about the sign, I can tell.'

'Frankly, that's the least of my worries,' Stephen said wearily. 'But never mind that. Come on, Chrissy, let's get you and our son somewhere civilized. The first tier of apartments is completed. Just wait till you see the one I've reserved for us.'

Crystal Springs Nassau was even more beautiful than her sister in Barbados. This time Stephen had more money, more experience and a better site. The buildings rose eighty feet above sea level, cantilevered in a crescent shape down a lush hillside. Wide balconies curved around every apartment building, and fell in pink and lavender bougainvillaea-clad tiers to a white crescent-shaped beach. Every room had a magnificent view of the hillside behind and the sea below.

Stephen had introduced the palest of peach hues for the main building and restaurants, one of which rose out of the ocean bed suspended on twenty-foot stilts overlooking a natural lagoon.

Roberto Sabortini, the landscape designer, had excelled himself – but, as he admitted, nature had provided him with the most wonderful back-up: abundant species of rare trees and plants and two natural lakes.

Meanwhile, Stephen had to give Paul credit for the most spectacular pool he had ever seen. The water sprang from a stone fountain hewn into the hillside sixty feet above the sea, dropping ten feet into a shallow, sparkling ornamental lake surrounded on three sides by clumps of swaying pampas, before it cascaded down twenty feet of natural rock-face into a narrow stream and spilled gently into the softly curved swimming-pool. An ornamental carved Japanese stone bridge crossed one corner of the pool and overlooked a miniature oriental water-garden packed with orchids of every hue. It was an architectural triumph which would be recognized as such eighteen months later with a well-deserved award.

The neon sign was removed and replaced by two solid brass embossed plates discreetly placed either side of the huge hand-carved doors. The hotel's opening night was a lavish affair, completely orchestrated by Susanna Belford-Cellini. She flew in Maine lobster, beluga caviar, fresh oysters and Cristal champagne – along with private-jet-loads of glitterati as her guests.

Stephen was furious, informing Antonio angrily that he personally could foot the bill for his wife's extravagance.

At the party, adulation and gushing praise poured from sycophantic socialite lips, along with genuine admiration from people who really mattered.

Susanna and Antonio basked in the praise. Stephen, whose taste and style and managerial skills had made the development the success it was, seemed in a strangely dislocated mood. He obviously felt none of the euphoria and sense of personal triumph he had when Crystal Springs Barbados opened.

Perhaps, thought Christina, it was because he had always known, despite Robert Leyton's original stake, that the Barbados hotel would one day be all theirs. She had a hunch, and felt that Stephen did too, that Antonio would be a whole lot harder to dislodge.

'This isn't working out, is it?' she said to Stephen when they were back in their suite that night. 'I can see you're finding it almost impossible to get on with Antonio, yet he's already talking about a new site in Phuket. If you want out, I think you should say so now.

'Antonio could raise the money to buy you out, presumably? Finance doesn't seem to be a problem for him.'

Stephen laughed bitterly. 'Oh, no, he's got all the money in the bloody world – and not the least fucking idea how to use it. You've seen what he's like. No taste. No style. All he's interested in is the next deal.'

'Then maybe that's what he should concentrate on,' she suggested. 'It's a waste of time your both working on a project simultaneously, treading on each other's toes and duplicating effort.'

'Like putting up and tearing down that bloody sign!'

'That and a thousand other things. Face it, you don't get on and never will. But if Antonio isn't creative, he's got a good eye for real estate. The Phuket site looks really promising – you said so yourself.'

'Yes,' he grudgingly admitted. 'And he's mentioned that the Concordia chain's in trouble in the States. It's not public knowledge yet, but Antonio's information is always right where money is concerned.' Stephen's voice held a bitter edge, but Christina could tell she'd started a train of thought.

'Maybe if you split the operation . . . Antonio in charge of acquisitions, while you oversee their development and day-to-day running?'

He raised an eyebrow.

'Aren't you forgetting something? I thought we were a team, Chrissy?'

'Well, as far as Barbados goes, we are; I'm talking about Platinum Hotels.'

Stephen seemed to reach a decision. 'Listen, I'm going to stay with Antonio.' He paused, 'I have to, in fact.'

'Have to? Why?'

He fobbed her off with a casual wave of his hand. 'Oh, some covenant or other; part of the way the equity deal was structured.'

Christina wasn't entirely convinced, as he went on, 'Besides, I may not like the guy, but I really believe that together we can go far. You do realize, Christina, from here on out it's going to be development after development, lots of travelling, a lot of new beginnings. I need you with me, Christina.'

'You know me, Stephen, always was a glutton for punishment. I wouldn't have married you otherwise.'

She threw a cushion at him then, he retaliated, and the evening ended far more pleasurably than it had begun.

When they put the plan to split the acquisitions side of Platinum Hotels Inc. from the development and management, Antonio seemed unperturbed.

'Sounds okay to me; I won't interfere with you, Stephen, if you return the favour.' He winked, and the two men exchanged knowing looks.

'We are going to have one of the biggest hotel groups in the world,' Antonio said.

'We're going to have the best, Antonio, if I've got anything to do with it.'

Stephen held out his hand, and Antonio gripped it firmly, their eyes locked.

'Just as long as you remember, Stephen, we are in this thing together.'

'How could I ever forget?'

Chapter Nineteen

FIVE YEARS LATER

'Mummy, come here quickly! Look at the snow.'

Christina joined Adam, who stood on tiptoe pointing at the huge snowflakes swirling in flurries past his bedroom window in the rented Upper East Side apartment they called home while they were in New York. She knelt behind him, hugging him and ruffling his red-brown hair, still wet from a recent bath. She breathed in deeply, enjoying the clean baby-smell of him.

'I bet it's cold out there. Aren't you pleased you're cosy and warm in here?'

She hugged him closer.

'I want to go out in the snow, Mummy. Why can't I go to the party with you?' Adam asked petulantly.

'I've already told you, it's for grown-ups.'

'But Vicky's going,' he wailed, turning to face her with big, pleading eyes, his lightly freckled face set in a stubborn scowl.

Christina sighed.

'I've told you before, Adam, Victoria is a big girl now.'

'She still goes to school,' he retorted.

'She goes to college. That's different.' Christina decided to change the subject. 'I promise to buy you the big Lego set you want tomorrow if you're a good boy now.'

It worked. Adam jumped up and down.

'The big one with all the lorries and trailers?'

'That's the one,' she said, leading him towards the bed.

He scrambled up and continued jumping up and down, shouting, 'Where's Gogie? Where's Gogie?'

Christina searched frantically for Adam's comforter, an old raggedy doll he had had since he was a baby. She knew she would have to find it before he would go to sleep.

'Perhaps Pat knows where it is,' she said, and was about to call for the nanny when Stephen walked into the room.

He had one hand behind his back as he approached the bed. 'Guess what I found in the bathroom?' Stephen pulled out the tatty doll. 'He actually fell in the water while I was in the bath.'

'Gogie.' Adam grabbed his doll. Jumping up and down he squealed: 'Gogie had a bath! Gogie had a bath!'

'I think Gogie and Adam should both go to sleep now, don't you?'

Christina settled her son down. He slid under the covers and she tucked him in, leaning over to stroke his brow before she kissed it.

'Night night. Sleep tight.'

'Night, Mummy. Don't forget about the Lego.'

She smiled. 'I doubt you'd let me.'

Stephen leaned forward as Christina stepped away from the bed.

'Night, Adam. Sleep tight.'

'Do the Nip Nip bug, Daddy.'

'Not tonight, darling, we're late for an important dinner.'

'Please, Daddy. Just once.'

Stephen sighed and slid his arm inside the bed as Adam pretended to be asleep, suppressing his laughter.

'Here is Mr Nip Nip, who bites all the bed bugs,' Stephen said, gently pinching and tickling Adam, who wriggled and shook with uncontrollable giggles.

'Again, Daddy. Again,' he urged as Stephen withdrew his hand.

'No, Mr Nip Nip has to go to a party now, and you have to go to sleep.'

'Can Pat read me a story, please?' Adam looked at his mother with wide, appealing eyes and, as always, she melted.

'Yes, but only for five minutes,' she said as she left the room.

Christina found Pat, their invaluable nanny, watching television in the cosy den off the vast drawing-room of their New York apartment.

She had been Adam's nanny since he was five months old, and Christina had often wondered how she would have managed without her during the last six years when so much of their lives had been spent travelling and living out of suitcases.

'Pat, could you read Adam a story? But not for too long; he's very tired.'

'Yes, of course, and I'll make him his favourite hot chocolate drink.' She stood up and stretched. 'Will you be late?'

'I expect so. Don't wait up,' Christina said, and glanced behind her at Stephen, walking across the wide hall towards the cloakroom.

'I'll just get my bag,' she called down the hall.

She selected a small Hermès evening purse. Taking a lipstick from her dressing-table, she applied a fresh coat of gloss to her full mouth. Studying her face in the long mirror, she was pleased with the reflection. Apart from a few tell-tale lines around her eyes, and a slight thinning of her cheeks, she did not look her age – thirty next birthday.

Christina took one last glance at her still-slim figure, pleased with the cut of her new Donna Karan silk jersey-dress and matching jacket. The long-style jacket hid her slightly rounded stomach, and the short, straight skirt flattered her slim hips and long, shapely legs.

She patted her hair into place. It swung to her shoulders

in a perfectly cut bob – the businesslike look she had
cultivated since joining Stephen in the work of adminis-
tering Platinum Resorts. Her fingertips touched the brilliant diamond necklace glittering at her throat, before she
switched off the light and joined Stephen. He was already
dressed in his Vienna overcoat, waiting impatiently in the
hall.

'Come on, darling, we're late.'

He held her ankle-length cashmere wrap open and she
slipped into it. Tom, the night porter, held an umbrella
over their heads as the limousine driver opened the door
and they slid into the dark, warm, plush interior of the
stretched Cadillac. It purred into life and moved slowly
through the congested streets.

Stephen rubbed the window and looked out as huge
gusts of heavy snow whirled past his line of vision.

'What a night! I hope this storm isn't going to last.'

'They said in the news earlier it would snow heavily
tonight and thaw tomorrow.'

He didn't reply, and they sat in silence for about five
minutes until she spoke again.

'Is something bothering you, Stephen? You seem to
have been very withdrawn all day.'

He ran a hand across his brow, pressing his temples
where a headache was developing.

'Antonio bothers me, as usual. We had a very heated
meeting yesterday and today. He was being difficult,
opposing all my plans for the new project in Australia.'

'Can't you buy him out?' Christina had suggested this
option many times before. Platinum Hotels had turned
out to be an incredibly successful venture, and she was
sure that Stephen could raise the money to buy back
Antonio's 24 per cent, even at its current value. 'It would
be so much easier without him around. You two have
always disagreed, but lately you seem to be at daggers
drawn.'

He sighed deeply. 'It can't get any worse. I only wish I *could* buy him out.'

'Can't you?' she asked.

Stephen stretched across the seat of the car and squeezed her hand so hard she winced.

'It's not as easy as you think.' She was about to pursue the conversation as the limo pulled up in front of the Pierre on Fifth Avenue and they climbed out. Caught in an icy gust, they ran under cover into the warm, inviting foyer.

A sign directed them to the conference room where the hotel awards ceremony was being held.

Christina left her coat in the cloakroom and joined Stephen in the reception area. Several people waved as they moved through the packed room, and Stephen excused himself to talk to Brett Hunter, the managing director of American Airways, who were staging the awards in conjunction with Leisure International.

Christina spotted Victoria in the corner, talking to Antonio. She had blossomed from an attractive teen-ager into a beauty who could have graced the cover of any glossy magazine she wished, but Christina knew that Victoria had other plans for herself. She had made that patently obvious at her twenty-first birthday party last month, when, holding her father's hand and eyes, she had announced that she would be joining Platinum Hotels after she graduated from Brown the following year.

Tonight she looked stunning in a long, slinky black dress which clung to her curves and left nothing to the imagination. Christina eyed Victoria's figure with a mixture of envy and admiration, thinking that she had had exactly the same type of body before pregnancy had thickened her waist and feeding Adam had robbed her of her full, firm breasts.

Victoria threw back her head, her laughter loud and

lusty, long black hair falling down her back in thick, glossy waves.

Christina was about to speak to one of their ex-managers from London when she felt a tap on her shoulder.

'Hi, Christina.'

She turned, inwardly dismayed.

'Hello, Susanna.'

She looked Christina up and down before she said, 'I love your outfit. I would have liked that myself, but they didn't have my size.'

Christina wondered how the painfully thin Susanna, now dieted to a skeletal size four, got anything to fit her.

She had expressed her concern to Antonio recently, hinting that perhaps Susanna was ill or anorexic. He had merely shrugged and in an indifferent manner informed her that his wife had always eaten like a bird, and that as it was a long time since he had seen her undressed he hadn't noticed that she was any thinner.

'So how are you?' Christina feigned interest she didn't feel, but was forced to talk to the boring, self-obsessed wife of Stephen's partner.

'I'm fine. You know how it is – I have my charities, which keeps me busy. And since Mummy had a stroke last year she's become very demanding, and nobody seems to want to spend any time with her but me.'

'Poor old you,' Christina commiserated, and hoped it sounded sincere.

'It's just as well I keep occupied because lover-boy over there is never around.' Susanna shot a contemptuous look in Antonio's direction, her eyes filled with undisguised loathing. 'I've forgotten the last time we had a meal together, let alone anything more intimate.' A weary smile crossed her face.

Christina looked in Antonio's direction and saw Stephen approach Victoria, leaning forward to kiss her upturned face, which was charged with animation and affection the moment she saw him.

'She's very beautiful, isn't she?' Susanna glared at Victoria, her voice thick with jealousy.

'Yes, she is.'

'She's also my husband's latest conquest.'

Christina gasped and looked directly into Susanna's disdainful gaze.

'You're not serious, I hope?'

'Deadly serious, I'm afraid. He's had the hots for her since she was about sixteen, and I think – in fact, I know – they're having an affair.'

Christina grabbed Susanna's scrawny arm as she saw Stephen coming towards them.

'Whatever you do, don't tell Stephen!'

'Why not, darling? He might kill Antonio and do us all a favour.' Her mouth snapped shut and she smiled sweetly as Stephen kissed her.

'Susanna, you look fantastic.'

And you lie so well, Christina thought, as the chairman of Leisure International shouted above the buzz of conversation: 'Will you all take your seats in the dining-room? Dinner is served.'

Stephen and Christina took their seats at a round table for six with Antonio, Susanna, Victoria and a young stockbroker who was escorting her. He introduced himself as William Banford Jnr from Boston.

Christina looked at the huge blow-up photographs of different hotels around the room. One caught her eye. It was a particularly spectacular shot of the beach bar and restaurant at the Lani Bluff Hotel in Maui – a Platinum Resort.

Ten Platinum Resorts were nominated out of the fifty they now owned, one of them from the Mandalay group which Stephen had acquired three years ago. In that time he had personally supervised the transformation of twenty

371

shabby and run-down hotels into exclusive world-class retreats.

They were served a meal of smoked salmon mousse followed by consommé and a choice of medallions of beef in red wine or brill in champagne sauce. Dessert was a delicious *crème brulée* with wild berries. Coffee followed, accompanied by fresh cream truffles.

Christina noticed that Antonio drank more than usual. His behaviour had altered subtly, she realized. Normally he took pains to appear friendly with Stephen, on the surface at least. Tonight, whether it was the effect of their last quarrel or just the drink, he had barely a civil word for his partner or his wife. He had eyes only for Victoria, monopolizing her conversation – to the embarrassment and pique of her escort. Susanna looked on in grim acceptance, while Stephen merely looked grim.

Christina was biting into a truffle and half listening to William Banford, who was boring her with details of a killing he had made on Wall Street the previous week, when Brett Hunter mounted the stage and spoke into the microphone. His smooth voice resounded through the noisy room.

'First and foremost, can I thank you all for braving this terrible weather to be here tonight? As I look around me I see many famous and infamous faces from the world of travel.'

Several people laughed.

'As you are all aware, we are gathered here tonight to bestow an award for the best resort group of hotels in the world. The list, as you can imagine, is vast, and we had to do intensive research until we finally reached our decision.'

Christina had her fingers crossed under the table. She hoped Stephen would win – he deserved it – but there was some stiff competition and it certainly wasn't in the bag.

She could see a nerve twitch in his face as Brett Hunter opened the envelope with the name of the winner inside.

'I'm delighted to announce that the winner of the Paradise Found Resort Award is Platinum Hotels, owned by Mr Reece-Carlton.'

The applause was deafening. Stephen stood up and held Christina's eyes for a moment before making his way through the applauding audience to receive his award. Cameras flashed as he took his place in front of the microphone.

He spoke loudly and very distinctly.

'Firstly, I want to thank you all for being here. I also want to thank the travel agents for sending us so many clients – and incidentally our repeat client-list is now over 60 per cent. Platinum Hotels always strives to offer the best standards of accommodation and service, and in receiving this award I think it proves we are getting it right.'

He touched the cast-bronze statuette in the shape of the rising sun with pride.

'I am thrilled and honoured tonight to receive this accolade. Before I go I would like to thank my wife Christina, who should be up here with me, sharing this achievement. She has supported and helped me through everything I've ever done, and I know I couldn't have made it without her.

'Thanks, Christina, and my warmest thanks to everyone who voted for Platinum Hotels.'

He held the golden statuette aloft as he walked down from the stage to more applause.

Christina watched him trying to push his way through the crowds as people rushed forward to shake his hand and congratulate him. Her heart felt ready to burst with pride.

She didn't hear Victoria's sharp exchange with William,

nor did she notice her flounce out of the room, closely followed by Antonio. Susanna did.

Eventually Stephen made it back to their table.

Christina was already on her feet, and he hugged her so tight the starched collar of his dinner-shirt cut into her neck. 'Well done, Stephen, you deserve it,' she whispered.

'And so do you. Like I said, I couldn't have done it without you.'

She held him at arm's length.

'I suspect you could, Stephen, but thanks for saying what you did. It meant the world to me.' Her eyes were moist with emotion.

He winked, and a smile lit his pale face for the first time that day. 'You mean the world to me.' He looked around the table. 'Where's Vicky? I thought she might like to congratulate her old pa.'

'She was feeling sick,' William said in a slurred voice. And, lifting a glass of whisky, he added, 'She went to get some fresh air.' He seemed to consider that statement and then said, 'I think', in an uncertain voice.

Susanna smiled, a sly expression curling the corners of her mouth.

'I saw her going in that direction.' She pointed towards the door. 'And, by the way, congratulations, Stephen. I want you to know I believe the accolade is all yours. Whatever Antonio may think.'

'Thanks, Susanna,' he said, thinking how ill she looked. Still holding the award he added, 'I'd better try and find Vicky; see if she's okay.'

Christina took one look at Susanna's face and decided to go with him. She had a sneaking suspicion that Victoria was with Antonio.

Stephen was asking the doorman if he had seen his daughter and describing what she was wearing as Christina joined him in the lobby.

'I think somebody fitting that description went towards

374

the powder-room, sir,' the man said, pointing in that direction.

'Christina, could you go and see if she's all right?' Stephen asked as they walked down the long corridor towards the ladies' room.

'Of course.' She nodded, and was about to leave him when they heard the sound of Victoria's laughter and Antonio's voice coming from a half-closed door to their left.

'Take it, Victoria, baby, it's great stuff. You know I only have the best. You'll be flying, and as soon as I can get rid of Susanna we'll . . .'

'You'll what, Antonio?' Stephen shouted, and burst into the room.

Victoria jumped up from a sofa, desperately trying to adjust the buttons at the top of her dress, which gaped open, exposing most of her left breast.

Her lipstick was smudged and dark-red marks showed clearly on the smooth skin of her neck. She was trying to hide something behind her back as Stephen strode the few feet that separated them and grabbed her wrist, wrenching from her grasp a tiny cellophane bag containing white powder. He sniffed it, and Christina gasped as he slapped his daughter full and hard across the face. She fell back, bumping into a low table.

Antonio jumped to his feet.

'You bastard!' Stephen's voice shook with rage. 'Supplying my daughter with cocaine!'

'It's harmless, Stephen. Good, pure stuff. Nothing but the best for Daddy's little girl,' he sneered. 'Anyway, she loves it, don't you, Vicky baby? Fucks like a demon when I . . .'

He didn't finish the sentence. Stephen swung the heavy statuette towards Antonio's face. It caught the side of his mouth, and blood spurted from his bottom lip as he reeled back, losing his balance.

Christina and Victoria both screamed as Stephen hit him again before he could recover, knocking him to the ground this time.

'You fucking piece of slime, Toni! I'll get you for this if it's the last thing I do,' he snarled, and without so much as a glance at Victoria's stricken face he stormed out of the room and into the foyer, Christina running in his wake.

'Could you please go back in there, Chris, and tell them all I've got a migraine or something? Anything! Invent something. I can't face them.'

Stephen was experiencing difficulty controlling his voice. His face was drained of all colour and he was shaking. Christina touched his arm gently.

'Of course, Stephen, don't worry.'

He nodded gratefully. 'I'll wait in the car.'

She made their excuses as apologetically and briefly as possible before grabbing her wrap to run out to the car, where Stephen was sitting silently. He didn't speak at all on the journey back, the award on his lap. He lifted it to eye level as the car pulled up in front of their apartment building in Sutton Place.

'What does it all mean?' He stared at the golden sun mounted on a bronze plinth, with the words 'Platinum Hotels. Best Hotel Group in the World 1992' engraved underneath.

The driver opened the car door and an icy breath of wind carried snow towards them. Christina shivered as she alighted.

'Where are you going, Stephen?' she called as he began to walk across the road.

'I'm going to put this in the trash where it belongs,' he shouted. She could barely hear his voice above the gushing wind.

She pulled her coat closer to her and watched him, sadness growing within her as he threw the award into a trash can on the opposite side of the street.

His head was bent against the wind as he walked back across the road. His hair was blowing wildly across his eyes, and she wasn't sure if they were wet from the snow or something else.

'Why, Stephen?'

'Because it's over,' was all he said.

Christina didn't understand, but he refused to be drawn into any further conversation about Victoria or Antonio.

'I need a drink,' he said as they entered the apartment and switched on the lights.

'I could do with one as well – I'll have a brandy, Stephen. I'll go and check Adam first. Be with you soon.'

She crept into her son's room and stood over his bed. The soft night light fell on his peaceful, slumbering face; one small hand was wrapped around Gogie, lying next to his tousled head. He looked so small and vulnerable that she was overcome with love.

He stirred and turned over. She was tempted to kiss him, but dared not for fear of waking him.

'Sleep tight, my precious,' she whispered, and blew a kiss at his flushed face before backing quietly out of the room.

She heard Stephen's voice on the telephone as she came out of the bedroom, and wondered who he could be talking to at this time of night.

Walking quietly down the hall, she stopped and waited, listening.

'Contact number 5892209. I'm ready to talk but I must leave New York as soon as possible. I'll await instructions.'

Christina rounded the corner as Stephen put down the receiver.

'Who were you talking to?'

He jumped and spun round to face her. She could see from his expression that he was startled.

377

He recovered quickly. Holding out his hand, he led her to the sofa, handing her a goblet half full of brandy.

'Sit down, Christina,' he said. She did as she was told, holding her brandy goblet in both hands to stop them shaking.

Stephen sat down next to her. He drank half of the brandy in his glass before he spoke.

'There's something very important I must do. It's been on my mind for a while, and now the time has come.'

'What is it, Stephen?' she asked in a small voice, afraid of the answer.

'I'm sorry, Christina, but I can't tell you. Not at the moment, anyway.'

'Is it dangerous? Can you tell me that much, at least?'

He thought about her question for a long time before he replied in a serious voice: 'There's an element of danger in life itself, in everything we do, unless we shut ourselves up in a vacuum.

'Remember, Christina, when you live as close to the edge as I do, there's always the risk of falling off. Or of being pushed. Take care, my darling. I may not always be around to protect you.'

'What do you mean, Stephen? Please tell me; I'm scared.'

'There's nothing to be afraid of. No one is going to harm you, believe me.' He moved along the sofa to where she sat, still gripping her brandy glass. He prised it gently from her hands and placed it on the table.

Taking her in his arms, he kissed her with a hunger and passion she thought had left him years before.

'Everything will be fine. I'll sort it out. What have I always said?' he asked her.

'It will be all right on the night.' Her voice was tremulous as he kissed her cheek. 'You're going to be okay, aren't you, Stephen?'

'Of course. You know me – nine lives,' he laughed.

She began to speak. He stopped her words with another kiss.

'Let's go to bed,' he urged. She agreed, and they walked to the bedroom, hand in hand. He watched her undress and then made love to her with a peculiar mixture of manic energy and tenderness. She felt almost as if she were in the arms of a stranger, but it was Stephen's voice she heard as she held him tight, and he shuddered as he came, calling out her name again and again.

Christina lay awake most of the night, her mind re-running the events of the evening and Stephen's odd behaviour. She fell into an exhausted sleep at 5.30, and did not hear him get up an hour later.

Adam woke her by bashing Gogie in her face at eight o'clock. He was still in his pyjamas.

'Mummy, Mummy, wake up! We're going to get the Lego now.'

Christina half opened her eyes and grabbed him. 'Come on in here for a couple of minutes while Mummy wakes up.' She lifted the covers and Adam climbed in, snuggling up to her warm body.

'Have you seen Daddy?' she asked.

'Yes, he's in his study on the telephone. Daddy's not coming with us to get the Lego.'

'Oh, why not?' Christina was instantly alert.

'Daddy's going back to Barbados today.'

She sat up and Adam joined her, swinging his feet out of the bed.

'How do you know that, Adam?'

He jumped off the bed.

'Because Daddy told me. He said I was to be a good boy and look after you while he was gone.'

Christina slid out of bed and crossed the room to the bathroom. 'Go and tell Daddy I'd like to see him, will you please, Adam?'

'What time are we going to get the Lego?' he asked.

'The shops aren't open yet. We have lots of time. Please, go and get Daddy for me.'

Adam ran off and returned a few minutes later, leading Stephen by the hand and chattering incessantly about the present he was going to get.

'And Pat has promised to take me skating this afternoon.'

'I'm not sure about that. You've never ice-skated before,' Christina said.

'I have so.' Adam pouted.

'That was for a couple of minutes. I'm not sure I want you to go.'

'But Mummy . . .'

'Don't argue, Adam.' Her voice was firm, and Stephen lifted the boy above his head to distract him, throwing his light body high into the air and catching him amid noisy squeals of laughter.

'What's this about you going to Barbados today? Was Adam making it up or is it true?'

Stephen threw Adam onto the bed. Sitting down next to him, he tickled his stomach as the boy kicked and struggled to escape.

'It's true. I've ordered the jet to be ready for take-off at eleven from JFK.'

'Why the rush? I thought you were staying here until your meeting next Tuesday, and we were all travelling down together the next day.'

Stephen stood up, lifting Adam in his arms. He steadied him on one hip. 'Come here, my darling,' he said, and with his free arm pulled Christina towards him, holding her close.

Stephen hugged them all into a tight knot, kissing first Adam's brow and then hers.

'My family. You are all I've got.'

'What about Vicky? You've got her too, Daddy,' said Adam.

Stephen looked distracted for an instant, and an odd expression crossed his face.

'So I have, Adam. Mustn't forget Vicky.'

Christina could not believe her ears. Stephen forgetting his precious daughter! At long last it seemed that Victoria had fallen from her pedestal.

'Like I said, I want you to look after Mummy while I'm gone, and I'll see you both in Barbados on Wednesday. I'll send the jet back for you.'

'Will Jimmy be flying the plane, and can I help him again?' Adam sounded excited.

Stephen ran his fingers through the boy's unruly hair.

'Yes, of course. You did a great job last time.'

'You still haven't answered my question. Why are you going back to Barbados so soon?' Christina insisted.

Stephen slid Adam to the floor and took both her hands in his. He looked deep into her eyes, a troubled expression in his.

'You must trust me and believe me when I say that I can't tell you at the moment, but you will find out very soon. Just remember, Chrissy, I love you. I have since the first day I met you, and I always will.'

Stephen left the apartment only minutes before Antonio rang, asking to speak to him. Christina informed him in clipped tones that Stephen had gone back to Barbados on urgent business.

An hour later she took a call from Victoria, who asked in a subdued, plaintive voice to speak to her father. Christina told her to contact Stephen at Crystal Springs. Neither of them discussed the previous evening.

The remainder of the day was spent with Adam. They bought the Lego set in the morning, and most of the afternoon was taken up with building an enormous construction site in his bedroom.

The weather changed at midday. A weak, watery sun appeared, bringing with it a warmer wind to blow across Manhattan, pushing the storm-clouds up-state.

Ice-skating was out of the question, so, as an alternative, to give Adam some fresh air, Pat suggested a walk in Central Park. They wrapped up well in warm coats, hats, scarves and woollen mittens, and had a short snowball fight with wet, dirty snow which was thawing fast.

Afterwards they bought hot dogs and ate them ravenously, returning to the apartment at teatime, flushed and invigorated.

Pat made steaming hot chocolate and Adam ate three of his favourite chocolate éclairs whilst watching children's television. Stephen rang at nine o'clock. He said goodnight to Adam and repeated what he had said earlier to Christina.

'I love you, darling, don't ever forget that.'

'If you keep on telling me at this rate, Stephen, I'm not likely to.'

He chuckled and said, 'Take care, Chrissy, my darling. I'll speak to you soon.'

She watched a James Bond movie with Adam and Pat, but couldn't concentrate. Her thoughts kept returning to Stephen's unusual behaviour. Something was wrong, very wrong, and she wished fervently that he had been able to share whatever it was with her before he left.

She put Adam to bed and went herself not long after, falling into an exhausted sleep almost immediately, only to wake a couple of hours later, sweating profusely and aware that she had had a bad dream, though she was unable to recall it.

She tried to go back to sleep, but a sense of unreality gripped her. This couldn't be her, this lonely woman tossing and turning, in the grip of a fierce sense of foreboding.

The telephone rang at seven o'clock. She was wide awake, and knew instinctively, before she reached across the bed to pick up the receiver, that it was bad news.

'The Prime Minister will speak to you now,' said his secretary in lilting Bajan tones.

She recognized Danny Bascombe's voice instantly, yet it sounded different this morning. She knew why moments later.

'Christina, I have some bad news for you. You're going to have to be very brave.' He paused, and she held her breath, knowing what was to come before he said it.

'I'm sorry to have to tell you that Stephen is dead.'

Chapter Twenty

22 SEPTEMBER 1993

Unusually, there were only four other people in the front cabin with Christina as Concorde taxied down the runway at JFK, New York, *en route* to London Heathrow. The exhilarating roar of the supersonic engines drowned any other sound as the aircraft became airborne within seconds.

Leaning back, she closed her eyes, thinking about the meeting yesterday and the shocking revelation that Edward Harrington owned 28 per cent of Platinum Hotels. She couldn't understand why Stephen had given away such a large part of his company to a man he had disliked intensely. There had to be a powerful motive.

Christina intended to investigate, convinced it had something to do with her husband's death, but in the meantime she had seven days in which to raise enough capital to buy Edward's shares and secure Platinum Resorts for herself. She was determined to do so, positive that this was what Stephen would have wished.

Concorde landed on schedule at 9.30 p.m. local time. She had brought hand baggage only, and walked through an almost deserted concourse to be greeted by her new chauffeur, Robin. She had met him only once before. He seemed pleasant and drove well.

Traffic was light on the M4 and it took only thirty-five minutes to reach the house in Wilton Crescent that Stephen had bought three years before. Carmo, the Portuguese housekeeper, opened the door.

'Welcome back. I am very sorry to hear the sad news.'

'Thank you, Carmo. And how are you and José?' asked Christina.

'We are well, thank you. Will you require any supper, madam? I was not sure. I had no message.'

'No thanks, Carmo. I'm not hungry. I think I'll go straight to bed. What I would like is a nice pot of tea and some mineral water, please.'

Christina climbed the four flights of stairs, holding the polished oak banister, until she reached the door of her bedroom. A gas log-fire burned brightly in the antique marble fireplace, and Carmo had turned back the covers of the Regency four-poster.

She walked into her dressing-room, careful to avert her eyes from the photographs of Stephen and herself displayed in the bedroom. She knew that in time she would be able to look at them without tears, but at the moment it was impossible.

Carmo carried a tray into the bedroom ten minutes later, calling to Christina, who was in the shower. She heard the housekeeper's voice as she stepped out, grabbing a towel from the heated rail.

'That's all for tonight, thanks.'

Carmo called goodnight and closed the door quietly as she left.

Christina dressed in her favourite cotton pyjamas and padded barefoot into the bedroom. She helped herself to a glass of water and took a sleeping-tablet. She had been taking them since Stephen's death, though they did nothing to dispel the terrible dreams. Then she poured herself a cup of tea and, placing it on the bedside table, slid between the cool linen sheets, stretching her long legs across the wide expanse of bed. Her feet encountered only emptiness, a dull reminder that there was no warm back to snuggle up to or cold toes to tickle; no goodnight kisses or early-morning cuddles; no reassuring hand in the night to comfort and protect.

Christina curled her legs up to her chest, feeling a big lump forming in her throat. She chided herself inwardly.

Stephen wouldn't have wanted you to feel sorry for yourself. If the situation were reversed he'd have come out fighting, and that's what you must do.

She thought about the two meetings she had scheduled for the following day; the more she thought about them, the more daunting they seemed.

One was with the finance director of Citicorp Bank, and the other with the managing director of Melville Stamford. Both banks had expressed interest in funding the share-purchase of Platinum Hotels on the strength of her collateral – sole ownership of Crystal Springs and the Wilton Crescent house.

She sipped her tea, feeling drowsy, and soon drifted into a deep, tranquillized sleep. It was her first night free from nightmares since Stephen's death.

'I have put a proposal to our credit committee, Mrs Reece-Carlton, and will have a reply for you on Monday.'

Christina was sitting in an austere office on the top floor of the offices of Melville Stamford Bank in Haslett Square, opposite a Mr Charles Sanderson, who surveyed her with bland blue eyes. He was the third banker she had seen from the same firm over the last three days.

'Thank you, Mr Sanderson.'

'Please, call me Charles.' His manner was too smooth for her taste, and the thin smile he offered failed to reach his eyes. She disliked him intensely.

'Do you think I have a good chance of getting a positive response? As you know, I have to bid on the twenty-eighth.'

'Not a lot of time to secure rather a lot of money.' He scribbled something on a pad. 'To be honest with you, Mrs Reece-Carlton . . .' She didn't invite him to call her Christina. '. . . the risk factor is not so great. Platinum

Hotels has been trading at a substantial profit margin for years, and with the security you have on your own two properties, I doubt they would turn you down. I personally have recommended the proposal for approval.'

He sat back in his chair, waiting for her to thank him. She could see his rounded paunch protruding under a loose button on the bottom of his pin-striped waistcoat.

'Thank you.' She hesitated. 'Charles.'

She stood up, tall and elegant in an understated Armani suit.

Charles Sanderson walked round his desk to stand close to her. Too close, Christina thought.

'I'll call you on Monday as soon as I have some news.'

He held out a hand so small it looked childlike. She gripped it, surprised to find that it was as cold as ice. He scrutinized her with an incomprehensible expression, and she was undecided as to whether it was, as she suspected, lascivious or merely amicable. In the short time since she'd been widowed, she'd been surprised by the predatoriness of the men she encountered.

'I'm going down to the country this afternoon for the weekend. I'll be there on Monday. I believe you have that number?'

Charles Sanderson glanced at some papers on his desk and read the number aloud.

'That's correct.' Christina smiled nervously.

'Don't worry; as soon as I have some news I'll contact you directly.'

Christina was eating a light lunch in the breakfast room when the telephone rang. Carmo took it, and a few seconds later poked her face round the door.

'Excuse me, but there's a gentleman on the telephone. Says it is urgent he speaks with you.'

'Take a message, Carmo, and tell him I'll call back as soon as I've finished lunch.'

387

'I already say that, but he say to tell you it is very important.'

Christina slammed down her fork, irritated, and moved out of the breakfast room into an adjoining sitting-room where there was a telephone on a small side table.

'Hello, Christina Reece-Carlton speaking. Can I help you?'

'Hello, Christina.' James Morris's voice was unmistakable. The line was very clear. It did not sound as if he was in the Caribbean.

'James, where are you?'

'I'm in England. Just got here yesterday. I'm staying with a friend in Surrey and was hoping I could have a meeting with you, if you're not too busy?'

'I didn't know you were coming to England. Is everything all right at Crystal Springs?' He could hear the concern in her voice.

'I didn't know I was coming over myself until a few days ago.' He hesitated. 'I need to talk to you urgently about the future of the hotel. Would it be possible for us to meet later today?'

Christina had planned to meet up with Adam and his nanny at Purley Hall, spend the afternoon riding, and later take in a movie perhaps.

The phone call was a nuisance; she hadn't bargained on seeing James Morris, but as she had just used Crystal Springs as collateral for a loan application she could hardly refuse to discuss something that obviously concerned the hotel.

'Can you come down to Purley Hall this evening?' she said, thinking that Pat could take Adam to the movies alone, and that they would be able to talk in peace.

'Yes, that would be fine. What time?'

'About 7.30 would be good for me, if that's okay with you?'

'Seven-thirty it is, Chrissy. I'll look forward to it.' She

was annoyed by his familiar abbreviation of her name, but said nothing. James was the first person she intended to get rid of as soon as she had sorted out the business with Platinum Hotels and could get down to managing the rest of her property.

She put down the receiver and called for Carmo to make her coffee whilst she changed out of her business suit and into jeans and a cashmere sweater for the journey down to Sussex. Before leaving the house, she collected her mail, and after settling into the back of the Rolls-Royce began to plough through the stack of letters which consisted mainly of invitations and circulars.

One slipped from her knee to the floor. Stooping to pick it up, she recognized Martin Ward's handwriting. She tore it open and began to read.

Dear Christina,

I feel compelled to write to you with my condolences on Stephen's death.

I lost my mother last year. I was very close to her, and know how the finality of death leaves us all feeling hopeless and defeated – but only for a while. Time heals, as I'm sure you will find for yourself.

I want you to know that I have thought of you often over the years, and that you are in my thoughts now more than ever.

Look after yourself, Christina, and call me if you need a shoulder to cry on.

Yours ever,
Martin

She read the short letter several times, visualizing him the last time she had seen him on the banks of the Seine, his pale face taut with a mixture of anger and hurt. She had never been able to erase that image.

She'd read in the newspapers that he'd married a fellow

PR person, so he must be over his feelings for her. He was offering friendship, that was all, and she could do with a friend now more than ever. Picking up the phone, she glanced at the letterhead and punched out the telephone number. It must have been his private line, because he answered after two rings.

'Martin Ward.'

'Martin, it's Christina Reece-Carlton here.'

'Christina! What a surprise. Where are you?'

'I'm in London. Well, I'm in the car, actually, travelling down to Sussex. I only got back a couple of days ago and I've just opened your letter.'

'I was sorry to hear about Stephen's death. It must have been a terrible shock for you.'

'It was. Thanks for the letter. I appreciate it.'

'I can't tell you how I feel just hearing your voice, Christina. After so long.'

There was a pause, and she realized that there were a lot of things she wanted to say to Martin – more than could be discussed on the telephone with Robin only a few feet away.

'How long are you going to be in England?' he asked eagerly, and before she had time to reply, added, 'Perhaps we could meet for a drink or dinner? Catch up on all the news.'

'It will have to be a long dinner, Martin. We've got almost seven years catching up to do.'

'Okay, let's make it several dinners and throw in a few lunches, if you like. How long are you going to be here, Chris?'

'That's the problem. I have to go back to New York next week for an important meeting.'

'Oh, no. I'm going away tomorrow afternoon, for a week, and it's something I can't put off.'

'Don't worry. I'll call you some other time and perhaps we can get together then.'

390

But Martin was loath to miss the opportunity of seeing her.

'What about tonight? I know it's short notice, but I could make it if you could.' He sounded hopeful.

'Well, I've got James Morris coming to see me this evening. But he's coming early and I don't anticipate him staying long. Why not come down to Purley Hall for a drink and a bit of supper?' The line went dead for a moment.

'Martin, are you there?'

His voice crackled and then became clear. 'Still here.'

'Could you make it tonight? It's the housekeeper's night off, so you'd have to make do with something I rustle up.'

'Sounds great to me. You made me a mean spaghetti once in Manchester,' Martin reminded her.

'I'd forgotten about that. I don't know how you can remember such things.'

'I can remember everything about you,' he said simply.

She felt flattered but also slightly wary. Her motive in asking him to Purley Hall was that she was lonely and needed a friend. She hoped he wouldn't read anything more into it. It was far too soon after Stephen's death.

'James is coming at 7.30, so if you can make it about 8.30 that would be fine.'

'You'll be alone with him, then?' Martin asked, concerned.

'Well, yes. He wanted to discuss the hotel.' Christina's voice became uneasy as she thought about the insidious suggestions James had made in the past.

'He's not a very savoury character, you know, Chris. There were stories on the island . . . I think I might come down a little earlier, if you don't mind?'

'Okay, Martin. That's a good idea, now you mention it. Actually, I feel a lot happier knowing I won't be alone for long with him.'

'You've got a date.'

It was not the way she would have described it, but nevertheless she was comforted by Martin's eagerness to see her, and the intuitive way he had picked up on her reluctance to be alone with James.

'Bye for now,' she said, and then rang Purley Hall to speak to Pat, asking her to check with Mrs Barnes that there was spaghetti in the pantry and minced meat to make bolognese sauce.

She would show Martin that even after all these years she could still make a mean spaghetti.

'We're leaving now, Christina,' Pat called from the hall. Christina appeared round the kitchen door wearing a big striped butcher's apron.

The nanny was kneeling in front of Adam, fastening the last button on his coat and tying a long woollen scarf twice around his neck.

'What are you cooking, Mummy?' he asked, wrinkling up his nose as she came towards them.

'Your favourite, spaghetti bolognese. I'll save some for you and Pat to eat for supper when you come back from the movies.'

'Why can't you come with us? Ben told me it was the best film he's ever seen.'

'I'm sorry, Adam, I'd love to see it too, but James is coming to discuss some important things with me. You can tell me all about it when you get back.'

He pulled the scarf from his neck and handed it to his nanny. 'I don't want to wear this, Pat, it tickles.'

She looked at Christina, who nodded.

'Make sure he puts it on when he comes out of the cinema, though. It will be cold then.'

She crouched down in front of her son and pecked him on the cheek.

'Mummy, when's Daddy coming back?' he asked out of the blue.

Christina was momentarily taken aback.

'I thought I'd explained that to you, Adam. He's gone to heaven.'

'I know, but when's he coming back? He promised to take me snow-skiing.' Adam looked at her in wide-eyed innocence.

Christina took a deep breath, her voice faltering a little as she said: 'Daddy is never coming back, but I don't want you to worry about him because he's safe and I know he'll be fine.'

Adam thought about what she said, digesting every word. 'Okay, I understand, so will you take me snow-skiing instead?'

Christina smiled, thinking how wonderful it was for the very young with no real conception of the finality of death. They could pick up the pieces so easily, looking only ahead of them.

Christina held her son's clear amber gaze with her own.

'I promise to take you skiing, cross my heart.' She made a cross on her chest with her forefinger.

'You, me and Pat will go, just as soon as I have sorted out Daddy's business affairs.'

Adam whooped. 'Can we go tobogganing and ice-skating as well? And could I take Ben with me?' he rushed on.

She ruffled his hair.

'If Ben's mummy says yes, then we can most certainly take him.'

'Can I call now and ask?'

'No, Adam.' She glanced at the hall clock.

Pat took her cue. 'We don't want to miss the start of the film now, do we, Adam? You can call Ben later.' She grabbed his hand and guided him to the door.

Adam waved to his mother.

'Ben told me they shoot lots of people and blow up a big building at the beginning.' He pretended to shoot

Robin, who obligingly acted dead, falling across the bonnet of the car.

'Have fun,' Christina called as the car door slammed shut. She waved to her son until the Rolls reached the iron gates at the bottom of the drive.

Then she went back into the kitchen and, tasting her bolognese, decided it needed just a hint more garlic and black pepper. She added the ingredients and stirred the thick meat sauce, moving the pan onto the Aga hot-plate to simmer. Then, taking off her apron, she hung it over the back of the kitchen chair and poured herself a glass of dry white wine. She left the kitchen and stopped to check her appearance in the tall, gilded hall mirror.

Her shoulder-length hair was tied up in a bun on top of her head. Several wisps had escaped, falling across a face that was flushed from cooking.

Her simple grey ribbed wool-knit dress clung to her now slightly rounded stomach. She sucked it in and, turning sideways, glanced at her reflection, wondering whether she should change.

Christina had been self-conscious about her protruding stomach since Adam's birth. She had exercised, but to no avail. She was reduced now to sucking it in or disguising it. Stephen had dismissed her moans, saying he liked her better with a bit of flesh. It made her more cuddly.

A dying log-fire crackled in the hearth as Christina entered the warm living-room. She threw a couple of large logs on top of the white-hot embers and watched the flames lick instantly into glowing life.

Her ears caught the crunch of car tyres on the gravel drive outside. Approaching the window, she peeped through a crack in the heavy curtains and saw a dark-blue Ford Escort park outside. After a rather long pause the doorbell rang. She picked up the intercom, full of trepidation yet unsure why.

'James, is that you?'

He answered in a muffled voice, and she pressed the buzzer to open the door.

He stepped from the dimly lit porch. She could see that his eyes were very bloodshot and his face looked pinched with cold. She closed the door quickly, shutting out the freezing fog.

'How are you, James? Good to see you.'

She extended her hand. He ignored it and leaned forward instead, intent on planting a kiss on her warm cheek. His lips felt wet, and she wiped her hand quickly across her face as his eyes glanced in the opposite direction.

'I'm bloody cold. Not used to British weather any more. I think my blood has thinned.' He rubbed his hands together, and she noticed that the sleeves of his worn overcoat were far too long.

'Here, let me take your coat.'

He shrugged out of the oversized, threadbare garment which she hung up in the cloakroom.

'Come on into the drawing-room. I've got a fire going in there. We can have a drink. You'll soon warm up.'

James followed her.

'Sit yourself down.' She pointed to a sofa in front of the now cheerful fire.

He sunk into the deep cushions. 'Lovely room,' he commented, looking around the cosy, chintzy decor.

'What would you like to drink, James? I've got just about everything.' She stood behind the sofa next to a table laden with bottles of spirits and glasses.

'Whisky and a little drop of water. Don't you remember?' He sounded annoyed.

'Of course,' she said quickly, 'but people do change their drinks sometimes. I do all the time.'

Christina mixed the drink and managed a smile while handing him a tumbler half full of scotch.

'So what brings you back to England? I hope everything's okay at Crystal Springs?' Her voice was light, but he detected a note of anxiety.

'I've not been well lately. I came back to see a specialist in London.'

He drank half the whisky and smacked his lips. Christina doubted that he was telling the truth, and pushed him to talk about the hotel.

'James, will you please just tell me if everything is okay in Barbados? I've a lot on my mind at the moment, and would like to be reassured that Crystal Springs is running smoothly.'

'When I left all was well – the usual everyday niggles, but nothing that can't be handled by my assistant,' he said matter-of-factly.

'You said on the telephone you had something important to say to me?'

'I have.' He swirled his whisky in the glass and drank the remainder. 'That was good. I feel much better.' He reached across the sofa, the empty glass in his hand. 'I could use another, if you don't mind?'

Christina jumped up and poured him another large whisky, adding a splash of water.

His palms were stretched forward towards the fire when she handed the glass to him. He took it, crushing his hand on top of hers. She pulled away with mounting unease.

'Don't come the hoity-toity lady with me, Christina. I know all about you.' He nodded his head. 'Everything, remember.'

Christina shuddered. She sat down stiff-backed in a wing chair several feet away from him. Her heart began to thud.

'Could you please get to the point, James? Why have you come here?' she snapped, anger replacing anxiety.

'You listen to me for once, Christina.' James's voice was suddenly aggressive. 'And bloody well stop telling me what to do. I've had enough of that from your husband –

more than I could stomach. Years of doing his dirty work, years of taking all the risks. And for what, I ask you? For what?'

She could see the tumbler shaking in his hand as he continued, 'It was all for you, Christina. I stuck around hoping that one day . . .'

His voice had softened. She suppressed a gasp of horror. He couldn't be serious, could he?

He was staring into the fire as if she weren't there. 'I would have done anything for you. I was thrilled if you gave me the odd kind word or warm smile. But I wasn't good enough for you, was I, Christina?'

'I was in love with Stephen, James. I didn't even consider you in that way. You worked for us. You were married to . . .'

'It didn't stop you fucking Martin Ward, did it?' he interrupted. 'Like a fucking bitch on heat sneaking around the island after him. I watched you, I saw everything you did. Whore!' he spat.

A wave of nausea swept over her. She prayed that Martin would arrive soon.

'I don't think that's got anything to do with you, James,' she said, standing up, 'and I think if this is all you've come to say, you'd better leave.'

She spoke with more confidence than she felt, beginning to walk towards the door.

He stood in front of her, blocking the way. He pulled a crumpled envelope out of the pocket of his jeans and thrust it in her hand.

'Before I do, I think you'd better read this.'

She saw her name scribbled in Stephen's almost illegible scrawl on the front of the envelope, which had been torn open. With clammy hands, she pulled out a single sheet of paper. James stood very close, studying her reaction as she read.

Chrissy

This has to be in haste so forgive me if I put things badly – Adam isn't my son, much as I wish I could say he is. While I was married to Barbara I had a vasectomy. I've cursed myself since and saw someone once to see if it could be reversed but there were problems.

I knew how much you wanted a child and would have given anything to father one for you. Martin Ward did me a favour, I suppose, though I could have wrung his neck at the time.

I want you to know that although I am not his biological parent, in every other way I look on Adam as my son. I love him very much and am proud of him. I'm going to put this note in the safe and pray you'll never need to read it. But if something should happen to me, I want you to know the truth.

And always remember, my darling, how much you mean to me.

I love you more each day.

Stephen

There was shock first, closely followed by disbelief. Her eyes were full of unshed tears as she finished reading the short note.

'I can't believe it. Why didn't he tell me?'

'There were lots of things Stephen didn't tell you,' James said with a kind of malevolent glee.

She screwed up the letter and pushed it into her pocket. Covering her quivering mouth, she breathed deeply to quell the flood of tears welling up in her eyes. 'I can't believe it.'

'Well, you'd better believe it, because it's true. I checked it out. Stephen had a vasectomy after Victoria was born. Apparently his first wife had a very bad birth and persuaded him to do it. So your kid is Martin Ward's bastard. Unless of course you were playing around with someone else as well?'

'How dare you, James?' she screamed, shaking with such violent rage she thought she might strike him. What did any of this have to do with him anyway?

'Tell me how you got this letter. Did Stephen give it to you before his death? He says he planned to put it in the safe.'

'It's not important how I got it. What is important is that now you know the truth.' He paused and muttered, 'Or at least, part of it.'

Christina strode the few feet that separated them and glared into his dissipated face, looking a lot braver than she felt.

'Tell me all of it, James. I'm entitled to know. I need to know.'

He grabbed her arm and she winced. 'You want to know it all, my lovely Chrissy?' He imitated Stephen's voice, forcing her close. 'You want to know what your wonderful Stephen was really like? He was a fucking megalomaniac bastard who got in with the wrong people and pushed them just a bit too far. He believed his own legend. Thought he could take on anything.'

James stared right through her.

'Nobody stands against the Mob. Antonio's foot-soldier Santorini finished him off. Though, believe me, I'd have liked to.'

'Santorini?' she repeated faintly, ignoring James's threat, which she was sure was empty. Suspecting the circumstances surrounding Stephen's death was one thing. But hearing someone named as his murderer . . . And Santorini of the lean, cadaverous face and dead eyes? She shivered. She'd always feared him. Now she knew how right she'd been.

'But why, James?' she implored. 'And how?'

He sighed. 'Oh, come on, you know how. Gino broke

his neck and made it look like an accident. Child's play to him.'

He had her undivided attention now, and loosened his grip on her arm.

'As for why – Cellini's side of the business was getting out of hand. The deal was that Stephen would confine himself exclusively to the legitimate side of things, using Mafia money to finance the best hotels he could create. He could never have funded even a fraction of them borrowing from conventional sources.

'For Antonio, the hotels were legitimate cover for his racketeering. Hundreds of millions of dollars' worth of revenue from drugs and arms smuggling and all the other lucrative Mob sidelines were laundered through the hotels.'

'What?' said Christina in disbelief. She felt her stomach churn, and held onto the back of a nearby chair.

'Then Antonio started pushing to use Crystal Springs Barbados for a base to ship in dope from Colombia. Stephen refused. He had a deal with Danny Bascombe and wasn't prepared to jeopardize it. A little laundering may be fine. It could provide jobs, prop up the local economy perhaps, but Danny wouldn't stand for a major smuggling operation, and Stephen was protective about the place. It was always his first love. Believe me, you came a poor second.'

She couldn't take it all in. Danny Bascombe tainted with the same corruption? No wonder her friend Pauline had shrunk away from her. She must have believed that Christina knew everything that was going on, when all the time she'd been in blissful ignorance.

'I don't believe you, James,' she said weakly, though a part of her already did.

He grasped her face in one hand and squeezed so tight she could hardly breathe.

'I'm not lying. The last straw was when he found out

400

about Antonio's affair with Victoria. He didn't mind how much crack Antonio and his backers were distributing through the hotels, but when it came to corrupting his darling daughter and introducing her to the merchandise . . . well, Stephen flipped.

'He intended to grass to the DEA. They'd already approached him, tipped off by a former employee with a grudge.'

He laughed, a thin, high sound that set her teeth on edge. 'Ironic, really, wasn't it? I framed Michael Stein on a possession of drugs charge, and to get his own back Stein pointed the finger at Stephen to the DEA.

'He didn't have any concrete facts – Stephen joined up with Antonio after we'd pushed Stein out of the nest – but he knew the business. He knew the profits Platinum Hotels were reporting couldn't be strictly legit, and the little shit always did like to stir things. It was a pity in a way we didn't settle his hash permanently . . . but I suppose he did me a favour in the end. At least he got rid of Stephen for me.'

James's eyes looked cloudy and faraway. He wasn't restraining her now, but Christina stood rooted to the spot, stunned by the implications of all he had told her. She couldn't bring herself to believe it without an argument, and yet it all made a terrible kind of sense.

'Stephen had kept records of everything that had gone down with Platinum. All the files were in Barbados. He was going to hand them over to the authorities, but Santorini got there first. I'm afraid, my darling Chrissy, his treachery cost Stephen his life.'

She blinked back tears. Not trusting herself to speak or stand, she sat down on the arm of the sofa.

'How do you know all of this, James?' she said in a flat, controlled voice.

'I was with Stephen the night he died. As I was leaving Crystal Springs House, I saw Santorini go round the back.

401

He wasn't due on the island to do his bagman bit for another week, so I hung around, thinking something interesting might be going on. As it turned out it was – *very*. After Santorini left I found Stephen's body. The letter was in his desk drawer. Santorini missed it.'

She shook her head. 'I always suspected Antonio. I knew there was something . . . I told Stephen to buy him out countless times, but he always made an excuse. Poor Stephen dragged down into something so crooked. I suppose once Antonio had something on him he couldn't get out. I'm sure that was what he wanted to tell me the night before he died.'

She was talking to herself, lost in thought.

It was too much for James.

'Stephen Reece-Carlton an innocent victim?' he shouted. 'He was a bloody villain! How can you be so naïve, Christina? Don't delude yourself. Antonio and your husband were two of a kind.'

She shook her head vigorously, refusing to believe it.

'You're lying, James. You always resented Stephen because he was talented and a visionary. Flawed in some respects, I agree, but criminal, never.'

'Sit tight. I've something I want you to listen to.' He started to walk towards the door. 'Don't move,' he ordered, holding up his hand in warning as he left the room.

Christina seized her chance and, running to the far end of the room, picked up the telephone, frantically dialling 999. James walked back into the living-room as she was replacing the receiver.

'As a small precaution – I cut the wire before I came inside,' he said, looking at the telephone. Then, with his index finger crooked, he beckoned her towards the occasional table where he had placed a hand dictaphone.

James switched it on, turning the volume up to the highest level. 'Part of my duties for Stephen involved checking that his office and telephone weren't bugged,' he said conversationally. 'Stupid of him to trust me really, wasn't it?'

She heard Stephen's voice engaged in a heated argument with another man. At first she didn't realize who it was. After a few seconds of listening intently to the high-pitched voice, however, she realized it was Edward Harrington. It soon became obvious that he had the upper hand in the conversation.

He was blackmailing his half-brother.

'I warn you for the last time, Stephen, if you don't give me what I want I'll spill the beans – and what a bloody awful mess that will make! I can see the headlines now: "Stephen Reece-Carlton charged with the murder of Alan Randell in construction site cover-up".'

'Not just extortion but murder as well.'

'You know I didn't kill him.' Stephen's voice was weary.

Edward sighed. 'I know you didn't kill him personally, but you arranged his death. You forget, brother dear, I have contacts on the – shall we say – *rougher* side of town. Randell was putting the squeeze on you, threatening to go public with the story of how your mates on the council pushed planning permission through – for a price.

'That's good enough for the police, believe me.'

The tape went quiet as neither man spoke, then it crackled a little, and she heard Edward's voice again.

'I've decided I don't want just money – that would be too easy for you. No, I want something for the future, a nest-egg to see me into my old age. I want a share of the company.'

She heard Stephen's outraged voice.

'No, Edward, never! You get a hundred thousand, like I promised, or you can go and fuck yourself.'

'Do you really want to give up everything, Stephen? Your pleasure palace, your dear little wifey, your standing in the business world? Wouldn't it be far simpler just to part with a small share of the business? No one need ever know. I'd trust you to manage it for me, naturally.'

'What do you call small?'

'Oh, about a third should do it. No, wait, I'm not greedy. Now let me see . . . how old's Robbie? Twenty-eight, I think. Yes, let's say 28 per cent. Take it or leave it.'

James stopped the tape.

'Heard enough?'

Shock had rendered her speechless.

Slowly, she began to absorb the shattering revelations about Stephen Reece-Carlton: the man she had loved for all these years; the man she had never really known. Her foremost emotion was anger toward Stephen for the way he had cheated and lied. Had he also lied about his love for her? She had no way of knowing now.

When she spoke her voice seemed to belong to someone else.

'Why have you told me all of this, James?'

'For the same reason as Edward threatened to expose Stephen. Blackmail, my dear Chrissy. Blackmail.'

'Why should I want to buy any of this filthy information from you?'

'Because you stand to lose everything if I expose the company to the DEA. I know how much you'd like to be the major shareholder in Platinum Hotels, and if you refuse to purchase this information, I'll go to Antonio.'

'And what if I go to the DEA myself?'

'I wouldn't advise that, Christina. Look what happened to your dear departed husband.'

'Are you threatening me?' She started to get up from the sofa, but he pushed her back down.

'Of course I am. But don't worry, I'm not greedy. Not like Edward.'

He sat down next to her, one hand stroking her leg. 'Pleasure before business for a change.'

She knocked his hand away, shivering. Where, oh where, was Martin? The clock on the mantelpiece said 8.15. He should have been there by now.

'Are you cold, my darling?' said James, and stood up to throw another log on the fire.

Christina seized her opportunity. She grabbed a heavy cut-glass vase from the mantelpiece.

James spun round, knocking the vase out of her grip with one quick, violent blow. It shattered as it hit the bookcase, hundreds of tiny fragments scattering across the polished oak floor.

'Now that was silly. Very silly. Look what you've done to your lovely vase.'

James grabbed her wrist, forcing her to the floor, pinning her down with his full weight. She was powerless to struggle.

'Let go, James! You're hurting me.' She couldn't disguise the panic in her voice, and he smiled triumphantly at the sound. She could barely recognize the wild-eyed, congested face which loomed above hers.

'Don't you like it? Doesn't it turn you on like my bitch of a wife?'

He slapped her face, open-palmed. Christina felt sick with the pain of it.

'She wasn't so keen when I did it. She didn't want me either. Whore!' he shouted, slapping her again. 'You're all the bloody same!

'Elaine only got off when Sebastian Aguilar played his sick sado games with her. But I sorted her out. I made sure she never fucked anybody ever again.'

Christina saw madness in his eyes. Terror rose up in her throat, and she thought that if she began to scream she might never stop. This man had murdered her best friend, his own wife, and now she was alone with him, at his uncertain mercy.

He pushed his face close to hers. She could feel his

breath, hot and foul on her face, as he forced both her trembling hands to the front of his dirty jeans.

'I want you to suck me, Chrissy, like you did Stephen and Martin,' he hissed in a hoarse voice. 'I want you to suck me until I come in your mouth.'

He paused for breath, and she whimpered like a trapped animal.

'If you do that, I'll let you go. I won't hurt you. I promise, Chrissy darling. I promise. You know I love you.'

He released her hands and began to fumble with the zip of his jeans.

Christina rolled over. He grabbed her arm. She screamed as he yanked it behind her back, dragging her across the floor. Her head hit the leg of the coffee table.

She began to shake as blood seeped out of a gash on her temple.

Already struggling to breathe, she felt his hands close around her throat.

'I promise I won't harm you, Christina, if you just do as I say. It's not a lot to ask.' His tone had changed to one of pathetic wheedling.

He began fumbling at his clothes with one hand, holding her against him with the other. She squeezed her eyes tightly shut, praying he wouldn't kill her. As he forced himself upon her, she gagged, unable to control the bile rising in the back of her throat.

James did not seem to notice. He was moaning, his own eyes tightly shut now.

She flinched, and her eyes opened wide in alarm when a log dropped from the fire and landed on the hearth inches from her arm. She noticed that only one end of it was alight.

Christina slid her hand carefully across. She grabbed the cooler end of the log and, raising her head, thrust the flaming brand into James's groin.

His moans turned to ear-splitting shrieks. He fell back-ward, screaming and holding himself with both hands.

Christina fled from the house, his inhuman cries ringing in her ears.

Mist shrouded the headlights of the oncoming car. The driver spotted her just in time, and the car screeched to a halt with Christina on top of the bonnet, screaming hys-terically. Martin leapt out, closely followed by two uni-formed police officers.

'He's in there!' she screamed. 'James . . . I think I've killed him.'

She pointed back to the house with a hand that shook. One policeman ran off. The other watched as Martin put his arms around her, cradling her to him.

'Where were you?' she sobbed. 'He cut the telephone lines. I was so afraid . . .' A sob stuck in her throat, and she struggled to speak. 'I . . . I thought he was going to kill me, like he killed Elaine. I really did.'

'Shhh, Chrissy, it's okay. You're okay now,' he soothed her. 'I'm sorry I didn't get here sooner, but I had an accident in the car. The fog's terrible out there. I tried to ring several times from the police station. When I realized the line was dead I got them to run me out here.'

She looked up the drive. The policeman had emerged from the house and was using the radio. The second officer approached him and they spoke briefly before they split up, one man going back inside, the other letting them know what was happening.

'No need to worry, Mrs Reece-Carlton. The state he's in, he won't be a danger to anyone for a good long time. We've called for an ambulance; it won't be long.'

'I hope it hurts like hell,' she said vehemently, and looked defiantly into the police officer's horrified face. 'Believe me, after everything he's done, he deserves it.'

Christina thought of her dead friend and the cold, callous way James had faked her suicide and afterwards accepted their condolences and sympathy. She remembered the way he had framed Michael Stein, and then poked and pried about the hotel, looking for anything he could turn to his own advantage. He had stolen Stephen's letter to her, the last thing he had written before his death.

But at the memory of Stephen and all she had learned tonight, her thoughts spun out of control, refusing to focus. She felt the sharp sting of the cold night air in the cut on her temple, and the lights blazing from the house began to burn brighter, dazzling her . . .

'Hold her, sir!' the policeman warned, as Christina fainted in Martin's arms.

'You should have been a doctor instead of a footballer,' she commented. 'You've done that so well.'

They were sitting at the breakfast table, and Martin was tying a knot to secure the neat bandage he had applied to her hand and wrist. He'd covered the cut on her head with a plaster. It didn't look deep enough to need stitches.

'There, you're all done. They're only minor burns and should heal up in a few days, but I'd get your doctor to have a look in the morning.' He placed her hand gently on the table. 'I doubt whether James will heal so quickly.'

'I hope it hurts for a long time!' She sounded weary and bitter. 'Poor Elaine. I knew all along she'd never have killed herself.'

Christina rested her head on her good hand.

'I just can't believe all that has happened tonight. I feel I'm living some kind of horrible nightmare, and that I'm going to wake up any minute and none of it will be real.'

'It's been a terrible shock for you, I know. The police are returning first thing in the morning for you to make an official statement. I'll stay with you until then.'

'Thanks, Martin, I'd appreciate that. Pat and Adam will be home soon, and I think we should keep this incident quiet. Say I burnt my hand on the oven. What time is it?'

He glanced at his watch. 'Half-past nine.'

Christina looked worried. 'They should have been back by now. The movie finished at nine, and it's about a quarter of an hour's drive.'

Martin stood up and stepped the few feet to a deep bay window. He pressed his face to the glass.

'The fog's still very thick. I expect your driver's taking it easy.'

'I hope so. I've had enough shocks tonight to last me a lifetime.'

'Hang on, I think I can hear something,' he said, and seconds later they saw the dull beam of car headlights cutting through the blanket of fog.

'Remember, not a word.' She held up her bandaged hand. Martin nodded and stayed in the breakfast room while she went to the front door.

Adam was first into the hall. He ran to his mother.

'The film was super, Mummy, like Ben said. Really cool. Pat enjoyed it as well, didn't you?'

She nodded. 'Yes, it was great.'

'You'd like it, Mummy, and I wouldn't mind going again.'

He began pulling off his scarf and mittens. As Christina helped him with his coat, she could not help seeing him with new eyes. Martin's son, not Stephen's, as she had come to believe over the past six years. As she had wanted to believe, she reminded herself, and the thought was a bitter one. Fancy wanting to believe your child was the son of a man who dealt in drugs and corrupted politicians, laundered money for the Mob, and even stooped to murder to further his own megalomaniac ends . . .

Adam pointed to the bandage on her hand. 'What happened?'

'Silly Mummy burnt herself on the oven.'

'Does it hurt?' He touched it tentatively. 'No, not much, but I'm sorry to say I burnt the bolognese as well.'

'Oh, no, Pat and I were looking forward to that.'

'Never mind, I'll get Dorothy to make it for dinner tomorrow night. She makes it far better than I do anyway. There's pizza in the fridge if you're hungry. You can have that and then go to bed. You look tired out.'

'I'm not tired!' he yelled, and raced through the hall into the kitchen, stopping dead in his tracks as he encountered Martin sitting at the breakfast table.

The child stared at the strange man without saying a word. They weighed each other up before Martin broke the ice. 'You must be Adam. I've heard a lot about you from your mummy.'

Adam continued to stare, a serious look on his face.

'Did you have spaghetti bolognese before Mummy burnt it?' he asked eventually.

Martin's face broke into a smile. 'No. Like you, I arrived too late.'

Adam scrambled up onto a chair, kneeling on it so that he could be at eye level with their visitor.

'What's your name?' he asked.

'Martin Ward. I'm a friend of Mummy's. I knew her before you were born.'

'Do you like playing Lego?' Adam beamed, and Martin was reminded of the first time he had met Christina. The wide smile was identical.

'I've got some really cool Lego; we could play if you like?'

'You are going to bed, young man, so forget about playing Lego,' Christina said as she walked into the room.

'I'm not tired and I'm hungry.' He jumped down from the chair and dashed into the kitchen, where Pat was busy putting pizza into the microwave.

'Take no notice of Adam. He's a typical six-year-old,

full of mischief and far too energetic at times, but I wouldn't be without him for the world. He puts everything in my life into perspective.'

'He's a handsome young man,' Martin commented as Christina sat down next to him. 'Looks like you.'

'You're right, he does,' she said, looking at Martin's strong jaw-line and deep-set hazel eyes.

Yet he grows more like his father with each passing day, she thought.

Adam arrived back at the breakfast table carrying a plate of pepperoni pizza, followed by Pat with the tomato sauce and two glasses of orange juice.

'I'm sorry, Martin. I didn't ask if you were hungry.' Christina frowned at her own forgetfulness. She'd asked him to supper, after all. It seemed like years ago.

He shook his head. 'I'm not, but I'd love a drink. A glass of wine would be great.'

'Okay,' she said, and got up from the table. 'We'll go into the den and leave these hungry people to polish off the rest of the pizza.'

He stood up too.

'Are you staying here tonight?' Adam spoke through a mouthful of pizza.

'Yes, I am.'

'Will you play Lego with me in the morning?'

Martin was about to say yes, when Christina cut in, 'Adam, will you stop pestering, please.'

'He's okay, really, Chris. I'll play if I get time, but I've got to get back up to London fairly early.'

Martin touched the top of Adam's head as he passed, thinking that the boy's hair was exactly the same colour as his own had been at that age.

Christina got a bottle of Chablis from the fridge and two glasses out of a kitchen cupboard. She led Martin into the small TV room. It was painted with a dark-green marble effect to enhance the drawings and paintings hung tightly together, interspersed here and there with one of Adam's childish attempts. A single huge sofa almost filled the floor space, packed with big squashy cushions.

Adam's toys were strewn across the floor. Christina stooped to pick up a couple of cars and dropped them into a big red wooden toy-box in the corner of the room.

Martin was staring at a Blue Period Picasso oil of a boy in a pierrot hat. He touched the frame reverently.

'Is this the real thing?'

Christina looked up from pouring the wine.

'Yes, they all are. Stephen was a great collector of twentieth-century art. He left the bulk of his collection to his mother. She collects herself, but in a much smaller way, I think. He knew she would appreciate it far more than I ever did.'

Martin glanced at a drawing by Matisse.

'This alone must be worth a small fortune.'

'His collection was valued at in excess of fifty million pounds.' She said the figure casually. She'd become so used to enormous amounts of money that fifty million no longer seemed to mean much. She realized with a start that the money she had heard discussed, which had bought Stephen's art collection and had paid for their ever more luxurious lifestyle, had been tainted. She had believed it all came from the hotels. How could she have been so naïve? Stephen had given her the good life, all right – but on the proceeds of drugs and arms smuggling. The thought sickened her.

She handed Martin a glass of wine as Adam bounded into the room.

'Pat says I have got to go to bed now.' He dived at her legs, clinging to them, almost knocking the glass out of her hand.

'Careful, darling.' Christina pulled him to his feet. 'It's way past your bedtime. Pat's right.'

'Will you read me a story, please?'

'No, Adam, it's too late. And anyway, I can't leave Martin sitting on his own.'

Pat came into the den holding a mug of steaming hot chocolate.

'Bed, you little scallywag. *Now.*' Christina's voice was firm, and Adam knew she meant it.

He tried one last shot.

'Can the nice man read me a story, then?'

Martin laughed. 'I'll say one thing for you, Adam, you don't give up easily.'

'He tries it on, you mean,' Christina retorted, smiling herself.

'Say goodnight to Martin, Adam.' She pushed him forward, but he stood his ground.

Martin knelt down so that he was the same height. 'You probably don't know, but I used to be a professional footballer. Do you play?'

Adam nodded his head vigorously, his eyes wide with admiration.

'I promise you that as soon as I can, I'll come down here and give you personal football lessons. How's that?'

'That would be great! Can my friend Ben come as well? He's a really good footballer.'

'Yes, he can come as well.'

Adam flung his arms around Christina.

'I can't wait to wake up so I can speak to Ben!'

'Well, off you go, then,' said Pat. 'It'll be morning before you know it.'

'Goodnight, Adam,' Martin and Christina called, as he ran out of the room grabbing Pat's hand and almost dragging her off her feet.

'Quite a handful,' Martin said, and folded his long body into the sofa.

She sat down next to him.

'Have you any children, Martin?'

When he shook his head and said no he went on: 'We've

413

been trying for the last three years, but no luck. My wife Maria has become obsessed, and to be honest with you, the whole thing has affected our marriage. We found out she had infertility problems two years ago. She started an IVF programme last year, which has been a terrible strain. She got pregnant once but then miscarried.

'It was very traumatic for us both, but for some strange reason she blames me. Anyway, after that we seem to have drifted further and further apart. She's staying with her mother this week in Gloucestershire because I'm going to Italy and Spain on business.'

'I'm sorry, Martin,' Christina said. After a story like that, how could she tell him he already had a son?

'Don't be. You've got enough problems of your own at the moment. The last thing you need to hear are mine.'

He sipped his wine and with his free hand found hers. 'Do you want to talk about it yet?'

She'd given him a rough outline of the revelations James Morris had made while they'd been waiting for Adam and Pat. Everything except Adam's parentage. She stared at the empty television screen and closed her eyes. 'I still can't completely take in all the things he said. I have to assume they're true, but they seem incredible, like something out of a movie.'

She opened her eyes wide. He could see that they were full of tears, but Christina refused to give way.

'The man I lived with and loved for all those years, the man I thought I knew inside out, was living a lie, a constant deception – almost living a double life. I saw only the good side, but the other was dark – horrible.' She shuddered with revulsion.

'Did you never suspect anything underhand or criminal was going on?' Martin found it hard to believe that she had had no idea.

'There were a few occasions when I found that Stephen

was being a bit underhand, and I never trusted Antonio. But Stephen always said you don't have to like the people you do business with and I accepted it. I was such a pushover for a man like that. So bloody stupid.'

The hurt of betrayal was so intense that she did not trust herself to speak again for a while.

Martin picked up the wine bottle and refilled their glasses.

'So where do you go from here, Chris?'

'I go to the Drugs Enforcement Administration and expose Antonio. What other choice do I have?'

'That could be dangerous. The alternative would be to back out of the deal in New York and let Antonio take over. Leave it for a few months until he's off-guard and then think about informing the DEA.'

'I can't, Martin. It's got to be done as soon as possible. Anyway, the authorities are already watching the company closely if James was telling the truth, and Stephen was poised to tell all.'

Martin moved closer and pushed some wayward strands of hair from her pale face.

'I'm only concerned for you, Christina. I always have been.' She saw him hesitate. 'I'm still in love with you.'

She pushed him away gently.

'I know, Martin, but this is hardly the time. You're married, and there's so much going on in my head right now, with everything I've found out about Stephen, I can't think about anything else.'

She stood up and paced to the other side of the room.

'I have got to get back at Antonio and Santorini. Stephen may not have been all he seemed, but he didn't deserve to die like that. No one should be allowed to wield the power of life or death.' She began to shake, an uncontrollable shuddering which refused to stop.

Martin jumped up and held her in his arms until the trembling stopped.

'I feel very tired all of a sudden, Martin. Do you mind if I go to bed?'

'Come on, I'll take you. Is there anything else you want?'

'Would you sleep in the next room, Martin? I'd like that.'

'Of course. You'd better tell me where we're going.'

'The first door on the left at the end of the landing.'

Christina walked wearily upstairs, leaning on his arm. Martin left her to undress while he went into his own room. After a few minutes he knocked on the door.

'I'll be right next door if you need me. Just call.'

'Thanks, Martin.'

'Goodnight, Christina.' He kissed her cheek, and started to back out.

She fumbled in her pocket. 'Before you go, there's something I haven't told you. I'm not sure that this is the best time, but I think you have a right to know.'

'What is it? You couldn't shock me any more than you have already tonight.'

He was wrong.

'You're a father, Martin. Adam is your child. Stephen left me a letter. I think you should see it.'

He was shocked at first, then angry, and finally full of pity. Not for himself and the way he had been denied knowledge of his son, and not for Christina, who he was coming to see was much tougher than he'd given her credit for. Surprisingly, he found himself feeling sorry for Stephen: the man who'd had everything, including the woman Martin loved, and yet had been unable to give her a child.

'I still haven't got this sorted in my mind,' he told her finally. 'But, you know, after everything I've learned tonight, all the nasty shocks – my own overwhelming

416

impression is that he loved you, Chrissy. No one fakes a letter like this, knowing it will probably be the last thing they do.

'Stephen loved you very much. You should hang on to that thought.'

It was a generous assessment of a man he had never liked in life, but to help Christina through the difficult times she faced, Martin felt he must speak up.

He didn't leave her that night. They talked for a long time about the difficult choices that faced them both. Christina was determined to see things through in New York, and he realized that he must let her, however much he feared the danger she faced there.

Christina begged him to have another try at his marriage, not to give up on it because he knew she was free again. With a heavy heart, he agreed.

Sometime around dawn they crept under the covers fully dressed and clung to one another, knowing that in a few hours they must part, perhaps forever.

28 SEPTEMBER 1993

A clear pale-blue sky greeted Christina as she pulled the heavy cord to open the drapes. Weak sunlight filtered through the trees onto the heads of a few early-morning joggers.

She watched a small terrier lift its leg against the gleaming chrome wheel-trim of a Bentley parked in front of the apartment building.

It was 7.30 in the morning, and she was already dressed in a sombre black trouser-suit and white silk shirt. She made herself a cup of coffee and wandered through the ten-room apartment. There wasn't a thing out of place, not a speck of dust or a cushion misplaced.

417

She had made her bed herself for the first time in years, and six packed suitcases stood in the hall. After her business was concluded, she would leave New York for good.

She washed up her dirty cup and left the apartment. Walking briskly up Sutton Place, she caught a cab on York Avenue.

'Madison and 58th, please,' she instructed the driver. As usual, he didn't speak English, and muttered something unintelligible as the dirty yellow cab bumped down the quiet streets to Madison Avenue and Platinum Hotels' head office.

She stared out of the window at a group of hoboes sleeping rough in a doorway, and watched a young black kid trying to steal a pretzel from a stand whilst the owner's back was turned. New York, city of promises and dreams, yet sullied and dissolute somehow, like a once glamorous film star clinging to her faded glory days.

Christina met Carol Rogers, Antonio's secretary, on the way into the Platinum Hotels block.

'Morning, Mrs Reece-Carlton. How are you on this lovely morning?'

'Fine, thanks. And you're right, it is a beautiful day.'

She followed Carol's Gucci-clad feet into reception. 'You're in early,' Christina commented.

'Mr Cellini left me a lot of work last night. I was going out to dinner so, rather than work late, I thought I'd catch up this morning.

'Would you like me to bring you a cup of coffee?' Carol asked politely.

'No, thanks.'

Christina took the lift up to the thirty-sixth floor. She flicked a switch at the side of the door to illuminate what she considered to be one of the most stunning offices she had ever seen.

Stephen had had great taste; it had emanated from him, and this room was pure Stephen, from the hand-picked veneers and custom-made American cedar-panelled walls and bookshelves, through the mellow oak floor, beautifully inlaid with ebony, to the exquisite Aubusson rugs lying on either side of the office.

Stephen had designed his hand-made cedarwood desk himself. It dominated the room.

She looked up at an old framed photograph of herself and Adam slotted in between a Dégas and a Chagall. She had always thought it incongruous up there with the masters, but Stephen had insisted.

She walked round the desk, past a floor-mounted sculpture by Henry Moore, and sat down. All his things were as he had left them, untouched. A solid bird's-eye maple humidifier still held three havanas. There was an antique clock, a silver desk lighter, and the new Cartier pen she had bought him last Christmas.

She swung round in the chair and looked out of the window. A dazzling winter sun glinted off the acres of glass stretching as far as the eye could see. One lonely cloud floated across her line of vision, carrying with it a solitary bird. Christina turned away sharply. She had things to do and not much time in which to accomplish them.

'Mr Cellini is here. Shall I send him in?' a secretary's voice announced over the intercom an hour later.

'Yes, Cara, that will be fine. And ask him if he'd like coffee.'

Christina flicked off the intercom and walked round the desk, ready to greet Antonio. With everything she had recently learned, she wasn't sure she could look him in the face without allowing her revulsion to show. But she knew she must, for just a little while longer.

He strode confidently into Stephen's office, handsome and affable as ever.

'Good morning, Christina. How are you?'

God, how could she ever have fallen for his 'regular guy' act, the flowery compliments and shit-eating grin? The man was a criminal and a cold-blooded killer. And she had to let him kiss her.

'I'm very well, Antonio. Are you?'

'Great. On top of the world. Looking forward to having this auction over with. I've come up with a deal I know Edward Harrington can't refuse. No hard feelings, Chrissy.'

Her face gave nothing away.

'Victoria and Edward should be here soon. And our favourite Swiss lawyer.'

He scowled, and sank into the soft cream sofa, his expression more guarded. He sensed something different about Christina this morning; something he had never detected in her before. It was confidence, he realized with surprise; an aura of supreme confidence.

They both looked up as Victoria walked into the room unannounced. She was wearing a sexy short, straight skirt and a big boxy jacket, her dark hair woven into a single long, sleek plait.

'Good morning. Not late, I hope?'

'No, I am early,' Antonio assured her, and showed her into a chair next to Christina's from which he would have a great view of her legs.

The intercom buzzed. It was reception.

'Mr Edward Harrington is here, with Mr Klein and Mr Wagner. Shall I send them up?'

'Send them to the boardroom, please, Jane. We'll be there in a few moments,' Christina replied in a crisp voice.

She faced her adversaries head-on. 'Okay. Are you ready?'

Antonio stood next to Victoria. 'As ready as I'll ever be. Let's get this thing rolling.'

The boardroom was located on the same floor, and they met Edward Harrington and the two lawyers coming out of the lift.

'Good morning. And what a wonderful morning it is,' said Edward jauntily. He looked even fatter, Christina noted, and seemed to have started dying his hair since she'd seen him last – in Barbados, during his trip there to blackmail Stephen, she thought, repressing a shudder.

'Good morning,' said Nicolas Wagner in a deep monotone. He inclined his head slightly in their direction, unsmiling.

Edward walked briskly, rubbing his hands together. He looked ridiculously elated.

Kingsleigh Klein kept a perceptible distance from him. As a top-of-the-tree corporate lawyer, he did not often come into contact with stockholders like Edward.

They all entered the boardroom, and the Swiss lawyer placed his briefcase on the table. Clicking it open, he took out a stack of documents and share certificates. He pushed his glasses onto the bridge of his nose and said: 'Shall we proceed?'

'I can't wait,' said Edward, grinning. 'Which of you lucky people is about to make me a very wealthy man, I wonder?'

'The procedure is simple. This is a share auction for the purchase of 28 per cent of Platinum Hotels Inc. owned by Mr Edward Harrington. The bidders involved are Mr Antonio Cellini, Mrs Christina Reece-Carlton, and Miss Victoria Reece-Carlton. They must deposit their bids in sealed envelopes, to be opened by me and checked by my colleague here.

'Obviously, the highest bid purchases the shares. In the event of two or three of the bids being equal, we will ask you to bid again.'

'If you would like to wait in the adjoining office, Mr

Harrington, we will call you when the bidding is over,' said Kingsleigh Klein.

Edward backed reluctantly out of the office.

'Can I have your bids, please?' said Nicolas Wagner.

'Certainly.' Antonio took a sealed envelope out of his jacket pocket and handed it to the lawyer with a wide smile.

Victoria pulled hers out of her briefcase and slapped it on the table.

Christina didn't move. Her heart was beating so loudly she thought everyone present must be able to hear it. She found her voice, and to her own surprise it sounded distinct and did not falter once when she said: 'I won't be bidding.'

Everyone looked at her in surprise.

'May I ask why not?' Nicolas Wagner took off his glasses and peered at her from owl-like eyes.

'Because there is nothing to bid for. The company is worthless.'

'What are you talking about?' Antonio was first to recover and came out fighting. 'What do you mean, worthless? Are you insane?'

'No, I'm not mad, Antonio. I have never felt more in control.'

'Would you care to explain your statement, Mrs Reece-Carlton?' asked Kingsleigh Klein.

'Platinum Resorts Inc. is under investigation by the Drugs Enforcement Administration at this very moment.'

Both lawyers momentarily registered shock. Victoria clasped her hand to her mouth. Antonio's face, slightly smiling, was unreadable.

'James Morris, our former manager in Barbados, is in custody in England. He has made a highly incriminating statement, and there is conclusive proof that Platinum Hotels was being used to launder illegal revenue from drugs and arms smuggling and other organized crimes.

This man . . .' – she pointed at Antonio – 'masterminded the entire operation.'

'How dare you accuse me?' he demanded. His voice was barely raised, but all the more threatening for that. 'I know nothing about drugs deals or money-laundering. If Stephen was into that sort of stuff, he never told me.'

Her stomach churned as Antonio faced her, cobalt-blue eyes hard and frightening now. She knew she must not show a trace of weakness or all might still be lost.

'So where's this evidence you say you have?'

'With the DEA. You didn't get it all, you see, Antonio. Stephen kept two sets of records. The ones in Barbados you already have, but he left a copy at our house in England. And very interesting reading it made while I was over there.'

It was a lie.

He came very close to her. 'I don't believe you, Christina. You're bluffing.'

His eyes pierced hers.

She returned the gaze, unflinching, and in a voice that was stronger than she felt, said: 'Talk to Danny Bascombe about whether I'm bluffing or not.'

She was pleased to see his sallow skin pale.

'Danny's agreed to talk *in camera*, Antonio. The game's up; accept it.'

She paused, and a deathly hush descended on the boardroom.

'James Morris saw Santorini kill Stephen, on your orders, and Danny told me everything when I was in Barbados two days ago.' She prayed it would work, and that in his arrogance he had not had her movements monitored. She was thrilled to see a flash of fear enter his eyes for a split second.

'Fucking Bascombe! I told Stephen we should have got rid of him years ago.'

Christina sensed that she was winning. She could almost feel Stephen's powerful presence urging her on.

'But I didn't kill Stephen, you can't pin that one on me,' Antonio insisted.

'You arranged for his death. That's as good as,' she snapped.

'I told Santorini to warn Stephen, not to kill. Gino's a fucking killing-machine. I can't be responsible if he gets off on it.'

'I think you'd better explain that to the authorities,' Christina said, going towards the next-door meeting-room, where she had helped them to hide before the auction began. She prayed she'd given them enough to go on.

As the men filed in, displaying their badges, Victoria flung herself at Antonio, kicking him and clawing at his face.

'You killed my daddy! You bastard, you killed my daddy!' she screamed hysterically, pounding his chest with her fists.

Antonio slapped her face with the back of his hand, and she reeled backward, falling against one of the DEA men, who restrained her.

Antonio adjusted his tie and pulled his jacket straight, touching a long scratch on his cheek as one of the agents stood in front of him.

'Antonio Lorenzo Cellini, I hereby inform you . . .'

'Okay, okay. Cut the routine,' he said with contempt, staring straight ahead. 'I'd like to call my lawyer.'

'You can do that down-town.' The agent took hold of his arm. He shrugged it off and turned to stare at Christina.

'Well, congratulations. I admire your guts. You're going to need them. Nobody pulls the plug on Antonio Cellini and gets away with it.

'I want you to know, Christina, that I'm glad Stephen's

424

dead. And that you haven't seen the last of me. *Ciao, bella*. Till we meet again.'

Two agents hustled him out. Kingsleigh Klein had gone into an urgent damage-limitation conference with their superior. Nicolas Wagner nervously shuffled papers back into his briefcase.

Christina knelt down next to Victoria, who had flopped onto the sofa. She put out her hand tentatively and pulled away the long plait that had fallen over her face.

'Are you okay, Victoria?'

'Yes. Just shocked.' She sat up and looked at Christina. Her eyes glistened with tears.

'It will take a bit of getting used to, that's all. I still can't believe my father was involved in all this. He was a cultured and sensitive man. It will take me a long time to accept it . . . if I ever do.'

'If it's any consolation to you, Victoria, I think he never intended to become involved. He thought he could make a pact with the devil while playing his own tune. At the beginning, Antonio offered him all the money he could ever need to build the sort of dream hotels he loved to create. Stephen thought he could stay on the fence, leave Antonio to deal with the dirty side of things alone. It didn't work out like that, and your father became very unhappy.

'But it was when he saw Antonio supplying you with drugs that he finally decided he wanted out. It was because of that he decided to risk his life and go to the authorities as they'd asked. He loved you very much, Victoria.'

Christina had decided not to tell her about her father's past crime. She would leave the memory of that buried with Stephen.

Her stepdaughter shook her head.

'He loved you, Christina, much more than me. I knew that from the very first day I met you. And he told me a few weeks ago that Adam was not his child, but that he

425

could not bear to lose you, so was prepared to bring him up as his own. He made me swear never to tell you. I suppose it's okay now.

'My father said to me that he had never in his entire life loved anyone or anything as much as he loved you. I think you should know that, Christina. I don't know whether the knowledge makes anything better for you. It certainly doesn't for me.'

She smoothed back her hair and wiped her face with a tissue. When she got to her feet she was composed again.

'I'll never be able to accept that either.'

The words were said in the old vituperative tone, and Victoria was a little girl again, all the years of festering jealousy and resentment distorting her beautiful face.

'I'm so sorry, Victoria,' Christina sighed, suddenly extremely tired. 'We could have been such good friends.'

'It would never have been possible, Christina. You see, you stole the only person I have ever loved.'

She left the room quietly, and Christina doubted they'd be meeting again.

Turning to the bewildered faces of the two lawyers, who had witnessed the whole scene in astonishment, she asked: 'So who gets the pleasure of telling Edward Harrington his shares are worth zilch?'

A sense of desolation gripped her as she sat once again behind Stephen's desk. When they had all finally left her – statements made, legal advice given, threats issued – she was left alone with her memories.

She studied a photograph of Stephen with a mixture of love and remorse. He was laughing and triumphant at the opening of Crystal Springs in southern California, receiving an architectural award.

The pale eyes stared confidently out, as opaque and unreadable in the glossy photograph as they had been in life.

'It's over, Stephen. At last it's over,' she said to his lifeless image. 'Now I can bury you once and for all and begin to live again.'

Epilogue

DECEMBER 1994

'Adam, you little pest!' Christina squealed as he poured water over her bare stomach and ran off down the beach laughing.

'Catch me if you can!'

She took up the challenge and chased him into the sea, trying to catch hold of his leg. He was too quick for her, diving into the waves, as lithe and fast as a flying-fish.

She paddled in the shallow water, waiting for his return, planning to duck him when he least expected it.

She watched him swim far out but wasn't concerned. He was an island child and a strong swimmer.

Wading ashore, she sat in the soft white sand at the waterline, letting the warm sea lap over her long, tanned legs. Since abandoning Platinum Hotels she had retreated to Crystal Springs and now lived quietly. Managing one hotel was excitement enough for anyone, she'd decided, and she aimed to make a success of that if of nothing else in her life.

Today the hotel was 90 per cent full and the beach was busy. It was a perfect December day with a cloudless blue sky and calm, aquamarine sea, cooled by a temperate trade wind.

She glanced along the shoreline to where a young honeymoon couple, who had been married at the hotel a few days before by Father Edward, were walking hand in hand. They waved, and Christina waved back, her eyes catching the figure of a tall blond man behind them. He looked familiar . . . or was it just wishful thinking?

It wasn't until the newly-weds ran into the sea that she could see him properly. With heart beating wildly, she experienced a crazy, overwhelming sense of joy.

'Mummy – come in!' Adam shouted, and waved to her from the water.

She waved back, pretending not to hear him.

'How are you, Christina?'

Martin sat down next to her. He was bare-chested and wearing faded blue denim cut-offs that revealed the cruel scars on one of his powerfully muscled legs.

'I'm fine. And you?'

She held her breath, not daring to look at him for fear he would see the yearning in her eyes.

'I was wondering if you had a room in the hotel for a while?'

He looked out to sea, shading his eyes from the sun's reflected glare. 'My divorce from Maria was finalized last week, Chris. I'm a free man.'

Neither of them had time to speak again before Adam ran out of the water and flopped down by his mother's feet. Grabbing her ankles, he kicked and splashed his legs in the sea.

'Look who's come to stay with us, Adam,' Christina said unsteadily.

The boy's bright eyes gazed at Martin, recognition sparking in them.

'I remember. You came to our house in England once. You play football, don't you?'

Martin nodded.

'Will you have time to teach me?'

'I think, Adam, you and I are going to have all the time in the world.'